Rules of Murder

A DREW
FARTHERING
MYSTERY

Rules
—of—
MURDER

JULIANNA
DEERING

BETHANYHOUSE
a division of Baker Publishing Group
Minneapolis, Minnesota

© 2013 by DeAnna Julie Dodson

Published by Bethany House Publishers
11400 Hampshire Avenue South
Bloomington, Minnesota 55438

Bethany House Publishers is a division of
Baker Publishing Group, Grand Rapids, Michigan

Printed in the United States of America

ISBN 978-1-62490-655-8

Scripture quotations are from the King James Version of the Bible.

Cover design by Faceout Studio
Cover illustration by John Mattos

Author is represented by Books & Such Literary Agency

To the One who makes
all things new

— One —

Farthering Place stood, as it always had, deep in the grove of oaks at the end of a long curving drive, half hidden from the main road and prying eyes. Nestled in the Hampshire countryside, the old manor house exuded respectability and permanence rather than great beauty, but it had a certain pleasing symmetry that saved it from outright stodginess. Even now, when it was little more than a looming shadow in the darkness, it had a dignified grace of line. Perhaps more so now. Now the lights that would have illuminated any ill-considered behavior had been extinguished and even the heartiest of the revelers had stumbled into a bed of some description.

A midnight-blue 1932 Rolls Royce slowed to a stop as it turned into the drive. Behind the wheel, Drew Farthering took a moment to look over the grounds, bracing himself before going down to the house. Before going home. Judging by the number of cars in the drive, his absence hadn't prevented Constance from throwing one of her weekend bashes. He hadn't told anyone to expect him.

Motionless, he surveyed the scene awhile longer. Then he nudged the figure sprawled, sleeping, in the seat next to him.

"We're here." He didn't know why he whispered.

His companion struggled into a more dignified posture and raked one hand through his sandy hair, making it stick up more than it already did.

"Still there, is she, Drew?" he asked through a yawn, and Drew nodded gravely.

"Farthering's still there, Nick. Always there."

In another moment they were at the front door and then inside the dimly lit entry hall. Dennison was prompt to answer the bell. As always, he was perfectly groomed and suitably grave, his only concession to the lateness of the hour being the robe and slippers that had supplanted his usual formal attire. Somehow he made even those look dignified and utterly appropriate.

"We weren't told to expect you, sir. Do come out of the damp."

He took Drew's hat, and Drew seized his hand. "How are you, Denny? You're looking grand."

"Very well, sir, thank you. I trust Nicholas has remembered his place with you."

Nick grinned.

"In the middle of whatever mischief I've made is his usual place," Drew said. "He never forgets that."

Nick threw his arm around the butler's shoulders and gave them a strong squeeze.

"Propriety," Dennison reproved.

"Great to see you, Dad," Nick said, his spirits undampened. "How is the old place?"

"Much less secure since you've arrived, I can assure you."

The two young men laughed.

"Good old Denny," Drew said. "Farthering wouldn't be home without you."

Nick picked up the bags they had brought in from the car. "I'll haul these up to our rooms, shall I, Dad? You go back to bed."

Dennison turned to Drew, displaying a rare expression of discomfort as he cleared his throat. "As I said, sir, we weren't told to expect you. Madam has her guests in for the weekend and—"

"And you've had to put someone in Nick's room. Never mind. He can kip on the divan in my study, can't you, Nick?"

Nick grinned. "It's not just my room, is it, Dad?"

"I regret to say, sir, but Madam—"

"She's put someone in my room." Drew's expression grew cool. "And may I ask—"

"Dennison? What's that noise down there?"

Drew looked up to the top of the gracefully curved stairway. Constance Farthering Parker squinted down at him, straining to see without the glasses she was too vain to wear.

"The master's come home, madam," Dennison informed her.

She clutched her pink satin wrapper more closely around her tall frame and, with majestic hauteur, swept down to the entryway. In her middle fifties she still managed to look young and rather pretty in the right light.

"We weren't expecting you, pet."

"So I hear," Drew replied, touching his lips to the rouged cheek she offered. "I hadn't realized reservations were required."

"Of course not. It's just we've nowhere to put you and—" she peered at Nick, who beamed at her over Drew's shoulder— "and young Dennison."

"I thought we'd agreed my room was off-limits, Mother. Especially after the last time."

"Now, pet, Honoria couldn't help it if she was ill."

"Perhaps she wouldn't have been ill if she'd stopped at something less than a quart of gin that night."

Nick snickered and then, under Constance's glare, coughed decorously.

"And just who have you put in my room this time?" Drew pressed.

"A friend of Mason's." Constance looked down and then up at him again, her eyes wide with innocence. "Really, Ellison, we didn't know you were coming this weekend, and we'll be full up with guests after tomorrow."

Drew scowled. His mother was the only one who called him Ellison. No one else dared.

"I suppose, as usual, my wishes weren't to be considered."

"Now, pet, really. Couldn't you—?"

"You'd think, with all the rooms in this house, you might have put him somewhere other than my room. That's not asking too much, is it, in view of—"

"In view of the fact that you are lord of the manor and I'm only living here on your charity?"

Her voice cracked with sudden anger, and Drew resisted the urge to snap back at her.

"In view of the fact that it *is* my room, I was going to say, Mother. Who is it anyway?"

"I told you, a friend of Mason's." Again she looked away.

"Who?"

"He's only staying the weekend."

"Who is it?"

"It doesn't matter," she said with a defiant lift of her chin, and Drew turned to the butler.

"Who is it, Denny?"

"A certain Mr. Lincoln, sir," Dennison said in his most impersonal tone.

"Lincoln!" Drew stared at his mother in disbelief. "By Harry, I'll not have him in my house, let alone my own room."

He took the steps two at a time, deaf to his mother's demands that he come back and collect himself. He'd heard what was said about his mother and Lincoln two years ago in Monte Carlo. He wasn't about to let that sort of thing go on in his own home, right under his stepfather's nose.

He pushed open the door to his room, and a shaft of light from the hall fell across the heavy four-poster bed. He could see Lincoln clearly as he slept—tall, powerfully built, his blond hair slicked back to show his broad aristocratic forehead. An ostentatious ruby ring gleamed on his right hand. Drew hated him cordially and regretted ever having been introduced to him.

He strode to the bedside, took hold of the muscular arm that lay over the sheet, and dragged Lincoln out onto the Persian rug. Sputtering and cursing, Lincoln sprang to his feet, but Drew didn't give him a chance to protest.

"Collect your things," Drew said, his voice tight and low. "I want you out in five minutes."

"Look here, Farthering—"

"Five minutes and not an instant longer."

Lincoln took a step toward Drew, who only eyed him with cool disdain.

"Drew, please." Mason Parker came into the room, bringing with him his usual air of calm sensibility. "I'm sure Mr. Lincoln meant nothing of the kind."

Seeing Mason, Lincoln's expression abruptly turned from anger to good-natured bewilderment. "I think we've had rather a misunderstanding—"

"Hardly!" Drew spat.

"He is our houseguest after all, Drew," Mason said. "I trust you will treat him as such."

"But, sir," Drew protested, his consideration for his stepfather wrestling with his anger. "This man—"

"Drew." Mason put his arm around his stepson's shoulders and took him aside. "Your mother told me what you've heard about Monte Carlo, and I can assure you none of it is true. Mr. Lincoln and I have some business dealings to attend to, and I asked him to stay the weekend with the others. I hope that doesn't inconvenience you too much."

Drew pressed his lips together and quickly counted ten. "Sir, listen to me." He lowered his voice, seeing Nick and Dennison and Constance were clustered in the doorway looking on. "I don't like to see you deceived, especially in your own—"

"Drew!" His stepfather was as close to being angry as Drew had ever seen him, though he too kept his voice low. "Don't let's quarrel now. I refuse to listen to idle gossip and trust you will do the same. You of course have the right to eject from your home anyone you do not wish to entertain. But I hope, for your mother's sake and mine, that you will remember yourself and manage a little hospitality while Mr. Lincoln is our guest. Please."

Drew counted ten once more, this time letting each number squirm and simmer before passing on to the next.

"I want my room back," he said at last. "And Nick's."

Mason smiled and turned to Lincoln. "Sorry about the mis-understanding."

"Not at all. Not at all. I'd no idea I was putting anyone out," Lincoln said, his smile sheepish. "Bit embarrassing and all that."

"I hope you'll let bygones be bygones and stay with us for the party. Dennison will see you have another room."

"Thank you, Mr. Parker." Lincoln put a robe over his silk pajamas. "No harm done."

Mason patted Constance's hand. "There, my dear. No harm done."

"I'm so glad, darling," she said, her expression meek and worshipful as she clung to his arm. "Good night, Mr. Lincoln."

"Mrs. Parker," Lincoln said with a formal bow.

Mason led Constance away, and Dennison came into the room to gather Lincoln's things.

"This way, sir," he said after a moment. "It's just through those doors and up the stairs."

Drew was standing near the door, his arms folded across his chest, begrudging every minute the other man spent in his room.

"Good night, Farthering," Lincoln said as he followed Dennison out into the hallway, the knowing nastiness in his expression belying his mild words. "Should be a charming weekend, eh?"

"Charming," Drew replied, managing a cool, brittle smile of his own. "So good to have you. You must come again sometime."

Lincoln walked away, chuckling to himself, and Drew slammed the door behind him, making the old leaded windows rattle in their frames.

"Steady on, old man," Nick said, and then he grinned. "No place like home, eh?"

Drew could only laugh.

Drew had breakfast out on the terrace with his stepfather the next morning. It was sweetly June, balmy and green, but the mist still clung to the ground in wisps. It hadn't yet burned off the rolling meadow behind the house, and last night's revelers hadn't yet left their beds.

He smiled over at Mason. The old boy looked the perfect picture of comfortable middle age—thinning on top, thickening in the middle, kindly laugh lines at the corners of his uncritical eyes—a middle age that asked nothing but tranquility and graciousness.

"I apologize for last night, sir," Drew said, spooning honey into his tea. "But I hadn't expected of all people—"

"Don't let's go into that again," Mason said briskly. "Tell me, how was the seaside? You and young Nick look in top form."

"I hope I won't sound too spoilt and all, but I'm beginning to find it rather a bore. All they do is sit and drink and gossip about the latest scandal. That is when they're not stirring one up."

"And, it goes without saying, you young chaps never get into any deviltry yourselves."

Drew answered his stepfather's indulgent grin with a shrug and a mischievous smile of his own.

"Can't say Nick and I haven't got up to a prank or two, sir. Just now and again."

Mason laughed. "And no young lady you've wanted to bring home?"

"What, out of that lot?" Drew made a face.

"What about Colonel Saxonby's daughter?" Mason offered. "Or that Pomphrey-Hughes girl? She seems to like you. Surely there must be some decent girls in society."

Drew stirred more honey into his tea. "Of course there are. I just haven't been introduced to them yet. Still, for a dance or a drink or a day on the beach, there's nobody can touch them. But when I get serious about a girl, I'd rather it was one who hadn't already strolled round the corner with all of my friends."

Mason looked away, and Drew cleared his throat.

"I'm sorry, sir." He rattled his teacup back into the saucer. "I do tend to ramble on when I get talking. Truly, the coast was very nice. Beautiful weather. The sea was lovely, and Bunny, you remember Bunny, sir—"

"Please don't."

"Sir?"

"Don't talk airy pleasantries to me. Heaven knows I've enough of that as it is. People talk to me for hours and say absolutely nothing."

"Sir—"

"And must it always be 'sir,' Drew? I've been married to your mother for more than ten years now. Must it always be 'sir'?"

Drew shifted in his chair.

"I suppose I never knew what else I should call you," he said, making his tone light. "I always thought 'Mr. Parker' a bit Victorian and 'Mason' rather cheeky. What do you suggest?"

"I wouldn't presume to ask you to call me Father, knowing how you feel about your own. And I know I've not been much of a father to you as it is. Dennison's seen to you all this while. I don't know, my boy. I suppose it's just that 'sir' seems so distant."

Drew gave him a small, warm smile.

"If it is, I don't mean it to be. You're one of the finest men I know, and I've more respect for you than just about anyone else in the world."

He knew as he said it that he'd lied, but it was a lie of kindness. He couldn't really respect anyone who let Constance walk over him as Mason did, but Drew did have a tremendous liking for him all the same.

"I expect you are the closest thing to a son I'll ever have," Mason said, "and I've a great deal of affection for you. I realize we've never been all that close, but I should like us to be friends if that suits you."

Drew knew only too well how living with Constance could be. He remembered when Mason had courted his mother. He'd been recently widowed and there had been no children, no family save a young niece living somewhere in America—no one to fill the empty space in his life.

"I'd be more than honored, sir," Drew said finally, and Mason gave his shoulder a squeeze.

"It's good to have you home again, my boy. The old place just isn't the same without you."

"I daresay I've livened things up a bit. I *am* sorry."

"Well, never mind. It doesn't matter now. But I wish you wouldn't have such wrong ideas about your mother. You know how people love to gossip, especially those with little else to occupy them."

"One of the hazards of being in society," Drew agreed, but this time his smile had a touch of bitterness in it. "I just can't bear to see her hurt you, sir."

"I trust her."

Silent for a moment, Drew watched a pair of robins hopping in and out of a flowering rhododendron.

"Well, I shan't make any more scenes with your guests," he said at last. "If you're certain they're *your* guests."

"That's good of you. Rushford will be in later today, and you can see for yourself."

"Very well then. I'll just have a pleasant time and play guest in my own home. It might be fun." Drew waved away the plate of eggs his stepfather offered him and took another piece of toast instead. "Yes, it will be a change from drinking and dancing and strolling on the beach. Here, we can drink and dance and stroll in the garden." He sighed in exaggerated contentment. "Ah, variety *is* the spice of life."

"Perhaps you should come into business with me," Mason suggested. "Farlinford is doing some excellent things with refining that might interest you. Could revolutionize the industry. And we've redone the directors' offices. You should come have a look."

Drew laughed. "I'll do that, certainly, but I think I'm far too young yet to work for sport and not nearly that desperate. Oh, I say," he added, sobering, "I read about McCutcheon in the news last week. He was in research, wasn't he?"

Mason nodded. "Bad business, that. Such a young man, as well. He knew his way round a laboratory, though, and I can't imagine him making that sort of mistake. Not a man of his experience. It wasn't a pretty way to go."

"Did he have family?"

Mason shook his head. "No one in the world, it seems. Very sad."

"I expect he was part of the new developments you were telling me about," Drew said. "Anything especially good?"

"I don't know," Mason admitted. "He said he was on the verge of something big. Then again, he always said that. I never really saw anything come of it. Shame, really. He showed such promise."

"Well, I remember precious little of my chemistry classes, but I'd not mind seeing what you do out at Farlinford. Perhaps I could help your little revolution. Still, not this weekend. I think I'd like to mingle with some new people for a bit. Maybe I'll find that girl you were asking after."

Mason stood up and tucked the morning paper under his arm. "That reminds me. My niece, Madeline, and some friends of hers from America will be driving down from London for a few days. Perhaps one of them will suit. It would be a great favor to me if you'd show them about the place a bit."

Drew raised his teacup in a toast. "We aim to please."

Once Mason had gone, Drew sat alone at the table until, seeing sturdy Mrs. Devon hovering at the terrace door, he stood up.

"Morning, Mrs. D. You haven't come for the breakfast things, have you?"

"If you've done, Mr. Drew," she said, scurrying out with a tray.

"What's happened to Ivy?"

"Nothing at all, love," Mrs. Devon said as she began stacking dirty plates. "I told her I'd clear away this morning. I wanted to make sure you had everything you wanted, your first morning back and all."

"Yes, lovely, Mrs. D. You're a wonder with the eggs as always. Nick'll be sorry he slept in."

"Oh no, sir. The scamp was in the kitchen before dawn, snatching bangers right from the skillet barely cooked through, if you please, and then out the door for the Lord knows what mischief."

"Yes, the Lord and the Lord only," Drew said with a laugh, and then a sudden clatter from the front of the house made them both jump. "That was never Nick."

Drew hurried to the terrace railing and looked down over the front lawn. Coming up the drive with three girls crammed inside was a little roadster meant at best to seat two. The car lurched, making the girls giggle and shriek almost loud enough to cover the sound of the sputtering motor. About fifty feet further, the engine died and then kicked back into life amidst the jeers of the passengers and the driver's half-growled cursing. Why a woman could never be trusted behind the wheel of an automobile, Drew didn't know, but he was certain it was true nonetheless. When the car slowed to a stop, he went round to the front of the house and down the steps.

The driver waved, smiling up at him with wide blue eyes and a coquettish tilt to her bobbed blond head. "We're here," she called in a high, babyish voice that was a world away from the one she used for cursing.

"Welcome to Farthering Place, Miss Parker," he said with polite reserve as he opened the car door for her.

All three of the girls giggled, but the dark-haired one in the middle looked swiftly away, pretending to look for something in her handbag. Realizing his error, Drew walked around the car and opened the passenger door.

"Miss Parker," he repeated, reaching over to take the brunette's hand.

She surprised him with an impish grin, a firm grip, and an intelligent pair of eyes that just happened to be the color of periwinkles. "You've found me out at last."

"Hey, you found me out, too!" protested the girl to her left, the one Drew had unthinkingly crowded even further into the corner of the seat when he had reached over to Madeline.

"A thousand pardons," he said, smiling at the diminutive redhead and bringing her to her feet with flourishing gallantry. He helped Madeline out next. The blonde at the wheel merely sat smiling at Drew, thrusting out her hand once he had released Madeline's.

"Don't forget baby," she cooed.

"Have they named baby yet?" he asked, putting his hands contemplatively behind his back. "Or shall we simply put 'Baby Girl Horwitz' on your place card at dinner tonight?"

The other girls giggled again. With a knowing grin on her red lips, the blonde slid over to his side of the car and got to her feet, putting her arm through his.

"It's Brower. Muriel. But *you* can call me Baby Girl. How ever do you drive these cars on the wrong side and everything? And, yes, I'd love you to show me the grounds."

The little redhead rolled her eyes. "Oh, brother."

"Charmed, Miss Brower, I'm sure," Drew said, smoothly disengaging her arm as he turned to the other girls. "And your other friend, Miss Parker?"

"Carrie Holland is the one you nearly crushed."

"Think nothing of it," the redhead said with a grin.

He found the grin infectious and gave her one of his own. "Miss Holland, a pleasure."

Muriel sidled up next to him and took his arm once more. "Now you can show me your castle, sweetie, and we can go from there."

"Perhaps we can arrange for the three of you to see the place after you've got settled in," Drew said as he again disengaged himself. "For now, I'd best fetch someone to take up your luggage and—"

"Uncle Mason!"

Madeline hurried up the stone steps to give her uncle a warm hug.

"Madeline, dear, how lovely to see you again." Mason drew her close to give her a fond kiss on the cheek. "And how nice to have your friends."

After another swift round of introductions, they all went into the house. Following behind everyone else, Drew couldn't help stealing another glance at Madeline Parker. She was tall, only three or four inches below his own six feet, gracefully slender and delightfully feminine. He'd seen the photograph on Mason's desk—a gawky beanpole of a girl, pirouetting on the beach in Atlantic City and smiling hugely. There was a world of difference between twelve and twenty-two, no denying that.

Perhaps there was hope for the weekend after all.

— Two —

Uncle Mason immediately entrusted Madeline and her friends to the capable Mrs. Devon, and soon the girls found themselves settled into a trio of rooms at the sunny south wing of the house. Madeline thought hers was particularly lovely with its wide bay window and huge four-poster bed draped in pale blue damask. It managed to be opulent and rich and yet light and airy all at once. She could hardly wait until it came time to nestle under the heavy coverlet and fine linen sheets like a princess in a fairy tale.

"Imagine," Muriel groused as she barged through the connecting door from the room she had been given, a copy of *Silver Screen* under her arm. "The three of us and only one bathroom. Is your room any better than mine?"

Madeline had been kneeling on the window seat, looking through the mullioned windows and admiring the lush rose gardens, but now she unfolded her long legs and swung around to sit on the edge of the seat and scowled at her friend.

The maid, a girl called Anna, looked up from her task of transferring Madeline's delicate lingerie from a suitcase to a bureau. "Is there a problem, miss?"

"Don't you mind her, honey," Carrie told her, a hint of South Carolina drawl showing through. "Some people wouldn't be happy in the governor's mansion."

"Yes, miss," Anna said, and she stood up. "I'll see your things are unpacked after luncheon has been served."

"We're lucky there isn't just one bathroom for the whole floor," Madeline observed once the girl was gone. "It's not like these old places were originally built with them, you know."

"And what's wrong with these rooms?" Carrie demanded. "They look just like rooms in an old manor house should. Velvet drapes and fussy old wallpaper and carved furniture that's been here just hundreds of years. I love my room. And did you see the view down toward the woods over there? It's just dreamy."

"I'll tell you what's dreamy," Muriel confided to Madeline. "That cousin of yours. Mr. Farthering."

Carrie breathed a little "ooh" of agreement.

Madeline laughed. Muriel always latched on to the best-looking man at hand. This time, though, Madeline didn't feel like letting her have everything her own way. Besides the thick dark hair and arresting gray eyes, besides the undeniably handsome face, there was something about Drew Farthering that was worth more than a second look.

"Oh, is he attractive? I didn't notice."

"You didn't notice," Muriel muttered, smirking.

"Besides," Madeline said, "he's not actually my cousin, you know. Uncle Mason's only his stepfather."

"Why didn't you ever tell us about him before?" Carrie asked.

"I never met him till now."

Muriel arched one finely penciled brow and lit a cigarette. "I'd say if there was any man I was glad was *not* my cousin, it would be that one. He's adorable. What's it they call him? Drew?"

Madeline nodded. "Short for Andrew, I think. But his first

name is something else, some stodgy family name he doesn't like."

"Drew's fine by me," Muriel said. "Adorable Drew. A real English gentleman and all that."

"He's probably like all the men, here and at home," Madeline said with an airy wave of one hand. "Full of hot air and applesauce."

"Who's on the cover this time?" Carrie asked, snatching Muriel's magazine. "Oh, Lucy Lucette. They'll put anybody on there."

"Ain't that the truth," Muriel said. "I hear dear Lucy will do anything to get her name in the paper."

"She's got a new picture coming out, doesn't she? *The Soiled Dove*?"

"No, they shelved that one 'cause they couldn't get a backer. This is something about a cage." Muriel reclaimed the magazine and flipped through the pages until she found what she wanted. "*Anabella's Gilded Cage*. Sounds decadent."

Shaking her head, Madeline went to the wardrobe, took out one of the evening gowns hanging there, and draped it over the bed.

Carrie "oohed" again and ran her hand over the pale green satin. "That's not the one from Giselle's, is it? Oh, you didn't!"

"I did."

"I thought you said it was too—"

"I changed my mind."

Muriel came over to inspect the garment in question. "Pretty sporty, if you ask me. A little out of your league, isn't it, doll?" She held it up against herself, dousing it in cigarette smoke as she did. "Now, on me it would be *trez chick*. And would the boys come running."

"*Tres chic*," Madeline corrected, taking the shimmering creation from her. "And why not on me? Uncle Mason had Madame Giselle create it especially for me, after all."

"Don't get me wrong, Madeline, honey," Muriel said. "You've got the stuff all right. But you're more the organdy type." She clasped her hands in front of herself and somehow managed to look demure. "White organdy with little puffed sleeves and a bunch of violets at the waist."

"Maybe forty years ago," Madeline protested with a laugh, and she held the daring gown up before her reflected image, wondering what Aunt Ruth would think to see her in it. "It *is* pretty, isn't it?"

"Pretty enough to make our Adorable Drew forget his stuffy English manners and sweep you off your feet." Muriel grinned. "Unless I get to him first."

"The poor kid," Carrie said.

Lunch was served, buffet style, on the terrace. Madeline had hoped she and her friends would meet more of her uncle's guests, but besides the three girls, only a few others had come to the table. The rest, having breakfasted late, had evidently decided to forgo the noon repast in favor of a hearty meal at teatime.

"Your uncle is meeting with his business partners for the afternoon," Drew told her, "and my mother has gone out driving and to the shops in Winchester with Mrs. Chesterton and Mrs. Laney."

"Oh, I had hoped to meet her right away."

"She should be in well before the party tonight." He picked up a plate for her at the serving table, and she couldn't help noticing how nice his hands were, perfectly groomed but not overly fussy—like his clothes, stylish but unselfconsciously masculine.

"Would you care for kidneys?" he asked. "Veal? Hashed meat?"

She hesitated for a moment, uncertain what sort of meat

would be in the hash and revolted by the thought of eating kidneys. "The veal, please," she said finally. "And some of that delicious-looking bread and cheese."

"Excellent choice," he said as he put some meat on her plate. "Now, which of the cheeses would you prefer? Red Leicester? Wensleydale? Cheddar?"

"The Lancashire." A pleasant-looking young man with sandy hair came up beside them, and after tucking his paperbacked novel under his arm, helped himself to a large serving of a pale yellow cheese. "If I were three years marooned on a desert island, Miss Parker, this would be what I craved the most."

She stared at him for a moment, wondering if he had lost his mind, and then she laughed. "*Treasure Island*! Oh, then I must have some of that."

Drew shook his head and served her a portion of the cheese in question, along with a slice of hearty brown bread. "I regret, Miss Parker, that I cannot present to you Mr. Stevenson's illustrious Ben Gunn. At the moment, all we have available is the equally unbalanced Nick Dennison. Mr. Dennison, Miss Madeline Parker."

Nick took Madeline's outstretched hand and made a flourishing bow over it. "Delighted, Miss Parker. And, before you ask, yes, the indomitable Dennison who serves as butler to Farthering Place has the honor of being my father."

He smiled as he said it, but there was a hint of a challenge in his hazel eyes. He was waiting for her reaction. So, evidently, was Drew Farthering.

"It's always a pleasure to meet a literary man," she said, squeezing his hand, and his smile warmed in return.

"Is that Stevenson you're reading now?" she asked.

"This? Oh no." Nick began helping himself to a variety of the hot dishes. "Do you like mysteries, Miss Parker?"

"Don't tell anyone," she said, lowering her voice, "but I love them."

"Capital!" Nick showed her the book he carried: *The Footsteps at the Lock*. "Have you read any Ronald Knox? I've only just started this one."

"I haven't heard of him," Madeline admitted.

"Some priest chappie turned mystery writer. I just got through *The Three Taps*. He tells a ripping tale, Father Knox. He's even got a list he calls his 'Ten Commandments' about what one should and shouldn't put into a proper detective story. I think he's jolly right, too."

Madeline took the book from him, examining it. "Do you read, Mr. Farthering?"

"I manage to make out most of the words," Drew said as he handed the plate to her and began filling his own.

Madeline pursed her lips, fighting a smile. "I mean, do you read mysteries? Have you read anything by Knox?"

He considered for a moment as he cut a slice of bread. "*The First Blast of the Trumpet Against the Monstrous Regiment of Women*?"

She tried to look severe but managed only to laugh. "Not John Knox. Ronald Knox. Do you never say anything meant to be taken seriously?"

"On the contrary," he said, "I'm quite a serious person."

"Monumentally solemn," Nick put in, reclaiming his book and tucking it into his coat pocket.

"Dare I say grim?" Drew asked, his expression thoughtful.

"I think you may go so far as grim," Nick said, "provided you do not venture past that and on to moribund."

"There," Drew told Madeline in triumph. "What would such a dour fellow be doing reading so frivolous a thing as a mystery novel?"

Nick looked at Madeline and tapped the side of his nose knowingly, saying in a loud stage whisper, "I have it on the best of authorities that Mr. Farthering has a complete set of Doyle in his study, several of Mrs. Christie's novels in his golf bag, and a stack of books by that Sayers woman in the boot of his car."

"I won't hear such outright falsehood!" Drew protested. "I've only got *Murder on the Links* in my golf bag. The rest of the Christies and all of the Sayerses are up in my study now, too."

"Oh, how wonderful!" Madeline exclaimed. "I love Lord Peter. I was just sure Harriet would break down and marry him at the end of *Strong Poison*."

"Well, don't despair," Drew said. "I've heard Miss Vane is to return in Lord Peter's new adventure, so all matrimonial hope is not lost."

"Shall we sit down?" Nick asked. "I believe Miss Parker's friends are missing her."

"Let me introduce you to them, Mr. Dennison," Madeline said.

"Yes, do that," Drew told her, a hint of distraction in his voice. The butler was standing portentously at the terrace door, obviously waiting to speak to him. "If you'll both excuse me, I'll be back in a moment."

Madeline watched him as he went to confer with Dennison.

"You and Mr. Farthering have known each other for a long time, haven't you?" she asked Nick.

"All our lives. My mother was parlormaid here when I was born. When she died, Drew's father was good enough to put me in the nursery with Drew and provide for me to be sent on to school with him up through Oxford. I can never repay either of them. I know my father will never leave here, and I suppose I'll be around, as well."

"Oh, really?"

Nick nodded. "Mr. Padgett, the estate manager, is letting me apprentice with him as it were. Totting up the bills, collecting rents, that sort of thing. Once he decides to chuck it all in, I'll be next in line. It's the least I can do for the old place, and fine use for my business studies, eh?"

"And Mr. Farthering—?"

"Joyous tidings," Drew said, hurrying back up to them. "Denny informs me that Minerva is now a happy mother made."

"Huzzah!" Nick cried. "Sound the trumpets and let the welkin ring! I had some sausages for her this morning and was wondering where she had got to."

"Minerva?" Madeline looked from one to the other of them, wondering who this Minerva might be and why Dennison had brought this news particularly to Drew.

"Minerva," Drew informed her, "is Farthering Place's resident feline."

"A cat?" Madeline laughed. "Dennison seemed awfully serious when he brought you the news."

"He was. Most grave."

"She's all right, isn't she?"

"Oh yes," Drew said, adding one last spoonful of green peas to his plate. "She's thriving, as are her five little ones."

"Then what was he so concerned about?"

"It seems she gave birth in the cupboard in my dressing room."

"Oh dear," said Nick.

Madeline looked at him and then at Drew. "Is that so awful?"

"I'm afraid, to Denny, it's no less than a tragedy," Drew said. "It seems Minerva decided there was nothing more suitable in which to swaddle her newborns than my new cheviot trousers."

"Shame," Nick murmured, popping a bit of cheese into his mouth.

"Yes, it seems so," Drew agreed, "especially since I told him he's not to move her off them for now. You'd think I'd suggested something reprehensible—murder or treason of some variety."

Nick nodded solemnly. "Or serving the Rothschild with the fish course."

"Well, come on then." Drew took Madeline's arm and turned her toward the table. "Lunch is getting cold, and your friends have too long been spared the pleasure of meeting young Mr. Dennison."

"Jolly nice to have some new girls about for the festivities and all." Nick shifted his plate to his left hand and used his right to smooth back his hair. "Oh, I say, Miss Parker, do either of your friends read mysteries?"

Madeline laughed. "Only *Silver Screen*."

The party that evening was lavish and suitably chic. Suave gentlemen in dinner jackets and black ties went to dinner in the company of elegant ladies dressed in diaphanous gowns cut to show off daring backs and bold décolletage. After the sumptuous meal came an offering of drinks and dancing in the ballroom, which evidently had once been a medieval great hall. This was to be followed by an extravagant display of fireworks on the front lawn. Although Madeline had attended a great many society functions since her debut four years before, some of them staggeringly gaudy in their ostentatiousness, none of them had been as opulent and grand as this. It would be the perfect evening if Drew weren't so busy with all the other guests and if she could escape the attentions of that odious David Lincoln.

He had introduced himself to her, bold, almost smug, and now, for the second time this evening, he held her crushed against him. She would be glad when this dance came at last to an end. He reeked of liquor and stale cigarette smoke, and his way of holding her too close and sliding his hand with just a shade too much familiarity down her bare back made her wish she had been more modest in her choice of evening gowns. Maybe Muriel was right and she was more of an organdy girl after all.

She glanced around for a means of escape and saw Drew in the middle of the room with none other than Muriel herself clinging to his arm, looking up into his face with guileless blue eyes, no doubt cooing over what a big, strong man he was. He was looking uncomfortable, obviously planning his own escape, and Madeline couldn't help a silent giggle.

"What is it, Miss Parker?" Lincoln asked, holding her even closer.

"What? Oh, I'm sorry. Really, it's nothing. Just, um—" She glanced up at him and then away. "I'm getting a little warm with everyone packed in like this. Do you think you could get me something to drink?"

"Of course," he said, his smile suave and insinuating. "If I'm going to leave a lady breathless, I'd rather it be when we're alone."

He left her with a bow at the far end of the room. Once his back was to her, she slipped into the hallway.

"As if I'd ever be alone with you."

She looked around, trying to gain her bearings. This wasn't one of the grand hallways leading to the other wings of the house. It was just a small one, still paneled in rich mahogany and floored with plush carpet, still grand in everything but scale. Surely there was some little out-of-the-way place she could find here, a library or a sitting room maybe, until Lincoln was otherwise occupied.

She tried the first door she came to and found it locked. Probably a broom closet or storage room of some sort. The next led to an austere passageway that looked as if it might end up in the kitchens. She might have to come back to that one if she didn't find anything more promising farther on. Finally she pushed open the door at the very end.

"Madeline, dear, do come in."

"Uncle Mason!"

Madeline found herself in a small study with a lovely vaulted ceiling and arched windows. Her uncle sat behind an untidy old desk ornamented with intricate carvings and stacked with ledger books and a jumble of papers weighted with an ivory-handled letter opener with a gleaming blade. In the overstuffed chair across from him sat a grandfatherly looking man in expensive but rumpled eveningwear. Both men stood to greet her.

"Come in, come in," Mason repeated, smiling. "Shut the door or we shall never be able to hear ourselves over the music."

Madeline did as he asked and then drew a startled breath to realize a third man was standing with his back to her, searching through a book that lay open on a side table.

"Mr. Lincoln, I—"

The man turned to face her. He wasn't Lincoln after all.

"I beg your pardon," Madeline stammered, one hand over her heart, "but I thought—"

The two older men laughed between themselves.

"Come here, my dear, and let me introduce you," Mason said, and then he nodded toward the older man across the desk from him. "This is Mr. Rushford, one of my business partners. Mr. Rushford, my niece, Madeline."

Mr. Rushford squinted as if his glasses were not strong enough to give him a very clear look at her, but his expression was kind. "How do you do, Miss Parker?"

"Very well, thank you, Mr. Rushford. I *am* sorry to have interrupted your business meeting."

"Not at all. Not at all. Such a lovely interruption is more than welcome."

"And," Mason continued, "this is my new secretary, Merton Clarke."

The secretary, the man she had mistaken for Lincoln, closed the book he was looking through and made a slight bow. "Good evening, miss."

She managed a smile. "Forgive me for staring, Mr. Clarke, but from the back you looked so much like—"

Her uncle nudged his partner. "I told you as much."

"Oh, I don't know." Rushford squinted at the secretary. "I suppose there's a bit of a resemblance. What's it matter anyway? The man's competent, isn't he? So long as Lincoln didn't recommend him just for one of his pranks, what's it matter?"

"Having a good time tonight, my dear?" Mason asked. "You seemed quite popular with the young gentlemen on the dance floor."

"Maybe a little too popular," Madeline said with a rueful laugh.

"Ah, so that's why you ducked in here. And who is it you're running from? Anyone I know? I'll have a word with him, of course."

Madeline squeezed his arm, grateful for his kindness. "Now, nothing so serious as that. I just thought I'd take a minute and see some of the rest of the house." A green marble clock, French by its look, ticked on the carved stone mantel. She couldn't help touching one finger to the figure that ornamented it: a lounging bronze lute player in the dress of an Elizabethan Romeo. "Everything is so beautiful."

"You stay with us as long as you like, Miss Parker," Rushford told her. "So long as you don't mind the company of a couple of crusty old badgers and one industrious little mole."

The others laughed, but Clarke merely blinked his pale eyes and did not protest the description. In evening dress and with his blond hair oiled and slicked back as it was, it was easy to see why, from behind, she had thought he was Lincoln. But his pasty complexion and almost nonexistent chin, oddly dimpled on one side, immediately put an end to the likeness. His stylishly thin mustache did little to improve things and only somewhat concealed the scar over his upper lip.

Madeline gave him her prettiest smile. "I understand you're leaving for Canada. Won't you tell me what you're working on, Mr. Clarke?"

His pale face turned pink, and he stammered something about pumping stations and pressure gauges until his commentary was interrupted by a knock on the door. Before anyone could respond, the door opened and Drew Farthering popped his head into the room.

"Ah, there you are, Miss Parker. We've been wondering where you'd gone off to."

Seeing him, Madeline felt her own face flush with pleasure. "Uncle Mason and his friends have been telling me about Farlinford Processing and the new system they're working on."

Drew put one gloved hand dramatically over his heart. "Good thing I've come to rescue you just in time." He nodded to the gentlemen in the room. "Good evening, sir. And to you, Mr. Rushford. And I don't believe we've met."

He offered his hand to the third man, who shook it briefly.

"Mr. Clarke is my new secretary," Mason explained. "Clarke, this is my stepson, Mr. Farthering."

"Pleased to meet you, sir."

"Likewise," Drew said, and then he turned to Mason once more. "But what happened to old Vickers? He's been with you just ages."

"Vickers suddenly decided to retire, so I've taken on Clarke. He's off to Edmonton, by the way, to see to some things there for me. I haven't told them he's coming." Mason winked. "See you manage a bit of work now and again, Clarke, when you're not fly-fishing."

"Only on the weekends, to be sure," Clarke told him, turning a bit pink.

"Ah. Well, best of luck to you, Clarke," Drew said. "Mind you keep your hand out of the till."

The other men chuckled, and the secretary's face went from pink to scarlet. "See here, Mr. Farthering, I would never—"

"Now, now, hold steady there, Clarke," Drew soothed. "Don't you mind me. Miss Parker will tell you I never say anything meant to be taken seriously." He gave Madeline a sly grin. "And she doubtless keeps a catalog of my faults close at hand lest any of them be forgotten."

"Oh, no," Madeline replied, all wide-eyed innocence. "I don't see any reason to keep a personal record of anything so well-documented and widely known."

"And that, Miss Parker, is why you're so desperately needed at the party." Drew tucked her arm under his. "Do you know, some of our guests, most notably your Miss Brower, are actually starting to believe I'm a charming fellow."

"No!"

"Yes!" Drew assured her, his face all earnest concern. "It's an absolute scandal, and there's no one but you to disabuse them of the notion. Now come along. There's someone I want you to meet."

— Three —

Mother, this is Miss Madeline Parker, your niece."
Drew presented Madeline to a stylish work of cosmetic art with chignon of platinum blond hair nearly as brilliant as the diamonds at her wrists and throat, a dazzling bird of paradise in black silk with plumes of electric blue.

"How are you, my dear?" Constance said, kissing the air somewhere near Madeline's cheek. "Mason's talked of nothing else since you wrote you were coming. Are you having a pleasant time?"

"Everything's wonderful," Madeline said. "And it's so nice to finally get to meet you. I'd love to—"

"You must come and have a chat with me tomorrow afternoon," Constance said, but Madeline could tell she was distracted, searching for someone in the crowd.

Drew cleared his throat. "Mother, Miss Parker—"

"Go get me a stinger, pet."

"But, Mother—"

"Shoo, shoo, shoo," she said, waving him away, "and tell Nelson to be sparing with the crème de menthe."

Drew made a dutiful bow. "Yes, Mother. Pardon me, Miss Parker."

Once he had gone, Constance grabbed Madeline's arm. "I saw you dancing with him."

"What?"

"I saw you dancing with him. David Lincoln." Constance's eyes were hard, a little frantic. "You'll stay away from him if you're a smart girl."

"Y-yes," Madeline stammered. "Of course. I wouldn't—"

"And then of course there's Mrs. Bennington's for hats," Constance said as Uncle Mason came up to them.

"Ah, I'm glad to see the two of you have met." He kissed Constance's cheek. "Would you care to dance, my dear?"

Constance's mouth tightened, but she managed a smile. "Not just now, Mason. I met the child only this very moment."

Mason chuckled. "And you were discussing hats. I should have known to keep my distance. Ah, there's Drew. Better warn him off."

"No, that's all right. I'm sure our dear Madeline will come talk to me later if she wants to know more, though I'll trust she'll rely on my advice." Constance's smile turned even more brittle. "About hats."

"Your drink," Drew said as he came up to them, and he handed Constance a milky beverage in a crystal glass. "Now, Mother, as I was saying, Miss Parker—"

"Oh, no, Ellison." Constance shook her head. "I really can't hear to talk over this music, and my head's a positive torture. I think Madeline and I have a lovely understanding for the moment. You really should take her round to meet some of the other young people."

"Sorry about that," Drew said when they got to the other side of the room. "Nights like this, Mother's always got something going on."

Madeline smiled. "Yes, it seems she does."

They watched Nick in flawless evening dress and Carrie in her stylish ice-blue gown whirl by on the dance floor.

Drew made a slight bow. "I think it time, Miss Parker, that you honored me with a dance or joined me in a Bucks Fizz."

Madeline smiled again. "A Bucks Fizz?"

"My girl! You cannot tell me you've never tasted a really fine Bucks Fizz! I believe they call it a mimosa in the States. Champagne and orange juice."

Madeline looked up at him, keeping her expression playful. "You realize that stuff is illegal at home, don't you?"

"I have heard mention of such things," Drew said, his tone very wise and knowing. "Do you think they'll send a policeman round to take you away?"

"I'll trust you to protect me."

"Does that mean you'll try one?"

"All right, but just a taste," Madeline said. "I'm not much of a drinker really."

Drew beamed at her. "Neither am I, to say truth. No use putting on a grand show like this and then not remembering it the next day, eh? All right now, just a taste of Bucks Fizz coming up."

Madeline smiled as he disappeared into the crowd, and then spent a moment watching Carrie and Nick still dancing, admiring the soft cloud of red fire that crowned Carrie's lovely head, set off to perfection by the ice blue of her dress.

"Thank you for waiting for me."

Madeline turned to see David Lincoln standing close beside her, something dangerous in the smile on his face and the touch of sarcasm in his voice. She took a step away from him and found her bare back against the paneled wall.

"Since you obviously didn't care to dance with me again," he said, "I thought I'd bring your drink here."

"That was very nice of you, Mr. Lincoln, but I really never drink much."

"I thought that might be the case with a violet like you," he said, his mouth curling up on one side, "so I brought you some water. Just to help you cool off."

Her mouth did feel dry all of a sudden, so she accepted the glass. "Thank you."

"Perhaps I'm not such a bad fellow after all."

"I never said you were."

"Perhaps you didn't need to say it." He moved closer to her, bracing one hand against the wall behind her, putting his well-built frame between her and the rest of the crowd. "There's no reason we couldn't be good friends, is there, Madeline? If something were to happen to me, you'd be sorry you weren't a little nicer, wouldn't you?"

She had no room to back away, so she lifted her chin and looked him in the eye. "I've been told, Mr. Lincoln, that a gentleman does not call a lady by her Christian name unless he has asked for and been granted that privilege."

His face was a little flushed, whether from drink or anger she did not know, but he managed still to smile. Then he braced his other hand against the wall, trapping her there between his muscular arms.

"Perhaps if you got to know me better, Madeline, there would be a number of privileges you'd grant me."

"Ah! I see you've met Miss Parker from America."

Drew set down the drinks he had brought with him and grasped Lincoln's hand, ostensibly in greeting, turning Lincoln away from her. Madeline breathed a sigh of relief, glad to see him and glad to see Nick and Carrie had finished their dance.

"You must come and meet some of our other guests, as well," Drew continued. "I don't believe you were ever properly introduced to Nick Dennison here, what with all the confusion last night."

"How do you do?" Nick also shook Lincoln's hand, turning him even further from Madeline. "Grand bash this, isn't it? I hope Dad got you nicely settled into your new room."

Lincoln's heavy brows came together. "Dad?"

"Yes, Dad," Nick said sunnily. "I'm sure you remember him, rather stodgy-looking older gentleman, very proper, very Victorian and that. Took your coat at the door, showed you into the drawing room when you arrived, moved your things for you when you changed rooms."

"Dennison?"

"Precisely. John Hanover Dennison, butler and proud father."

"See here, Farthering," Lincoln protested. "This man says his father is your butler!"

Drew shrugged. "Well, he would know, wouldn't he?"

Madeline and Carrie giggled at the indignation on Lincoln's face.

"You see," Drew added as he picked up one of the glasses he had just brought, "Mr. Dennison is the son of a gentleman's gentleman, which is much better, my dear Mr. Lincoln, than being, as you are, merely a son of a—" he took a slow sip of his Bucks Fizz—"gentleman."

Nick choked back a chuckle.

"You *dare* allow him into a society party," Lincoln sputtered, "knowing he's of the working class?"

"Why, he's not working now, are you, Nick, old man?"

Nick looked about for a moment and then shook his head in wide-eyed innocence. "Don't seem to be now, guv," he said, putting on a broad Cockney accent. "No, most definitely not."

This time Madeline laughed aloud, and Lincoln stiffened.

"I'll make sure everyone here knows about this."

"My friends already know," Drew told him, his expression cool. "And I haven't a care what anyone else thinks."

"Then I see *I* am the one out of place here," Lincoln said with grave condescension.

"I would say you are," Drew agreed. "And I would suggest you turn your attentions toward those who might welcome them."

Lincoln sneered. "Quite right. Perhaps I *should* go spend some time with your mother."

Drew's gray eyes flashed, but before he could respond, Madeline draped her arm across Lincoln's shoulders and smiled into his eyes, all demure innocence, still holding the drink he had brought her.

"Now, I think that's a lovely idea, Mr. Lincoln. I believe Aunt Constance is right over there."

She turned as she said it, indicating the place, and just happened to empty her glass down his immaculate shirtfront.

Lincoln's outraged oath could be heard over the music.

"Merely a slight mishap," Drew assured the startled onlookers as Lincoln stood there gasping.

Madeline put one hand over her mouth, covering a smile. "Oh dear, Mr. Lincoln! Now you see why I really shouldn't drink."

Nick took a dry serviette from the tray and stuffed it into the front of Lincoln's sodden waistcoat. "I'd help you clean up, old man, but I wouldn't want you to think I was working or anything."

Puffed up like an angry cat, Lincoln stalked off.

"I hope he didn't hurt your feelings, Mr. Dennison," Madeline said once he had gone, but Nick only laughed in answer.

"Nonsense," Drew assured her. "He's been offending the upper classes for years now. It's his favorite hobby."

He smiled as he said it, but there was still discernible anger in his taut face as he watched Lincoln make his way through the dancers and straight to Constance. Constance took Lincoln's arm, said something urgent in his ear, and the two of them went out the side door.

Madeline slipped her arm through Drew's. "I never did get to taste that Bucks Fizz."

"Ah, well, we can't have that, can we?" he said, and his smile was a little more genuine as he handed her a champagne flute filled with the bubbly orange beverage.

"Would you care to try one, Miss Holland?" Nick asked. "Or shall we have another dance?"

"I've never been one to turn down a dance," Carrie said, and the two of them disappeared once again into the throng out on the floor.

"All right now, Miss Parker," Drew said, raising his glass. "I would like to propose a toast to your lovely eyes, your fetching green frock, and your most subtle way of dealing with a cad."

She laughed. "It's not green. Not really."

"No?"

"According to Madame Giselle, it's *eau de nil*."

"Ah, water of the Nile. Well, I'm certain Cleopatra herself could not have done it more credit."

He touched his glass to hers and then waited as she took a sip. "And?"

"It sort of spoils the taste of the juice, doesn't it?" she said, handing the glass back to him.

He laughed heartily. "I expect it rather does. Well then, would you care for a dance?"

She listened for a moment, hearing the words in the smoky, mesmerizing tune: "Mad about the boy . . ." Perhaps this wasn't the song to choose for a first dance with a man as attractive as Drew Farthering.

"Or shall we go out into the garden for a bit?" he asked. "We're to have fireworks on the front lawn shortly, if you'd prefer that."

"I'd love to get away from the crowd awhile. I'd better tell Carrie and Muriel where I'll be."

"Oh, they're all right, aren't they? Look. Nick's looking after Miss Holland, and as for your Miss Brower . . ." He took a quick look around. "If she calls me Adorable Drew just once more—"

Madeline laughed. "Why don't you show me the garden?"

They strolled out onto the back lawn. The windswept night was made for sweet talk and stolen kisses, and Drew realized he wasn't immune to it. As they stood for a moment sheltered in the low-limbed wisteria, the music and the other guests seemed far away, not a part of their world at all.

"I love the smell of night," he murmured, breathing in the fragrance of the wisteria blossoms.

"It's beautiful," she said, and seeing her standing there, nymphlike in her diaphanous eau-de-nil gown, he could only echo what she had said.

"Beautiful."

She smiled and took his arm. "I was wondering, Mr. Farthering, if I could ask a favor of you?"

"Certainly," he said, putting his free hand over hers as they began to walk. "If it is in my power."

"I know we met just today, but we *are* family in a roundabout way."

"Yes. I suppose we are."

"Anyway, I was hoping you would start calling me Madeline." There was sweet appeal in her half smile and in her periwinkle eyes. "If you don't think that's too brazen of me."

"Not at all. Not at all. And I'll expect you to call me Drew, as well."

She laughed all of a sudden. "That was partly why I poured

my drink down Mr. Lincoln's front. He was being awfully familiar and pushy, calling me Madeline when I had hardly had three words with him and hoped to never have three more."

"I hope you and I shall have a great many words," he told her. "And dancing and dining and—"

With a thundering boom, a burst of white sparks illuminated the clouded sky.

"And fireworks!" she cried, throwing her hands up in joyous abandon, making him want to romp through the grass alongside her.

He caught her hand, and her fingers squeezed his at the next explosion, a shower of red, white, and blue. After four more red bursts, each more impressive than the last, Drew gestured toward a stone bench a little way ahead of them, and they sat down.

"Having fun?" he asked.

"Oh, yes. It's been quite an exciting night."

"Sorry about that unpleasantness with Lincoln earlier. I should have warned you about him."

"I've already been—" The blast of another round of fireworks overpowered her words and rattled the panes in the greenhouse standing about thirty yards away.

"That was loud enough for them to hear in London," he said once the echoing boom had died away. "Must have been two or three at once."

"We used to have this sort of thing all the time when we still had our house on Lake Michigan. The reflection of the fireworks on the water was the most beautiful thing."

"You don't still have the house?"

She shook her head. "When Mother and Daddy died, there was evidently a lot of debt to be paid, and the house went for that. I was ten, so I didn't know much about it. I'm just thankful Uncle Mason made sure I was taken care of. He's taken very good care of me since then, even if some of Mother's people thought he was a bit too extravagant."

He chuckled. "Protestant work ethic and all that, eh?"

"Something like that. Don't scoff now. There's a lot of wisdom in that school of thought."

"I wouldn't dream of scoffing," he assured her. "There must be something right in it if it produces such unaffectedly lovely creatures as you."

With a hiss and a boom, another rocket exploded over them, bathing them in red light. When it faded, there was still a becoming pink tint to her cheeks.

"And what about your Protestant work ethic?" she asked, a mischievous sparkle in her eyes. "Or perhaps the Church of England has its very own work ethic."

"I daresay it does," he replied. "I don't know how much it's rubbed off on me, though. I was raised in the faith, mind you, but you know how it is. One gets a bit old to be playing church." The sparkle in her eyes faded, just slightly, and he hastened to add, "Of course, lord of the manor and all, I still attend services most times. Funny old Bartlett, the vicar. His homilies never have a thing to do with the texts he chooses."

She smiled. "As long as he reads the text, I think it's a good start. No one can really listen to those words and not feel them inside."

"Perhaps that's so. Once my father passed on, though, none of it seemed quite the same to me anymore." He shrugged and looked down, not wanting her to see into his eyes just then.

"You loved him very much."

"He loved me," Drew replied with swift certainty. "And I never saw him do an unkind or dishonest thing all my life." He smiled a little wistfully. "As Hamlet said of his own father, 'I shall not look upon his like again.'"

She smiled, too. "My father was like that. I suppose every child of a loving father makes him into a bit of an idol."

"That may be so. At least you had your uncle to look after you. Losing my dad—I guess I've been rather at loose ends ever since."

"Uncle Mason has been awfully good to me. My faith meant a great deal to me too after I was left an orphan."

"I can understand how you felt." He looked up again, making his expression exaggeratedly sincere. "At the tender age of nine, *I* was left an orphan."

"You were not," she said with a giggle.

"I was," he insisted. "But, being so young, I hadn't a clue what to do with it, so I sent it back."

Her laughter was covered by the fireworks' grand finale, a last salvo of green and red and blue, hissing and booming, answered by thunder from the clouded sky. Then, save the faint sounds of music and laughter from the house, there was silence.

They sat for a few minutes not saying anything, and Drew felt as if he could stay there with her for a very long while indeed. He'd never felt quite this way about any girl before, especially not so suddenly. But did she—?

"Madeline?" he asked, trying to keep his tone light and conversational.

"Yes?"

"I think . . ." He reached over and took her hand. "I know we've only just met, but I've already grown terribly fond of you."

He waited expectantly, but she said nothing. She didn't even look at him.

"You haven't told me how you feel," he pressed after a moment, and she turned her face nearer to his, until their lips almost touched.

"Do I have to put it into words?" she asked, her voice low and languid, her eyes inviting.

He could feel the rush of blood in his veins. "Yes."

She moved even closer and then gave him a quick, childish peck on the cheek. "I think you're cute."

She jumped to her feet and stood looking down at him with a pixie grin. After a stunned moment, he stood beside her, glad for the darkness that covered his flushed face.

"I see."

She kissed the tip of one finger and pressed it to his lips. "I think you're awfully handsome, and I've never been attracted to anyone half so much, but that may be nothing but moonlight and Bucks Fizz."

Laughing softly, he shook his head and sat down again. "Fair enough."

"Well, I *am* a tease," she admitted, "and so are you, if you want the truth. Bringing me out here into this lovely garden and not even trying to kiss me. And looking at me through those long lashes. You should be ashamed."

He laughed again. "And if I *had* tried to kiss you?"

She put her hands behind her back, a coy little gesture that made her all the more enticing. "I might have let you."

"Or poured a drink down my shirt."

She grinned at him still. "You can never be too sure."

He drew one of her hands into his own and pressed it with a light kiss. "I thank you, mademoiselle, for returning me to my senses." Looking up at her, he kissed her hand again, this time with tantalizing deliberation. "We'll talk about this again one day."

With a flash of lightning and a rattling clap of thunder, the sky ripped open, releasing a torrent of rain.

"Quick!"

He grabbed her hand and ran toward the greenhouse. It wasn't far away, but by the time they reached shelter they were both soaked through with cold rain and warmed with running and laughter. The smell of earthy decay inside the greenhouse seemed stronger than usual. There was also the faint odor of fresh paint and another nasty smell too, but rain did that sometimes. He hunted down a lantern and a dry match, and soon they had a small circle of light.

"I'm afraid your lovely dress is spoilt," he said, plucking at her rain-spotted sleeve.

She laughed. "You're not much better." She pushed a lock of hair from his forehead and wiped away the little rivulet of water that had run down from it onto his nose.

"We shall look a sight, the pair of us, going back into the house like this." He dared her with a smile. "We could stay out here and create a scandal. Or, I should say, have one invented for us."

She pursed her Cupid's bow lips and leaned conspiratorially closer, clinging more tightly to his arm. "You mean when they find us out here frozen to death?"

"Oh, I say, what an idiot I am. Of course you're cold."

He began struggling out of his sodden dinner jacket, but she stopped him.

"No, thank you. I'm drenched enough as it is."

"Well—" He held up the lantern, shining its feeble light around the greenhouse. "Ah, just the thing. Come along."

He marched her over to a pile of mackintoshes tossed in the corner.

"We mustn't have you catch your death. It simply isn't done."

He picked up the coat on top of the pile and held it up for her to put on, but she wrinkled her nose, shrinking back. The nasty smell was stronger than ever now.

"It doesn't look entirely clean, does it?" he admitted, a bit embarrassed.

She took the lantern and examined the next one down. "This one's worse, I think. Smells sort of sickening."

"Hold that closer," he said, puzzling over the dark stain.

Something had spilled or soaked over the coat, and he pulled it back to see if the rest of the pile were in the same state. Madeline gave a sudden, stifled cry, and he grabbed the lantern and set it down before she could let it crash to the floor. She didn't make another sound, but she clutched his shoulder painfully hard, her breath coming in little smothered gasps.

He flung the coat back into place and stood up, as shaken as she.

"Come on. Let's go back inside."

"Drew, that's—"

"Come on," he urged, and he led her back to the house, through the kitchen door, and into the chair nearest the fire.

"Are you all right?" he asked, dropping to one knee on the stone floor beside her. "Here, give me that, if you please."

He snatched a drink from the tray Anna was taking to the guests and pressed Madeline's hands around it.

"Drink that down. You all right?"

"I don't—"

"Drink it," he insisted, and she managed a sip.

"Is the young lady ill, sir?" Anna asked.

Drew looked up, distracted. "No. Yes. Go and get Mr. Parker straightaway, if you would, please."

"Yes, sir." She bobbed a tiny curtsy and disappeared through the kitchen's swinging doors. A moment later, the doors swung again and Mason came into the kitchen.

"Drew? Madeline, my dear, what is the matter?"

Drew got to his feet. "We just found Lincoln in the greenhouse. I'm afraid he's taken a load of buckshot to the head."

— Four —

"W e're to touch nothing in the greenhouse and allow no one to leave the party until they arrive," Mason said as he replaced the telephone receiver.

"I could have told you that much," Drew muttered, wishing he could do something more than stand about waiting for the police. "Besides, it's too late about the greenhouse. No telling what evidence we've ruined."

"I'm sure the police can handle this," Mason said, his face pale. "We'd best tell Dennison what's happened. He can keep his eye on the guests, too."

"Nick as well, if you don't mind, sir. He can be quite useful from time to time."

"Very well. Send Anna for them both, if you like. No need to tell her what's happened yet. It'll be all over the village by morning anyway."

Soon Dennison, *père et fils*, joined them in the kitchen.

Keeping his voice low, Drew gave them the news.

"David Lincoln!" Nick said. "Of course, it stands to reason that someone would eventually—"

Madeline took a quavering little breath and hugged her arms around herself.

"Quiet, you brute," Drew growled. "Why don't you just make a general announcement?"

"Sorry."

"Give me that." Drew began to pull off Nick's dinner jacket, intending to put it around Madeline, but Dennison interrupted.

"No need of that, sir. I have just the thing. I'm certain Mrs. Devon won't object."

The housekeeper had an old flannel wrapper she liked to warm at the kitchen hearth before she retired in the evening. Dennison handed it to Drew, who quickly swaddled Madeline in its capacious warmth.

"Good work, Denny." He knelt again at Madeline's side. "Better now?"

She managed a slight nod and a trembling smile.

"Good girl. Sorry you had to see that. And sorry this cretin has upset you."

He glared at Nick.

"Now, see here, Drew," Nick protested, "I know this is no game anymore. A man's been killed, and the guilty party is most likely in the next room drinking Bucks Fizz. I think we should start questioning everyone."

"We?" Drew felt a tingle of intrigue in spite of himself. "You mean—"

"Please, boys." Mason glanced at his niece. "I've sent for Mrs. Devon to look after Madeline until the police have had a chance to speak to her. We can let them see to things from here on in."

"But, sir," Drew began, but he stopped when he saw the look on his stepfather's face. "As you say, sir."

Nick heaved a sigh of disappointment. "I suppose we shall

have to miss our opportunity to play Holmes and Watson, then, if the police are to see to things."

Drew grinned a little. "All for the best, my man, all for the best. Our Miss Parker wouldn't love us anymore if I took up smoking a foul-smelling pipe and you had a Jezail bullet in your shoulder or your leg. The stories aren't actually too clear on which it is, so perhaps you'd best have one of each. Just to be certain."

"Anything for our Miss Parker," Nick agreed. "Still, it seems a shame. We could solve the thing and then see if Father Knox would approve of our methods."

"We're more likely to break all of his fusty ten commandments," Drew said, "and that will make him so cross he'll never let you read another of his stories again."

"What shall I tell your guests, sir?" Dennison asked after he had given both young men a stern look.

Mason shook his head. "Nothing yet. No need to spoil everyone's good time, so long as no one tries to leave. If anyone does, ask him to step into my study, and I'll have a word with him myself."

"I shall have the staff keep watch."

"And post Peterson outside the greenhouse, if you would, please," Mason said. "Just to be certain."

"Very good, sir."

As it turned out, none of the guests, save the guilty party, realized anything was amiss. The drinking and dancing proceeded uninterrupted, Mrs. Devon came into the kitchen to fuss over Madeline, and soon there was a discreet tapping on the kitchen door.

Drew answered it himself.

"Evening, sir," said Police Constable Applegate. "I understand there's been a bit of trouble."

Drew peered into the darkness behind the constable's gawky

frame in disbelief. "They didn't send anyone down from Winchester?"

Applegate's freckled face flushed red. "Chief Inspector Birdsong's gone up to Skegness, sir. On holiday."

"So you're, ummm . . . it."

"Well, Hodges had to stay back at the station," Applegate said defensively. "But the chief inspector's been wired. He'll be down on the first train tomorrow."

Nick only partially concealed a chuckle, and Applegate lifted his chin.

"I *am* a fully qualified police constable, you know."

"Yes, yes, of course," Drew soothed. "Come in. It's just we rather thought the chief inspector would come for this sort of thing. We don't have much in the way of homicide round these parts, do we?"

"No, sir. I thought we'd never—"

Mason cleared his throat, and Applegate made his expression suitably solemn.

"Evening, Mr. Parker. I'm sorry to hear there's been an unfortunate incident." Applegate took out his official notebook and pencil. "I understand a Mr. Lincoln was the victim. Your houseguest, was he, sir?"

"That's right," Mason said. "And he was part owner at Farlinford. His father was one of my partners until he passed on."

Applegate made the appropriate notations. "I see, sir. And Mr. Drew found the body?"

Mason nodded. "That's right."

Drew went to Madeline's side. "Miss Parker and I."

"Miss Parker is my niece," Mason added.

"And the scene of the murder?" Applegate asked.

"The greenhouse." Mason gestured toward the kitchen door. "This way."

"If you'll come along, sir." Applegate motioned to Drew and then to Madeline. "And you, miss."

"I should say not!" Mrs. Devon kept her arm around her charge's damp shoulders. "And I will thank you, Jimmy Applegate, to ask the poor girl your questions straightaway so I can get her into some dry things and a warm bed. I fancy your mum would like to hear how you do your job without a thought for a young girl's sensibilities."

"It's all right, Mrs. Devon," Madeline said. "If they need me to—"

"Is it absolutely necessary for her to go back out there?" Mason asked.

The constable glanced at the uncooperative faces surrounding him. Mrs. Devon was positively bristling.

"No, I don't suppose so, sir," he conceded. "Perhaps just a few questions and then I don't suppose there would be any harm in just you and Mr. Drew going out with me. Has someone been watching the greenhouse to see it's not tampered with?"

"Our gardener," Mason said.

"That's all right then. Now, miss."

"I really don't know what to tell you," Madeline admitted. "We watched the fireworks and then it started to rain, so we ran into the greenhouse. Drew—Mr. Farthering was going to get me a raincoat from the pile there, but when we looked at them, we found . . ." She bit her lip. "We found Mr. Lincoln."

"And you knew Mr. Lincoln, did you?"

"Not really. I met him tonight. At the party."

"But you recognized him when you saw him there? In the greenhouse?"

She shook her head rapidly, closing her eyes as if to block out the gruesome sight. "Not really. His face . . . his head . . ."

She clung to Mrs. Devon, who was stroking her hair, making

little soothing noises even as she stared daggers into P. C. Applegate.

Drew knelt by Madeline's chair once more and took her hand. The poor kid. "Come on, Jimmy. She really didn't see any more than that."

Applegate sighed. "All right then, Mrs. Devon. I suppose that will be all."

"I should say," Mrs. Devon muttered as she led Madeline up the back stairs.

Drew watched after them until they were out of sight, then turned back to the young constable. "Shall we press on?"

"Right," Applegate said. "The greenhouse, was it?"

"This way." Nick hurried to the kitchen door to usher them all out, but Applegate held up his hand.

"Just Mr. Parker and Mr. Farthering, if you please."

"Don't be such a stick, Jimmy," Nick said. "Just one good look, eh? You know you're just aching to see. Why keep it all to yourself?"

"The chief inspector would never—"

"Oh, let him," Drew said with an air of sage resignation. "He'll only badger you until you do anyway."

"I will," Nick confirmed.

Applegate looked heavenward and heaved a great sigh. "Come on then."

"You're a positive ghoul, you know that," Drew told Nick as they followed the faint light of P. C. Applegate's torch through the dark garden.

"Evidence, man, evidence. How are we to find the murderer if we don't see the evidence?"

"The chief inspector will be up here in the morning. You know you'll never be able to push him about the way you do Jimmy."

Nick grinned. "That's why we have to have a look tonight."

Everything at the scene of the crime was just as Drew and Madeline had left it. The lantern still burned, the air was still thick with the sickly sweet smell of blood, and the body on the floor was still quite dead.

Nick crowded in to look over Applegate's shoulder as he pulled the soiled mackintosh away from the victim's mangled head. Then he turned away with a quick intake of breath.

"Too much for you, old man?" Drew asked with a smirk.

Nick gulped. "Not at all. It just doesn't take me long to look at a dead body." He gulped again and gave Drew an anemic smile. "He is rather a mess, isn't he?"

Applegate covered the body again and jotted down a few notes.

"I beg your pardon, Mr. Drew, but how is it you know this is Mr. Lincoln?"

Drew thought for a moment. "I suppose I just do. I mean, he's got Lincoln's build and fair hair and all. That's his ring, I'm certain. No gentleman of style would wear such a vulgar thing. Of course, it's a bit hard to tell one man from another in eveningwear."

"We'll have fingerprints taken, naturally," the constable said. "Is there family we should notify, Mr. Parker?"

"Not that I know of," Mason said. "His father died three years ago. His mother, some time before that. I don't believe there were other children."

"He wasn't married?"

"I believe there was a Mrs. Lincoln for a short while. Re-married and living in Ibiza now, as I recall." Mason rubbed his hands together. "I suppose we ought to have Dr. Wallace out. Or the mortuary."

"We've seen to that, Mr. Parker," Applegate said. "They

should be here anytime now to get everything put right. You did say Mr. Lincoln was staying the weekend?"

"That's right," Mason told him, looking relieved to be going back into the house. "Would you like to see his room?"

"In a moment, sir. First off, I have to ask if there was anyone in particular who would benefit from Mr. Lincoln's death. Or anyone with a grudge?"

"Of course not," Mason said, his expression bland. "Not that I know of anyway."

Applegate looked at Mason narrowly, and Drew could tell what he was thinking. The rumors about Constance and Lincoln were well known in the village. Applegate couldn't have missed hearing them.

"I see, sir." Applegate made a few more notes. "Now, as it's rather late, if I can just have a list of your guests, as well as everyone living at Farthering Place, including staff, we'll let you get to bed. Of course, we'll have to lock up the room Mr. Lincoln was using. And leave your gardener out here to keep watch. P. C. Benson will be on duty at six. He can take over for your man then."

"Naturally. Naturally."

Mason led the constable out of the greenhouse, but Drew stayed behind, staring down at the body. Thinking.

After a moment, Nick nudged his arm. "I say, Drew, hadn't we best get back to the house? I mean, I'm sure old Birdsong won't much like it if we're out here mucking things up worse than they already are."

"Evidence, man, evidence." Drew grinned. "Wasn't that what you said?"

Nick glanced at the stained mackintosh and grimaced. "Couldn't we look for evidence in the house?"

"I was just wondering about that ring of his," Drew said.

"You mean why the killer didn't take it?"

"No. Look at his hand." Drew held the lantern close to the body. The right arm wasn't completely covered up, and the third finger of the right hand had a band of flesh clearly lighter than the rest. The ruby ring glimmered just above the knuckle. "What would make it move up like that?"

"Gentlemen, if you please."

Drew and Nick turned to see Applegate at the greenhouse door, looking disapprovingly at them.

"Sorry, Jimmy," Drew said.

"We haven't touched anything," Nick added. "Just looking for evidence. Can't solve the case without evidence."

"I'm sure we'll thank you to leave the evidence to the proper authorities," Applegate said, drawing himself up to his full, very official height. "I need to dust for fingerprints and take photographs before they come round for the body, so if you'll kindly excuse me . . ."

"But, Jimmy," Drew said, "did you notice—?"

"I am a highly trained observer, Mr. Drew."

"As you say," Drew said with a sigh. "Come on, Nick. Let's see what else there is to be seen."

The festive atmosphere inside the house had turned somber. The band were packing up their instruments, and the guests huddled in murmuring groups, most with a cigarette or a drink to soothe the nerves. Per Constable Applegate's instructions, Dennison was dutifully taking the name of each of the guests, and Mason was at the back of the room talking to Rushford.

"It's horrible," the old man said as Drew and Nick came up to them. He removed his spectacles and wiped them with his handkerchief. "My word. Lincoln. I mean, the man was a bit of a cad, but you know what young people are nowadays. We never had such things happen in the old days."

"Certainly not," Mason soothed. "Are you sure you don't want anything?"

"Just some bicarbonate, if you don't mind too much."

"Seems everyone's at sixes and sevens right now, Mr. Rushford," Drew said. "Nick, old man, would you mind . . . ?"

"Not at all," Nick replied. "Just don't start without me."

"Start?" Rushford asked once Nick had darted off to the kitchen.

"Oh, nothing," Drew told him. "This thing with Lincoln has everyone a bit rattled."

"Terrible business," Rushford agreed. "What have the police said?"

"Apparently they don't answer questions," Mason said. "They just ask them."

"Quite right." P. C. Applegate joined them, notebook in hand. "First off, sir, I must ask where Mrs. Parker is at the moment."

"Mrs. Parker?"

"Your wife, sir."

Mason almost concealed his annoyance at this unnecessary revelation. "According to her maid, she has retired for the evening. She was quite understandably upset by what's happened."

"I see, sir. And were you the one to tell her about the, um, incident?"

"No," Mason said. "I don't know how she found out."

"Perhaps I might speak to her, sir?"

"Wouldn't the morning do just as well?" Mason asked.

Applegate eyed him narrowly and made some more notes. "That may be, sir. And when did you hear the news?"

"Drew sent one of the maids for me. I was in my study making a list of a few more things I wanted my secretary to see to once he arrived at our office in Alberta."

"That would be in Canada, sir?"

"When last I saw it, yes."

"Your secretary's name, sir?"

"Merton Clarke."

"And when was he expected to leave?"

"He already has, I believe. He took the train to Southampton, sailing on from there."

"So he left before you wrote your list, did he, sir?"

"Well, yes," Mason admitted. "It was all very last minute. I was going to telegraph it to him at the dock."

"And were you with him when he made this so-called list, Mr. Rushford?"

Rushford started. "Me? No. No, I don't remember a list. Were you making a list, Parker?"

"It was after you and Clarke had left the study," Mason said. "I came out to the party for a bit, saw my wife was in no mood for my company, and thought I'd best take care of a few more things before I turned in."

"How about you, sir?" Applegate said to Rushford. "When you and this Mr. Clarke left Mr. Parker, where did you go?"

"Why, Clarke went up to get his things together and call a taxi. I went into the library and played bridge with a Mr. and Mrs. Halloway and some foreign fellow called Adelante or some such until they called us all out here to tell us there'd been a murder."

"Was this before or after the fireworks, sir?"

"Oh, before. Well before, I'm sure."

Rushford wiped his glasses again and looked relieved at the arrival of his bicarbonate.

"Did I miss anything?" Nick asked as he handed Rushford the glass.

"I have to ask where you were tonight, Nick," the constable said.

"Me? Here and there, I suppose. After we rescued Miss Parker from Lincoln's unwanted attentions, I danced a bit, saw the fireworks on the front lawn, and then danced a bit more. It was Miss Parker's friend, Miss Holland, who was with me. That is until they sent for me and Dad. After the body was found."

"There was an incident between the deceased and Miss Parker?"

"Well, yes. Of a sort."

Nick glanced at Drew.

"Not much of one," Drew said. "He was coming on a bit too brash, and she let him know she wasn't interested. That's all it was."

"I understand you and Lincoln had something of a set-to yourselves last night, Mr. Drew. Is that so?"

"That was less than nothing," Mason put in. "Merely a misunderstanding about the room Lincoln was in. It was quickly sorted out."

"And the last time you saw Mr. Lincoln alive?" Applegate asked Drew.

"It was when Miss Parker sent him packing. Nick and I made sure he understood she meant business. Last he said, he was off to have a word with my—"

P. C. Applegate looked up from his notebook. "A word with whom, sir?"

Drew bit his lip and glanced at Mason. "With my mother, I'm afraid."

"Pardon my asking, sir, but about Mrs. Parker." Applegate looked at Mason, and his freckled face flushed scarlet. "Was Mrs. Parker . . . was she acquainted with Mr. Lincoln, sir? I mean . . ."

"Mrs. Parker was well acquainted with Mr. Lincoln," Mason said coolly. "As I said, his father was one of Farlinford's founding partners, as was Drew's father. We've all known each other for ages."

"I mean, sir . . ." Applegate's face was now beet red. "I mean, there's been talk, just rumor mind you, about Mrs. Parker and Mr. Lincoln in Monte Carlo. I wouldn't dare repeat such a thing if it didn't have bearing on a murder investigation."

"The rumors are just that," Mason said, his usually mild face taut. "Is there something you'd like to know about that actually pertains to the case?"

"Perhaps it would be best to send for Mrs. Parker after all, sir. Just to clarify things."

"Don't you think she's upset enough as it is?"

"I can appreciate that, sir, but under the circumstances . . ."

"Shall I send Anna up for her?" Drew asked.

Mason did not reply for a moment, but then he nodded. "Yes, perhaps that is best."

Drew excused himself, found Anna in the kitchen gossiping about murdering Bolsheviks lurking everywhere, and sent her upstairs.

When he returned to the ballroom, Dr. Wallace was there talking to the others.

"I'm afraid I can't tell you more than was already obvious. Instantaneous death from a shotgun blast to the head. No more than two hours ago. Your fireworks display, Mr. Parker, must have been what masked the sound of it. No other marks or injuries on the body. No weapon at the scene. Marks & Blackistone's have come to remove the body, Constable, if permitted."

"Yes, all right. I've dusted for prints and found nothing but what was on the lantern, probably Mr. Drew's. No weapon found, as you say."

"You did fingerprint the corpse as well, didn't you?" Nick asked. "I mean, just to be sure."

"Yes, I do know my job, thank you. Nothing more there to see. I'll tell Mr. Blackistone he may carry on."

"But, Jimmy," Drew began, "what about—?"

"Doctor! Oh, Doctor!" Anna raced down the front stairway, something Mrs. Devon never allowed. "You must come at once!"

"What is it?" Dr. Wallace asked, hurrying to her.

"It's Mrs. Parker, Doctor. She's dead."

— Five —

The bottle on the night table was marked *Veronol*.

It was empty.

"Did Mrs. Parker typically use this?" P. C. Applegate asked.

Drew narrowed his eyes, studying the expression on the face of the girl standing at his mother's bedside. Beryl had been Constance's personal maid for nearly five years and knew her mistress's habits well.

"She did. If she couldn't sleep or her head was bothering her, she'd take it and go right out." Beryl crumpled her apron in both hands and used it to blot the tears from her round face. "She'd go right out. I didn't think anything of it when she didn't wake at first, but then I saw she was stone dead."

Applegate nodded. "And you helped her dress for bed?"

"Yes, sir. I always did. But she was in a terrible state tonight. I couldn't hardly get her to sit still long enough to let me brush her hair and take off her makeup."

The constable made note of that. "Did she say what had upset her?"

"No, she wasn't much like that. Not one to confide as some ladies are."

"But she had heard about Mr. Lincoln being killed?"

"I'm sure I don't know. I only heard about it just now."

"You didn't go downstairs with the rest of the staff after Mrs. Parker had retired?"

"No, sir. I had my program on tonight. Mrs. Parker was always kind enough to let me listen to *Gert and Daisy* on her wireless, the one in her sitting room."

"So you'd know if there was anyone else up here this evening? After she'd come up to bed?"

"Oh yes, sir. There wasn't nobody. I'd've seen if someone come through the sitting room, and she always kept the hallway door locked."

The girl glanced at the lifeless, negligec-clad form that lay with one bare white arm thrown gracefully over its head. Mason was kneeling beside the bed, patting his wife's cold hand. Drew stood behind him, one steadying hand on his stepfather's sagging shoulder.

"Poor Mr. Parker and Mr. Drew," Beryl sobbed.

"All right," the constable said over another torrent of weeping. "That's all for now."

Anna and some of the other girls were clustered, whispering, in the hallway. But when Beryl came out, they gathered around her and, clucking and consoling, led her away to her quarters.

"This has already been fingerprinted and photographed," Applegate said, and he handed the little bottle to Dr. Wallace, who put it into his black bag along with his stethoscope.

"I'll run some tests to make sure the contents were the same as the label and to make sure it's what's in her system," the doctor assured him. "I see nothing to suggest it wasn't an accidental overdose of the stuff. For now, we'll say death by misadventure."

"Thank you, Doctor," Mason said, not taking his eyes from his wife's waxen face.

"Will you be all right, Parker?" the doctor asked. "I could give you something to help you relax, if you'd like."

"No," Mason murmured. "No, that's all right."

Dr. Wallace snapped his bag shut and came over to the bedside. He looked closely at Mason, and then he lifted Drew's chin so he could better peer at him.

"How about you, son?"

"I don't need anything." Drew patted Mason's shoulder. "I wish you'd get him to bed, though."

"Not yet," Mason said. "Not until they come to—to take her."

"I'll be taking her now," the doctor said, his voice gentle. "There will have to be an autopsy, I'm afraid."

Mason clung a little more tightly to the lifeless hand he held. Then he sighed, released it and stood up. "Of course. Of course."

It was a relief when Mason's man, Plumfield, appeared and led him away.

"I'll let you carry on then, Dr. Wallace," Applegate said. "If you'd like to come along with me, Mr. Drew, I do have a few more questions."

With one final look at Constance, Drew followed the constable out into the now-vacant hallway, shutting the bedroom door behind him.

"You heard what the maid said," Applegate began. "Was there any of that that didn't seem right to you?"

Drew shook his head. "No. Mother's often mentioned taking something to help her sleep some nights. Dr. Wallace prescribed it for her himself, as he said. And Beryl does listen to *Gert and Daisy* every week without fail. I had a friend who acted in it once, and she worried me to death with questions about him."

"Not to be indelicate, sir," Applegate said, "but it would be stretching coincidence if the two deaths were unrelated."

"I suppose it would," Drew agreed. "But we don't even know if my mother knew about Lincoln's death. All the same, earlier on—"

He caught himself, remembering what Mason had said when the constable had first suggested sending for Constance. *According to her maid, she has retired for the evening. She was, quite understandably, upset by what's happened.* Beryl never would have told him Constance was upset over Lincoln's death. She hadn't yet heard about it. Had Mason been mistaken about what she said, assuming the murder was the cause of Constance being upset, or had he lied?

"What is it, sir?" Applegate pressed.

Drew shook his head. "Oh, um, earlier on Mother did complain of a headache. That could be why she went up to bed and took something to help her sleep. It never took much to put her into a state, and everyone knew it."

"I suppose we can't prove whether or not there was a connection until we've had a chance to go through Mr. Lincoln's things. You did have his room locked up after we found the body?"

"I believe my stepfather had someone take care of that."

The constable nodded. "I'd like to see it now, if you please, sir."

Drew rang for a maid, and in another moment they were unlocking the door to Lincoln's room. As it happened, P. C. Applegate's precautions proved futile. There wasn't a fingerprint on anything—not Lincoln's or anyone else's.

"Clean as a whistle," the constable observed. "Are you certain this room was locked up, Mr. Drew?"

"I'm assuming it was, but at the best that was sometime after the murder. With the party going on and all, I expect just about anyone could have come in here and tidied up before Lincoln's body was discovered."

"I did find this in the inside pocket of one of his bags," Applegate said, "in with the handkerchiefs and socks and, er, unmentionables."

He set a thick envelope on the little table next to the bed. Drew opened it to reveal a slip of paper wrapped around twenty ten-pound notes.

This is the last, David, the paper read. *I'm serious this time. I expect he'd find it a relief to know anyway.*

It was Constance's handwriting.

"What do you expect that means, Mr. Drew?" Applegate asked once Drew had told him who had written the note.

"The same as you do. He was blackmailing her."

"And why would that be?"

"Don't be stupid," Drew snapped. "You've heard the gossip. Why do you think he would have?"

"Presuming, then, it was the . . . Monte Carlo incident—I hate to be blunt, sir, at a time like this, but do you think she might have killed him over it?"

Drew sighed and sank down into the overstuffed chair in the corner of the room. "I don't know. I wouldn't have thought so. But then I would have thought her too vain to take her own life."

He drew a slow, deep breath and resisted the urge to bury his head in his arms and cry. His mother was dead. It didn't matter that she had never been much of a mother to him or whether the fault of that was in her or in himself. She was gone and so was the possibility that things between them would ever be any different.

"And the 'he,' sir?"

Drew knit his brow. "What?"

"The 'he,' sir. The one she says would be relieved to know. Who do you think she means there?"

"My stepfather would, I think, be the obvious choice."

"I see," Applegate murmured, and he made another notation in his book.

"Is there—?" Drew steadied his voice. "Is there anything else in Lincoln's things we ought to know about?"

Applegate shrugged. "Apart from a rather large quantity of brilliantine and other gentlemen's toiletries, just the usual clothes and things, sir. A bill from his tailor, racing tips, the odd box of matches. I will ask if you recognize this, sir."

He produced a photograph of a young woman. She could have been no more than twenty-two or -three at the time the picture was taken, though judging by the style of her clothes and hair and the fading portrait itself, she was at least twice that old by now. She was rather pretty.

Drew studied the photo for a moment and then turned it over. In neat block letters, someone had written MARIELLE.

"Not a clue," Drew admitted. "Perhaps Mr. Parker or Mr. Rushford would know."

"I will be talking to them," Applegate assured him.

"Not tonight," Drew said. "Please. Not my stepfather anyway. He can wait till morning, can't he?"

"That'll be all right," Applegate agreed, his voice a touch less official. "Maybe you ought to have a bit of rest as well, sir. And, um, I'm sorry about your mum."

Drew managed a thin smile. "So am I, Jimmy."

It was after three in the morning when Drew finally made it to bed and nearly six before he slept. At a quarter after eight a discreet knock woke him from an insensible sleep. A moment later, Dennison came into the room.

"You wished to be dressed before nine, sir."

Drew didn't respond at first, hoping for just another instant of oblivion, but then he opened his eyes.

It wasn't Denny's usual job, but now he stood over Drew with a tray laden with ham, eggs, and tomato grilled to perfection, along with toast, double cream, and a steaming cup of tea.

"Mrs. Devon's made your favorite, sir, and she's sent up some honey for your toast, fresh from Mr. Cranston's hives, as you like it. For your tea as well, of course."

Drew only stared at him, very stupidly, he was sure, and then he managed a nod.

"That was good of her, Denny."

He struggled into a sitting position, and Denny set the tray across his lap.

"And may I," Denny continued, "on behalf of all of us belowstairs, sir, express our deepest sympathies regarding Mrs. Parker."

Drew closed his eyes. He didn't want to think about Constance, not quite yet, but it would have to be dealt with sooner or later. He managed another nod. "Yes, thank them all for me if you would, Denny."

"Will there be anything else, sir?"

"Not at the moment, no," Drew replied, expecting Denny's usual *very good, sir* and circumspect departure. It was not forthcoming.

Drew looked up at him and saw something more behind the impersonal correctness of his demeanor.

"I'm all right, Denny," Drew told him, surprised at the thickness in his own voice. "Really."

"Very good, sir," Denny said. "I'll just lay out your morning things and draw your bath."

Shortly before nine, Drew was groomed and dressed and in his stepfather's study.

Mason looked weary. Inexpressibly weary. It came as something of a surprise to Drew that there was nothing more in his stepfather's expression. But neither was there anything more in his own. Constance was dead. The idea seemed strange yet.

"Did you sleep?" Drew asked.

Mason shrugged slightly. "Off and on. I don't much remember."

"Has the chief inspector been in yet?"

"Not yet. I'm sure he'll be here and asking for me anytime now, though." Mason sighed. "More questions."

"I can get them put off a day or so if you like, I expect," Drew offered, and Mason patted his arm.

"No, best have it over at once." Mason sighed again and stared into the little fire that had been laid to take the Sunday morning chill from the room. "Not that I can tell them much of anything."

"You could talk to them about the blackmail."

There was a long, thick silence, absolute but for the crackling of the flames. Then the French clock whirred and began tolling the hour in delicate little pings. *One. Two. Three. Four. Five. Six. Seven. Eight. Nine.* For a moment afterward, the sound still resonated in the room. When there was again perfect silence, Mason lifted his eyes to Drew's.

"Blackmail?"

His voice was bland and quiet, almost studiedly nonchalant.

"I see you're not surprised by that, sir," Drew said. "Perhaps you arranged to have it paid for her. I've known some while, so there's no need to shield her now. Especially not from me."

"You've known what some while?"

"Well, not about the blackmail, not till now, but about the reason for it."

His stepfather's dispassionate expression did not change. "You mean you've assumed you know the reason for it."

70

"Come, sir, I'm no longer a child. I know what I've seen and, if I didn't, I've had enough people point it out to me over the past two years."

"People who know no more of the truth of the matter than you, I'm afraid, Drew."

"You mean people not hiding from the truth, don't you, sir?" Drew asked, his words sounding sharper than he meant them to.

"No. People who don't know the truth."

"Then they should be made to know the truth," Drew insisted. "I, at the very least, have the right to know it."

"There are some things she did not wish to have brought up. They are in the past and digging them up now could not benefit anyone. Trust me, son, they have no bearing on this case. She did not wish to have them discussed, and I mean to abide by that now she's gone."

"But she *is* gone! How can it hurt her now?"

"You're a Farthering, Drew. The name means something. Surely you can understand her reasons for keeping it out of that sort of scandal."

"If she wanted the name kept out of scandal, she should have kept herself out of scandal."

"There really is nothing more to discuss here," Mason said, his voice taut. "I mean to honor what your mother wanted. As her husband, it's my place to protect her interests."

"Hers or your own?" Drew said, the words barbed. "It's humiliating for a man to have to admit he's been cuckolded, I'm sure."

Mason pressed his lips together and did not answer.

"I'm sorry, sir," Drew said after a moment. "I sometimes say more than I ought."

Still Mason said nothing.

"We like to believe the best of those we love," Drew added,

hating that he had hurt the man. "I know it isn't easy to accept it when they aren't always what we think they should be."

Mason peered at him. "No. No, it's not."

"But knowing the truth doesn't mean we can't still love them."

Mason nodded. "So you would rather have the truth, would you? Even when the thing is past and done and changes nothing?"

"I would."

Again his stepfather peered at him. "How old are you now, Drew? Twenty-four?"

"Yes. Why?"

"So you know why she was being blackmailed, do you?"

Drew nodded, suddenly not as sure as he had been.

"Tell me why," Mason urged.

"I don't mean to upset you, sir, but I'm sure you've known as well as anyone."

"About?"

"About her and Lincoln. I've no doubt he was taking money to keep quiet about their affair two years ago."

Mason shook his head. "I've told you time and again. There was no affair."

"And I thought you were going to give me the truth now," Drew said tightly.

"Will you listen to me, or have you already decided you know everything?"

Drew bit back a hasty retort. Mason had the calm air of a man who was sure of his facts.

"I'll listen. Of course."

"You know Lincoln's father was partners with me and Rushford and with your father when we started the company, back in ninety-eight. Connie and your father had been married only a few months. He was like many young men, then and now, eager to build his empire and his great name. He did it too, and, as usually happens, paid the price for it. By the time the company was on its feet, he and Connie were practically strangers, and she had no interest in intimacy with a man she rarely saw."

He peered at Drew again and then continued.

"He poured himself more and more into the business, no doubt hoping she would relent in time and be proud of his success." Mason smiled a little. "Being 'in the right,' of course, she held her ground and kept her distance."

Again Mason paused.

"You know your father was a good man, Drew. I'd never dispute that with you."

Drew merely looked at him, feeling a growing uneasiness inside himself, a feeling that he had pressed too far into what he did not truly want to know.

"But he was a man, no more than that," Mason said. "Even the best make a false step now and again, especially when things aren't going well at home."

Drew frowned, less out of displeasure than from the desire to keep his lips from trembling. "What are you telling me? That it was my father who was unfaithful?"

"It was not long after your grandfather died, and I imagine your father was still in need of comfort on that score. He stopped into a little hat shop on the *Rue de la Paix* one night, when he was in Paris on business, thinking to bring Connie back some sort of peace offering. The girl there was sympathetic and kind. He told Connie later that she had a sweet, simple way about her that made him feel he could confide in her."

Drew's frown deepened. "Then Mother knew about her. Soon after, I suppose."

"He and the woman were together only a week. He came back and told Connie everything, begged her forgiveness, and promised never to stray again. As far as I have ever known, he kept that promise until he died."

"And Mother never forgave him, I suppose," Drew said.

"You're wrong there. She did forgive him. He let the rest of us run the business more and more after that and spent more time with her. She told me later that it was like a honeymoon all over again, even better than the first."

"That seems little enough for her to pay blackmail on all this time. Granted, it wouldn't be good for the company if it got out, but it was years ago. I can't imagine—"

"There's more."

Drew didn't like the look on Mason's face. "More?"

"Three or four months after your father's return, he got a letter from Paris, from the girl in the shop."

"I suppose it was the rest of the old story, then." Drew turned up one side of his mouth. "She was going to have a child. And wanted money."

"Not just a child, Drew," Mason said slowly. "You."

— Six —

Along with breakfast, Anna brought Madeline the news that Constance was dead. Unable to choke down more than a bite of toast and a few sips of hot coffee, Madeline got out of bed, threw on a suitably somber dress, and went to find Uncle Mason. As she headed down the front stairway, she saw Drew cross the marble floor of the entry hall and start up the stairs. He hadn't seen her yet.

"Drew," she called, keeping her voice low.

He glanced up at her and just as quickly away.

She called again and then hurried down to him.

"Hullo," he said, sounding a bit dazed.

She took both of his hands, wishing she could take him into her arms. "I'm so sorry. It must be such a shock about your mother."

She was surprised by the cynical smile that touched his lips.

"Yes. Yes, it is."

He said nothing more, and for a moment she could think of nothing else to say.

"Is Uncle Mason in his study?" she asked finally, and Drew nodded.

"But the chief inspector is with him. I don't think they'd let you see him at the moment."

Poor Uncle Mason. He must be heartbroken.

She looked up into Drew's eyes, but they refused to reveal anything.

"Is he . . . Is he all right, Drew? This has to be terrible for him. For both of you."

"I suppose it is terrible. I'm a bit stunned myself. Things are never quite as they seem."

Puzzled, she waited for him to go on, hoped he would, but he did not.

"Just going to look in on the newborns," he told her, not quite meeting her eyes.

"I'd love to see them," she said, "if you don't think that would upset Minerva too much."

"She's always trusted me, and Nick bribes her with sausages, so I think she wouldn't mind letting us peep in on her."

She went with him back up the stairs and down the hall to his dressing room.

Minerva, a small tabby cat with very large green eyes, lay at the bottom of the cupboard, still nestled in Drew's navy cheviot trousers. Her five kittens, their bellies round with milk, slept against her. Two of them were tabby-striped like their mother, two were marmalade, and one was, at present, almost entirely pink through its fine white fur.

"Oh, they're such little darlings," Madeline whispered, and Minerva responded with a slow, smug blink of her eyes, as if it were obvious that nothing less was to be expected.

Drew sat cross-legged on the floor, watching the little family. "It goes on, doesn't it? Life? Look at this little blind fellow," he said, pointing out the pink one. "Before long, he'll be snow-white. 'Lord, we know what we are, but know not what we may be.'" He smiled again, that cynical little half smile. "And sometimes we don't even know what we are."

She got down on the floor beside him, curling her legs under herself and slipping her arm through his, wanting somehow to comfort him.

"Life does go on," she said. "Even when it's hard."

"There's a mixed blessing."

After another moment of silence, she turned to him once more. "Drew?"

He seemed lost in thought, so she gave his arm a little squeeze. "Drew?"

"Sorry. I guess I was just thinking about—about everything."

"We don't have to talk if you don't want to," she said, though she wanted him to want to talk to her, "but I am a good listener."

"Yes, I expect you are." He blinked a few times before he faced her. "I don't know that you'd want to know what a sordid mess we are here, though."

She held his arm a little more tightly, remembering the maid's half-whispered intimations. "Was it . . . was it suicide?"

"The police think she killed Lincoln and then herself over a lovers' quarrel." His voice, low and empty, was so unlike his normal voice that she had to look at his face to be sure it was coming from him. "Or, possibly, your uncle murdered him in a jealous rage, and she couldn't face living without him."

"No." Her heart squeezed into a hard, painful knot inside her, but she forced herself to smile a little. "It's just not true. I know Uncle Mason wouldn't do anything like that. He couldn't."

"How do you know?" he asked, his gray eyes hard. "How does anyone know what someone else may be or do?"

"He's just . . . he's just not that way," she insisted. "He'd never hurt anyone."

He laughed, but it wasn't his usual infectious laugh. It wasn't so nice as that.

"We forget sometimes that parents—even uncles—have lives of their own. Worlds of their own. Sides of themselves we never see and never dream are there. Even when someone describes those lives to us, we can't believe them. We *know* better." He jerked his head toward the sleeping kittens. "They know nothing but that she's there to feed and wash and warm them. They don't once think of her as a hunter or their father's mate or our pet."

"But, Uncle Mason—"

"I'm not saying he's guilty. I'm just saying one can't know. One can't know for certain."

"I think you can," she said. "You can see a man's character in his life. He can't keep that secret. Not forever."

"Character," Drew said, his face marred with an ugly sneer. "Shall I tell you about character? What do you think of this house?"

"The house?" She knit her brow, struggling to follow his splintered conversation. "I think it's a beautiful house. I love how your family has built it up over so many hundreds of years, adding to it but leaving what was there before."

"It's a sham." There was something rather brutal in his soft voice. "All of it. It looks as though it's been here since the fifteen hundreds, but it's barely eighty now. My great-grandfather had it built to look as if the Fartherings had lived in it for the past four centuries. He had the architect design it in three different styles, using bits he'd bought from other old houses about to be torn down, as if it had been added onto over the years. The village was called St. John Woodlea until 1857. That was when Great-grandfather Henry used a little financial persuasion to have the name changed to Farthering St. John. All of it is a sham." His smile turned bright and brittle. "Like me."

"You?"

"Ellison Andrew Farthering, heir to Farthering Place, and absolute fraud. I thought I had everything figured out. I knew my father. I knew my mother." He took a shuddering breath. "I knew myself."

She didn't want to press for more than he wanted to tell her, but obviously there was more. "I don't understand."

"My mother's not dead."

Had he lost his mind? "But—"

"No. My mother is not dead. At least she's not at Dr. Wallace's surgery waiting for Marks & Blackistone's to take her away."

"What?"

"Constance Farthering Parker, née Ellison, was not my mother. I am the product of a sordid little tryst between my father and a French shopgirl. That makes me a Farthering, certainly, albeit on the wrong side of the blanket."

She didn't know what to say to that. What could she say?

"Mother—Constance—Blast it, I never seem to know what to call anyone." He scrubbed his free hand over his eyes, and she nestled more closely to him. "Anyhow, I always wondered why she never quite took to me. I could tell she wanted to sometimes, especially after my father died, but it never seemed quite the same as it was with other boys and their mothers. After a while, I guess I decided I wouldn't much take to her, either. I always thought she was jealous of the attention my father paid me. Now I see it was just that I was a constant reminder of his infidelity."

"How did she manage to make everyone believe you were hers? I mean, wouldn't the family or her friends have known?"

"She and my father were rather clever about that, it seems. Four months before I was born, he told everyone he had business in Paris, and he took her with him. After my arrival, they engaged a nurse to look after me and came back to Farthering Place, *fait accompli.*"

"What happened to the girl in the shop?"

He shrugged and then took a faded photograph from his coat pocket. "The police let me borrow this. It was in Lincoln's things. He was blackmailing Constance over my checkered past. I can't help but wonder . . ."

She took the picture from him and turned it over. "Marielle. A French name." She turned it to the front side once more. "And she might be the right age. Uncle Mason couldn't tell you more about your mother? Not her name or anything? Or whether or not this is her picture?"

"He said Constance never spoke of her except in the most general terms. I'll contact my solicitors to see what they can find out for me—birth records or anything that might identify my mother. One would suppose she's still alive somewhere."

Madeline studied the face in the picture and then Drew's. "She doesn't look very much like you. Maybe a little bit in the eyes and nose. It's hard to tell with these old pictures."

"They always said I looked like my father."

She smiled. "He must have been beautiful."

That made him smile too, but there was bitterness in it. "I don't know what to make of it or of this blackmail business. Or of Constance herself."

"She must have felt something for you if she raised you from a baby," Madeline offered.

"I suppose she did try. She must have tried if she agreed to pretend I was hers in the first place. Maybe it was just for my father's sake. Maybe it was for her own pride. But still . . ."

"What?"

"She paid Lincoln to keep it quiet. So I wouldn't know about my father. So I wouldn't think less of him even if it meant I would think less of her." He reached down to stroke the cat, not looking at Madeline. "And I thought the worst of her."

"Because of Lincoln," Madeline murmured, and he looked at her again, his expression startled at first and then wry.

"So you heard the rumors, as well. I suppose you were bound to. Farthering St. John is a small place, and the really succulent gossip is too rare to be allowed to die too hastily."

"She warned me about him," Madeline said, just then remembering.

"What did she say?" he asked, his expression keen.

"She said I ought to stay away from him, but I thought it was just because she was jealous. He'd been after me all night."

"Was that all?"

"Yes."

He was silent for a moment, and then he said, "I suppose one tires of paying blackmail."

"Do you really think she did it? I mean, do you think she could have?"

"I don't know. Maybe the lovers' quarrel theory is wrong, but he was blackmailing her. It must get old after a time."

"But to kill him that way . . ." She shuddered.

"The police think that's why she did away with herself. They think she couldn't bear what she'd done. Still, it's not typically a woman's crime. Not with a shotgun like that."

"It's so awful."

"Otherwise, that leaves Mason, but he never thought they were involved in the first place. Even if he killed Lincoln for Constance's sake, she wouldn't have known about it yet. Why would she kill herself the same night?" Drew's face hardened. "Unless he was lying to me about the whole thing. Unless he killed them both."

"Why would you think that?" she asked, trying not to be

angry with him. "He's lived here for ten years. You know him. Has he ever done anything to make you think he would even be capable of murder?"

Drew shook his head. "But I thought I knew my father, too. I would have wagered my life on it." Again he smiled a brittle smile. "On his character."

"Your father made a mistake," she said gently. "People do make them, you know, and learn from them. You said yourself how the gossip flies in a small place like this. Don't you think there would have been talk if there had been more than just the girl in France?"

"I don't know," Drew admitted. "I don't know why I'm telling you all this, anyway."

"Sometimes it helps to talk to someone."

"Talking about it doesn't change anything. It doesn't change who and what I am."

"No, it doesn't," she agreed. "You're exactly who and what you were before. What God made you to be."

"So I'm to thank Him for making me a bastard?"

She bit her lip, and he was quick to apologize.

"Rather bad form to use that sort of language in a lady's hearing, isn't it?"

"Not quite fair, either," she said, her heart softening once again at the apologetic pain in his eyes.

"No? I think it's an extremely equitable assessment."

"So you think God forced your father and mother to have an affair?"

He laughed a little. "No. Put that way, I suppose it would be absurd."

"I think He makes it pretty clear that He'd rather no one did that kind of thing." She made bold enough to caress his cheek. "Because He knows the hurt it causes even to the innocent."

Drew didn't say anything, but he didn't move away, either.

"Besides," she added, "that's something between each of them and God. It's not your fault. It doesn't make you any less precious in His eyes." *Or mine.*

He put his hand over hers, pressing it still against his cheek. Then he pressed her palm tenderly to his lips.

"I don't know what to think anymore," he murmured, his breath warm against her skin. "Or what to do."

"You don't have to do anything," she soothed. "Not right now. The police are investigating things, and they'll figure it out in time."

He squeezed her hand and then let it go. "Nick will be disappointed. He so wanted to solve a real mystery, but this is a bit close to home for a frolic."

"Nick will be all right," she assured him. "I want you to be all right."

He ventured to pet one of the sleeping kittens, the little pink one he'd pointed out earlier. "Are *you* going to be all right, Madeline?"

"Me?"

"If the police should find out something you'd rather not know, I mean." He stroked the kitten still, not looking at her. "If your uncle was . . . involved somehow in all this."

"You said you didn't think he was guilty," she protested.

"I said I wasn't prepared to say he was guilty."

Tears sprang to her eyes. "Have the police found something against him?"

"No. Not that I know of, anyway. But it's possible that they will."

"Did you talk to him about it?" she asked.

"No. I didn't like to yet. Not with everything that's happened."

"I couldn't ever believe it of him," she said, her heart churning inside her. "I know he's just a man and no man is perfect, but he's not a murderer. Not Uncle Mason."

Twin tears rolled down her cheeks, and he slipped one arm around her shoulders.

"There now," he said as he blotted her face with his linen handkerchief. "I never meant to make you cry. Fancy you coming all the way here from America just to have everything turn out perfectly awful, and here I am making it all the worse. Don't you mind me. You said yourself I never say anything meant to be taken seriously."

She couldn't help smiling at that, and he gave her shoulders a gentle squeeze.

"I've always liked your uncle," he added. "And seeing that he's *your* uncle, he must be all right."

"We just have to let the police figure it out," she said. "And pray they do it quickly."

"Ahem."

Drew and Madeline looked up to see Dennison standing in the dressing room doorway.

"I beg your pardon, sir," he said, "but your presence is required in Mr. Parker's study."

Drew sighed. "Tell him I'll be there straightaway."

Feeling her cheeks turn warm, Madeline moved out from under his arm. "Do they want to speak to me, too?" she asked as Drew helped her to her feet.

"They haven't said, miss," Dennison replied.

"I'd best toddle along then," Drew told her, releasing her hand with another little squeeze. "I don't want you to let all this worry you. It will be sorted out one way or another."

Drew knocked at the study door and was immediately admitted. Mason sat in his usual place behind the desk, and across from him, in the chair that had been Rushford's the night before, sat a tall, stoop-shouldered man in a brown overcoat.

"Chief Inspector, this is my stepson, Drew Farthering," Mason said. "Drew, this is Chief Inspector Birdsong of the Hampshire Police."

The other man stood. "Good morning, Mr. Farthering."

"How do you do, sir?"

Drew shook Birdsong's hand. It was a hard hand, a workman's hand, a fair match with the inspector's craggy, mustached face.

"I'm sorry to have to trouble you at this difficult time, Mr. Farthering," Birdsong said. "I realize the family is in mourning, and I'll be as brief as possible."

"Sit down," Mason told them both. "Please."

"I've read Constable Applegate's notes from last night," the inspector said as he made himself comfortable, "and Mr. Parker here has confirmed them. I'd like you to tell me what happened from the time Mr. Lincoln and Mrs. Parker left the party last night."

Again Drew repeated everything he remembered, the fireworks and the thunderstorm and the blood-soaked body under the mackintoshes in the greenhouse.

"How do you suppose someone let off a shotgun not thirty yards away from you and the young lady without your hearing it?" Birdsong asked, his gimlet eyes narrowing.

"It must have been the fireworks, just as I told Jimmy, er, Constable Applegate. I do remember one sounding particularly loud at the time. It could have been then."

Birdsong nodded. "And who was in charge of the fireworks, Mr. Farthering?"

"I believe it was Peterson, our head gardener, and one or two of his men."

"I see. Would they be the only ones to have access to them?"

"No," Drew said. "Just about anyone could have, I suppose. He set it all up in the afternoon so it would be ready for the party."

Again, Birdsong nodded. "And does anyone on the estate have a gun of any sort?"

"As best I know, Peterson has a shotgun, and my stepfather has a little Webley he brought back from the war."

"I've shown him that," Mason put in. "It hasn't been fired in years."

"And that's all?" the chief inspector asked.

"As best I know," Drew confirmed.

"And when did you last see the gardener's shotgun?"

Drew crossed his arms over his chest, considering. "I don't know if I could say for certain. Ages ago, I expect. Do you think that's what was used on Lincoln?"

"We have to consider every possibility, sir," Birdsong said. "Do you recall when you saw it last?"

Drew shook his head. "I couldn't tell you the date. It was last summer, I believe. He had it out to deal with some moles that were making a mess of the rose garden. I don't believe he ever fired it, though."

"Are you aware that it was missing?"

Drew sat up straighter. "No. You say it *was* missing. Does that mean it's been located since?"

Birdsong nodded. "Thrown in the brush at the edge of the woods. Wiped clean, of course."

"What does Peterson say?"

"According to Applegate, he claims it was locked in the shed as usual. He didn't even know it was gone."

"You don't think he would have done such a thing, do you?" Mason asked.

"It doesn't seem likely, sir," the chief inspector replied. "And Applegate checked his hands last night. None too clean, mind you, but nothing to indicate he'd fired a gun, and no reason to. But it's early days yet."

"Then who do you think killed Lincoln?" Drew asked.

"We'll come to that in time, Mr. Farthering. For now, I'd like you to tell me about you and Mr. Lincoln. Not the best of friends, were you?"

Drew stared at Birdsong in disbelief. "I didn't kill him, if that's what you mean. I'm not saying I feel any great bereavement over his passing, but I've never thought murder a very sporting way to settle an argument."

"So you did argue."

"I suppose you could call it that," Drew admitted. "If I wanted the man gone that badly, I could have simply ordered him off my property."

"Certainly," Birdsong agreed. "Although that wouldn't be much in the way of defending your family honor, now, would it?"

A protest sprang to Drew's lips, but then he smiled, knowing the inspector was watching for a reaction from him. "I have yet to see anyone's family honor improved by premeditated murder."

"You know it was premeditated, do you?" Birdsong asked, and Drew still smiled.

"As well as you do, Inspector. He had to have known somehow when that last burst of fireworks was to be let off so he'd know when to fire. None of the single bursts would have covered the sound of the gun."

"Very true, very true," Birdsong murmured. "Very well then, Detective Farthering, who is it you think is most likely to have killed Lincoln?"

"I suppose the obvious candidate would be my—would be Mrs. Parker." Drew glanced at his stepfather's drawn face and hurried to add, "But I don't think she did it, sir."

"According to Peterson, she was the one who gave order for the fireworks."

"We almost always have them at summer parties," Mason put in. "Everyone knows that."

"Lincoln was blackmailing her," Birdsong reminded him. "More than one woman has found that cause enough for murder."

"I'm sure you've seen the note," Drew said. "She said she wasn't paying anymore. She didn't care what Lincoln made public. Why kill him now?"

"And why was he blackmailing her?" the inspector asked.

Feeling a sudden tightness in his chest, Drew again glanced at Mason. "He, uh, Lincoln found out that I wasn't her son. I suppose he meant to tell me about it, if she didn't pay." Would Mason have told Birdsong as much already?

"Did she ever adopt you legally, Mr. Farthering?" the chief inspector asked.

Mason must have told him or he would surely have had a great many more questions. "I don't know," Drew admitted, looking to his stepfather.

Mason shook his head. "I don't believe so. No."

"So," Birdsong mused, "if you weren't legally her son, that might affect your inheritance later on, mightn't it?"

Drew felt the hot blood rise in his face. "If you would care to check, Chief Inspector, Farthering Place and everything in it, as well as a good portion of Farlinford Processing, was left to me by name under the provisions of my father's will twelve years ago, and held in trust until I reached majority in 1929. It has always been my assumption that my mother's separate property would go to her husband unless she made a particular bequest to me."

"And did she?"

"A few items, but nothing of great monetary value. Our solicitor's office would be glad to provide you with the details. It's Whyland, Montford, Clifton and Russ in London."

"I'll be certain to check with them, sir," Birdsong replied, and a bit smugly, Drew thought.

"Dennison will get you the number."

"I don't wish to appear unfeeling, Mr. Farthering, but do you think Mrs. Parker took her own life?" The chief inspector gave the question a veneer of solicitousness.

Drew glanced at his stepfather. There was a glistening film of sweat on Mason's upper lip.

"Dr. Wallace says it could have been an accident." Drew wasn't sure he sounded all that convincing even to himself. "If she were upset and all, she might easily have taken more of the Veronol than she realized."

"And was she upset, Mr. Farthering?"

His stepfather's words came back to him again: *"She was, quite understandably, upset by what's happened."* It was such a little bit of a thing. . . .

"I don't know," Drew answered truthfully. "When I saw her last, she was a bit on edge, but then what woman isn't with a houseful of guests?"

Drew decided not to say anything more. Not at this point. There was no need to cast suspicion on his stepfather over what may have been no more than a misunderstanding. He'd ask Mason about it himself when he had the opportunity. The man deserved that much from him.

"And when was it that you saw her last, sir?"

Drew hated it, this game of cat and mouse, but he supposed it had to be done. There had been at least one murder, and the murderer had to be found.

"It was after Miss Parker sent Lincoln packing." Drew gave the chief inspector a knowing glance. "I'm sure it's in your notes. He went off to talk to Mrs. Parker, and they both left the party straight off. I didn't see either of them again."

"And you feel sure Mrs. Parker wouldn't have killed Lincoln?"

Drew had to think for a moment. "Not sure, perhaps. But I would never have thought so."

"We've taken a cast of the shoes Mrs. Parker was wearing last night, as well as Lincoln's. It appears Mrs. Parker walked across the lawn toward the greenhouse, then hurried to catch someone up before she got there. They both stopped a moment, evidently exchanged a few words, and afterward she went back into the house."

"So she never actually went inside the greenhouse?" Mason asked.

"It doesn't seem so, no," Birdsong said. "Not last night."

"Thank God for that," Mason breathed.

Drew looked at his stepfather. Could he have been wondering about Constance all this while? Wondering if he were married to a murderess? *"I trust her,"* he had said just the day before, but did he really?

"The other set of footprints belonged to Lincoln, I suppose," Drew said, but Birdsong shook his head.

"They were definitely made by a man's dress pumps, the size of Mr. Lincoln's but not the same style."

Drew knit his brow. "Any clues as to whose they might be?"

"None as yet, but we did find something rather interesting when we removed Mr. Lincoln's shoes to make a cast of them." He lifted one eyebrow. "There's a mark down the back of his left stocking where he must have backed into one of those little tables in the greenhouse. Looks like it had recently been painted."

"Nothing too odd in that, is there?"

"No, except there was no corresponding mark on the back of the shoe, and by rights there should be."

"Our Mr. Lincoln was provided with a new pair of shoes."

"It appears so."

None of them said anything for a moment.

"Anything else untoward about Lincoln's body, Inspector?" Drew asked.

"Not that we've come across yet. Nothing apart from him being blown to bits and all."

"Yes," Drew observed, "that would certainly be untoward."

"Anyway, those footprints were all over around the greenhouse, what your man Peterson hadn't spoilt with tramping about." The chief inspector turned to Mason. "I understand, sir, that there was a death at Farlinford Processing last week, as well. A Mr. McCutcheon, one of the research scientists, and acute benzene poisoning, was it?"

"Yes," Mason said. "Evidently he was doing an experiment with it and had a spill. He should have known not to work with the stuff in a closed room like that. The vapors overwhelmed him almost at once. Ghastly thing, I'm sure. We had to clear everyone out of the building as a precaution."

"And what day was that, Mr. Parker?"

"Last Thursday, the twenty-sixth."

"And you were where at the time, sir?"

"At my office, as usual," Mason told him. "Mr. Rushford and I were there discussing business when we heard the commotion, but he was dead by the time we got to him."

"And you, Mr. Farthering?" Birdsong asked.

"I was at the seaside," Drew said. "Just came home this Friday night."

"Did you know this McCutcheon, sir?"

"No," Drew said. "Never met the man to my knowledge."

"He'd been at Farlinford almost three years," Mason said. "I'd met him, but not too much more than that. Not much more than to say good morning and to ask how the work was coming. Research and development was always Lincoln's father's specialty, when he was still with us. But he and Rushford and I didn't usually work with the men directly."

"This Mr. Rushford, sir, he is your partner as well, I take it?"

Mason nodded. "He's the head of our financial department. He sees to our investments and mortgages and that."

The chief inspector jotted something in his notebook. "And what is your job, may I ask?"

"I suppose you'd say I'm rather over everything at Farlinford. I make sure we have money to operate our plants and refineries and ship our products to our distributors with enough to spare for research and some outside investments that, in turn, bring more money into the company so we're able to start the process all over again."

"What about young Mr. Lincoln?" Birdsong asked. "What was his position at Farlinford?"

Drew opened his mouth and then shut it again at the chastening look on his stepfather's face.

"He didn't really have a formal position in the company," Mason told the inspector. "I mean, he had an office, the one his father always had, and he was, of course, a director, taking his father's place, but he seemed fairly content to collect his share of the profits in the company and leave it at that. He really wasn't in the office all that much, not on a regular basis."

"Was he acquainted with Mr. McCutcheon?"

"I suppose it was quite possible that they had met," Mason said. "Not that I know of, though."

"Lincoln never did much at Farlinford besides eye the secretarial pool," Drew put in.

Birdsong consulted his notes once more. "There was another death at your company, wasn't there, Mr. Parker?"

"We've had some accidents now and again, as does any industrial concern, but the last one was well over five years ago. A pump exploded and—"

"I mean a murder, sir. At your offices in Canada."

"Oh." Mason nodded, his face grave. "That was a sordid business. A young Chinese girl was found dead in a storage closet."

Birdsong's businesslike expression remained unchanged. "Beaten and then strangled to death, I understand."

Mason looked a bit white around the mouth. "Turned out her uncle worked for the company, sweeping up and such, and was displeased to find a white man had been keeping her as his mistress. Killed her to save face, they suspected."

"I never heard about that," Drew said.

"It was well before I came to Farthering to live, fifteen years ago or more now."

"What happened to the murderer?"

"Sentenced to hang," Mason said. "And then, because of some uncertainty in the evidence, the sentence was commuted to life in prison."

Birdsong shuffled through his papers. "He was killed in a prison brawl a year ago."

"Ah," Mason said, and then he clasped his hands in his lap and said nothing more.

"What does any of this have to do with what happened last night?" Drew asked the chief inspector. "Do you think there's a connection between this incident or McCutcheon's death and Lincoln's?"

"No," Birdsong said. "I shouldn't think there's any connection, but it's early days yet. Early days. Now, if you will kindly start at the beginning, Mr. Farthering. When you came home and found Mr. Lincoln in your room . . ."

The chief inspector questioned Drew and Mason for some while longer, mostly repeating the same questions but slightly rephrased, noting, Drew was certain, any variations, any hesitations in the answers. Before Drew was absolutely determined to strangle the man, it was over.

"I'd like to see this gardener of yours," Birdsong said. "This Peterson."

Mason rang the bell. A moment later, there was a knock at the study door.

"Come in, Dennison."

Dennison complied. "Something you wished, sir?"

"Send Peterson to me."

"In here, sir?"

"Yes, please. At once."

Raising his eyebrow a disapproving quarter of an inch, Dennison bowed. "Very good, sir."

Before long, Peterson shuffled to the study door, peering inside like a wary old badger at the mouth of a trap. Eventually he bared his head, revealing lank, greasy curls shot with gray, and then took two steps inside.

"Afternoon, Mr. Parker. Mr. Drew."

"Good afternoon, Peterson," Mason said. "Chief Inspector Birdsong would like to ask you a few questions about last night."

Peterson nodded his head, worrying his worn cap in his hands.

"Come on in, Mr. Peterson," Drew urged. "It's all right."

The gardener nodded once more and, after taking a moment to buff the toes of his battered boots against the back of his trouser legs, ventured four steps closer.

"Your name, please," Birdsong began.

Peterson pursed his lips. "Well, didn't he just call me by it?"

"For the record, if you please."

"Peterson. Arwel Peterson."

"And your profession?"

Peterson displayed his grimy hands, dark with the sun and his work in the earth. "I didn't get these of keepin' the accounts, now, did I?"

Mason cleared his throat. "If you please, Peterson."

"No disrespect, sir," Peterson muttered, still worrying his cap. "I'm head gardener here at Farthering, Inspector. I never had me any truck with the p'lice. You'll pardon me if it sets me a bit on edge."

Birdsong peered at him. "You have anything that ought to be worrying you?"

"No. What do you mean?"

"Something you'd rather not speak with us about?" Birdsong looked into his ever-present notebook. "No?"

Peterson shook his head and swiped a hand across his stubbly upper lip.

"Tell me what you did last Friday."

"The whole day?" Peterson asked.

"The whole day."

The gardener scratched the side of his head with one grimy fingernail. "I gets up round five, as I reckon it, and gets dressed. My old woman, she give me beans on toast fer breakfast and a bit of black pudding and tea. Then I goes down to the shed fer my spade and such."

"Is that the shed where you kept the shotgun?"

"It is."

"Go on."

"About then I sets Mack and Bobby, my men, you see, I sets them on to weedin' and that whilst I tends to the roses. Mrs. Parker, God rest her, sir, Mrs. Parker was that fond of her roses, and I liked to keep 'em nice fer her. So I were mixing some top-class muckings from the stables into the soil round them, just to perk 'em up like. Took me nigh unto noon to do 'em all."

"All right," Birdsong said. "And did you see anything during that time?"

"I seen some of them has aphids."

"I mean anything unusual," Birdsong pressed.

"That *is* unusual for my roses."

Drew bit his lip.

"Anything else?" the chief inspector asked.

"There's moles or somethin' digging round in the bed nearest the forest."

Birdsong's voice was most terribly patient. "Anything *not* to do with your roses."

Peterson shook his head.

"And after you finished with the roses?"

"I stopped round home to have my dinner. My old woman, she give me—"

"And after you ate?"

Peterson sniffed, his grubby face the picture of disdainful offense. "Well, I touched up the paint on a few of the tables in the greenhouse, and then I went round to do the fireworks, didn't I?"

"Touched up the paint?"

"I painted the whole lot last week, but there's always some bits needing a touch here and there."

"All right," Birdsong said. "Was anyone with you when you set up the fireworks?"

"I had Mack helping me put up the little stand we use to fire 'em from. Mostly it were me."

"Mr. Peterson," Drew asked, "when you arrange the different ones, do you have any particular order you do them in?"

"Order, sir?"

"I mean certain types together or anything like that?"

"Not really an order as I would say, Mr. Drew. I know your mum, God rest her, sir, she didn't like them the same color together, if you know what I'm saying. She said it weren't artistic-like."

"So you arranged them ahead of time."

"That's right, sir. I laid them out the way they should be. Then, when the time came to fire 'em off, I didn't have to try seeing which were which there in the dark."

"Capital," Drew said, and the little gardener gave Birdsong a smug little nod.

"Did anyone tamper with them?" the inspector asked.

"Tamper with them?" Peterson scratched behind one ear. "I can't say as they was tampered with, though I suppose I got some out of their proper order. Right there at the last were three or four reds together, bold as brass, I may say, and me trying to be so careful for Mrs. Parker."

Drew shook his head, commiserating. "And when you had them in order, what did you do with them?"

"Like I always do. I put 'em in a trunk and put it up by the side of the house. That way they'd be ready for the party and still be out of the weather, if we was to have any."

"Did you stay there with the trunk afterward?" Birdsong asked.

"Stay with it? Well, it weren't going to wander off, were it? Stay with it? I can see you're gulling me now, sir."

"No, that's all right, Mr. Peterson," Drew soothed. "What did you do after you put them in the trunk?"

"I goes back down to see how Bobby and Mack are getting along with the weeding and such. Then I brought round some peonies from the greenhouse to put in that bed under the library window. The ones that were there were looking a mite peaked, so I thought—"

"Yes, that's all very well," the inspector said. "So you did your gardening until . . . ?"

"About teatime it was. My old woman . . ." Peterson looked at Birdsong. "Then after I'd had tea, I went to ask Mrs. Parker, poor lady, when she wanted the fireworks let off. She told me about an hour after they'd had their supper. Now, being an early riser as I am, I knowed straightaway I'd be worth nothing the next day if I didn't have some rest beforehand, so that's exactly what I done."

"And you slept till when?" Birdsong asked.

"Near ten it were. I come up to the house, let off the fireworks, and hurries on back to my bed. I didn't know nothin' of what happened up to the house till they rousted me out to come watch over the greenhouse so no one made any mischief with the evidence."

"You said you got some of your tools from the shed that morning, is that right?" Mason asked.

"Yes, sir."

"Did you have the shotgun locked up then?"

Peterson shook his head. "I can't say as I did, sir. But I can't for certain say as I didn't."

"Did you see anyone around the shed who oughtn't to have been there?" the chief inspector asked. "Anyone at all?"

"No, sir."

Again, Birdsong scanned his notes. "I see you told Constable Applegate that you kept the gun locked in the shed. Was that in a cupboard of some kind? Or was it the shed that was kept locked?"

"No, sir, I didn't as a rule lock the shed. Bobby and Mack would need to get tools and such from it in the usual doin' of their work. But I were always careful with the gun. I didn't want none of the village children as might be poking about to light on it and think it a toy."

"So you kept it locked in what?"

"An old crack-bottom steamer trunk." Peterson frowned and stroked his unshaven chin in thought. "As I remember, it were once used by Mr. Elliot Farthering, Mr. Drew's grandfather, when he traveled across to Canady. The split in the bottom don't hurt it none. It's as safe as a bank vault, that trunk."

The chief inspector nodded. "And you keep the key to it?"

"I do, sir. I believe Mr. Dennison has one as well, along of all the household keys. And Mr. Parker."

"Anyone else?"

"Not as I know, sir. No one."

"And you're certain it was locked?" Mason asked.

"Oh yes, sir, Mr. Parker. I'm not a man to be reckless with firearms. You ask anyone, sir."

"I know he fairly tanned my hide when I got hold of one when I was a boy," Drew said, smiling.

"And well I should, sir, beggin' your pardon," the gardener replied, "and your father, God rest him, said as much at the time."

"Back to the matter at hand," Birdsong said. "Did you know the murdered man, Peterson?"

"Know him, sir?" Peterson shook his shaggy head. "Knew of him, I s'pose. His father and Mr. Drew's father being partners and all, young Mr. Lincoln were about the place from time to time over the past many years. But he weren't much the sort to pass time o' day with them that was beneath him as it were."

"Do you remember seeing him about when you were doing the fireworks? Or before that?"

"No, sir. I can't say as I seen him at all during the weekend."

Birdsong made a few notes. "And what about Mrs. Parker? When did you last see her?"

"The last time was when I asked about when she wanted the fireworks, sir. Directly after tea as I remember."

"All right then," Birdsong said, looking rather more peeved than when he had begun the interview. "Can you think of anything more that might be of use to us in this matter? Anything at all?"

"No, sir. That day were just the same as any other to me. Apart from the unfortunate happenings, begging your pardon, Mr. Parker. Mr. Drew."

"What about your men?" the inspector pressed. "Jackson and Haywood, are those their names?"

Peterson nodded. "That's them, and if they seen anything, they said nothing of it to me."

"Very well," Birdsong said. "If you remember anything more, you get word to me. Understand?"

"I'll do that, sir. Sure certain, I will."

"Anything else, Mr. Farthering?" the chief inspector asked once Peterson was dismissed. "Anything you think might help us solve the murder?"

Drew sighed. "I just don't know, Chief Inspector. I can hardly believe it's happened. I wouldn't have believed it, but there it is."

"All right then." Birdsong stood, and Drew and Mason followed suit.

"I'm sorry we couldn't be of more help," Mason said, shaking the other man's hand.

"You never know, Mr. Parker. Sometimes, when they've had a bit to think, people start remembering things." The chief inspector gave Drew and Mason each one of his cards. "Now, if either of you should think of something, you ring me up. Even if you're not sure that it means anything, you ring me up. And,

Detective Farthering"—he shook his index finger at Drew—"you and that young Dennison scamp mind you don't interfere with police business. Do all the clever thinking you want, and when you get an idea, I'll be happy to hear it. But you let the police do the investigating. Do I make myself clear?"

"Why, Inspector, I never—"

"You two and Applegate might be old mates, but that holds no water with me. I'll not have you spoiling any evidence."

"Upon my honor, Inspector, I will not spoil any evidence."

— Seven —

His questions finally exhausted for the time being, Chief Inspector Birdsong left Drew and Mason to themselves. After a few awkward moments, Drew cleared his throat.

"I have to ask you something, sir, and I hope you won't take it wrongly."

"You want to know if I killed Connie."

Drew looked down. "I hate this. All of it. I couldn't imagine you doing it, sir." He looked up again, straight into Mason's eyes. "But I couldn't imagine her killing Lincoln or herself, either."

"I don't mind you asking," Mason said. "I'm quite sure the police have me at the top of their list at the moment. But to answer the question, no, I didn't kill her or Lincoln or anyone. I guess the most damning bit of evidence against me is that no one can imagine who else would have."

"That is the question, isn't it, sir?" Drew asked with a weak smile.

"I suppose we'll just have to let the police sort this all out."

"What are you going to do in the meantime?"

Mason sighed. "Keep on with my work, I expect. Still things

to clear up on McCutcheon's desk now he's gone. Lincoln never did much of anything of consequence, so no worries there."

"What happens to his share in the company?"

"He inherited his father's share according to the original partnership agreement, and that's still in force. Everything goes to the three of us—you, me, and Rushford—since he left no heirs. None we know of anyway, though I expect there will have to be some sort of public notice to any possible claimants before that can be settled. That's for the solicitors to hammer out."

"Any way I can be of help, sir?"

Mason's expression warmed, losing some of the distracted, harried look that had been in it since the night before. "That's good of you, but I don't know what you could do in such a matter."

"I mean to see what I can find out. Obviously the chief inspector is hard at work on the case, but we can't be the only matter he's got to see to. Who knows? Maybe I'll stumble on something he's missed."

Mason looked uneasy once again. "Do you think you ought? Murder's no game."

Drew grinned. "Don't worry, sir. I'm not planning to get myself bumped off, as they say in the cinema."

"I shouldn't like something to happen to you, Drew. I'd say we've had enough of death here for some while, wouldn't you?"

There was something pleading in his stepfather's eyes, something grieving, something not wanting to grieve anymore.

Drew nodded, his own expression sobering. "More than enough. I'll stay out of trouble."

❦

"There you are." Nick sprang up from the chair he had dragged into the corridor so he could wait in relative comfort. "I thought you'd be all day about it."

"You mean it's still Sunday?" Drew asked as they went into the library, squinting and blinking as if he had just emerged from outer darkness. "What's happened to Miss Parker?"

"Old Birdsong found her out there and has been at her ever since."

Drew turned to the windows that looked out onto the garden. Madeline and the chief inspector were sitting on the same bench where she and Drew had sat the evening before. Birdsong was gesturing toward the greenhouse, and Madeline was shaking her head emphatically, her face flushed and her periwinkle eyes fiery.

Drew frowned. "Poor kid. She's hardly been here a day and this is what she gets."

"I like her," Nick said. "She's not one of these wilting little flowers who'd melt in a drop of rain, but she's not out to make herself over into a man like some of these modern girls, either. I like her."

Drew's expression softened. "So do I. Better than anyone I've ever met. I wish I could get her away from all this." Frowning again, he shoved his hands into his pockets and paced in front of the windows, glaring at the chief inspector.

"Steady on now," Nick said. "He's got to do his job. And there *is* a murderer loose somewhere."

"Don't be too kind. He'll have you in next."

"What's the theory so far, may I ask?"

"We have rather a neat explanation for all events as it stands," Drew said. "Either *A*, scorned and blackmailed woman kills her lover and then herself, or *B*, jealous husband disposes of faithless wife and her blackmailing lover. Who else would have killed either of them?"

"Have they brought up the possibility of murder?" Nick asked. "Of your mother, I mean."

"Not as such, no. But as the inspector reminds me, it's early days yet. Dr. Wallace has called it death by misadventure so far."

"Bit of a coincidence to happen just last night, isn't it?"

"Birdsong is asking me if I didn't do for them both," Drew admitted, and Nick raised one eyebrow.

"Because?"

"Because," Drew said, his voice artificially melodramatic, "Lincoln had stained the family honor and because I didn't want to lose my inheritance."

"Your inheritance?"

Drew shook his head, not wanting to wade through the story yet again. "There's not much you don't know about me, Nick, old man, but this I didn't even know myself."

He told Nick about Constance paying Lincoln's blackmail to cover up Drew's father's indiscretion. When he had done, Drew looked at his friend, waiting for his reaction.

"French, English, or Byzantine," Nick said, "what's that matter? I'd still put my last fiver on you against all comers at eighteen holes of golf."

Drew laughed. "I'm a rotten golfer, and you know it."

"Bit sticky finding this out just now though, isn't it?"

Drew exhaled heavily. "Rather. So I suppose I'm C, erstwhile son kills to keep sordid family secrets hush-hush."

"It couldn't have been you," Nick said with his usual wry grin. "Father Knox specifically says the detective must not be the murderer. It just wouldn't be right."

Drew couldn't hold back a little grin of his own. "Still on about Father Knox, are we? Anyway, Birdsong's the detective in the case, and he'll brook no interference from civilians."

"That's as may be, but we mustn't forget D," Nick said. "Willful murder by person or persons unknown. Lincoln was such a charming fellow, he must have had just droves of admirers."

"But if someone we don't know killed Lincoln, why would he kill Constance, as well? Or why would she kill herself over it?"

Nick shrugged. "Perhaps she saw something she shouldn't have."

"No," Drew told him. "If that were the case, the murderer wouldn't take the chance that she would go up to bed and take the Veronol without telling anyone what she saw."

"Unless it was someone she thought she ought to protect, and that someone decided she couldn't be trusted to keep quiet."

There was a sick feeling in the pit of Drew's stomach. "Mason."

"I didn't say that," Nick insisted. "I did *not* say that."

"Who else then?" Drew asked. "Who would have a reason to kill Lincoln and Constance? Her suicide makes sense only if she was the one who killed him in the first place. If she didn't, then we have to assume the same person killed them both."

"I saw the inspector had old Peterson in, too. Was he any help?"

Drew shrugged. "Not much. Said the fireworks weren't the way he'd laid them out and his roses have aphids. He'd never even met Lincoln, so he hadn't much to say in that respect."

"Really? I'd have thought Opal would have had him to dinner some Sunday. Perhaps Lincoln was more the sort to wait for a girl in the street."

"Opal knew Lincoln?"

"If local gossip is to be believed. I never saw them together, but I didn't really know Opal myself much more than to speak to."

"I thought she'd gone away."

"She did. Months ago."

"I guess Peterson didn't say anything about her. I suppose there's more than one father not wise to his daughter's goings-on."

"True enough. But that's not going to help this case. What we need is evidence. We just don't know enough yet." Nick's voice took on that mischievous tone Drew knew only too well. "But it doesn't mean we can't find out."

"I mean to find out," Drew assured him, his grim expression returning. "I mean to find out a great many things."

"I don't know if the chief inspector will take much to the idea," Nick said. "He's not likely to want a couple of nosey Parkers poking about."

"We won't interfere with them," Drew assured him. "I've given my word on that point."

"All right then, where do we start?"

Drew considered for a moment. "If Lincoln was blackmailing Constance, it's not much of a reach to imagine he had other *clients* as well. I don't suppose there's any way they'd let us look at his bank records."

"Not half," Nick said with a snort.

"So then, what can we find out? The police aren't likely to let us search his flat or anything so helpful as that, but they can't stop us from talking to people. I wonder if Mason would know who his friends are."

"Mightn't Rushford?" Nick asked.

"Possible, I suppose, but not too likely. Rushford's a bit fussy to be spending his off hours with a bounder like our Mr. L. We could get his address from someone at Farlinford. They must send his dividend checks somewhere. Chelsea, if I remember."

"There's always a garrulous landlady or maid of all work at the flat of anyone recently deceased, isn't there?" Nick asked.

"We can only hope," Drew replied.

"Hope what?" Madeline smiled as she came up to them, but there were traces of red in her cheeks along with a hot touch of temper in her eyes.

"Did the inspector give you a bad time, darling?" Drew asked, and she shrugged.

"I guess that's his job."

"Shall I punch his nose?"

She laughed and took his arm. "I'd rather you took me for a walk around the countryside. I've hardly seen any of it."

"Time to cool off a bit, eh?"

"It wasn't that bad." She pressed her lips together, chin quivering. "I didn't like what he was asking me about Uncle Mason."

Drew's eyes narrowed. "What was he asking?"

"If he and Aunt Constance had been quarreling. If I saw him talking to Lincoln anywhere around the greenhouse or the garden shed."

"Hmmm. Nothing too unusual."

"He asked about you, too," she added.

"I see. But that didn't bother you?"

"Oh, that's all right, Drew," Nick said. "He probably doesn't think you're clever enough to plan a murder, anyway."

"Nick, old man, your confidence in me is most gratifying. Come along, Madeline." Drew patted the hand that rested on his arm. "I think a bit of fresh air is well indicated for both of us." He led her toward the French doors that opened onto the garden, and then he stopped. "I say, Nick? You may want to ring up Miss Stokes in personnel for that address we were wondering about."

"Right," Nick said. "Straightaway."

Responding to the question in Madeline's eyes with nothing more than a smile, Drew took her across the rose garden, along a wooded path and out onto the meadow.

"There aren't many things I really love," he said after they had walked awhile, "but I love this place. I don't know what I'd do if it weren't here for me to come home to."

"It's so beautiful, the mossy stone walls and the sheep and

cattle, and everything is so green." She sighed. "I can understand why you love it. It's a wonderful place to call home."

They walked awhile longer in companionable silence.

"What else do you really love?" she asked finally.

He smiled. "You'll only think me foolish."

She tucked her arm under his and looked up into his eyes. "Tell me."

"Oh, I don't know. I've a friend or two I love, I suppose."

"Nick?"

"Nick's stuck with me through a lot, especially these past ten or fifteen years," Drew said. "And Denny's taken me in, more or less, since my father died. By rights, I should have my own valet, just as your uncle does. But Denny's looked after me so long, I can't imagine having anyone else. I fairly much see to myself most of the time, anyway. Much simpler that way, even if it is a local scandal. Now, don't laugh. You'd have to have a personal maid too if you were to live here. I mean, lady of the manor and all."

She squeezed his hand. "You're sweet. Not the least bit subtle, but very sweet."

They reached the top of a rise in the road, and Madeline pointed down toward the village. "Is that Farthering St. John?"

"In all her glory."

"How perfect," she sighed, and then she turned to him, beaming. "How wonderfully perfect."

"Is it?"

He looked over the village again, trying to see with new eyes something he'd seen practically every day of his life. There wasn't much to it really—a few rows of houses on the main road, some better kept than others, some shops, a garage, a chemist, and a minuscule police station nearly large enough for the two officers typically on duty there. It was home, of course, and dear to his heart, but he knew too that there was nothing there over which the average person should marvel. Then again, Madeline came from a country that boasted little more than three hundred years of civilized history. He'd have to make allowances.

"Yes. Absolutely perfect," she said. "Look at the sweet little gardens they all have. And what a lovely old church."

"That's Holy Trinity. Actually, it's The Church of the Holy Trinity and All Angels, if you want its full title. It's mostly Norman still, but you can see a little of the Georgian and Victorian, too. Not enough to spoil it, though."

"I hope you'll take me there sometime."

"I expect we'll all be going there soon enough."

"Oh." She looked a bit flustered. "Oh yes, of course."

He hated to remind her of that, of the funeral and what had led up to it. He hated to remind himself, but there it was.

"Look here," he said, taking her face in both his hands so he could look into her clear periwinkle eyes. "I don't want you to worry about all this. Just—" His voice caught. What was it about her that made him so quickly feel he could trust her? "Just stay close."

She melted into his arms, soft and warm, yet strong and lithe and altogether right. He stood there just holding her, being held by her. With his cheek against her fragrant hair and her head nestled on his shoulder, he pressed her close, letting some of the tightness in his lungs disperse into the grass-scented air.

After a time, he turned her face up to him again.

"Look here," he repeated, making his expression stern. "I don't want you to think I'm always such a ninny as this."

He loved the understanding warmth in her eyes and the little tremor in her smile. Maybe what he felt was too new and untried to be real, but the fresh possibility of it was a sweet, dizzying distraction from all the unpleasantness of the last few hours.

"It won't do to get off track at this point," he said. "I mean to find out what's happened here. To Lincoln and to Constance. After that, we can carry on learning how perfect we are for each other."

"Do you know what I like best about you?" she asked, taking his hand and swinging it between them in a lazy arc as they began walking back toward the house. "You're so shy and unsure of yourself."

He smiled in spite of himself and held her hand more tightly. It was insane, but it was the most wonderful, intoxicating insanity he'd ever felt.

"You don't . . . you don't have someone waiting for you, do you? I mean, somewhere in the wilds of America?"

Her only answer was a careless shrug. Maddening.

He stood still where he was, forcing her to stop alongside him. "Well, do you or don't you?"

She grinned. "Nobody."

"No?"

"Absolutely no one." She nestled close to him. "And if I did, I don't think I'd want it to be anyone but you."

She lowered her lashes and then looked up again, coy and challenging, and he pulled her even closer. He could feel her heartbeat and the rapid catches of her breath as he held her against him. Or was that his own heart and breath? No, he wouldn't kiss her. Now was hardly the time to fall in love. There were serious matters to be seen to. Still, he let himself drink in the moment just awhile longer. Then he released her.

"We ought to be getting back, I expect. Mrs. Devon will be waiting tea."

"All right."

He offered her his arm again and then spun her back toward him. "Look here."

That same coy look was on her face. And blast it if there wasn't a knowing little smirk keeping it company.

"Look here," he said again. "I said we ought to go back, and I meant just that. I can't waste all my time swanning about with strange girls, no matter how perfectly charming they may be. Now mind."

She shook her head. "You're wonderful. I've never been scolded in such a complimentary way. And I promise I won't waste any more of your time." She backed toward the house, pulling him by both hands and still smiling up at him. "Hurry. We don't want to keep Mrs. Devon waiting."

"Hold on. Hold on." He pulled back the other way. "I absolutely demand that you waste *some* of my time. At least a little of it."

"I don't plan for the time we spend together to be wasted at all. I'm going to help you solve this case."

She leaned up and kissed his cheek, then turned and scampered into the house.

What could he do but dash after her?

— Eight —

Drew and his stepfather were sharing the newspaper the next morning over an early breakfast when Denny came out onto the terrace.

"Chief Inspector Birdsong to see you, sir."

Mason looked up from the financial section. "Show him into my study, Dennison. I'll be there in a moment."

"I'd rather we talked right here, Mr. Parker," Birdsong said as he strode out to them. "You and Mr. Farthering will want to hear what I've found out."

Drew straightened in his chair and abandoned the society page. "I daresay we will. Do take a seat, Inspector. Would you care for some breakfast? Tea?"

Denny relieved the inspector of his hat and returned to the house, discreetly closing the terrace doors behind him.

Birdsong accepted a cup of tea and sat down. "I've just spoken to Dr. Wallace. He's completed the autopsy on Mrs. Parker."

He leaned forward to peer at Mason.

"Yes?" Mason prompted.

"He found traces of Veronol in the bottle we took from Mrs. Parker's bedside table."

Mason nodded. "Yes. And?"

"There was Veronol in your wife's body as well, but not enough to kill her."

"What?"

Mason looked helplessly at Drew.

"Then what did kill her?" Drew asked.

"Wallace isn't certain," Birdsong said. "All he can say is that something made her stop breathing."

"But wouldn't the Veronol account for that?"

"Not according to the doctor. He said what she had taken could have done no more than put her into a deep sleep. Different folk react in different ways, of course, but you said she'd taken this many times before."

"Yes," Mason breathed.

"And never had a problem?" Birdsong pressed.

"No."

Drew narrowed his eyes. "She couldn't have just had some natural breathing difficulty, could she?"

"Not according to Dr. Wallace."

"And there was nothing else in her system?"

"A little alcohol. I understand you brought her that, didn't you?"

"I brought her one drink, yes. She sent me for it."

"I see."

"I have no idea what else she drank that night. I somehow doubt that stinger was the only one she'd had."

Birdsong's expression remained bland, benignly attentive. "Did you happen to notice what she had that night, Mr. Parker?"

"No. I was mostly in my study, though. I couldn't say for

certain what she drank. She liked a drink now and again, no denying that, but she was never vulgar about it."

"No, sir. Of course not. I'm sorry to have disturbed you so early. Dr. Wallace has released the body. Marks & Blackistone's will see to everything for you now. I hope that meets with your approval."

Mason sighed and rubbed his eyes. "Very kind of you, Inspector, I'm sure."

An hour later, when Mason had long since shut himself up in his study and Drew was still mulling over recent events and tea, Nick came and sat down at the table with a plate of eggs and toast.

"Morning, old man. How are things today?"

Drew smiled, only half listening. "Tolerable, I suppose."

"I heard old Birdsong was in again. Any news?"

"Dr. Wallace has done with the autopsy on Constance and released the body. I expect we'll have the funeral tomorrow."

"Anything I can take care of for you?"

"I'll talk to Mason about what he wants. I'm sure there are all sorts of arrangements to be made, but I don't know what they are yet."

"What did the doctor find?"

"Nothing, really."

"He doesn't know what caused her death?" Nick asked.

"No, except that she stopped breathing. And, yes, I know Father Knox says there aren't supposed to be any unknown poisons in the case."

Nick put down his fork. "Really, Drew, I wouldn't have dreamed of mentioning it, you know. I try to not always be an idiot."

"I know, old man. It's a deuced puzzle, though. And hang me if I know where this piece fits. Or if it even goes into the same puzzle as the rest. Still, something killed her, and it wasn't the Veronol. And there were no other drugs found nearby. Nothing peculiar in her bloodstream, either. I'd say that pretty much puts the suicide theory to bed."

"And she hadn't had any tea or anything to eat before she slept?"

"Not according to Beryl. She sometimes would have some chamomile of an evening, but she didn't that night. Nothing anyone knows of after that stinger I brought her at the party. And I made that myself."

"I suppose Birdsong was on you about that."

"Not as such, no, but I could hear his little brain ticking along behind that beetle brow."

"Well, I suppose there's nothing for it but for us to figure out what's been going on."

"Yes, and we'll have a bit of company, as well."

"Company?"

"The charming Miss Parker has announced her intention of joining the investigation."

Nick's face lit. "Has she? Oh, jolly nice."

Drew scowled. "No, it is *not* jolly nice. I shall never find out anything if she's along."

"Be fair. She doesn't seem the sort of girl to be squeamish or go chattering on about hats or operas or anything."

Drew stared into his cup. "It's not that."

"What then?"

"It's . . . well, it's just not the type of thing a girl ought to be involved in. Man's work and all."

Nick laughed. "You can't fool me, you know."

"What?" Drew protested.

"You just don't want to be distracted."

Drew put his head in his hands. "Is it that obvious?"

"I'm afraid so."

"How can I concentrate on this case when she's all I can think of? When one pert look turns my spine to blackberry jam?"

"Blackberry?"

Drew looked up. "Oh, yes, I'm certain it's blackberry. I don't like blackberry."

"She *is* most awfully pretty."

"Yes, and knows it, worse luck, but I've been around beautiful girls before. Remember Elsie Martinson?"

"Do I remember Elsie. You had it bad, and I thought Bunny was going to blow his brains out over her."

"When he could remember her name was Elsie and not Eleanor or Myrtle." Drew shook his head. "Poor Bunny. Good thing he got distracted by that new Lagonda he bought right after. But Elsie was a stunner, no question. Still, it was hard to stay keen on her once you'd known her awhile. She liked to pull the wings off fellows just to amuse herself. I shouldn't be surprised to find she had a complete set of old beaux in a glass case, pinned through the heart onto corkboard and properly labeled as to date and place collected."

"Bah. Miss Parker's nothing like that."

"I know. That's precisely what makes it so hard for me to keep my mind on the task at hand."

Nick snickered. "I have a feeling that if she wants in on the game, she'll be in on the game."

Drew groaned and buried his head in his hands once more.

The day of the funeral was clear and warm, a fresh June day with no hint of rain.

Standing at the graveside, surrounded by black-clad mourners, Drew listened to the vicar's words—God's words, he'd always been taught—and wondered if Constance was standing before Him now. Or, having hardly given Him a thought during her life, was she forever separated from His presence?

Drew didn't know.

He breathed out a sigh, glad that burden was not his. He had only to account for his own soul.

And what of his own soul? Could it stand before a holy God and not be found wanting? It was an old-fashioned notion, to be sure. One that he had been taught he was too sophisticated and erudite to believe. And yet, even as many of the professors scoffed at the idea, there was still that inescapable infusion of belief all through Oxford. *Dominus illuminatio mea* ran the school motto. *The Lord is my light.*

There was a God of some sort, surely. Someone had made the world and all that inhabited it. But how did one reach Him? And what did He really want?

The vicar spoke on, intoning the familiar funeral words, "'In the sure and certain hope of the Resurrection unto eternal life . . .'"

He glanced at Madeline as she stood next to her uncle, clinging to Mason's arm in gentle comfort. She nodded now and again, eyes closed, a look of sweet peace on her angelic face. She had that sure and certain hope and found no fear in death. What would Constance have thought had she known death would come for her as she slept?

Madeline walked with her uncle back to where the cars were parked. He opened the door for her, but she urged him inside first.

"I'll be right back."

Drew was still standing beside the grave, his hands behind his back, his face devoid of emotion. He didn't look at her when she came up to him. He kept his eyes on the freshly turned earth.

"I don't suppose I ever understood her. I'm sure she never understood me."

She pressed his hand. It felt oddly cold there on that warm morning, but it responded to her consolation, returning the squeeze.

"She was scandalized by my being friends with Nick. Even when I was very young." He surprised her with a smile. "I remember once, I must have been seven or eight then, she was complaining to my father about him. She said there had to be at least one little boy of a better class for me to play with. My father laughed and said perhaps Henry or George or John would ask me round to play. 'They're a bit older than the boy,' he said, 'but very well connected. I think even you'd be pleased.' She was eager to meet the family until he told her their surname was Windsor."

Madeline smiled too, just a gentle little smile that wasn't inappropriate for the circumstances. "Perhaps King George's sons would have been too much of a step down for you."

"I would have striven to be gracious to them nonetheless," he said, tucking her arm under his.

"Grace is a lovely thing."

Again he surprised her. There was something in his face that responded to that word just now. *Grace.*

He was quick to look away. "Yes, I suppose it is."

When she was sure he wasn't going to say anything more, she squeezed his hand again. "Uncle Mason is waiting for us."

The day after the funeral, following an early breakfast, Drew and Nick sped up to Chelsea to take a look at Lincoln's flat. Just as quickly, they were on their way back to Farthering Place.

"Well, that was seventy-five miles wasted." Drew shoved the car into gear and pulled out onto the main road headed west. "That Mrs. Wilsdon, she can't be a proper landlady."

"Not in the least," Nick agreed. "She wouldn't be charmed, wheedled, bribed, or bullied."

"I don't know if you can claim that 'I say, Mrs. Wilsdon, if you don't let us see Mr. Lincoln's flat, we'll be rather vexed' is actually bullying."

"Well, be fair. She was under orders from the police. You did promise not to spoil any evidence."

Drew scowled. "I wasn't going to spoil any of their wretched evidence."

They drove in near silence until they took the turn south toward Farthering Place.

"How are we supposed to solve this thing if they won't let us investigate?" Drew asked and not for the first time.

"Perhaps Birdsong will give you permission to have a look if you'd ask."

Drew considered this for a moment. "He'd likely tell me to mind my own job and let him mind his. Who could blame him?"

"Surely he wouldn't blame a chap for wanting to know who's behind a couple of murders in his own home."

"He might not, I suppose."

Drew wrenched the car to the side of the road, throwing Nick against the door.

"I say, steady on."

"Well, you said we should go talk to Birdsong."

"I did?"

Drew turned sharply into the road and then backed up,

narrowly avoiding putting the rear wheels into the ditch. With another sharp turn he had the car facing back the way they had just come, north toward Winchester. Before long, they were pulling up in front of the police station and were soon admitted into the office of the chief inspector.

"Well, if it isn't Detective Farthering."

"Good afternoon, Inspector. I trust you are doing well this fine afternoon."

"I've been in this job long enough to know when someone wants something."

Drew held his hat over his heart. "I see the inspector is as wise as he is kind."

Birdsong gave him a sour look. "And what is it now?"

Drew smiled. "Chief Inspector, we come to you, hat in hand . . ." He elbowed Nick, who scooped off his own hat. "We come to you, hat in hand, and—"

"No, you may not have a look at Lincoln's flat. And, yes, Mrs. Wilsdon rang up to say you'd been asking."

"There it is," Nick grumbled.

"But you said we could help," Drew protested.

Birdsong looked stern. "I said you could bring me any clever ideas you might have."

"How are we supposed to have any clever ideas if we can't see the clues?"

"I'm sure you'll think of something."

"But, Inspector, it's just not—"

"Mr. Farthering, if you please, I simply do not have the time to deal with amateurs in the middle of a murder investigation. I appreciate your willingness to be of help, but I'm sure you can understand my position here."

"So you won't let us have a look?"

"No."

"Not just a tiny peek?"

"I'm afraid not."

"Can you at least tell us what you've found?"

"Nothing."

"That's hardly cricket, Inspector. Not even the most infinitesimal hint?"

"I'm telling you. Nothing. There was absolutely nothing."

"The flat was empty?"

"No, but there was nothing there to tell us anything. His things were still there, presumably as he had left them, but there wasn't anything unusual in the least. It all looked as if he had just gone away for the weekend, as indeed he had."

"Then why is everything guarded like the crown jewels? We weren't going to make off with Lincoln's cravats or anything."

"My men are having trouble getting any clear fingerprints. What with his room at Farthering Place being wiped clean, we want to have something to clearly identify the body."

"You're not saying everything was wiped clean at his flat as well, are you?"

"No, nothing like that. But thanks to an overly conscientious charwoman, there's not a clear print in the place. My men are still checking it over, but we hardly need any uninvited guests to muddle things even more."

"I see. Well, then there's no need of us interfering there."

"I'm glad you can see it my way, Mr. Farthering."

"Has anything else turned up?"

"We haven't solved it yet, if that's what you're asking, but it's early days still."

"Yes, so you've said. But surely you've uncovered some juicy tidbit of which we are as yet unaware."

"We did have Lincoln's bank account checked. It seems he's deposited several rather large sums of money in the past few weeks and then, two days before he was killed, took it all out in cash."

"Interesting."

"I doubt he was killed for that, though. It's not as if he had it on him that night. I'd be interested to know your theory, Detective Farthering."

Drew glanced at Nick.

"I can't say I have one altogether, sir. I can't help wondering if it all had something to do with Lincoln's blackmailing schemes. It's hard to believe Mrs. Parker would be the only one he had his hooks into."

"Perhaps not. But that doesn't explain her murder, if in fact she was murdered."

"No, that is a bit of a sticking point, isn't it?"

"And then of course there's the question of her involvement with Lincoln."

"My stepfather explained that, didn't he?"

"Do you believe him?"

Drew didn't answer for a moment.

"Well?"

"Of course I do. He's just not the sort to murder anyone. Especially not the wife he was mad about."

"And if that wife betrayed him?"

Drew looked at him coolly. "By all accounts, the rumored betrayal was more than two years ago. Shouldn't he have killed her then?"

"Not necessarily. Still waters, as they say. There's been more than one case put across my desk where a man or woman has waited, decades at times, to have the perfect revenge."

"If that's the case, his revenge wasn't all that perfect. Killing them both the same night?" Drew shook his head. "Not really all that subtle, I'd say."

"It can be very effective to hide in plain sight, sir."

"It would seem, then, that you don't have any other suspects."

"There is still the possibility that Mrs. Parker made away with Mr. Lincoln."

"And then? I thought suicide was ruled out."

Birdsong pursed his lips. "Possibly."

"And don't forget me and the family honor."

"Oh, we're not likely to forget, Mr. Farthering. The picture will no doubt become clearer as time passes. Leave it to us."

"'Leave it to us.'" Drew stalked across the library floor at Farthering Place. "Leave it to them, Nick, and they'll have Mason hanged in a month."

"Or you."

"Yes, well, there is that distinct possibility. Dash it all, there should be more clues. There should be just acres of suspects and something like a hollowed-out table leg or uneaten biscuit that's the key to the whole thing. And there should be a mysterious Russian or a man with a false beard."

Nick sighed. "Not even a sinister Chinaman to suspect, more's the pity."

"I thought your Father Knox specifically forbade the appearance of Chinamen in any capacity."

"True," Nick admitted. "And one can hardly blame him. It's been such an overused device in mystery novels in the past, making the exotic stranger the villain, no doubt he felt he must speak up."

With a discreet knock, Dennison came into the room. "Mr. Rushford's man has requested to see you, sir."

"Really? Well, send him in."

"Very good, sir."

Dennison vanished and reappeared with Rushford's servant close at his heels, but it was decidedly not Rushford's man Bristol. The stranger bowed.

"I have honor to serve Mr. Rushford in requesting worthy Mr. Farthering's presence at his home."

"We have our Chinaman," Nick said under his breath. The man's small stature and Oriental features were a match for his accent. He was a young man as well, certainly not much older than Nick or Drew himself.

"There *are* other Oriental nations besides China," Drew said softly.

Whatever his nationality, his inscrutable humility certainly gave him a sinister aspect. Or was it merely his entrance at that point in the conversation that made him seem so?

Drew stood. "You're Mr. Rushford's man? What happened to Bristol?"

"Mr. Bristol sought other opportunities, sir, before I came to Mr. Rushford's employ."

"And you are . . . ?"

The man bowed once more. "I am Shi Min. If you have your leisure, Mr. Rushford would very much enjoy to discuss some private matters with you."

Drew glanced at Nick and then back at Min. "Private matters? What private matters?"

"I regret, sir, my master did not take me into his confidence."

Drew smiled. This was intriguing. "All right then. Lead the way."

"I'd better come along," Nick said, eyeing the chauffeur narrowly, but the man's mask of inscrutability did not change. He never took his eyes off Drew.

"Unworthy servant would take much honor if revered Mr. Farthering would make entrance into humble vehicle of my master. Your footman will not be required."

"Footman," Nick growled.

With another bow, Min made his way to the door.

"I'll be with you straightaway," Drew told him, and then he turned to Nick. "Perhaps old Rushford's remembered something from the party or before. Or something about Lincoln. Heaven knows what other schemes he had going besides the blackmail."

"All right," Nick said. "As I am, ahem, not required at Rushford's, I suppose I'll poke about a bit here and see what I can turn up."

"Good man," Drew said, giving him a slap on the shoulder. "Just remember, we're not to spoil any evidence. Now mind."

"Let me make note of it," Nick said, taking out his list of commandments and the stub of a pencil to scribble on the back of the list. "No . . . ev . . . i . . . dence . . . is . . . to be . . . spoilt. Got it."

"Lovely." Drew shook his head. "I'm certain your good deeds will not go unpunished. Oh, and look after our Miss Parker while I'm gone, see she doesn't get bored. And tell Mrs. Devon I'll ring up if I won't be back in time for tea."

— Nine —

It was only a short drive to Rushford's home in Winchester. Drew would have liked to see what information he could casually extract during the trip, but his seat in the back of Rushford's limousine was partitioned from the driver's seat by a pane of glass, and carrying on a conversation via the speaking tube beside him would have been awkward at best. Now he had no opportunity to do anything but follow Min from the drive and into the house.

Min showed Drew into a large, sunny room that looked as if everything in it had been there for the better part of five decades. The wallpaper above the dark wainscoting was a faded print of curled acanthus leaves, a perfect complement to the rest of the Victorian décor. Rushford was sitting at a little secretary desk, reviewing a ledger book.

"Come in, young man. Do come in." He closed the book and rose to shake Drew's hand. "Good of you to come. I hated to trouble you to come up, but I thought we might best be able to talk freely here."

"It's no trouble, sir. How may I be of service?"

"Oh, and please have a seat. Would you care for anything? Tea? A spot of brandy?"

"A bit early in the day, isn't it?" Drew said, smiling as he settled into a fussily upholstered Morris chair. "Tea would be lovely, though."

"Tea, Min," Rushford ordered, "and have Cook send in some of those little cakes, as well."

Min bowed and disappeared into the hallway.

"I was surprised to hear that Bristol had left you," Drew said as his host pulled up a chair, "but this Min fellow seems to have stepped right in for him."

"Min's a wonder. I get a driver, gardener, and houseboy all on one salary." Rushford smiled. "There are a great many of his sort in Canada, don't you know."

Drew had a sudden recollection of Mason's conversation with Chief Inspector Birdsong. "Were you there when the Chinese girl was killed at the Edmonton office?"

Obviously a little puzzled by the sudden turn in the conversation, Rushford nodded his head. "That was horrible, just horrible. But it was, oh, some fifteen or twenty years ago. How did you hear of it?"

"The chief inspector was asking my stepfather about it. He wanted to know, other than poor McCutcheon two weeks ago, if there had been any deaths associated with Farlinford. Apart from an accident now and again, he said the only one he knew of was this girl."

"Funny you should mention it," Rushford began, lowering his voice, "but Min's father—"

"Your tea, sir."

Min stood no more than a foot behind them, holding a silver tray laden with cakes and biscuits and a steaming teapot.

Drew didn't dare guess what he may have overheard. There was certainly no clue in the man's face.

"That was certainly quick," Drew said. A little unnerving too, truth be told.

Min bowed and set the tray on a side table. "I have good fortune to meet the maid in the corridor. She had been sent by the cook, knowing Mr. Rushford had a guest."

"Thank you, Min," Rushford said somewhat too heartily. "I'll pour out."

"As you wish, sir." Min bowed once more and left the room, closing the door firmly behind him.

"That was a bit awkward," Rushford admitted as he filled Drew's cup. "Lemon?"

"Honey, if you please," Drew said. "I take it Min's father was involved in the murder in some way?"

"Yes, poor devil. He worked at the plant, porter or night watchman or some such. The girl was his niece."

"Mason says he killed her for his family honor. Because she was a white man's mistress."

"True, although he never admitted to the killing. Rather passionately denied it, in point of fact. Of course, he barely spoke to be understood as it was. Precious little to tell what he was saying half the time."

Drew took a slow sip of his tea. "And the girl's lover?"

"He was one of our junior engineers. Seems he hanged himself at his home three weeks after the trial. Ugly affair all the way around."

"How did Min come to be in your service?"

Rushford smiled indulgently. "Funny thing, that. He was only a little chap when all that business with his father was going on. I didn't hear anything more of him for years. I'd quite forgotten the whole incident, to be quite honest, and then he appeared at my door asking for a position."

"All the way from Canada? That's a bit far to go just to look for work."

"No doubt," Rushford agreed, "but he said he wanted to repay me for what I had done for his father." The older man looked a little embarrassed. "I had spoken for him to the court, as there was no eyewitness to the crime and the evidence was no more than circumstantial. Min's been with me only a short while now, and I can't think how I ever managed before he came."

"It's like that with Denny. I can't imagine Farthering Place without him."

Rushford's face clouded. "Have the police learned anything more about the . . . the unpleasantness out there?"

"I suppose they're working on it. There seems to be rather little to go on."

"I couldn't be certain, but I was almost sure I had seen that photograph the police found in Lincoln's things, the one of the girl. I wish I could remember where." Rushford smiled. "Well, never mind. It'll come to me in time."

"I hope so, sir."

The old man sat gnawing his lip, staring silently at the crackling hearth. Drew spent the time enjoying an excellent lemon tart and wondering why Rushford had sent for him. Eventually the last crumb of the tart was gone, and Drew cleared his throat. "Sir, I—"

"I suppose I ought to get on with what I have to say."

"When you're ready, sir."

Rushford took a deep breath and then let it out, making a sound as old and weary as the lines on his face. "I have to tell you something that doesn't make me proud." He looked around as if expecting to find someone eavesdropping on him in his own home. "Your mother was not the only one Lincoln had on the hook."

Drew leaned forward in his chair. "I rather thought as much. Had he gotten ahold of you, too?"

Rushford slumped over, his elbows on his knees and his head in his hands. "It's been a nightmare," he moaned. "It wasn't the cash so much as everything else, and he didn't ask all that much money really. He wanted me to sponsor him at my club and introduce him to people of importance and guarantee his debts. I couldn't refuse him. The scandal would have ruined me."

"What was he blackmailing you for?"

"I . . . heavens, I hate to say it, but it seemed such a little thing at first."

Drew waited, not speaking.

"I took some money from the company. I had heard of a sure thing in some investments, and as I was going through a rough patch in the old bank account just then, I thought it couldn't hurt anything to simply borrow it. But the investments went bad, not really a surprise given the way the economy's been, and then lost more trying to make it up. I finally did make it up, mind you, and it was deuced hard too, but that was after Lincoln had found out about it. I couldn't have him tell Parker about it. I couldn't."

"How much was it?"

The old man's face was colored with shame. "Nearly eighty thousand pounds."

Drew almost choked on his tea. "Eighty thousand? Well, theft is no small matter in any amount, but eighty thousand? Still, it's hardly worth a bullet to the brain, is it?"

"I don't know what possessed me. I've never had a blot on my record."

"Perhaps you should just have come to my stepfather and

fessed up. No doubt he'd have made it good, at least loaned you the money until you could repay it. Better than letting anyone blackmail you over it."

"Perhaps I should have, but I hated to trouble him. No one has all that much to spare these days. But he's the sort of chap who would be understanding that way, isn't he?"

Rushford looked so utterly miserable, Drew couldn't help feeling sorry for him. "Have you told the police?"

Rushford wrung his hands. "That's just it. I'm afraid the police will find this out and think I had something to do with Lincoln's death."

"And if they find it themselves, it'll look worse, is that it?"

"Exactly so."

"I can see why you wouldn't want anyone at Farthering to overhear us, but what can I do for you?"

"I thought perhaps with you and that young constable being friends and all, you might speak to him about it, not naming names, mind you, and see what he thinks the police might say about such a situation. Then perhaps . . ." He closed his eyes and shook his head. "No, no. It sounds so childish now I say it aloud. Like asking one of the senior boys to speak to the headmaster about a prank one's done oneself, fearing the consequences."

"I shouldn't worry too much about it," Drew said. "You ought to ring up Inspector Birdsong and tell him just what you've told me. If the money's long ago been paid back and there's nothing else suspicious in the books . . ."

"Nothing I know of, no."

Drew took the inspector's card from his trouser pocket and slid it across the table. "Ring him up. It's the best thing."

Rushford hesitated and then took the card and slipped it into the pocket in his waistcoat. Drew took a swallow of tea, waiting for him to say something more, but the old man merely grabbed a piece of almond shortbread and began nibbling it round the edges.

"Anything else the police ought to know?" Drew asked finally.

Rushford sighed. "I can't think what. I've been over it all a hundred times, and I can't think of anything else that might be of help to them. Not that this will make anything about the murders any clearer, but at least they'll know about it."

"Best be aboveboard and all," Drew said. "And try not to worry."

"What an ugly world it's become." Rushford abandoned the ravaged biscuit and sipped his tea. Then he sighed. "Already gone cold."

"I understand you came here from Canada," Drew said as he followed the chauffeur down the front steps to the waiting limousine.

Min nodded in assent, not slowing his short, shuffling steps.

"Were you born there?" Drew asked.

Min turned to face him as he held open the car door. "Your servant was born in Peking," he said, keeping his eyes focused at some point beyond Drew's left shoulder. "Revered sir will care to enter, please?"

Drew considered for a moment, and then he moved around Min and opened the passenger door in the front of the car. "I believe I'll ride up here this time."

Now Min actually looked at him, his eyes bulging.

"No, please. Gentleman ride in back, please. Not proper to ride in front with unworthy driver."

"Nonsense."

Grinning, Drew hopped into the front seat and shut the door after himself. Min stood there for a moment more, still holding the back door. Then, muttering something in Chinese, he shut the door, walked around the back of the car and got into the driver's seat. An instant later, the engine purred to life and they were headed down the drive.

"This is much cozier, wouldn't you say?" Drew asked.

"If it pleases you, sir," Min said, but it was obvious he remained unconvinced.

Drew shifted in his seat, trying to keep his knees from bashing against the glove compartment. It was certainly more comfortable in the back, but not nearly as enlightening.

"I've never been to Canada," Drew said. "It's rather a long way, isn't it? Expensive trip as well, I daresay."

Min said nothing.

"You must have saved for some while before you came."

"I save many month to travel to New York City, then work on ship laundry to pay passage to Liverpool."

"My, my. Was she a large ship?"

"Very large, sir. Called *Britannic*. She have just made voyage from England and now was returning home."

"And all that just to work for Mr. Rushford."

"Mr. Rushford very good to Min's family."

"So I've been told." Drew watched the other man's face as he drove through the countryside. "I understand he was of some help to your family about that unpleasantness back in Edmonton."

Min's eyes did not leave the road. "He speak to judge so they not hang Father. He give Mother one hundred dollar Canadian to help after Father taken away. Mr. Rushford do more than Min was able to repay then."

"You couldn't have been more than a boy."

"Ten year old. Old enough to remember. Old enough to repay someday."

"It must have been difficult for you and your family. I understand it was your cousin who was killed."

"That is so."

"Do you remember her much?"

Min slowed to maneuver the car around a sharp bend in the road. "She was called Lan Jing. You would say Perfect Orchid."

Drew smiled at him. "That's rather lovely, isn't it?"

The other man still did not spare him a glance, but when he finally spoke, his voice was not as impersonal as it had been. "She came with us from China. Was as daughter to my mother and father, as gentle sister to me. But, for some, it is as nothing to crush a harmless sparrow."

Drew could see the driver's hands were tight on the steering wheel, and his lips were pressed into a hard line. Perhaps a change of subject would be wise here, but he couldn't help feeling for the ill-fated little Perfect Orchid.

"Did your father have any idea who might have killed her?"

"No." Min's voice was hard again. "He say only it was someone who did not break in."

Nick had been very uncooperative when Madeline asked where Drew had gone. She hadn't forgiven either of them for not taking her to Chelsea with them. Now it was well into the afternoon, and she still hadn't seen Drew. Impatient, she rang for Anna.

"Do you know when Mr. Drew is supposed to be home?"

"I believe he's in his room, miss."

Madeline thanked the girl and went down the hall and into the west wing. She found the door to Drew's bedroom standing open and him sitting cross-legged on the floor, the towel on his lap full of sleeping kittens. He looked up, and a smile lit his face. "Hullo."

She forced herself not to smile back. "I should be very angry at you, leaving me behind this morning."

"Now, darling, don't be cross. Come see."

She went over to him, unable to keep from cooing over the babies. "The little angels. And where's Minerva?"

"Anna took her down to the kitchen for a treat. In the meantime, Denny has cleared the cupboard of the trousers she was nesting in. He's just now arranging a much more suitable blanket of some sort for her to sleep on."

"That's nice of him."

"Yes, well, I'm not altogether certain he's forgiven her for her choice of a place to bring her progeny into the world, but I told him if he was to retrieve the trousers, he'd have to arrange a suitable replacement himself." Drew patted a spot beside him on the lush Turkish carpet. "Pardon me for not getting up, but I'd love for you to join me."

She stood there a few seconds longer, smiling after all. As flawless as he had looked the night of the party before the rain had ruined his eveningwear, she thought him even more so now. Lounging there before the huge open windows in a white shirt and wheat-colored slacks, the soft breeze teasing the dark locks of his hair, and the lazy summer sunlight spilling over him and his tiny charges, he was irresistible. She had to make this moment of perfection last. It would be gone too soon as it was.

"What is it?" he asked finally, and the addition of a puzzled smile to his handsome lips made him all the more appealing.

"Nothing." She tucked her skirts under her and sat on the floor beside him. "Just that you look cute."

"Cute again, is it? Hmm. I suppose that's better than ghastly."

"It certainly is. How are the children?"

"Doing very nicely, Mummy. All as fat as ripe little plums."

"And napping in Daddy's lap, not a care in the world."

She laughed, and his eyes met hers. *"I've already grown terribly fond of you."* He'd said it before, there in the garden on that terrible night Lincoln was killed. It was written still on his face. She felt a warm flush creep to her cheeks, knowing his expression was a mirror of her own.

"I wanted to let you know . . ."

Her voice sounded unsteady, even to herself. How could she say what she didn't ever want to say?

His smile had faded, replaced with that pensive uncertainty from the day of the funeral. "What is it?"

"I've been talking to Carrie and Muriel," she said, and she knew he could hear the reluctance in her voice.

"I suppose you're all going." His lips were pressed in a firm line now. There was nothing soft and laughing about them anymore.

"We've had our reservations for weeks and weeks now."

"I thought you were going to help us solve the case."

"If it were just me, I would stay until things were figured out, but Carrie and Muriel have wanted to tour Europe for a long time. They only came down here to Hampshire for a few days to please me."

"Of course, that's to be understood. You'll be wanting to see London and Paris and all, not just some stodgy little village where nothing happens."

Much more had happened here at Farthering Place than she would have expected even from London or Paris, but those events had been tragic and harrowing, not at all the pleasant vacation they had planned. And there was much more that she hadn't anticipated.

"I hate to leave." Her blush deepened. "Leave Uncle Mason, I mean."

"He'll understand. He's that way, you know. Never expects anyone to bother about him."

"Please don't." Tears burned behind her eyes. Did it have to be tears? This was awkward enough.

"Don't what?"

She couldn't tell if his carefully controlled expression covered anger or hurt or indifference. No, it wouldn't be indifference. Indifference never made an effort to strike back.

"Uncle Mason—"

"I'll look after him. Truly, he'd be the first to tell you to go on your holiday. There's nothing you can do here anyway, especially if you don't care to stay." He smiled a little once more, and the hardness had gone out of his expression. "Truly."

"It's not that I don't care to stay," she told him, and he looked down at the sleeping mound of kittens in his lap.

"They'll miss their mum." He put his hand over hers. "As will I."

With a little sob, she pressed her face against his shoulder.

"Don't go," he whispered, slipping his arm around her waist. "Don't go."

"But—"

"Your uncle needs you," he breathed against her hair. "Darling, I need you."

He kissed away the tear that had slipped from the corner of her eye. Then he touched his lips to hers, and she could taste the faint saltiness on them.

"You can't go," he told her, and she pushed away from him.

"You shouldn't have done that." Never mind that she had wanted him to. "You know it doesn't mean a thing."

There was a flicker of hurt in his eyes. "I don't know that, actually."

"I've enjoyed spending time with you, Drew. It's been fun,

but we both know it's nothing more than a little holiday fling. I have to go back. If I don't go now, if I stay until the police have everything figured out, I'll still have to go back before long. You'll pick up with someone else, and—"

"No." His gray eyes were stormy now. "Do you think I'm this way with every girl I meet? I know it's utter madness. I know it's far too soon. But I also know I can't bear the idea of you walking away when you haven't given me a chance to prove I'm serious."

"Maybe I'm the one who's not serious."

That hurt him, she could see it, but he only nodded. "Fair enough. I won't presume to say that you don't know your own mind. But be honest with yourself. If you won't be honest with me, be honest with yourself. Are you sure there isn't something? Something real?"

She bit her lip and looked away from him. "I won't say I don't have feelings."

"Feelings?"

She dropped her head. "For you. About you. But we'd both be foolish to make any permanent decisions based on something as fleeting as feelings, don't you think? After just a few days?"

He touched one finger to the underside of her chin, turning her face up to him. "And what if they aren't fleeting?"

She shook her head, unable to say anything.

"I'm not asking you to make any promises, Madeline. I just don't want you to go. Unless you're already sure there's no future for us."

"No," she whispered. "I'm not sure of that, either."

"Then, please, stay awhile at least. Truly your uncle does need you. He's bound to have it rough these next few days. You're all he's got left. Stay and have a bit of fun with me. If that's all it ends up being, at least you'll know."

"Oh, Drew."

"You can't go," he told her again. "Not until you're sure. You can't go."

She shook her head, clinging to him. "I can't go. Oh, Drew, I can't go."

"Not yet, darling. Not yet."

She didn't like to make promises, not so soon, but it did feel right, so very right, to be with him, to tease and romp with him, to find comfort in the shelter of his arms and taste the warmth of his lips. They were on hers again, and she closed her eyes, drinking in the sweetness of it all.

A moment later, he flinched and then chuckled. She opened her eyes to see Minerva standing with her front paws on his leg, inspecting her kittens and looking annoyed to find that they had been tampered with. She nudged one with her nose, and an instant later all five were awake, protesting their late dinner with a cacophony of piercing cries. Minerva picked up the little white one by the scruff of the neck, meaning to carry it off, but Drew quickly took it back from her.

"Hold on, old girl. Hold on. Denny? I say, Denny?"

There was a clatter from the dressing room and then Dennison appeared, coatless and rubber-gloved to the elbow. "Sir?"

"Have you finished in there? Minerva's getting a bit restless."

The kittens were still crying piteously, and Minerva was pacing back and forth beside Drew, meowing and trying to get at them.

"Just done, sir," Dennison said. "Your cupboard has been sanitized and lined with oilcloth, a generous portion of lamb's wool, and a down comforter. The nestlings should be quite at their ease."

"Excellent."

Drew stood, cradling the towel full of kittens in both hands, and followed the butler back into the dressing room. Minerva ran a few steps ahead of him, only to come back and try to insinuate herself between his feet.

"Steady on, girl," he said. "We'll soon have the family reunited."

He was as good as his word, and a moment later Minerva was settled in the newly refurbished cupboard, with her kittens greedily making up for the delay in their noon repast.

"You did a fine job, Mr. Dennison," Madeline said, but the butler merely sniffed.

"I fear, miss, that all was not good news."

"No?"

"The cheviot trousers were quite past redemption."

The next morning, Dennison arranged for Carrie's and Muriel's things to be packed into the trunk of the little roadster that had brought them to Farthering Place.

"I wish you were coming," Carrie said for the hundredth time as she and Madeline stood in the front drive and hugged in farewell. "You know Muriel and I need someone to referee for us."

Madeline tried not to think too much about what she would be missing by staying behind. "The two of you will have a wonderful trip. Just take lots of pictures, send me a ton of letters, and no whirlwind romances."

Carrie laughed. "You should talk."

Madeline giggled and then followed Carrie's glance up to the top of Farthering's front steps to see that Drew and Nick were there. Nick was looking particularly glum.

"I'll try to behave," Carrie promised her, and Madeline could have sworn her friend's voice was just the tiniest bit louder now, "but if I end up eloping with a lord or something, it'll be because you didn't come along and keep me sane." She glanced at Nick again and then scampered up the steps. "It's been awful nice meeting you both."

"A delight, Miss Holland," Drew said. "I hope you'll forgive us for robbing you of a very charming traveling companion."

Madeline smiled. Drew was such a dear.

"But you must also ask pardon," he added with a bow to Carrie, "for robbing us of a very charming houseguest."

"How you do go on, Mr. Farthering," Muriel said as she hurried out the front door. "You English boys sure do know how to talk to a lady."

She held out one hand, gloved in a leopard print, and Drew bowed dutifully over it.

"Miss Brower, it's been a revelation."

Muriel smirked and flounced down the stairs, swaying her hips. Drew gazed heavenward.

Carrie laughed and shook her head, then turned to Nick, her eyes soft and warm. "I've had such a good time. I mean, besides all the trouble, you know."

"It's been grand," he said, clasping the hand she offered him. "You must come back one day, when things are a bit less out of order."

"I hope I can."

He hesitated for a moment, but he didn't release her hand. "Please don't."

"What?"

"Marry a lord, I mean. Don't do that."

"He's right, you know," Drew told her. "You'll end up with half a dozen offspring just like our friend Bunny."

She laughed. "Bunny?"

Nick rolled his eyes. "Clive St. John Pontisbright Marsden-Brathwaite. Bunny when at home. He has the brain of a peahen, but lots and lots of money."

"He's a good chap for all that," Drew said. "Stout fellow, give you his shirt in an instant, but rather likely to forget your name or where he's left your car."

"Don't do that," Nick repeated, a sudden earnestness in his eyes.

Carrie smiled, promising nothing, but she squeezed his hand before letting it go. "I'll send you a postcard."

Watching them, Madeline smiled to herself. *She'll be back.*

"See you soon," Muriel said, pressing her cheek to Madeline's. Then, with a quick glance at Drew, she winked. "Keep your eyes open, Madeline, honey. That one's a real smoothie." She got behind the wheel and started the car. "Come on, Carrie, or we'll be driving all night."

"I'd better go," Carrie told Nick.

He escorted her down to the car, opened the door, and helped her inside. "Do be careful."

"I'll try my best," she said, and without warning, the car lurched into motion.

"Toodles," Muriel called, and then with the grinding of gears the little roadster clattered away.

Madeline stood there with Nick, watching until the sight and sound of it were no more, and then Drew came down the steps and linked arms with them both.

"'How now, my hearts!'" he quoted. "'Did you never see the picture of "we three"?'"

Nick laughed, but Madeline was only puzzled.

"What's that?" she asked.

"Merely a bit of Shakespeare," Drew said. "A little quip from *Twelfth Night*."

"Oh, now I remember," she said. "But I never did understand that line."

"They say it's likely based on a public-house sign picturing two fools with the inscription 'We Three.'"

She pursed her lips. "I'm sure I'll hate myself for asking, but if there are only two fools in the picture, where's the third?"

"Well, darling, *someone* had to be looking up reading the sign."

Madeline smiled.

"And I'm sorry to say it, Miss Parker," Nick added, "but you've been standing here looking up at two fools for at least five minutes now. Shall we go in to lunch?"

This time she laughed.

They spent the meal puzzling over recent events, and afterward, while Madeline chatted with her uncle about his last visit to America and the adventures they'd had, Drew pulled Nick aside.

"Keep your voice down," Drew said.

"What is it? What's wrong?"

"Shh. Nothing. I thought you'd like to motor up to Winchester with me."

"What for?"

"I've been thinking, added to everything else, it's a bit of a coincidence that we had another death just two weeks ago."

"McCutcheon." Nick glanced over at Madeline. "I thought the police hadn't found anything all that suspicious there. Just an accident."

"I don't know. I'd feel better, though, if we had a look round his flat and his office."

"You know his address?"

Drew tapped his breast pocket. He'd charmed the information from the breathless Miss Stokes in personnel via telephone just that morning.

Nick grinned. "What about our Miss Parker? She'll want to come."

"I told you about that. It's too distracting."

"She won't like it, knowing she's been left once more to fend for herself." Nick glanced toward her again. "She's coming. What are you going to tell her?"

"Just keep quiet. I'll think of something."

"We're going to look at the horses," Madeline announced as she strolled up to them, Mason in tow. "We may go riding. We went all the time when he used to come visit me at school. I think it will brighten up both of us."

Drew smiled. "That sounds good. I'll get my hat."

"No. I mean . . ." Madeline bit her lip. "I'd love for you to come. Always. But I thought this time just Uncle Mason and I . . ." She put her hand on his arm, appealing, consoling.

Drew let his smile fade. "Well, of course, darling, if you don't *want* me along . . ."

Nick grinned and then quickly began studying a loose thread on the sleeve of his coat.

Mason patted Madeline's hand. "Perhaps you young people ought to—"

"No," she insisted. "I've hardly had you to myself since I've been here. You understand, don't you, Drew?"

Drew felt a pang of guilt at the pleading look in her eyes. His expression warmed, and he stroked her cheek with the backs of his fingers. "You go, darling. Have a lovely time, both of you." He nodded at Mason. "Do you a world of good, sir."

Mason looked at Madeline with a fond smile. "Yes, I believe it will. Shall we go, my dear?"

Madeline gave Drew a swift, grateful peck on the cheek, and then she and her uncle went out across the garden.

"You hound," Nick breathed once they had gone. "The poor girl thinks she's broken your heart. Or at least bruised your ego."

Drew hurried with Nick into the corridor, toward the garage and away from the stables. "I doubt she'll give it another thought."

But, dash it all, the girl could make him feel like the most abysmal scoundrel with just one trusting look. Little wonder he'd made no headway in the case. Still, it was a pity this was such a serious matter. It would be profoundly satisfying to spend his days doing real investigations instead of just trying to solve made-up cases one step ahead of the detectives in the novels he read. So much more engaging than the usual empty whirl of high society.

"Come on," he told Nick. "I want to see what we can turn up at McCutcheon's."

— Ten —

Arthur McCutcheon had been hired on at Farlinford Processing fresh out of college based on his exceptional promise as a chemical engineer. But despite his perpetual assurances that he was on the verge of a great breakthrough, his three years with the company had proved unfruitful. Then in one careless moment, he was gone.

Drew had found out that much from talking to Mason and Rushford. He shared the information with Nick on the brief drive to Winchester and the nondescript block of flats where McCutcheon had lived.

The door, appropriately marked MANAGER, was opened by a stubby little boy of perhaps ten. Bespectacled and fussily dressed, he looked annoyed at being disturbed when more than half of his Marmite sandwich was yet to be eaten.

"Yes?"

"Hullo," Drew said with a cheerful smile. "Might we speak with the building manager?"

"I am the manager," the boy told him. If it were possible for anyone to look down his nose at someone of a greater height than himself, Drew was certain this boy would have done as much. He'd make a fine civil servant one day.

"Are you?" Drew asked, not altogether concealing his surprise. "That must be an interesting job."

"Not very. Is there something you wanted?"

"I'd like to see number twenty-seven," Drew replied, still smiling. "Mr. McCutcheon's flat."

"And I'd like a motorized bicycle," the boy said disdainfully, "but I'm not likely to get that, either."

Nick grinned. "Well, aren't you a cheeky little—"

Drew cleared his throat. "Might we have a word with your father?"

"Certainly," the boy replied, and then he smirked. "He's at his office in London."

"Your mother, then," Drew said, a little less patiently.

The boy jerked his head toward the street. "She's across the road, listening to *More Scenes of Domestic Bliss* on the wireless with Mrs. Dunlap, and you won't half catch it if you go to see her before it's over."

"Oh, that twaddle," Nick muttered.

"Look here," Drew told the juvenile manager, "this is a serious matter, and it's quite important that I have a look round up there."

"I'm not to let just anyone into any of the flats unless it's the police or someone of that sort. Are you with the police?" the boy demanded.

"No, not as such," Drew admitted, and then he lowered his voice conspiratorially. "But you give me five minutes up there, and I'll give you a shilling."

The boy shook his head.

"A pound?" Drew offered.

"A pound!" Nick protested. "Half the population of Britain doesn't make that for a day's work."

"A motorized bicycle," the boy countered.

"What?"

The boy crossed his arms over his stocky chest, endangering his fine shirt with the sandwich he held. "A motorized bicycle. Get me one, and I'll let you in."

Nick glared. "Well, I like that."

"Now, Nick, old man, let's hear him out." Drew smiled sweetly at the boy. "So, if I get you a motorized bicycle, you'll let me up in Mr. McCutcheon's flat, no questions asked?"

The little scoundrel nodded his head. "All right."

"I would be very happy to give a deserving and helpful lad a nice new motorized bicycle," Drew said, still smiling. "But you're a nasty, greedy little toad, so you shan't have one. Come on, Nick. We'll pop round to this Mrs. Dunlap's and see if the lady of the house mightn't be more reasonable."

With a tip of his black Homburg hat, Drew turned and, with Nick in tow, made his way back into the street. The boy shot out after them.

"Wait! Wait! I'll let you in! I'll do it for a pound!"

"I fear that offer has been withdrawn," Drew said sunnily as he tapped on the front door of the house opposite.

"A shilling then," the boy pleaded, unwittingly squeezing his sandwich into a pulpy mess. "Don't! Her program is on!"

The little girl who opened the door merely stared at the two strangers. Drew could hear a man and woman talking from the radio inside.

"Good afternoon," he said with a slight bow. "Might I inquire whether this is Mrs. Dunlap's residence?"

The girl nodded solemnly.

"And is there another lady with her right now? Listening to the wireless?"

Again the girl nodded. Then she looked at the boy and very quietly asked, "What's he done now?"

"He's been good enough to send me over to talk to his mother," Drew said, and he handed the girl his card. "If you would be so kind, please take that in and ask her if she would come have a word with me."

"Her program's not over," the girl said, still solemn.

"Susan!" a woman's voice scolded from inside the house. "What did I tell you about talking to salesmen?"

"I'm not selling anything," Drew called back. "I've just come to speak to the lady who looks after the building across the street."

The little girl scurried inside with the card, and a moment later a dowdy-looking woman wearing bright red lipstick came to the door.

Drew removed his hat. "Good afternoon, Mrs. . . . ?"

"Newton," the woman said, eyeing him with suspicion. "Is there something you wanted?"

"I do beg your pardon for disturbing you. My name is Drew Farthering. You were letting rooms to a Mr. McCutcheon who worked for my family's company, Farlinford Processing."

"That's right. So you're *that* Mr. Farthering. Well."

"I'd like see the flat for a moment, if that's possible. I was hoping to gather some information about a project McCutcheon was working on for us."

"Is that all? The police came round when he passed over and then locked everything up tight until yesterday. I couldn't even go tidy much less show the place to be let again." She turned to her son. "Clarence, show the gentlemen number twenty-seven."

"We'd like to ask a few questions as well, if we might," Nick added, and the woman glanced back into the house. The couple on the radio were arguing viciously now to the accompaniment of melodramatic music.

"Well . . ." she began.

"Or," Drew offered, "dear Clarence could let us into the flat and then we could come back later and talk to you." He looked at his watch. It was eight minutes to the hour. *More Scenes of Domestic Bliss* would be over soon. "Say in about ten minutes?"

"That would be lovely," the woman told Drew, obviously relieved. "Go on, Clarence," she scolded. "You could have just taken them up to Mr. McCutcheon's without disturbing my program, couldn't you?"

She hurried back inside, the little girl shut the door, and an unwilling Clarence trudged across the street once more. Drew and Nick followed him back to his own flat to fetch the key to McCutcheon's rooms, and then the three of them went up to the first floor.

Number 27 was an unassuming little flat at the back of the building, overlooking a burgeoning vegetable garden and the unrelieved brick of the block behind it. Pajama bottoms were strewn across the rumpled bed, and an unwashed plate and teacup had been left in the sink, signs of nothing more sinister than a hurried departure for a usual day's work. There were a number of books on chemistry, physics, and mathematics, along with a dog-eared collection of fantasy and horror novels. Other than a reproduction of a hideous surrealist painting, there were no pictures on the walls, only a little framed photograph on a side table. It was signed *To Mackie always*.

"Looks as if he left someone behind, after all," Drew said.

"I'm sure she has a jolly nice personality," Nick observed, studying the face of the bespectacled young woman with impossibly bushy hair and a crooked smile.

Drew responded with an impatient frown. "I say, Clarence, has anyone been in here since the police came?"

The boy sneered at him. "Of course not. Do you think we let just anyone poke about our flats?"

"Well, that's all right then." Drew smiled and pocketed the key. "We'll let you know if we need anything more."

"But—"

"You go back to your sandwich, there's a good lad, and we'll make sure to give the key to your mother once we've finished up here."

"And we'll make sure to tell her what a great help you've been," Nick added, and he hustled the boy into the corridor and shut the door after him.

"All right," Drew said. "See if there's anything in that bureau."

It didn't take them long to go through the sparse furnishings. The contents told them nothing but what they knew already: Arthur McCutcheon was mired in his work and had little interest in much of anything else.

"What exactly are we looking for?" Nick asked as he rummaged through a shoebox full of old papers he had found in the top of the wardrobe.

"I don't know exactly. Anything that would show a connection between McCutcheon and Lincoln or Constance. Besides Farlinford, of course."

Nick opened an envelope and looked at the slip of paper inside. "It seems Mr. McCutcheon's debt to the Winchester Bank & Trust in the amount of twenty pounds was paid in full on the twenty-seventh day of April, 1931." He put the slip back into the box and took out an engraved invitation. "Elizabeth Myrtle Cubbins and James Arthur Davies requested the honor of his presence at their marriage this past February."

"More to the point, if you please," Drew prompted as he rifled through the drawer of the writing desk, and then he picked up a stern-looking tome that must have belonged to a student of the law sometime in the past fifty years. "Hullo."

Nick looked up. "What?"

"Very interesting," Drew said, scanning the book. "It's marked at the part about blackmail and the penalties therefor."

Nick looked over his shoulder at the underlined passage. "Hardly a coincidence after what's happened with Lincoln, eh? Do you think it's motive for murder?"

Drew frowned again. "I don't see how, if McCutcheon was locked up in his lab when the benzene spilled. I don't know. Shall we talk to Mrs. Newton here and then have a quick look at Farlinford?"

Mrs. Newton made it perfectly clear that her tenants' personal entanglements were their own business and none of her own, just as she had told the police. She could say nothing of Mr. McCutcheon except that he was a man of quiet habits who paid his rent on time and caused her no trouble. That seen to, Drew and Nick made their way to McCutcheon's office, which was a little more than two miles from the flat.

Drew told Mr. Baumann, the third floor manager, that he just wanted to look at McCutcheon's laboratory, just to see it for himself, and Baumann obliged.

Once he and Nick were left on their own, Drew looked for a place to start. The room was very typical of the research labs at Farlinford, all white and stainless steel, cabinets filled with files and notebooks, worktables covered with test tubes and chemicals marked with ominous warning labels. It looked as if nothing had been disturbed since McCutcheon had last been at work.

"According to the police, McCutcheon typically holed up in here all day with the door locked," Drew said. "Everyone says he was one of those intense chaps who lived for his job and always claimed he was on the verge of something big. When the benzene spilled, he couldn't get the door unlocked before it killed him."

Nick made a face. "Ghastly way to go west, if you ask me. But suppose it was murder. Suppose he found out about Lincoln somehow and was going to report him. Perhaps Lincoln would kill him to shut him up, but how would he manage it in here?"

"The police say this Adams who has the office next door heard McCutcheon fall, heard him trying to get out and rushed right over. They had to break down the door." Drew took hold of a piece of wrought iron that barred the window and gave it a firm shake. It didn't budge. "There aren't any other ways in or out. McCutcheon's is the last door in this wing, so no one could have gotten out without Adams or Baumann or someone seeing him."

"Still, suppose someone spilled it on purpose."

"Rather an odd way to dispose of someone, but I guess it would work in this environment, especially if it was meant to look as though an accident. But there's the getting in and out to be accounted for." Drew considered for a moment. "We've been through McCutcheon's flat. Nothing there to speak of, apart from that law book, and that may not have anything to do with anything. Maybe there's something in his files or tucked away in a drawer that will shed some light on things."

"The police went through it all and found nothing of note," Nick reminded him.

Drew opened another cabinet. "Maybe they didn't know what to look for."

"Right," Nick said. "They're just the police. What would they know about solving crimes?"

"Quiet, you."

The two of them searched through the remaining cabinets and drawers and found nothing of interest.

"You'd best start on that filing cabinet in the corner," Drew said. "I'll look through these notebooks."

Nick's shoulders sagged. "It'll take a week to get through all that."

"Then you'd best get at it, old man."

Nick trudged over to the filing cabinet. "I thought detecting was supposed to be all mysterious and exciting," he muttered as he yanked open the top drawer.

Overbalanced, the heavy cabinet began to topple, and Nick just managed to catch it.

"I say! A little help here!"

Drew hurried over to lend a hand, but stopped short, staring at the floor behind the files.

"Good heavens."

"Drew," Nick urged. "This is heavy."

"Oh, right. Right."

They pushed the drawer back in and made sure the filing cabinet was stable. Then they pulled it away from the wall again, and Drew bent to retrieve the object he had seen.

"Looks as if the police weren't quite as thorough as advertised."

He handed Nick an old photograph of a young woman. A young woman whose clothes and hairstyle would have been fashionable a quarter of a century earlier. It wasn't the same picture as the one in Lincoln's bag, but it was of the same girl. Taken the same day as the other too, judging by the clothes and the room.

"That's the girl. Marielle." Nick turned it over, but the back of this one was blank. "What would McCutcheon be doing with this?"

Drew reclaimed the photo and studied the woman's face,

searching for something familiar in it, something that resonated with the image he saw in his own mirror. She was smiling this time, and there was a hint of a dimple at the corner of her mouth. Any man might be led astray by such a smile and such a dimple, even a good one. Drew slipped the picture into his coat pocket.

"For now, we need to see what else the police might have overlooked. This cabinet shouldn't have tipped over so easily."

He bent down and opened the bottom drawer. It was empty.

"Curious," Nick said. "The police didn't say anything about this in their investigation, did they?"

"Not to me. But I haven't really asked them about McCutcheon yet. Birdsong may not wish to discuss it with me, at any rate."

"Can't hurt to ask, can it?"

"I'll give it a go next time I see him, but for now let's check the desk. There's precious little else in the room we can look behind."

With Nick's help, Drew pulled the desk away from the wall. Other than some paper clips and a long-forgotten fountain pen, there was nothing behind it.

"Dash it all," Nick said. "I was hoping to find the killer's confession, complete with gory details, back here somewhere."

Drew narrowed his eyes, staring for a moment, and then he ran his hand over the wall.

"Didn't Father Knox have something to say about secret passages?"

"What?"

Drew showed Nick a crevice in the wall, a barely visible crack that ran from the baseboard up the wall about three feet and then turned at a right angle to go about two feet across and then, with another right angle, back down to the baseboard. It would have never been noticeable with the desk in its proper place.

"No," Nick said, with an incredulous shake of his head. "It's probably some sort of access for workmen. You know, electrical or something to do with the plant."

"If it is, it's deuced inconvenient to get to. Besides, we'll never know if we don't try it."

Drew pressed on the wall near the top right corner of the crevice. Nothing happened. He was equally unsuccessful no matter where he pressed.

"Must open from the inside," he concluded.

"Or it's just a badly done patch for when some experiment went wrong and blew a hole in the wall. Or . . ." Nick produced his penknife. "Perhaps it opens outwards."

"Ah."

Drew took the knife and pried the blade into the crevice. With one quick twist, the panel popped out, exposing a small crawl space.

Nick picked up the panel, inspecting it. "Handle on the inside. Makes it easy to close it after one's gone in."

"Shall we?" Drew asked.

"I suppose we fairly much have to at this point, but I will register a formal objection." Nick pulled out his list of commandments. "There aren't to be secret passages, and if there must be one, it should be in a place that is likely to have such a thing. This isn't the sort of place at all."

"Your objection is noted but irrelevant. With or without Father Knox's approval, there is a secret passage that could have been used in dispatching McCutcheon, and I plan to find out where it goes."

"Perhaps we should put the desk back in place," Nick suggested. "No need to be found out before we get a few answers."

"Capital idea."

They centered the desk back over the opening. Then Drew crawled under it and into the passage.

"It's rather dark," he called. "I don't suppose you thought to bring a torch."

"I didn't expect I'd need one in a laboratory," Nick called back. "Shall I see if there's one somewhere about?"

Drew backed out from under the desk, his hands grimy and the knees of his crisp white trousers smudged with dirt. "That seems to be in order. Heaven knows what might be in there, but at first glance it reminds me of nothing so much as the much-vaunted outer darkness."

"Back in a jiff," Nick promised, and he was, bringing a torch with him.

"Ah," Drew said. "Success."

"I got it from one of the stenographers. She keeps it in her desk in case the electricity goes out."

Drew nodded. "Clever girl. Now back into outer darkness."

He crawled under the desk and into the passage with Nick at his heels.

"I don't envy you explaining the state of your clothing to Dad once we get out of this mess," Nick said as he pulled the panel closed behind them.

Drew grimaced. "It is a bit dusty. I don't suppose the char-woman gets by here much. But do keep your voice down. It's hardly worth having a secret passage if one announces it to the world, you know."

He was relieved to find the crawl space ended just a few feet farther on, and the passage, though only wide enough to wriggle through, became high enough for them to stand up.

"That's better," he whispered. "Now, where exactly are we?"

He shone the torchlight on the wall in front of him. It was painted and had a decorative molding at the ceiling. At about eye level there was a rectangular space that was brighter and less worn-looking than the rest.

"There was a picture or something hanging here once," he said, fingering the nail hole at the top of the rectangle. "This used to be the front side of a wall. Probably original to the building."

With some difficulty he managed to twist himself around to look at the wall at his back. "Ah. And this one is new and obviously faces out the other way."

"Didn't they have the offices remodeled a bit a few weeks ago?" Nick asked, his voice barely audible.

"Precisely. Perfect opportunity for someone to add some custom features. Now, just where does this go?" Drew flashed the torch ahead of them and saw that the passage stopped at a dead end. "Not there, obviously."

"Unless the door there is disguised," Nick offered, but Drew shook his head.

"Why would anyone conceal a door *inside* the passage? But . . ." He turned the torch downward. "Why not something similar to what we've just come through?"

There were three handles in the newer wall, about twelve feet apart, and one at the far end of the passage in the opposite wall. All of them were only about two feet from the floor.

"Well, well," Drew mused. "Which shall it be? The lady or the tiger?"

"I say the one by itself there," Nick suggested, pointing to the handle in the older wall. "The other three likely go to the same sort of place. This one's different."

"*Vive la différence*, eh?" Drew put a cautioning finger to his lips and listened at the wall. "I don't hear anything," he whispered. "Let's just take a quiet little look."

He switched off the torch and, without a sound, opened the panel little by little until he could see into the room beyond. Then he pulled it silently shut again.

"What did you see?" Nick asked, his voice soft and urgent.

Drew switched the torch back on. "It's rather what I thought. The accounting department. The panel opens under a desk as in McCutcheon's lab. That means access to all the ledgers and other records. Now let's see where the other doors lead."

"Well, don't stand about all day. It's beastly stuffy in here. Pick one."

"I say it's wise to take the middle course," Drew said.

Once he had plunged them back into total darkness, Drew cautiously opened the center panel in the recently built wall and found himself in darkness still. He covered the end of the torch with his left hand to block most of the light and switched it on again. He was staring at the hem of a gentleman's overcoat. He pushed it to one side, and after crawling over a pair of what he considered rather shabby dress pumps and a sturdy pair of galoshes, he stood up.

He was still for another moment, listening, and then, finding a doorknob, he turned it and stepped noiselessly into an office. He immediately recognized the man at the desk with his back to him.

"Good afternoon," he said as he switched off the torch.

With an audible gasp, Rushford spun to face him. "My word! Where did you come from?"

"Your coat closet, I believe, sir," Drew said sunnily. "I hope you don't mind. Oh, and I've brought a guest." He went back to the closet. "Come on through, Nick, old man."

"My word!" Rushford repeated as Nick emerged from the darkness. "What were you doing in there? And how in the world did you get in?" He mopped his forehead with his handkerchief. "My word."

"We came from McCutcheon's laboratory," Drew answered. "Did you know there's a passageway back behind your office?"

"No," Rushford said, startled patches of red on each of his pale cheeks. "Behind *my* office? But whatever for?"

"That is precisely what we are attempting to ascertain. Would you care to see?" Drew asked. He pulled back the overcoat and shone the torch toward the small opening in the back of the closet.

Rushford blinked a few times. "You came through there? I could never do it, even if I managed to fit. It would be too ghastly in a tiny, dark hole like that."

Drew refrained from smiling. Rushford was not a particularly large man, but he was shaped rather like a grape. The passage might be a bit of a tight fit for him at that.

"I understand your office was recently redone," Drew said. "Was that your idea?"

"Mine?" Rushford's laugh was a little unsteady. "Not as such, no. Parker and I had talked about it for some time, but nothing ever came of it. Then we decided it would be something good for Lincoln to see to. Keep him out of mischief and all." He blotted his upper lip with his already-sodden handkerchief. "Well, one shouldn't speak ill of the dead, I know, but he could be rather a trial when he had a notion to come up here and *work*."

"Yes," Drew said, "I've heard my stepfather mention that. Do you happen to know the firm he engaged to do the work?"

"I'm afraid I don't remember. It wasn't really much to do with me. I was in York that week on business. Somebody and Son, I daresay, but then it's always an 'and son,' isn't it?"

"I suppose it is," Drew replied.

"Would someone in accounting have a record of it?" Nick asked.

"Oh, certainly," Rushford assured them. "Go and see a Mr. Evans in disbursements. He can show you everything from the original estimate to the final payment. They're quite particular about that sort of thing, though I'm not usually in on the details of each minor transaction."

"That's all right," Drew assured him. "My father always said the only thing the owner of a business has to know is how to find the right people. The rest will take care of itself."

"Too true," Rushford agreed. "Too true. Still, it seems harder every day to find someone who can be trusted."

The red patches had faded into his cheeks, and he seemed to have recovered from his fright.

Drew nodded. "Alas, that is also too true."

It was past teatime when Drew and Nick returned to Farthering Place. The door to the library was open, and Drew could see Madeline sitting on the divan, reading.

"She's not going to be pleased with you, old man," Nick said, half under his breath. "Not when she finds out where we've been."

"She's not going to find out."

"No?"

"You're not going to say anything," Drew said, his expression firm. "And I know I won't."

Nick laughed softly. "You're still a hound."

"Yes, but I don't mean her to find that out quite yet." Grinning, Drew straightened his tie and strode into the library. "Hullo, darling. Did you have a pleasant afternoon?"

She glanced up, smiling briefly, and then turned again to her book. "Yes, we did, actually. Uncle Mason and I had a very nice talk. You have some beautiful horses."

"They are fine, aren't they?" He sat on the divan next to her. "Did you see Charlemagne?"

"Hmmm?" She didn't look up.

"Charlemagne. My Arabian. Did you see him?"

She turned the page. "Mm-hmm. Very nice."

Frowning, he stood up again. "I won't interrupt your reading, then."

She kept reading. "All right."

"I'll just keep my adventures to myself, shall I? Don't suppose you'd like to know where I've been all afternoon?"

"Oh, have you been out?" Still she didn't look up.

"I have."

She turned another page. "That's nice."

"I've been to McCutcheon's flat, I'll have you know, and to his laboratory."

From his station at the library door, Nick burst into laughter, and that smug, pixyish little grin was on Madeline's face, as well.

She closed her book. "And here I thought I'd hurt your feelings by not asking you to come with me and Uncle Mason. Don't tell me you hadn't already decided to go up to Winchester."

Drew sank into a chair. "Do you see, Nick? I'm reduced to drooling idiocy by her mere presence."

"You know you don't have to take me along if you don't want to," she said. "Maybe I can do some investigating on my own."

She knew very well he couldn't allow that, not with a murderer at large, no matter how innocently she batted those long lashes. He tried his best repentant expression.

"Now, darling, you know I always want you along. I just thought it was likely to be rather a bore, and I knew you and your uncle wanted some time together, and—"

"And was it? A bore?"

"Not half!" Nick chimed in, coming properly into the room. "There's a secret passage from McCutcheon's lab to the accounting department and to the directors' offices. And maybe his accident was no accident. And he had a photograph of the same girl Lincoln had."

"Marielle?"

"Seems so," Drew admitted. "Although it's not clear why. He may have been going to report Lincoln to the police, or they just might have been in on the whole thing together."

"Why else would he have her photograph?" Madeline asked. "Strange, him and McCutcheon both being dead now."

"It's quite possible that Lincoln spilled the benzene on purpose and then escaped through the passageway." Drew frowned. "Too bad McCutcheon died before Lincoln. Otherwise he'd be a prime suspect in our murders here."

Nick sat himself on the divan and leaned toward her. "That secret passage at Farlinford, quite inappropriate according to Father Knox, but it's there all the same."

"And no one's found it before now?"

Drew shook his head. "They've redone the offices, your uncle's, Rushford's, and Lincoln's. Lincoln was in charge of the project. Looks as if he gave himself access to all the financial records, the other directors, and McCutcheon. The chief inspector will be quite interested in our discoveries, no doubt."

"We tracked down the invoices for the builders, Chatterton and Son," Nick said. "Of course, there is no Chatterton and Son."

"And of course," Drew added, "Lincoln authorized it all."

"Could he do that?" Madeline asked. "Make those kinds of decisions by himself?"

Drew hesitated, not wanting to bring up anything that might prove unsettling to her.

"Well, could he?" she pressed.

"No, actually. The company is set up to require the signatures of two directors for unusual expenditures." Again Drew hesitated, and then he took a deep breath. "The other signature was your uncle's."

Madeline's eyes flashed. "But that doesn't mean—"

"No, that doesn't mean anything." He squeezed her hand. "It doesn't mean he knew what Lincoln was up to. Lincoln was put in charge of the project. It would be perfectly natural for him to have your uncle countersign the authorizations for it. Don't let it trouble you, darling."

She managed a trembling smile. "No, of course not."

— Eleven —

Drew was forced to leave Madeline to her own devices all the next morning while he and Nick and Mr. Padgett took care of some estate business. Fortunately they were through by lunchtime, and he was quick to claim Madeline afterward. He found her in the library, intent on another book.

"Hullo," Drew said.

She started and then laughed. "Don't you know better than to sneak up on someone who's reading a murder mystery?"

"Sorry, darling. Who is it today?"

"Agatha Christie. Yours, I'm sure."

She held up the book, *Peril at End House*, and he tried to take it from her.

"I didn't pay seven and six for that only to have someone else read it first."

"How much is that in real money?" she asked, smirking as she held it out of his reach.

"Now, now. Give me the book, there's a good girl."

She shook her head. "You didn't even know it was here."

"That's as may be, but Mrs. Harkness at the bookshop always

sends me out the month's selection from the Mystery Mavens' Newsletter. It's the only bright spot in my otherwise dreary existence."

She seemed unmoved by his piteous expression, but there was a sparkle of mischief in her eyes.

"You can have it after I'm finished."

He sat on the divan beside her and tried to read over her shoulder, but she turned to block his view.

"Be fair," he protested. "At least tell me what it's about."

"I've read only a few pages, but according to the dust jacket, it's about a girl who lives in a run-down old house on the coast, and someone is trying to kill her."

"Probably because she goes about taking other people's books."

Madeline made a face at him. "All right, I'll read it to you. 'No seaside town in the south of England is, I think, as attractive as St. Loo. It is well named the Queen of Watering Places and reminds one forcibly of—'"

He cleared his throat. "You know, this would be lovely if it were after dinner on a cold January night. But just now it's far too nice out to stay indoors, isn't it?"

She eyed him narrowly. "What did you have in mind?"

"I thought you might like to spend the afternoon with me. You've been shut up in the house with nothing to do all this time, and I was positively abominable to you yesterday."

"And after you begged me to stay."

He hung his head. "I'm quite paralyzed with self-recrimination." Then he looked up at her, a mischievous glint in his eye. "Shall we take the grand tour? Farthering St. John and environs? Afternoon walking tour only a tanner, tuppence for the kiddies?"

"Oh, can we, please? I've been just dying to see it."

"Then it's high time you did." He took the book from her,

set it on a side table, and tucked her arm under his. "Of course, you're likely to be gawked at. We don't see many strangers in Farthering St. John."

As Drew had expected, they passed a few people along the road, people who looked at Madeline with unabashed curiosity but offered only a tip of a hat or a brief "good afternoon" before continuing on their way. But the lady working in the garden of one of the first houses they came to stopped her work and met them at her gate.

"Good afternoon, Mr. Farthering," she said, brushing the dirt from her hands. "Lovely day."

Drew tipped his hat. "Good afternoon, Mrs. Beecham. It is indeed. May I introduce Miss Parker? She's staying with us at Farthering. Madeline, this is Mrs. Beecham. She grows the loveliest dog roses in all of Hampshire."

"I can see she does," Madeline said. "So nice to meet you, Mrs. Beecham."

The older woman's round face glowed as she looked over the well-loved pale pink blooms. "Why, thank you, Miss Parker, though I'd rather call them briar roses. So much prettier, don't you think?"

"Well, yes, I—"

"Aren't you Mr. Parker's niece? Poor Mr. Parker, and you, Mr. Farthering. I hope you're getting on all right, now your mother's gone. Mrs. Harkness from the bookshop was just asking after you. She's so fond of you, dear. Anyway, such a shame a tragedy like that happening right there at Farthering Place."

"Yes, certainly," Drew said, and all at once the day didn't seem so perfect. "Tell Mrs. Harkness we're all very well, thank you."

"And aren't you a pretty thing?" Mrs. Beecham said to Madeline. "American, aren't you? That's a perfectly charming hat.

I don't know why they say American girls have no style about them. Of course, I've never thought any such a thing, but you know how people talk."

Drew cleared his throat. "Yes, well—"

"You know, I believe there are some Americans staying at the Queen Bess just now, Miss Parker. Do you know them?"

Madeline shook her head. "I don't think so."

"Are you sure? I'm certain I heard they're from America."

"America is quite a large place, Mrs. Beecham," Drew said pleasantly. "Who are they?"

"Oh, I couldn't say, dear. I've got my garden to take care of, you see. I haven't time for idle gossip. All I've heard is that they're two Americans come to the Itchen to fish for trout, a Mr. Whiteside and a Mr. Flesch. Mr. Flesch lost his wife this spring, and his friend Mr. Whiteside, he's in business of some sort, brought him here to cheer him up a bit because Mr. and Mrs. Flesch's tickets couldn't be exchanged. It's understandable Mr. Flesch might want to keep a bit to himself, losing his missus and all, but Mr. Whiteside has been rather a favorite with the ladies of the Women's Institute. Not a stripling anymore, you'd have to agree, but not one to give in to the rust and rot, as they say. Now there is a young man staying at the cottage Mrs. Chapman lets out, a Mr. Barker, but then he's not an American at all, so I don't suppose you'd know him, would you, dear? Are the two of you off to see the village?"

Seeing Madeline could manage only a bewildered smile after all that, Drew answered for them. "Miss Parker wanted to go down to the shops and all and take another look at the church."

"Oh, my dear, do," Mrs. Beecham told Madeline, gushing only minimally. "It's not Winchester Cathedral, of course, but our little church can be quite charming in its own right."

Madeline smiled. "It's lovely."

"Thank you, Mrs. Beecham," Drew said, tipping his hat. "It's been nice chatting with you."

"So nice to meet you, Mrs. Beecham," Madeline added as he turned her once more toward the village.

"Oh, do take her to Mrs. Leicester's for tea!" Mrs. Beecham called after them. "She does a lovely sherry trifle!"

Drew didn't look back. "Thank you, Mrs. Beecham. I'll do that."

"She was nice," Madeline said once they were out of earshot.

"I'm certainly glad she doesn't poke about in anyone's business," he said with a smile.

She giggled. "Be good. If you're going to grow up to be a big detective someday, you'll be lucky to have people like her who notice every detail, even if they don't have a clue as to what those details mean."

"You're right as always, darling. Henceforward, I shall cherish the gossips, the busybodies, and the meddlers, binding them to my heart as with hoops of iron."

They walked along the high street, and the houses eventually gave way to the little row of shops and other businesses that, along with the church and the train station, formed the center of the village.

Drew stopped and made a courtly bow before a two-storied building with black and white half-timbering, mullioned windows, and, swinging above the door, a weathered image of Queen Elizabeth herself, ruff and all.

"The Royal Elizabeth Inn, my lady, known locally as the Queen Bess."

Madeline looked up at the sagging roof. "Is it going to fall down?"

"It's managed to stand, by one means or other, since its namesake wore the crown. And that, my dear, was well over three hundred years ago."

"That's not three hundred years old," she said, pointing to the addition at the right side of the building that more than doubled the inn's size.

"That? No, that's practically brand-new. Mr. Muns, the proprietor, tells me his grandfather added it on about thirty years ago. Shall we go call on your friends, the fishermen?"

Madeline giggled. "Does she think I know everyone in America?"

Drew squeezed her hand. "Well, she's a good old soul, even if she does mind everyone's business but her own."

"Someone's up to no good," Madeline observed, looking above and behind him, and Drew turned to see a scrawny little boy climbing down the trellis at the back of the inn.

"Hi there!" Drew called. Panicked, the boy dropped into the back garden and out of sight.

"What do you think he was after up there?" Madeline asked.

"There's no telling with small boys."

She took his arm again. "As you prove every day."

He grinned. "Shall we take Mrs. Beecham's advice about the trifle?" He looked up at Holy Trinity's tower. "'Stands the Church clock at ten to three? And is there honey still for tea?'"

She pursed her lips. "It's only twenty after two."

"I promise not to tell if you won't."

"I do still want to see the church and some of the stores," she said. "They won't be closed, will they?"

"Not for a while yet. And though it's rather early, we'll be all the better for a bit of nourishment."

"Is it nearby?"

"Just across the corner there." Drew pointed out another half-timbered building set snugly between the tobacconist's and the post office, this one considerably smaller than the Queen Bess.

"All right. It might be a good idea, after all." She looked ruefully at her little buff-colored pumps, now smudged with dust and grime. "I knew I should have worn my walking shoes. Next time I'll be better prepared."

He took her arm and escorted her across the way. "I'm sure it's nothing a nice cup of tea won't put right."

The sign above the shop read *The Rose Garden* and, in smaller letters, *Cream Teas*. The inside was all lace curtains, crocheted doilies, and bone china with ladylike floral patterns and gilt edges. It was exactly what Madeline would expect it to be, and he was certain she would love it. Six tiny tables were all the room would hold. None of them was currently occupied.

"Hullo, Mr. Farthering," the waitress said, flashing brazen blue eyes at him, and then she looked Madeline up and down and her expression turned very cool indeed. "Two of you then?"

"Yes, thank you, Kitty."

The girl showed them to the table in front of the window. "Will you have the cream tea or would you like to see a menu?"

"The tea would be lovely, thanks," Drew said. "And perhaps some of your watercress sandwiches. Or do you prefer cucumber, darling?"

"Just tea for me," Madeline decided. "I want to try some of that trifle Mrs. Beecham was talking about, even if I'm not really sure what it is."

Kitty smirked. "It's sponge cake soaked in brandy, miss, with strawberry preserves, custard and cream."

"Is it as good as Mrs. Beecham says?"

"I hope so, miss," the girl said, her smug look belying her modest words. "I hate to say with my own cooking."

She strolled back into the kitchen, swinging her lithe hips.

"That's old Mrs. Leicester?" Madeline gasped, lowering her voice.

"No, old Mrs. Leicester died eight months ago. That is the new Mrs. Leicester."

"Why, she couldn't be more than twenty-two."

"A fact of which I believe old Mr. Leicester is most appreciative."

Madeline shrugged. "He might not be so appreciative if he saw the way she looked at you."

"You needn't worry, darling. I'm certainly not looking back." He put his hand over hers. "Not as long as I have someone so much more attractive to look at."

A touch of pinkness came into her cheeks, but she bit her lip. "She's not someone you, um, used to know, is she?"

"Please, give me a bit of credit here."

"She is pretty," Madeline admitted. "Well, prettyish. In an obvious sort of way."

"That may be so, and she certainly can cook."

"Yes," Madeline drawled, "I bet she can."

No sooner had Kitty brought in their tea and scones, flirting outrageously with Drew as she did, than the little bell above the front door jingled and the door opened to admit three stout middle-aged ladies and a florid-looking older gentleman with a white mustache. The man was smiling roguishly, and the ladies were all tittering like schoolgirls.

"Four, please, Kitty," one of the women said, and she giggled again when the man said something too low for anyone else to hear. Frowning, Kitty excused herself to see to them.

"What do you eat in a place like this?" the man asked, befuddled, and Drew and Madeline looked at each other, trying not to laugh as they realized who he must be.

"One of your fishermen, by his accent," Drew murmured, spreading a generous amount of clotted cream and strawberry jam on a bite of scone.

"They're not my fishermen," Madeline hissed.

"At any rate, he certainly can't be the recently bereaved Mr. Flesch. At least he oughtn't to be. So that leaves only jaunty Mr. Whiteside." The group at the table across the way burst into fresh gales of laughter, and Drew nodded. "Decidedly Mr. Whiteside. Shall we introduce ourselves?"

Madeline sighed. "I suppose we might as well. Everyone seems to assume I know him, anyway. But I want my trifle first."

Once they had finished their tea and scones, along with a generous portion of very excellent sherry trifle, they went over to the other table.

"Good afternoon, ladies, lovely to see you all," Drew began, bowing slightly. "I beg your pardon, sir, but I couldn't help noticing that you're from America, and I thought you might want to meet a countrywoman of yours."

The older man stood, and his face split into a wide smile. "Well, sure I would."

"I'm Drew Farthering, and this is Miss Madeline Parker from Chicago."

"Pleased to meet you, ma'am," Whiteside said, swallowing up her hand in both of his. "My name's Whiteside. Jonas Whiteside."

Madeline returned his smile. "Hello."

"Jonas Whiteside, the architect?" Drew asked, and then he shook his head. "Of course! You don't know me, sir, but I believe you've done some work here and in Canada for our company, Farlinford Processing, haven't you?"

"Why, yes, I have. Drew Farthering, did you say? You must be Mason Parker's stepson."

"That's right." Drew shook his hand. "And Miss Parker here is his niece."

"Well, I'm awful pleased to meet you both." Whiteside gestured to the table. "Why don't you join us?"

"Oh, no, no," Drew said. "We wouldn't think of disturbing you. You ought to call up at Farthering Place if you're ever at loose ends, though. I'm sure my stepfather would very much like to see you again."

"That'd be real nice. I knew he had an estate somewhere around here, but I didn't realize we'd landed right on it."

"Just up the road," Drew assured him.

"Perhaps I will come for a visit sometime. I was going to send flowers, anyway. After I heard about your loss."

"Very kind of you, sir. Thank you."

"Are you sure you won't join us?"

"Actually, we must be off. I promised Miss Parker I'd take her to look at our church and let her nose about some of the shops before they shut for the day."

"Well, if you ever want to talk to somebody from home, ma'am, you let me know." Whiteside winked at her. "Maybe we can find us a real iced soda pop somewhere around here."

"That would be nice," Madeline said. "Of course, if you come up to Farthering Place, perhaps I'll see you then."

After Drew made another apology to the ladies and they both made their farewells, he and Madeline went back to their own table. He reached up and jiggled the bell over the door, and Kitty hurried out of the kitchen.

"Oh, it's you." She dipped her chin so she could look up at him in that knowing way some girls had. "Something else?"

"Just the bill, if you would, please, Kitty."

She scribbled a few numbers on her pad and then tore the page off and gave it to Drew with a sly grin. He handed her some coins and told her to keep the change. Then, with a tip of his hat to Mr. Whiteside and the ladies, he escorted Madeline out into the high street.

"How odd that it would be the Mr. Whiteside who designed

our new plants," he said as they walked toward the church. "I'm surprised Mrs. Beecham didn't know that beforehand, as well."

"Maybe she does by now. It's been at least half an hour since we spoke to her."

He shook his finger at her. "Cheeky."

She giggled at his mock sternness. "Does everyone here know everything about everybody?"

"Almost without fail, darling, so you'd ought to be on your best behavior. Good thing we're on our way to church. In fact, I'm sure it will do wonders for your reputation to be seen going. Evidently, it doesn't matter why you're going so long as you are seen."

"Do you think everyone's a hypocrite?"

"Of course not. But there seems to be a great many of them in the church."

"There are a great many of them everywhere, in case you haven't noticed. Maybe church is the best place for them, anyway." She smiled up at him in that pert, challenging way she had. "It's not the healthy people who need the hospital, you know."

They walked across the road and down to Holy Trinity. Headstones, as weathered and mossed over as the ancient oaks that shaded them, were scattered through the churchyard, and Madeline went along reading the names and dates, admiring a weeping marble angel here and a slumbering cherub there, musing over the lives of children who had died young and men and women who had lived long. They steered clear of the newest grave.

"How old these headstones are," she murmured. "And how many there are too for such a small place."

"We've had rather a long while to collect them," Drew reminded her. "Shall we go in?"

They went up the walk and to the massive wooden door at

the front of the church. He opened it for her and, removing his hat, followed her inside.

"There's not all that much to it, I'm afraid. And you've been here once already."

"But that was different. I didn't get a chance to really look at things then."

It was no more than a small parish church, one that might be found in any village in Hampshire, or indeed in all of England, but she seemed fascinated by its every detail. She opened the door to one of the old pew boxes and sat down.

"What must they have felt all that time ago when this was first built and they began to worship here? When they first looked up and saw the light through that window?"

He followed her gaze up to the arched window above the altar, its richly colored panes depicting Christ in glory, His arms outstretched, His eyes merciful, His pierced hands beckoning. The late-afternoon sun shone through, illuminating the glass like a page from a medieval Bible. Drew had never noticed such richness in it before, but he didn't allow any of the wonder in Madeline's expression to be reflected in his own. No need getting silly over a woman's fancies.

Her eyes shone as she looked up at it. "I've been wanting to have another look at that since the funeral."

"I'm afraid that stained glass came a good four or five hundred years after the church, darling."

"It's still wonderful."

He came and sat down beside her in the pew. "If you like this, I'll take you up to Winchester one day and show you the cathedral. I daresay one could fit a dozen or more of our little Holy Trinity inside it."

She took his arm and hugged herself against him. "Oh yes, please. I'm sure it's glorious. But, in its way, I think it would still be the same as it is here. It's as if the fragrance of the prayers of all those hundreds of years still lingers here in these stones and in these pews, saying God still bends down to hear and answer."

"I suppose it all must have been easier to believe back in those days." He shrugged and helped her to her feet and out of the pew. "Now modern science explains everything away and, in time, one wonders what it's all for."

"How very sad," she said as they walked up to the altar, toward the pulpit inscribed with the words *Woe unto me if I preach not the gospel.*"

He smiled. She was pitying him now. "Not so sad as that. I believe in God and all. I just . . . I suppose I just don't think of it much."

"Really?"

"It's not that I don't think He's out there. Somewhere. I just don't know if He's really all that interested in what each of us is doing. I mean, I'd say He's rather too busy to worry about if I've gone to a service and sung hymn 196 and given to the collection and all. No doubt He'd like us to be good to one another, help the poor, not run off with another man's wife or murder her or any of that sort of thing, and if we've done a kindness here and there, that's all for the better."

"So just do a little more good than bad, is that it?"

"No, not exactly. I just think if God is a God of love and mercy as they say, He'll know I mean well and see I'm taken care of."

"But you don't want to actually ask for His love and mercy. Or thank Him for it."

"It's not that. I just, well, He's got better things to see to, hasn't He? I'd think it rather cheeky of me to be wasting His time day in and day out."

"Or is it that you don't want Him wasting your time?"

He laughed, and her face turned scarlet.

"You don't much mince words, do you, Madeline?"

She looked down. "Sometimes I forget we've really only just met."

"I'm glad you forget. I like that you speak your mind to me, but I won't suddenly become religious just to please someone else." He squeezed her hand. "Not even you, darling."

She looked relieved, not angry as he had feared.

"I wouldn't have it any other way." She tilted her head back and smiled up at him again, a mischievous sparkle in her eyes. "In fact, I wouldn't want you to be religious at all."

She laughed and tried to pull away from him, but he pulled her closer instead.

"Just what are you?" he asked, cupping her face in his hands. "And why have you come here only to drive me mad?"

"I came here, Mr. Farthering, to visit my uncle and see your beautiful country." She wrinkled her nose at him and pulled away. "Driving you mad is just a little bonus."

"I see." He wagged one finger at her. "That's very naughty of you. And you'll be sorry, too."

She slipped her arm through his and started them walking again. "And why is that?"

"If I'm mad, I'll have to be looked after for the rest of my life. And since you'd be the one responsible for my condition, it only follows you'd feel obliged to do the looking after. Assuaging the crushing guilt and all, you know."

"If anyone should feel guilty, it's you."

"I? Madam, I protest."

"Yes. For keeping all this to yourself this whole time."

"That was bad of me, wasn't it?" He dropped to one knee before her. "I make a present of it to you. All of it."

"Get up, silly."

"All right," he said, complying, "but don't say I didn't try to make it up to you. And don't expect the same offer when we go up to see Winchester Cathedral."

"When will we?"

"Oh, once all this mess with Lincoln has been cleared up. I don't know. Right now I feel as lost and confused as a striped tie on a plaid shirt."

"I don't think your Mr. Dennison would approve."

"Oh, definitely not. He looks askance at me if I decide to wear charcoal socks rather than black, and heaven help me if I break away entirely and choose argyle."

She giggled. "You always look very nice."

"You must thank Denny for that. He says anything less reflects badly on him."

"I'll put that on my list."

"Your list?"

"Of things to thank Mr. Dennison for."

"Have you a list?"

"Sure I do. He's made sure that you dress stylishly without being a dandy. You told me he practically raised you after your father passed away, so he must have had something to do with you being not nearly the snob someone with your looks and money usually is."

"Not nearly?"

She grinned and smoothed his tie, blushing a little as she did. It was very becoming.

"I think your Mr. Dennison has more of a sense of humor than he lets himself show."

"Who? Denny? The man's a mausoleum."

"He's not fooling anyone. I've seen you and Nick with him."

"All right, I'll confess. I did see him smile once. It was the twelfth of August, 1909. I remember it quite clearly."

She laughed. "You're such a liar. And here in the church, too."

"What?"

"In 1909? Were you even born then?"

"I was a year old, thank you, and quite mature for my age."

"Pity it didn't last."

"Now, that's no attitude to take."

She took his arm again. "Come on. You promised to let me do some shopping before it's too late."

"And here I thought you were going to explain everything to me before we left the church."

"Why should I tell you what you already know?" She took a book from one of the pews, the *Shorter Catechism*. "'What is the chief end of man?'"

He laughed. "All right, perhaps I do remember that one."

"Well?"

He cleared his throat and stood very straight, reciting, "'Man's chief end is to glorify God and to enjoy Him forever.'"

"There. You see? And it isn't even my church. Don't make it more difficult than it is." She returned the book to its place. "Come on."

"Madness," he muttered as he followed her into the street. "Absolute madness."

— Twelve —

It was nearly five o'clock when they got back to Farthering Place.

"Mrs. Devon has been waiting tea for you, sir," Dennison said as they came in through the kitchen.

"Tell her that's all right. I took Miss Parker to tea at The Rose Garden."

"Very good, sir. And Mr. Parker said he would like to have a word with you the moment you came in."

"In his study?"

"I believe so, sir. He said it was rather important."

"Well, then, I'll go straightaway. Come along, darling. You'll want to change before dinner. I'll just nip in and have a word with your uncle."

"I'll come with you. Just for a minute, don't worry. I just want to say hello and make sure he's doing all right."

"Well, come along then."

They went to Mason's study, and Drew tapped on the open door. Mason looked up from the papers scattered across his desk amid a cloud of cigarette smoke.

"Oh, Drew. There you are." Seeing Madeline, he got to his feet. "Good evening, my dear."

"Hello, Uncle Mason. Don't get up. I do wish you'd take a break from working all the time."

He managed a faint smile and sat down again. "I can't just now, my dear, but soon."

"All right, but I'll take that as a promise."

Drew sat himself on the edge of the desk. "I say, sir, did Nick tell you about our visit to the office?"

"He did, in point of fact. I don't know what to make of that passageway being there all along, but who would think to look for something as outlandish as that?"

"Precisely. Lincoln must have been planning this for some while." Drew watched his stepfather's eyes. "He and whoever's in it with him."

"True enough," Mason said.

"Did you hear about the missing files, as well?"

Mason pursed his lips and folded his hands on the desk, effectively blocking Drew's view of the papers he had been working on. "Nick said one of McCutcheon's file drawers was empty."

"But it wasn't when the police searched the lab earlier, or at least the chief inspector didn't mention it." Drew glanced at Madeline and then back at Mason. "What would anyone want with that sort of thing?"

"Best leave that to the experts," Mason said, and he began stacking pages. "Let's see to our own business while we still have one, eh?"

"I'll let you get to whatever important business you need to talk to Drew about," Madeline said. "I don't want to interrupt."

"No, no. No interruption in the least, my dear. I just find

myself in a bit of a difficulty, and I'm hoping Drew won't mind helping me out."

Drew studied his stepfather's weary face. "Anything the matter?"

Mason sighed. "With everything that's happened, I forgot one of our French clients, a Mr. Latendresse, will be stopping by tonight."

"Tonight? The funeral was just three days ago. Are you up to that sort of thing yet?"

"I'll have to be, won't I? I'd forgotten he was coming until he rang up to say he was about an hour away."

"Can't he make it another time?"

"I'm afraid not. He's on his way up to London and then off to the Netherlands for a fortnight. I really can't cancel on him now after he's come all this way. I'm sure he hasn't heard about . . . about anything here."

"All right, if you think it's best."

"Can I help at all?" Madeline asked. "I'd be happy to play hostess for you, if you want me to."

"I was hoping you would." Mason seemed to brighten a bit. "I don't really want to have to carry all the conversation tonight. Don't worry. I'll handle the business end of things."

"I don't mind hanging about if you'd like, sir," Drew said. "Between the three of us, I'm sure we'll have your Mr. Latendresse purring like a kitten and eager to throw all his business to Farlinford."

"Actually, I was hoping you'd see to something else for me."

"Certainly."

"Rushford was to be here tonight as well, but his car has refused to start. His man is looking to it, but I'm afraid he won't have it repaired in time to get Rushford here before Latendresse has to leave. Denton has the night off or I would send him, and Peterson . . ." Mason looked pleadingly at Drew.

"And Peterson is just not quite the ticket for a business matter."

Mason exhaled. "Precisely. Do you think you might run up to Winchester and get him?"

Drew smiled. "Don't see why not. I can be there and back in half a jiff."

When Drew got to Winchester, he found Rushford waiting for him.

"I've just had a call from Parker. He wants me to stop by the office and pick up some equipment specifications and other papers he'd like to discuss with Latendresse. I hope it doesn't put you out to stop on the way."

"Not at all. Not at all." Drew steered him out the front door and to the Rolls. "We'll have you there and then to Farthering Place in no time at all."

It was a pleasant drive on a fine night, even if Rushford was rather dull company, talking only of business matters.

"You needn't come up," Rushford said as he got out of the car at the Farlinford building. "I'll be just a moment."

"Very well, sir. Take your time."

Drew watched as the old man unlocked the door and disappeared inside, and then he looked up at the window that marked Rushford's corner office. After a while, the light went on.

Drew sat for a moment, whistling a vague tune and tapping the steering wheel. Then, switching from whistling to humming, he looked himself over in the rearview mirror. Tie straight, hair in place, teeth sparkling, all was as it should be. Perhaps once the business portion of the evening was over, he could manage a bit of time alone with Madeline. She was going to have to explain herself and in no uncertain terms. Religion was a complex and personal matter, and she had just boiled it down into two basic ideas: glorify God and enjoy Him. She was absolutely stark staring mad.

He couldn't wait to get back home to her.

When he looked up at the window again, it was dark. Several minutes passed, but Rushford did not come out.

Drew glanced at his watch. A quarter of an hour now. Perhaps the old boy had stumbled in the dark.

Drew shut off the engine and went up to the door. Rushford hadn't locked it behind him.

"Mr. Rushford? Sir?"

There was no reply, so Drew went around to the stairwell and opened the door. At least Rushford hadn't fallen down the stairs.

"Mr. Rushford?"

Drew hurried up the three flights to the top floor, where everything was dark.

"Hullo?"

He switched on the lights and went across to tap on Rushford's closed door, and then he pushed it open.

"Mr. Rushford?"

Rushford lay on the floor, bleeding from his temple onto his white tie and boiled shirt. His hands were tied behind him with an electrical cord, pulled from the desk lamp that lay smashed on the floor at his feet. He groaned when Drew felt for a pulse at his throat.

"Steady on, sir," Drew said as he cut the binding from his wrists with his pocketknife. "We'll have you up in a jiffy."

Rushford was puffing and wheezing by the time Drew got him into a chair.

"Dear, oh dear, I shall never be the same again." His eyes were red-rimmed and full of tears, and he patted his coat with both hands, searching blindly for his handkerchief.

Drew gave him his own and then poured him a shot of brandy from the credenza behind the desk.

"Drink that down. There's a good fellow." He pressed the old man's hands around the glass and helped him raise it to his lips. "Go on."

Rushford took a sip, coughed, and then emptied the glass. Then he just sat, his breathing so jerky and labored, Drew thought he might be sick, but he soon quieted.

"That's better," Drew soothed. "Now, can you tell me what happened?"

Rushford slumped forward, his elbows on his knees. "I don't know."

"What do you remember?"

Rushford shook his head, muttering something unintelligible.

"That's a nasty knock," Drew observed, and he dampened a serviette from the credenza with some brandy and dabbed the wound on Rushford's head. The old man made a startled, hissing sort of sound.

"Sorry, sir. I know that must sting."

"It's all right. Oh dear, I can't believe it. It just can't be."

"Can you tell me what you remember?" Drew urged.

Rushford tipped the glass again, draining out the last amber drop, and then he sat turning it in his hands. "I came in, sat at the desk, and opened the bottom drawer. That's the one where I keep my little lockbox. I leaned over to put the key in the lock, and something struck me across the side of the head."

"I should say it rather did." Drew dabbed once more at the cut on the man's temple.

"I didn't remember anything else until I came to on the floor there."

"And you didn't see anyone?"

Rushford shook his head. "But I heard . . ." He paused and shook his head more violently. "It couldn't be. It just couldn't."

Drew got down on one knee so he could look into the old man's face. "What did you hear?"

"Someone talking. On the telephone. A man."

"What did he say?"

"I couldn't tell much. He said he'd got it and they'd share out after he'd taken care of things at the bank."

"It? What did he mean by 'it'? What had he got?"

The old man sighed. "I don't know."

"Anything else?"

Rushford's only answer was a shake of his head.

"He didn't say what bank?" Drew pressed.

"No, nothing like that." Rushford blotted his face with Drew's wadded-up handkerchief.

Drew checked the bottom drawer. "Well, there's no lockbox here now."

"Oh dear. Oh dear . . ."

"What was in it?"

"Some bonds. Bearer bonds. Worth quite a lot. I only opened it because Parker said he wanted the total values and the companies they were with. He said Latendresse had asked if we had the capital for the joint venture they're considering and wanted detailed proofs." The old man's eyes darted from the empty drawer to the broken lamp to the papers strewn all over the room. "Heaven knows what else they've taken."

"Don't you worry yourself, sir. It'll all be put right in time. Just relax now."

Drew telephoned the police, and soon two constables were there to take down Rushford's story and examine the crime scene. That done, they assured Drew they would investigate thoroughly and, without further ado, dismissed him and the victim to their homes.

"We'd best go on now," Drew told Rushford. "I expect Latendresse has long since left for London. We ought to ring up and let Mason know what's happened."

"Yes, yes, of course."

"Then I'll take you back to your place. We can telephone the chief inspector from there and let him know what's happened."

Rushford gnawed his lip and didn't say anything.

"Is that all right?" Drew asked.

The old man swallowed with difficulty. "I suppose that's best."

He got to his feet and then sank back into the chair with a groan.

"Are you all right, sir?"

"I can't . . ." Rushford's bloodless lower lip quivered, and his eyes filled again with tears. Then he smiled. "I suppose I'm a bit more shaken up than I realize."

"Come out to Farthering for a few days, sir. We'll ring up your man, have him pack some things for you, and meet us there once he has your car put right."

"Farthering? No. Oh, my word, no. It's terribly kind of you, but I couldn't possibly think of putting you all out like this. Min can look after me."

"Min can look after you just as well at Farthering Place."

Over Rushford's faint protests, Drew telephoned Min and made the arrangements. He then called Mason and told him what had happened. After he hung up, he rescued Rushford's hat from behind his desk and handed it back to him.

"Now we'll get you home and have Dr. Wallace see to you."

"I hardly think a doctor will be necessary," Rushford said, touching his fingertips to the darkening lump on the side of his head.

Drew steadied him as he stood and then helped him into his hat and coat.

"We'll let old Wallace decide that, shall we?"

Drew led him like a child down to the car and bundled him inside.

"Oh, I didn't lock the door," Rushford said, struggling to get out of the car again, but Drew pushed him back into the seat.

"It's a bit late to worry over that now."

"Oh dear," Rushford moaned.

"Don't you mind, sir," Drew soothed. "The inspector will see that this all gets put right before long. And I have an idea or two of my own."

Rushford didn't say anything more, but he did not look at all convinced.

Drew made the trip back to Farthering Place as quick and easy as possible. Rushford wasn't disposed to saying much and understandably so. Drew didn't press him. He had enough to think over as it was.

Denny must have been watching for them. He came out to the car the moment they pulled into the drive.

"Good evening, Mr. Rushford. Good evening, sir."

"Hullo, Denny." Drew hopped out of the car and went around to open Rushford's door. "Listen, Mr. Rushford here has been knocked about rather badly at the office tonight."

"Yes, sir. So Mr. Parker informed me."

"He's going to stay on at Farthering a few days. Where shall I put him?"

"It's being seen to, sir. Perhaps Mr. Rushford would care to have coffee in the parlor until his room can be arranged?"

"Capital." Drew helped the old man to his feet. "Come through here, sir. We'll soon have you settled in. I suppose Mr. Latendresse has gone?"

"I regret so, sir. The gentleman was evidently on quite a rigorous schedule."

In another minute, Rushford was sitting before the parlor fire with his hands around a cup of Mrs. Devon's stalwart coffee. He had refused food or anything stronger to drink.

"This is too good of you," Rushford said. "I hate to put you all out this way, especially since I never got to meet with our client."

"Nonsense, sir. It's no trouble in the slightest. I'm sure my stepfather's seen to everything as far as the company business goes."

"Oh, and I never did get the things Parker wanted." Rushford sighed.

"You rest easy now and don't worry yourself."

"So kind of you," Rushford murmured. "I think I could have a bit of something to eat, after all."

"What's this? What's this?" Mason came into the room, his voice hearty despite the concern in his eyes. "Whatever has happened to you, old man? Did you see who it was?"

Rushford shook his head. "No, they were on me before I knew it."

"They?"

"They or he, I don't know. Whoever it was took the bonds and, either way, my office and yours have been torn up, and I didn't get those papers you wanted."

"Papers I wanted? I thought you went there for something *you* wanted to show Latendresse."

Drew looked from Rushford to Mason and back again. They both looked equally puzzled.

"No," Rushford said. "I was going to come straight here until you called."

"I didn't call. You called here, said your car had refused to go, and I said I'd send someone up for you. I didn't ask you to bring any papers from the office."

"No, it was after that. I was in the bath, and you told my man to give me the message."

"Min said I called?"

"Yes, I'm certain he did."

"I tell you I never made any calls after I first spoke to you."

"Hold on," Drew said. "This can all be cleared up in a moment. What's the number to your house, Mr. Rushford?"

Rushford told him, and Drew dialed. A moment later, he heard Min's voice on the other end of the line.

"Mr. Rushford's residence."

"Hullo, Min. Drew Farthering here."

"Yes, Mr. Farthering? I was about to leave here with Mr. Rushford's things."

"Yes, very good, Min, but I'd like to ask you something. Did anyone ring you up there before I came to get Mr. Rushford tonight?"

"Yes, sir. Someone called from Mr. Parker, wanting to leave a message for Mr. Rushford. I assure you, I gave him the message."

"Oh yes, I know, Min. That's all right. But who was it that left the message?"

"I'm sorry, but I do not know. He said only that he was calling for Mr. Parker."

"Thank you, Min."

Drew hung up the phone. Mason and Rushford both were looking at him expectantly.

"He said it was someone claiming to be calling on your behalf, sir."

Mason knit his brow. "But who? I didn't ask anyone to call."

"Someone obviously wanted Mr. Rushford to open the office

and to open his safe," Drew said. "Someone who knew what was there to be had or who was hoping to find something in the offices."

"Lincoln," Rushford breathed, breaking into a fresh sweat.

"Lincoln?" Mason repeated, his eyes wide.

"I mean this must be tied to Lincoln's murder somehow." The old man cleared his throat. "Yes. Yes, it must be. Don't you think, Parker?"

"I suppose it would be too much of a coincidence to think it wasn't," Mason said. "But what in the world were they after at the office? The bonds, certainly, but why tear through the files, especially mine? I suppose I'll have to go up there first thing tomorrow and see what else is missing."

"No doubt the chief inspector will be back down here too, once he gets a report on tonight's goings-on," Drew said, studying Rushford's face. "Pity you didn't see who hit you or recognize his voice."

The old man merely looked into his tea and sighed.

— Thirteen —

Chief Inspector Birdsong returned to Farthering Place the next morning and requested an interview with Rushford. It was singularly unproductive, and Drew could add little that was of any use. Of course, he did have a bit of an idea about what may have happened, at least some of it, but he wasn't quite ready to have it sniggered at by the police. Nor was he desirous of being told yet again that he ought to leave the investigation to the professionals. If he could unearth enough support for his theory, there would be plenty of time to bring it to the attention of the worthy chief inspector.

He was about to go see if Rushford had remembered anything more about the incident at Farlinford when Denny came into the parlor.

"Peterson would like a word with you, sir."

The gardener peered into the room. "Good morning, sir."

At a stern look from the butler, he belatedly removed his hat. Then, with a bow, Denny left the room.

"What is it, Mr. Peterson?" Drew asked.

"I can't say for certain, sir, but it seems there might be poachers about."

"What makes you think that?"

"I'm certain I saw someone last night, sir. At the back edge of the rose garden. I don't know what he might have been after there. He didn't take none of the roses as I can see."

"Did he see you?"

"He must have done, sir. He was at the garden and made for the greenhouse and then, of a sudden-like, he bolts into the woods. If the p'lice hadn't taken my gun, I'd've warned him off with it. As it were, I couldn't do more than holler after him that if he didn't stop, well, I'd know the reason why."

"What did he look like?"

"Well, I couldn't rightly say, sir. It were a dark night and all, and he seemed all over in black, as well."

"You couldn't tell anything about his face? The color of his hair?"

"No, sir. Nothing like that. He was there and gone in a twinklin'. I'm sorry I can't be no better help, but I thought you'd best know about it. Mr. Parker and Mr. Padgett have gone into the village to talk to the council about using the meadow for the fair next month, so I thought I'd best tell you about it."

"Quite so. Quite so. Anything else you noticed?"

"No, sir, other than the moles have been at the garden again. Do you think the p'lice will be giving me back my gun before they've uprooted the whole lot?"

Drew smiled. "I'll see what I can do about it. Don't you worry. Have they done much damage?"

"Not as I can see, sir. Just digging about in the dirt and all. More a nuisance as yet."

"Well, thank you, Mr. Peterson. You and your men keep a watch out, and let me know if you see anything else."

"Right you are, sir."

Peterson replaced his hat, gave the brim a tug, and strode out of the room.

Drew took a sip of his tea, looking out over the grounds from the rose garden to the greenhouse and then to the wood. It made little sense for a poacher to be this near the house. There certainly wouldn't be any game as nearby as this. But if it wasn't a poacher, who would it be? And for what would he be looking?

"Beg pardon, Mr. Drew."

Drew turned to see Anna at the terrace door, her eyes round and her hands clasped together as if she had to hold them still.

"What is it, Anna?"

"I'm sorry, sir, but I couldn't help hearing what Mr. Peterson said. About somebody being in the garden and at the . . . the greenhouse, sir."

"Did you see something last night?"

"Oh, no, sir. I was in my bed with the door locked and my chair propped against it and the covers over my head, like I been ever since that Mr. Lincoln and the missus was taken."

"I see," Drew said, keeping his expression solemn and concerned. "Well, there's no need for you to worry about it. Mr. Peterson and his men will see that there's no one about who shouldn't be."

"But what if it wasn't a poacher, sir?"

"What?"

"Well, I mean, sir, what if it was someone come to do some mischief in the house, robbers or . . . or worse."

"Whyever would you think that?"

"It does happen. Sometimes an innocent is carried off in the night."

Drew chose a discreet cough rather than what might have

appeared to be insensitive laughter. "Now, who do you know that was ever carried off in the night?"

"Well, it *does* happen, sir. Look at that cinema actress, that Lucy Lucette."

"Oh dear. Must I?"

"But, Mr. Drew, the poor thing. The papers say she was at home having her beauty sleep, and when her maid came to wake her the next morning, she just wasn't there."

"Wasn't she? Perhaps the maid was looking in the wrong bed. Who's her leading man these days, anyway?"

"It's not funny, Mr. Drew." Anna's chin quivered, but she stuck it out all the same. "It's not a fit world we live in."

"Well, not to worry. I imagine poor Lucy will be found. Besides, the kidnappers of American cinema stars are quite unlikely to turn up in Hampshire."

"But Mr. Peterson saw—"

"Now, don't you mind about that, Anna. Whoever Mr. Peterson doesn't catch outside, Mr. Dennison and I will see to inside. Fair enough?"

"Just as you say, sir."

"There's a good girl. Now, kindly run and ask Nick if he won't meet me down at the rose garden, if you would. We'll see if there's anything you ought to be worried over."

"Yes, sir," she said, clearly unconvinced and uncomforted. "Thank you, sir."

Drew took one last sip of his tea, ate two very fine ginger macaroons, and then headed down to the garden. Nick was already there, peering at the ground.

"Hullo there. Anna tells me there were some unauthorized shenanigans about the grounds last night."

"So Peterson says." Drew examined the area. "What's it look like to you?"

"Well, I'm fairly sure Mr. Peterson doesn't go about doing the garden on his tippy-toes."

"A fair assumption," Drew agreed. "Clearly our visitor either treads very loudly and didn't want to be heard in the night, or more likely, he decided half a print is much harder to match to a delinquent foot than a whole one. Shall we see where he was off to?"

They followed the tracks from the garden to the greenhouse and then to the edge of the woods.

"Peterson said he must have startled the man near the greenhouse because he dashed off then and into cover here."

Drew and Nick looked about for a while longer, and then they followed the tracks into the trees and out onto the road, only to lose them in a jumble of foot and tire marks. Clearly at a dead end, they retraced their path back up to the house.

"There's only one set of prints," Drew said, "and Peterson saw the man run into the wood, so we know he wasn't going the other way. But where did he come from?"

"Perhaps he got onto the walk that goes round the house from the drive."

"I suppose, but where would he have come from before that?"

Drew studied the footprints in the flower bed once more.

"Suppose he wasn't coming up to the house."

Nick drew his brows together. "Then how could he have left these marks?"

"Suppose he was leaving the house."

"Oh, I say. You don't suppose—"

"I think a good look round would be in order, don't you?"

"I'll run down and get Mack and Bobby," Nick said. "They can watch the house to see no one gets out."

"Good idea. I'll have Denny tell the staff to keep watch inside."

"Look here, oughtn't we have old Birdsong in on this?"

"Yes, I suppose we should. Still, it wouldn't do anyone much good if we were to ring him up and then have to wait for him to motor down from Winchester or wherever he's off to and, in the meanwhile, let our man get away, now, would it?"

Nick grinned. "It would be deuced irresponsible, I'd say."

Drew gave him a hearty pat on the back. "Good man. Now, you see to Mack and Bobby, and I'll get Denny."

Nick loped out toward the greenhouse, and Drew hurried inside.

"What are you two up to?" Madeline asked. She was standing there halfway up the front stairway.

"Up to? I don't have the slightest notion what you mean," Drew said.

She nodded, clearly unconvinced. "I saw the two of you looking around in the yard and then running off into the woods. You've found something."

"Nothing that need worry you, darling."

She came down to him. "I'm not worried. I just want to know what's going on."

"Well, if you must know, Mr. Peterson saw someone run from the house and into the wood last night. He couldn't see who it was, just someone all in black."

"But what could he have wanted?"

"I don't know."

"Where did he come from?"

"I'm afraid I don't know that, either. But since his footprints go only from the house to the woods, I'm thinking maybe he's been hiding here all along."

"Here? In the house?"

"A bit unnerving, isn't it?"

"I'll say it is."

"Not to worry, darling. If there is anyone untoward here, we'll soon flush him out."

Drew rang the bell, and Dennison made an immediate appearance. Although he did not look entirely convinced of the sagacity of Drew's plan, he responded to it with only a slight bow and his usual "Very good, sir."

"Mack and Bobby are at their posts," Nick announced as he came back inside. "Where shall we start?"

"Lovely." Drew rubbed his hands together. "As soon as the staff are in place, we'll start down here and work our way upward. What do you say?"

"Excellent. Will you be joining us, Miss Parker?"

"You're not leaving me behind with a murderer in the house."

Drew put her arm through his. "You'll be safe with me, darling."

♦

Drew paced before the library fireplace. "Well, that was a bust."

"And I had such hopes," Nick said, and he flung himself into an overstuffed chair.

"You're driving me crazy stalking around like that." Madeline forced Drew to sit beside her on the divan. "And you shouldn't have scared poor Mr. Rushford that way. He's rattled enough as it is."

Drew frowned thoughtfully. "Poor blighter. I did hate to go in there at all, but we had to at least take a look around. Now he'll likely have the jitters worse than he did to start with."

"Well, it's certain he didn't see anything," Nick said with a grin, "or we'd have heard the howls across two counties. But at least *I* didn't come away empty-handed."

Drew leaned forward to peer at him. "What's that?"

There was a spark of mischief in Nick's eyes as he patted the little red leather notebook he'd taken from his pocket.

"I nicked it when we were in old Rushford's room."

"What is it? His diary?"

"Says so on the cover."

Madeline's mouth dropped open.

Drew's jaw tightened. "You stole his diary?"

Nick shrugged. "*Stole* is a rather harsh term, isn't it?"

"But a man's diary—"

"Exactly. If he's our man—"

"If he's our man, he's not likely to write it all down and leave it for anyone to find. Besides, didn't your Father Knox say we weren't to know the inner thoughts of the perpetrator?"

"Don't be daft. But he might have put down something that will give us a clue, don't you think?"

"I suppose that's possible." Drew held out his hand. "Let's have it."

Nick handed him the book. "Or he may have seen something he forgot to mention."

Drew thumbed through until he found Saturday, the fourth of June. The page was blank.

Nick narrowed his eyes. "Suspicious, don't you think?"

"No, he's written about it the next day: 'Terrible tragedy. David Lincoln was murdered last night at Farthering Place. Parker's wife dead, too. Possible suicide or overdose of her sleeping medicine. Awful thing.'"

"Not very helpful," Nick muttered.

"No, and stop reading over my shoulder."

Nick made a little huffing noise and sat up straight, his arms crossed over his chest. "Fine."

Drew scanned a few more pages. "Nothing but everyday happenings. Here's a bit about the case: 'Still no word on Lincoln's killer. Unnerving to know a chap and have him murdered, even if he was a scoundrel. World's gone mad since the war.'" Drew skipped further ahead. "How about last night?"

Nick leaned forward again. "Well?"

"Nothing."

"The poor man," Madeline said. "You really couldn't expect him to feel like writing after what he'd been through."

"No," Drew agreed, "but he made up for it today: 'It's a wonder I wasn't killed. The office robbed and our bearer bonds taken. It's been such a frightful experience, I don't know if I shall ever recover. I'm still so confused. I don't know whether or not I heard properly. It must be this blow on the head. Anything else is impossible.'"

Nick frowned. "Is that all?"

Drew turned the page. "More or less. A mention of the incompetence of the police. A wonder that we've not all been murdered in our beds quite yet. Fear that the company will go under after the theft."

"What do you suppose he heard?" Madeline asked.

"Or didn't hear." Drew flipped back a page. "'I don't know whether or not I heard properly.' Heard what?"

"Perhaps we should just pop up and ask him," Nick said.

"Brilliant." Drew leapt to his feet. "And I know just what to say. 'Pardon me, Mr. Rushford, sir, but we've positively trodden on every duty we have as your hosts by stealing your private diary. Now that we've rummaged through it, we'd like you to answer a few questions. Never mind the head wound, this will take only a moment.'"

Nick gave him a sour smile. "All right. All right. It was just a thought."

"And have you thought, my good man, how you'll get the thing back into his room without his knowing it's been gone?"

"Well, not as such."

"Lovely."

"Can't the maid take it in when she takes Mr. Rushford his dinner?" Madeline asked. "Under a napkin or something?"

Drew shook his head. "I don't want any of the staff to know what's going on here."

"All right," she said. "How about Mr. Dennison? He could sneak it in, couldn't he?"

Nick's eyes widened.

Drew grinned. "Oh, that will be marvelous. He'll be delighted to know what we've been up to, despite his efforts to civilize us, won't he? Perhaps you'd like to tell him, Nick, old man."

"Fine." Nick squared his shoulders, chin held high. "I'm not afraid." He paused for a second. "Or, even better, we could try a new scheme I've just devised where we keep this all to ourselves for now. Then *I* could toddle up to Rushford's room with a pile of new books for his amusement, just happening to toss them onto the dresser where the diary was in the first place."

"That might work, unless he's missed it already." Drew thought for a minute. "Unless you were to accidentally toss a few behind the dresser and just happen to find the diary when you retrieved them."

Nick nodded. "I knew you were the clever one of the lot."

"Yes, and good thing, too. Don't expect me to cover your petty thefts after this."

Nick saluted. "*Oui, mon capitaine.* I shall see to it *tout de suite.*"

"Carry on." Drew returned his salute, then turned to Madeline. "Now that's taken care of, tell me what you'd like to do this evening. I'm afraid there's not much in the way of entertainment here in Farthering St. John, but we'll think of something."

"I thought Mrs. Pomphrey-Hughes was having her musical evening tonight," Nick said.

"Isn't there something you're meant to be taking care of just now?" Drew asked.

"I'm sure you're most especially invited, old man."

"Well, I don't think our Miss Parker would very much enjoy that, do you?"

"Why not?" Nick grinned in the most annoying fashion. "Mrs. Pomphrey-Hughes is known for her soirees. She once had Florence Easton sing Santuzza's aria from *Cavalleria Rusticana* right there in her drawing room. I'm given to understand it was quite a triumph."

Madeline's eyes lit. "I heard her sing in New York once. She was wonderful."

"I don't think there's any such triumph scheduled for tonight," Drew told her. "I mean, you can't expect a Florence Easton in Hampshire every week."

Nick's grin grew more annoying. "Perhaps not, but isn't Miss Pomphrey-Hughes expecting you?"

Drew glanced at Madeline, who was listening with rapt interest and narrowed eyes at the mention of a Miss Pomphrey-Hughes.

"Bah, I don't know why she should. If they sent me an invitation, I'm sure I had Denny send regrets some time ago."

Nick's expression of deep concern was more annoying still. "Oh, but your poor Daphne—"

"She is not, nor has she ever been, *my* poor Daphne. I doubt she has ever thought so, anyway."

"Could have fooled me."

"Any display of interest, I can assure you, Nicholas, has been manufactured by dear, sweet, acquisitive Mrs. Pomphrey-Hughes and no other. I'm sure she's a great reader of the classics and well aware of that 'truth universally acknowledged.' And knowing me to be single and in possession of a good fortune, who better to mend my most piteous want of a wife than her own daughter Daphne?"

"Don't you like Daphne?" Madeline asked.

Drew shrugged. "She's all right, I expect. Decently attractive girl and all that. Then she has to open her mouth and spoil everything."

"Well, her head *is* as empty as a balloon," Nick said, "but much more fun to play with." He nudged Drew. "Remember that time you took her to see *Othello*?"

Drew rolled his eyes. "Good heavens."

Madeline looked from him to Nick and back again. "What happened?"

Nick smirked. "He told her it was a comedy, thinking she'd know better and laugh at the remark. Afterward, he asked her if she had enjoyed the play. She owned that she had but said it never got to be all that funny."

Madeline stifled a laugh. "That was *very* bad of you. The poor girl."

"She's been to school, hasn't she?" Drew protested.

"Perhaps she had mumps that day," Nick offered.

"You're both very bad," said Madeline, and Drew tried to look contrite.

"Well, darling, if you'd like to risk one of the Pomphrey-Hughes's musical evenings, I would be quite pleased to escort you. They invite most everyone, so I don't think they'll mind if we pop in."

"Oh, that's all right. It's nice to have a quiet evening at home sometimes."

"There is a cinema in Winchester, if you'd care to motor up there. I believe there is a new film playing. All-star cast or some such."

"It's not that awful thing with Lucy Lucette, is it? If it is, there'll be a line round the block since she's disappeared."

"No, I don't think she's in it. And there's a lovely little French restaurant nearby for supper later on."

"That sounds wonderful. Let's do it."

"Oh, jolly nice," Nick put in. "I love the cinema."

Drew glared at him, and he cleared his throat.

"Ah, yes. Yes, I love the cinema, but I've got to get this diary back, you know, and I've just remembered some business I must see to here that will take all evening."

"Oh dear, what a shame," Drew said. "Are you sure it can't wait?"

"Well, of course, if you insist."

Drew lifted one eyebrow, and Nick rapidly recanted.

"No, better not. All play and no work and all that."

"Are you sure you hadn't rather spend the evening with Miss Pomphrey-Hughes?" Madeline asked Drew, all innocence. "With your Daphne?"

Drew answered her in kind. "Well, yes. Yes, I would. Thanks for being so understanding about it. Denny," he called, "lay out my eveningwear."

Madeline immediately took Nick's arm. "How would you like to take me to the movies tonight?"

Nick positively beamed. "Oh, rather!"

Drew shoved him out of the way. "Clear off, you. Now look here, Miss Parker, are you coming to the cinema with me or must I resort to violence?"

"Your charm has won me, sir. To the cinema it is."

It was almost midnight when Drew and Madeline returned to Farthering Place. A fast drive in the cool night air had put a glow in Madeline's cheeks and an extra brightness in her eyes. Dash it all, she was fetching.

"Oh, that was wonderful. The poor baron. What a tragedy! And Garbo was divine as the ballerina." She sucked in her cheeks and leaned her head back in seductive languor. "If only I could be so beautiful," she mourned in a heavy Swedish accent.

He shook his head. "I like women with a little softness to them. Surely with her money she could afford a few hearty meals."

She squeezed his arm, laughing. "She was glorious and you know it. Next you'll be saying Barrymore can't act."

He stopped short. "No," he said, lifting one cautioning finger in mock reproof. "I may say he'd do better with some fewer nights at the pub, but never, *never* will I say he can't act. I saw him do Hamlet in London when I was, oh, seventeen, I suppose. Gave me a new appreciation for the Bard."

Madeline's face turned abruptly sober, and he pulled her closer to his side.

"What is it, darling?"

"Oh, nothing."

"It most certainly is something," he said. "Come now, tell me. Even the confessional could not afford better protection for your secrets."

"It's silly of me, I suppose, but I got a postcard from Carrie and Muriel. From Stratford-upon-Avon."

"Did you?"

"Muriel especially told me to keep my eye on Adorable Drew."

"Oh dear."

"And they wanted to know if we'd heard about Lucy Lucette's disappearance."

"Nothing but."

Madeline sighed. "I don't know. I always wanted to see Stratford—Anne Hathaway's cottage and where the Globe Theater once stood and all the other sights we had planned. I suppose I'll never see them now."

"Nonsense. Once we get things here sorted out, we'll drive up to Stratford and see all the touristy places and perhaps even a play or two. Nick can come along as chaperone and low entertainment for the journey."

She laughed. "I don't know if Aunt Ruth would approve of him. Of course, she didn't really approve of the three of us girls knocking around Europe alone, either. I don't dare tell her what's happened here. Not now. She'd probably row herself across the Atlantic to drag me back home."

"She sounds rather formidable. But we wouldn't want her to think these awful things happen here on a regular basis. Farthering is such a placid place and we never—"

A shriek pierced the night.

Drew and Madeline both looked up toward the darkened house. Then Drew ran up the steps and flung open the front door. He switched on the light in the entry and bounded up the stairs, only to be nearly knocked down by Anna fleeing for her life.

He caught her by the arms. "What is it? What's happened?"

"I saw him, Mr. Drew! I saw him!" Her face was ghost white. "I *saw* him!"

"You saw who?"

"Him that was killed! Mr. Lincoln!"

"Don't be silly," Drew said. "What are you going on about?"

"I saw him . . ."

Madeline hurried up the stairs to them.

"Shh, Anna, it's all right," he soothed. "Whatever it is, it'll be all right."

Lights were coming on all over the house.

"Let's go down into the parlor and sort this all out," Drew said, keeping his voice low.

Dennison, in his robe and slippers, was waiting for them at the foot of the stairs. "Is there some trouble, sir?" The look in his eye was a harsh censure of the maid's lack of decorum.

"Everything's all right, Denny," Drew said. "Please go up and see to it that everyone goes back to bed. We'll look after Anna here. She's just had a scare."

"A rodent of some sort, sir?"

"Very likely, yes."

"It wasn't a rodent, Mr. Dennison," the girl protested.

"Thank you, Denny," Drew said. "That will be all."

"Very good, sir." Dennison bowed. "Miss."

Drew hurried the girls into the drawing room and shut the door. "Now, Anna, tell me exactly what you saw."

"I told you, Mr. Drew—I saw him! Mr. Lincoln!"

"Don't badger her." Madeline helped the girl to the window seat and sat her down. "Just take your time and tell us what happened."

Anna took a shuddering breath. "I was finishing up the laundry, putting the linens in the upstairs bathrooms. That's usually Beryl's job, but she was up in the missus's sitting room and listening to the wireless. Mr. Parker said he didn't mind her doing it; it was what Mrs. Parker would have wanted. But I don't know that I wouldn't feel all peculiar-like up there now at night. I mean *after*, you know. It just wouldn't seem right."

"So you were upstairs," Drew prompted.

"I was up in the back hall, putting away, like I said, and I heard something behind me. So I turned around and wasn't anything there. So I go on, listening and not hearing anything, until I heard someone creeping about. I called out because sometimes Tessa, she does the washing up, and sometimes, bless her, she has pain all down her leg and has to walk it off before she can sleep, so I called out, 'Tessa, is that you?' But it wasn't Tessa. So I called out again, 'Is someone there?' and the hall went dark." Anna's voice quavered. "Black as pitch it was, and then . . ."

"Then . . . ?"

"Then I saw him!" She burst into tears. "It was Mr. Lincoln, sir. I know it was."

Madeline slipped into the seat beside her, putting a comforting arm around the girl's shoulders. "It's all right, dear."

Drew paced in front of them. "Now be reasonable, Anna. You know it couldn't have been Mr. Lincoln. Mr. Lincoln is dead."

"Oh, but I saw him, Mr. Drew. He was lurkin' down at the end of the hallway, down by the door to the lumber room. And then . . . then he just wasn't!"

"Mr. Lincoln couldn't possibly—"

"He was lurkin'!"

"Did you see his face?" Madeline asked.

"Oh, no, miss. I couldn't see his face because he didn't have a head!"

This brought another torrent of weeping.

"Shhh. Don't think about that now," Madeline said.

"No, you *must* think about it now, and sensibly." Drew pulled a chair over and sat so he could look into the girl's face. "If he didn't have a head, how could you know it was Lincoln?"

"It was *because* he didn't have a head," Anna insisted, her chin quivering. "It couldn't be no one else, not after what was done to him in the greenhouse. And after what Mr. Peterson seen."

"You mean the poacher?"

Anna sniffled. "He says poacher. There are others would say different."

"Did Peterson tell you more than he told me?"

Anna dropped her eyes. "Not as such, Mr. Drew, but I could tell from what he didn't say. He said the man was all in black. Sounds to me it could have been evening clothes. What poacher goes about in evening clothes?"

"Just because he wore black, that doesn't—"

"And Mr. Peterson said he couldn't see his face. Nor tell what color of hair he had. Well, how could he of a man without any head? And what's a poacher doing at the greenhouse, I'm wondering, except he's Mr. Lincoln haunting the very place he was murdered?" She shuddered. "Now we're sure to be plagued with spirits and groanings and tappings in the night."

Three soft taps broke the silence, and Anna stifled a cry.

"Excuse me, Mr. Drew." Mrs. Devon poked her head into the room. "Mr. Dennison said I should come look after Anna, if you've done."

"Yes, I think so, Mrs. D." Drew helped Anna to her feet. "Go along with Mrs. Devon now. We'll see to things down here. And if you think of something you didn't tell me about, anything at all, you come tell me right away."

"Yes, sir, Mr. Drew. Thank you, sir."

"Come along, dear," Mrs. Devon said. "We'll go and have a nice cup of tea and see if that doesn't put things right."

"It was awful, just awful." Anna clung to her as they left the room, her voice still low and frightened. "I tell you, Mrs. D, he was lurkin'."

Drew shut the door after them and sighed. "So much for our lovely evening out."

"It was still a lovely evening," Madeline assured him, slipping her slender hand into his. "You don't suppose she really saw something, do you?"

"Not likely she and Peterson both dreamed it all up. Not on the same day. But we did check the house already."

"I can't help feeling a little unnerved now." Shuddering a little, she nestled against him. "I suppose poor Anna could have just imagined it after the excitement this afternoon, couldn't she?"

"True, she could." He held her tightly, just for an instant, and then turned her face up to him. "Are you going to be all right on your own tonight? Shall I send Mrs. Devon to stay with you?"

"No, that isn't necessary. I wish . . ." She pressed her face against his shoulder, and he lifted her chin once more.

"What did you say, darling?"

There was an extra touch of pink in her cheeks. "Don't think badly of me, but I . . . I wish you could stay with me. I know you shouldn't and you can't, but I wish you could."

Again he sighed. "I wish I could, too. No need to pretend otherwise. But best not play with fire, no matter how innocently it starts."

"I know." She stroked her fingers down the line of his jaw. "No matter how tempting it is."

"Besides," he added, "I wasn't figuring on you discovering what a cad I am at least until our silver anniversary."

"You never give up, do you?"

He grinned. "Do you want me to?"

She laughed, but there was a touch of longing in it. "You could still see me to my door, I suppose."

"That I certainly can." He tucked her arm under his. "And I can put a chair in the hall and watch it all night if you'd like."

"What if someone comes in through the window?"

"Hmm. I hadn't thought of that. I suppose I'll have to roust Nick out of his bed and get him to spend the night in the garden watching it."

"Where is he, anyway? I thought he'd be the first one down when Anna screamed."

"The man sleeps like a stone. Shall I go to his room and fetch him down?"

She laughed. "How about I just lock the door *and* the window and let both of you get your sleep?"

"Well, all right, but there's not much thrill in that. Come on then."

He accompanied her upstairs, and she left him at the door with no more than a peck on the cheek and a wistful glance.

Maddening.

— Fourteen —

The morning dawned bright and clear, and the sunshine gilded Farthering Place with a normalcy that was most welcome. The night before, once he had made sure Madeline was securely in her room, door locked, Drew had made another search of the house. In deference to the peaceful slumber of the other residents, it wasn't as thorough as he would have liked, but he saw no sign of anything untoward. He had even taken a peek into the lumber room at the top of the house, but it had obviously not been disturbed for some time. Not since Christmas at the very least. In the darkness, he had also managed to upset a Grecian urn on a hallway table, wake one of the footmen, and only very narrowly escape a thrashing. Once everyone's identity was sorted out and the contrite footman had returned to his bed, Drew had gone to his own.

Now he found himself rather eager to take Madeline into the village for Sunday services, another comfortingly ordinary event to counterbalance some of the recent unsettling goings-on at home. She had on a trig little frock made of some sort of gauzy material the color of Mrs. Beecham's dog roses. It was modest enough, showing just a fetching curve of calf and turn of ankle over dainty pink slippers, but it was still undeniably attractive.

Mason positively beamed as she walked between him and Drew, her arms linked in theirs, her eyes smiling up at them both.

Drew pressed her hand and looked away from those shining eyes. She might not forgive him if it happened that he was the one to prove her well-loved uncle a liar, thief, and murderer. He might not forgive himself. But the case was such a muddle yet. There was precious little evidence against Mason or anyone else.

The service itself was blandly forgettable. Old Bartlett, the vicar, had stumbled through the homily, expounding on a verse in the book of Revelation, the message to the church at Sardis: "I know thy works, that thou hast a name that thou livest, and art dead." Drew couldn't really follow the tenuous connection the vicar was trying to make between the verse and his experience with fox hunting, but Madeline seemed to glean something from it. Perhaps, as she had said the night of the party, the Scripture had force in and of itself.

He considered the possibility that someone who was thought to be alive, alive to conscience and to honor, could in actuality be dead. Who really was as he seemed to others? His father hadn't been. Neither had Constance. And Mason?

He glanced at Madeline as she joined in the closing hymn. No doubt she would need the stalwart assurance it promised if he were to destroy her faith in her uncle, and it was hardly likely she would turn to Drew himself for comfort under those circumstances. There had to be someone else worth suspecting, someone else with a name for honesty who was at heart a murdering scoundrel.

". . . *thou hast a name that thou livest, and art dead.*"

He could think of little else over the midday meal.

"You seem a bit off your feed, old man," Nick observed as

Drew picked at his half-eaten lamb chop. "Something on your mind?"

"Oh, just things." Drew forced a smile and took another bite of potato.

"Don't you like your nice courgettes, Mr. Drew?" Mrs. Devon asked as she cleared away the plates for the next course. "Mr. Peterson brought them in just today. You couldn't ask for better than that."

"No," Drew said, managing another smile. "No, you couldn't."

"Peterson's a good fellow," Nick said, "and an honest man of the soil, God bless him."

"Hear, hear!" Mason lifted his glass in a toast, and, laughing, Madeline and Nick joined him.

An honest man. Drew had always known the little gardener to be plainspoken and honest. He had denied meeting Lincoln, but was that strictly the truth?

Drew decided to slip away for a quiet walk after lunch. Soon he found himself at the gardener's cottage, a neat little thatched house with roses growing round the door. Madeline would have thought it perfect, too. Peterson ought to be finished with his Sunday dinner by now. Drew rang the bell, and soon the door opened to reveal a stocky little woman of middle age in an apron that looked as worn as she did.

Drew removed his hat. "Good afternoon, Mrs. Peterson."

"Mr. Drew. What a surprise." Mrs. Peterson turned to call to her husband. "It's Mr. Drew from up at the house."

Peterson hurried to the door, struggling into his coat and smoothing down his shaggy hair.

"Mr. Drew! Come in, sir. Come in. I was just sleeping off the Sunday roast."

"Sorry to have disturbed you, Mr. Peterson, but I was wondering if I might have a brief word with you."

"Certainly, sir. Sit yourself down. Bring the gentleman some tea, Mother."

"Don't trouble yourself, Mrs. Peterson. I'll be only a moment."

"Are you sure?" she asked, taking Drew's hat from him and laying it on a doily-covered side table. "I can have the kettle on in two ticks."

"I'm most awfully grateful, to be sure. Perhaps another time."

"Just as you say, sir. I'll get back to my washing up then and leave the talk to you menfolk."

"Sit yourself down," Peterson repeated, showing Drew to a faded armchair near the hearth. "Do forgive the mess. We wasn't expecting no company."

He snatched up his newspaper, the only discernible mess in the spotless little room, and folded it up before seating himself in the straight-backed chair in the corner.

"You should have sent for me to come up to you, sir, instead of coming all this way."

"'All this way' is little more than across the back lawn," Drew said, smiling. "I don't like to bother you on a Sunday, but I really must ask you about something, and I hope you won't think it impertinent of me."

"Don't suppose I'll know till I'm asked, will I, sir?"

"I suppose not." Drew was glad for the other man's good humor and hated the prospect of spoiling it. Well, there was nothing for it but to ask. "I'd like you to tell me about Opal."

Peterson's expression turned solemn, guarded. "What do you want to know?"

"Where is she, for a start."

"I dunno. She left home over a year ago. Not a word since."

"Why did she go?"

Peterson made a disgusted, huffing sort of sound. "Who knows with girls today? Nothing's ever good enough for them.

They have to be swanning up to London and heaven knows where with bobbed hair and skirts hardly long enough for a child of six and faces painted up like circus clowns. She went because she wanted to is all I know. Said she fancied taking up the stage. Takes her fine ways from the cinema nowadays, I expect. Can't look like a decent girl no more. Now it's got to be Greeta Garbo and Marilyn Dietrich and that brassy Harlow girl or that Lucy Lucette having everybody chasing about looking for her. Well, if they find her, they can have her, I say, and welcome. And Opal as well."

"I understand she was friends with Mr. Lincoln awhile back."

Peterson shrugged. "Might have been. All I know is she never talked about who she went with, not to me. She certainly never brought him home to supper like any respectable girl would do."

"Did they quarrel?"

"I wouldn't know. All I know is she were moping about for a week or two, then she were off. Not so much as good luck and goodbye to them as raised her all these years."

"You may as well tell him the truth, Arwel. He's sure to find it out in time." Mrs. Peterson stood slump-shouldered in the doorway to the kitchen, the platter from her best tea service wet and shining in her hands, along with a dish towel to dry it. "What's done is done."

"I can't tell you much more anyhow, Mr. Drew." Peterson's voice was suddenly humble. "Girls are such silly creatures, and no amount of warning seems to keep them out of mischief. Yes, she were walking out with Lincoln. I told her it warn't no more than a fancy of his that wouldn't last the month, but she wouldn't hear it. Well, I were wrong about that. It were nearly three month before he went his way, but not before he'd ruined her for good and all."

"And she went up to London after that?"

"That's right."

"And she never brought him home to meet you?"

"No. Thought she might once, but he never turned up. The roast were burnt black."

Drew nodded and then turned to Mrs. Peterson. "Pardon my asking, but I must know. Because of the case, you see. Was she . . . was she in trouble?"

Tears sprang to the woman's dull eyes. "No, thank God. She would have told me, I know she would. But I thought she would come back by now. Or at least write." She made a little sobbing noise, and Peterson went over and put his arm about his wife's shoulders.

"Now, Mother, buck up. Buck up. If she's decided to go on, we'd ought to let her be. We can't make her stay forever."

"I know, I know." She blotted her face with her dish towel and then took an uneven breath and dredged up a quavering smile. "I beg your pardon, Mr. Drew. I shouldn't let things get the better of me, I know I shouldn't."

"Not at all. Not at all. I must beg your pardon for bringing up such a painful subject." Drew stood and took her hand, the one holding the dish towel. "If there's any way I can be of help, Mrs. Peterson, do let me know. Promise?"

She closed her eyes, nodding a few times, and made a little curtsy. "It's too good of you, Mr. Drew, I'm sure."

"We'll see to our own, sir," Peterson said. "No need to trouble yourself, but thank you."

Drew picked up his hat from the tiny side table. "Well, if there's nothing more then—to do with the case, I mean—I suppose I'll be off."

Mrs. Peterson's eyes filled with tears once again. "You don't think our Opal would have anything to do with murder, do you, Mr. Drew?"

"No, no," Drew assured her. "Not in the least. I just had to know about Lincoln, you see? If we know the sort of man he was, we're more likely to find out why he was killed and by whom."

"Oh, yes, of course." She sniffed and blotted her face again. "You . . . you won't be telling anything about this, will you, sir? I mean, to anyone not in need of knowing. I don't mean the police and such, if they were to ask."

"You may rely on me, to be sure."

"Mr. Drew," Peterson said, "as you're here, I'd like to show you something as might be of interest down to the shed."

"Really? What is it?"

Peterson shrugged. "Might be nothing, but it's better shown than told of."

"All right then." Drew gestured toward the shed. "Lead on."

With a final farewell to Mrs. Peterson, Drew followed Peterson down the garden path.

"I didn't want to cause Mrs. Peterson any further upset," Drew said as they walked along, "but I would like to know where you were last Sunday but one. Bobby tells me that's the only day you've been away since Christmas?"

"I didn't like to say in front of the wife, sir." Peterson hesitated, staring out over the fields and fidgeting with the striped braces that held up his trousers. "A mate of mine, chap called Clancy, was in the Queen Bess a month or so ago. He'd been up to London and happened to see our Opal there."

"And?"

"She were . . . well, he said she were in one of them dancing halls, as they say, where the girls get a shilling a dance and heaven knows whatever else goes on." Peterson's face was red, and there was a tremor in his voice. "I couldn't let the wife hear about that, as you can well imagine, sir, but she was visiting her aunt a couple of Sundays ago, and as it were my day off, I thought I'd take the train up and see if I could find Opal."

Drew said nothing, waiting for the man to go on.

"I found her, just where Clancy said, working in that place and living with five or six other girls crammed into a mean little flat not fit for pigs. She wouldn't see me at first, but I pushed my way in, and there she were in a tatty old robe and slippers, looking thin and edgy and talking all shaky like, most faster than I could follow at times. What makes a girl like that? Maybe she were that mad at me. I don't know."

Drew kept his silence still. A man who'd rarely left the village in his entire life would not recognize the signs of cocaine addiction.

Peterson groaned. "I didn't care. Not what she done nor where she was. I begged her to come back, said we'd take care of her and get her all rosy again here at home. I told her that her mother had wept over her this whole year, but all she did was laugh, kind of crazy-like. She said she were still going to be on the stage and one day she'd be rich enough that we would all live better than the king. It were like she couldn't even tell the sty she were in."

"And all this because of Lincoln," Drew said, watching the other man's expression.

"Lincoln?" Peterson spat on the pathway. "I'd say rather all this because of me. My wife, she don't know it, but Opal and me quarreled, right after Lincoln threw her over. I told her she had no more than she deserved from him, and besides that, she were no better than she should be. What's a girl to do when her own father don't have no kindness for her? When she's already hurt past her young heart bearing?"

"Did you tell her to go?"

"No," Peterson said, his voice suddenly hoarse. "Might as

well have done. I been that ashamed this year now to even tell the missus what I done. I thought I could make it right and bring Opal home, but she won't have none of me now."

Drew wanted to say something to comfort the man, something to assure him that his child would be home again in time, as soon as she came to herself, but he wasn't as optimistic as that. There were too many of them, nice girls from good families, who tried the stuff for a lark and were never again free of it. A good many more than the ones who could take it or leave it alone.

"At least you tried," he said finally. "She knows where you are if she decides to come home. There's not much more you can do unless she wants to come."

"It's what my missus says. She says even God don't make us come to Him if we're dead set on living with swine, like the Good Book says about the prodigal son."

"But He watches for us to come home and runs to meet us when we do." Drew smiled a little to think he would remember that bit of his Sunday lessons in particular.

Peterson smiled faintly now, too. "True enough, sir. True enough. Here we are."

They had reached the shed. Peterson opened the door and gestured toward a small kit bag grimed over with fresh dirt that sat on the wooden table he used for his work.

"Where did you get that?" Drew asked.

"I thought the moles had been at that rose bush that's at the back of the garden, there near the wood. One side of it looked a bit peaked, so I thought I'd ought to give it a bit of looking after. When I dug round it, I hit this."

"Have you opened it?"

"No, sir. I thought you'd better know about it first."

"Have you seen it before?"

"Not as I can say, sir. I suppose it looks fairly much like any other of its kind, but I couldn't say whose it were."

Drew rubbed his hands in anticipation. "How about we have a look?"

The latch was fastened and locked, but Drew's penknife quickly made that of no importance. In another moment the bag was open and its contents spread out on the table.

It had belonged to a man, judging by the toilet articles and the gentleman's undergarments it contained. Other than some handkerchiefs, a book, and some packets of headache powder, there was nothing else inside.

Drew flipped through the book. Fly-fishing. "And you didn't find anything more?"

"No, sir. Not there, but I did find these."

Peterson reached down to the shelf under the table and brought up a pair of men's dress pumps. They were mangled out of shape and smeared with rubbish.

"Where were these?"

"That's the queer thing of it, sir. Mrs. Devon gener'ly saves me the leavings from the kitchen so's I can use some of it on the growing things. I dumps out the bin to sort through it all, and there they was."

Drew wrinkled his nose and prodded one of the shoes with his penknife. "How often does Mrs. D bring you this, uh, bin?"

"I usually collect it of a Saturday night, but last week, with the goings-on, begging your pardon, Mr. Drew, I didn't empty it until the Monday morning."

"So anything in here was put in sometime between then and last night?"

"Must have been, sir. Who'd've put shoes in there, though? A gentleman's shoes at that, and quite nice, I must say, till they was spoilt."

"Quite the sort to wear to a party, wouldn't you say?"

Peterson nodded. "Shall I polish them up, sir?"

"No. Best leave them as they are for now. The police will want to give them a look."

There were those footprints in the grass, along with Constance's. They might be well acquainted with this particular pair of shoes.

Drew used his penknife to turn the left one over. There appeared to be some dried egg yolk and something that looked like apricot jam on the heel, with a faint smear of white paint. No doubt the mark would match the one on the left stocking on the body in the greenhouse.

"Better put them in a box of some sort for me, and I'll see to them and the kit bag. Let me know if you find anything else, will you?"

"Oh, right away, sir, right away."

"And if I can be of any help about Opal . . ."

Peterson fidgeted with a button on his vest. "Very good of you, sir, but we sees to our own."

— Fifteen —

Drew spent most of the next morning in his study. Minerva was taking a brief holiday from her kittens, lying in the sunshine and watching him pace as he waited for an answer to the telegram he had sent to Canada. It was nearly eleven when Denny finally brought it up to him. He read the terse message and then went down to the parlor to find Nick and Madeline.

"Yes, it does," she said, and Drew recognized the pert, challenging look in her eyes that he found as intriguing as it was infuriating.

"No, it doesn't," Nick protested. "Who cares if a snake can actually hear a whistle? It's a ripping good yarn either way."

"But part of the fun is trying to solve the mystery before you read the solution. You can't possibly figure out what that whistle is for until the end of the story, because snakes just don't . . ." Madeline looked up at Drew. "What's the matter?"

"Bad news?" Nick asked.

Drew shook his head. "I was just wondering . . . suppose it really wasn't Lincoln in the greenhouse."

For a moment, the other two merely stared at him.

"What do you mean?" Madeline finally asked.

"That bag, for one thing. Suppose it was Clarke's. Why would anyone want to get rid of it? He wasn't staying the weekend, so he wouldn't have brought much up to the house. His real luggage would have been sent on to the ship. Besides, they weren't expecting him in Edmonton. According to Mr. Rushford, he was meant to pop in unannounced to see how things were going over there without anyone prettying things up in advance."

Nick wrinkled his brow. "What have the police said?"

"They haven't identified it yet. There's not much in there to go on. The shoes are a different matter."

Madeline raised one eyebrow. "Whose are they?"

"They don't quite know that either, but they are the same ones that made the footprints in the garden where Constance was that night. Don't tell this to anyone yet, but I think what Rushford heard at the office the night he was attacked was Lincoln's voice."

"Are you sure?" Madeline asked, her eyes wide.

Nick's only response was a low whistle.

"Remember when we were looking at the body, Nick?" Drew asked. "Before Jimmy shooed us off?"

Nick nodded. "Hardly something I'll soon forget."

"I've been puzzling about that ring ever since then."

Madeline frowned. "You mean it wasn't his, after all?"

"No," Drew said, "it was his all right. But there was something not right about it. It wasn't on his finger properly, only about halfway down, if you know what I mean."

"As if the killer tried to pull it off," Nick said.

"Or as if he didn't manage to get it all the way on," Madeline breathed. "Oh, Drew, you don't think . . . ?"

"Ever since the break-in at Farlinford, I've had suspicions." Drew took the telegram out of his pocket. "I got this just a bit ago. It's a reply to the one I sent yesterday to Canada."

"Hold on," Nick said. "You think Clarke—"

"He never got to the office in Edmonton," Drew interrupted. "He never got on the ship."

"What better way for Lincoln to avoid pursuit than being declared dead, eh?" Nick grinned. "And as a point of order, I must say it's hardly cricket for you to have suspicions and not lay them out for inspection. Father Knox wouldn't like it. But I suppose the question now is where has our charming Mr. Lincoln taken himself off to?"

"Poor Mr. Clarke," Madeline said. "I had forgotten all about him. I remember Mr. Rushford saying Lincoln had recommended him to be Uncle Mason's secretary. And he did look rather like Lincoln from the back."

"Did he?" Drew asked. "I guess I never saw him but that once, in the study. I don't recall that he looked like Lincoln at all. Rather an odd, pasty-looking fellow, as I remember."

"He did from the back," Madeline said. "It startled me at first. But I never thought of him again once I went back to the party with you." She shook her head. "I can see why Lincoln would want to disappear."

"Blackmail is no small thing," Nick said. "Maybe Mrs. Parker was going to turn him in to the local constabulary."

"Or," Drew offered, "perhaps another of his satisfied customers decided he'd had enough of paying blackmail and was out to shut him up permanently, and Lincoln thought it best to make his exit."

"Still, it's not right," Nick said grimly. "It's not right at all."

"Rather bad form to kill a chap just because he fits into your dinner jacket," Drew agreed.

"No, I don't mean that," Nick replied. "That's bad enough. But Father Knox didn't approve of doubles. Lincoln's doing it all wrong."

"The police have already checked his flat for clues. Perhaps we should take a look at Clarke's. Maybe there's something there."

"But the police—"

"The police don't know what I know yet. Or at least what I think I know. We can be in and out of Clarke's and them none the wiser. What do you say?"

"Oh yes," Madeline said. "I want to go with you."

"Are you in, Nick? I can ring up Miss Stokes and get the address, and we can be off."

"All right," Nick said. "But we're likely to find no more there than we did at Lincoln's."

"Now, now," Drew said. "Faint heart and all that."

"I'm afraid you have won the only fair lady at hand," Nick said. "Or at least you're set on winning her."

Drew winked at Madeline. "Quite right, and don't you forget it."

Once Drew had obtained Clarke's address from the overly inquisitive Miss Stokes, he and Nick and Madeline drove up to Winchester.

"This can't be right," Nick said, looking around at the row of seedy warehouses and tatterdemalion little shops that lined the street. "What number did you say?"

Drew glanced at the back of the envelope where he had jotted down the address. "Thirty-seven."

Number 37 housed the cannery that preserved for market Frye's Freshest Fish. No one currently at work there recognized Clarke's name or description. All of them were quite sure that no one was allowed to actually take up residence in the building.

"Heigh-ho," Nick sighed as they returned to the car. "And what now, mon capitaine?"

"Obviously a false address."

"And a fake name," Madeline added.

"Perhaps not. His file could have been tampered with in our

records. I certainly wouldn't put it past whoever's behind all this." Drew smiled. "I think, for now, I'd best have a little chat with our Mr. Rushford."

Rushford was sunning himself on the terrace when Drew returned to Farthering Place. It seemed a pity to upset the old boy when he was just beginning to get his nerves back, but there it was. He already had a glass of something in his hand, so perhaps he'd be in a mellow mood.

Drew pulled up a chair next to him. "Having a pleasant afternoon, sir?"

"Oh, hello, young man. Yes, very nice. Very nice. Perhaps I should have a country place of my own. Nothing like it for the nerves. Been thinking of going back to Canada one day. Pleasant place for an old man to finish out, what?"

Drew smiled. "Not for a good many years yet, I trust."

He was glad to see Rushford smiling, glad that fear was gone from his eyes. It was the worst thing to see in an old man—fear and uncertainty and helplessness. He hated having to bring them back to Rushford now, but it couldn't be helped.

"I'd like a word if I might, sir," Drew began. "About the other night at Farlinford."

Rushford's smile vanished. "I don't know of anything more—"

"I'd like to know about what you heard."

"What I heard? I never—"

"You said you weren't sure you had heard properly. Heard what?"

"I said I heard someone on the telephone. I told you that."

"But you said something couldn't be, that it was impossible, that you mustn't have heard properly. What did you mean?"

There was a flash of anger in the old man's eyes. "I never said such a thing. You must be mistaken."

"You wrote it in your diary."

Rushford's face went white. "You read my diary?"

"It's inexcusable, sir, I know, and I can't blame you for feeling misused, but we're dealing with murder here. I have to know what you heard."

"I don't know." Rushford put his head in his hands. "It's all so muddled, I can't say for certain."

"Just tell me what you thought."

"It was the voice, the one talking about sharing things out."

"What else did he say?"

"I didn't hear anything more, but his voice . . . No, it's madness."

"What about his voice?"

"I think . . . I think it was Lincoln. It *was* David Lincoln."

Drew nodded. "The chief inspector will want to hear this."

"They won't believe me," Rushford said. "I hardly believe myself, but that was what I heard." He looked up at Drew, his tired eyes pleading. "You believe me, don't you?"

"I do. I've always thought there was something peculiar about that body in the greenhouse. But if Lincoln is alive, why is he still here? I should have thought he would have decamped with the money the moment he was dead and buried."

"But if it wasn't Lincoln who was shot," Rushford said, "then who—"

"Mason's secretary, that Clarke fellow, God help him. He never turned up in Canada."

"Lincoln's bleeding us dry." The blood surged into Rushford's face. "The greedy little worm is bleeding us dry."

Drew gave him a moment to collect himself, and then he stood. "Well, I'll—"

"The police have got to be told. About Lincoln. They must be told."

"I'll see to it right away. No doubt Inspector Birdsong will want to speak to you about it."

"Yes, of course. I should have told the police about this before now, but it was so fantastic, I thought perhaps I was hallucinating back at the office." Rushford blinked rapidly. "I . . . I didn't want to say anything until I was sure I had my head about me."

"Perfectly understandable, sir."

There was something pitiful in Rushford's trembling smile. "Rather nice to know I haven't gone completely mad."

Drew rang up the chief inspector and listened as Rushford stumbled through his explanation of what had happened at Farlinford and why he hadn't mentioned anything about it until now. Then, chastened, Rushford handed Drew the telephone.

"He'd like to speak to you."

Drew grinned. "I suppose I'm in for it now." He put the receiver to his ear. "Well, Inspector, a rather interesting turn of events, is it not?"

"We've been turning our investigation along these lines for a while now, Mr. Farthering, though you might have informed us of your suspicions before today." The annoyance in Birdsong's voice was palpable. "No need to make our work any more difficult than it already is, wouldn't you think?"

"Terribly sorry, Inspector, but I hated to trouble you until I had a bit more to go on."

"That's as may be, Farthering, but do keep us in mind in the future. Perhaps we can be of some small assistance, and we'd be ever so grateful."

"Now, no need for spite, Inspector. I promise I shall mend my ways and lead a blameless life hereafter."

Birdsong made a small coughing noise that Drew could not help interpreting as an indication of disbelief. Nevertheless, the chief inspector continued, "I'd like you to come up to the station here in Winchester, if you wouldn't mind, sir."

"What about?"

"I don't like to say over the telephone, sir. I'll be happy to explain it all once you're here."

Drew offered Rushford no explanation, and he didn't tell Madeline or Nick where he was going. Denny had to know, but he was the only one. Before long, Drew found himself seated in a chair in a drab little interview room in the Winchester police station. On the table between him and the chief inspector lay a file folder. It was bursting with papers.

"Sorry to trouble you like this, Mr. Farthering," Birdsong said, "but something has come up."

"Yes?"

"It seems that some bearer bonds have been sold to the Chandlers Ford Merchants Bank and Trust."

"I expect that happens a great deal more than most people realize," Drew replied.

His grave expression went unappreciated.

"I take it you'll find this all considerably less amusing, sir, when you hear that those bonds properly belong to Farlinford Processing."

Drew was considerably less amused. "Chandlers Ford, did you say?"

"I thought, as a director of the company who is not currently under suspicion, you might want to accompany me to the Merchants Bank and Trust down there to see what we can make of the incident."

"I'd certainly like to go along," Drew said, "and I won't even take undue note of the tone you used in saying not *currently* under suspicion."

Birdsong eyed him keenly. "And I'll do all the questioning, if you please."

"Of course."

"Do you know of any other valuables gone missing, sir?"

Drew leaned forward in his chair. "What kind of valuables?"

"Bonds? Stocks? Anything that might be sold for ready cash?"

"Nothing of which I am aware, Inspector. Has something turned up?"

"According to Mr. Platt of your accounting department, it seems a number of negotiable instruments normally kept in the company vault are no longer there."

Birdsong shuffled through the papers in the file and finally pushed one toward Drew. It was a list of what had gone missing and, even more depressing, the values of those items.

"And the delightful tidings keep rolling in." Drew sighed. "Anything else I ought to know?"

"Not so far. I'm only telling you this so you can keep your eyes open. Oh, and I've done some research into your findings in Mr. McCutcheon's flat and laboratory."

"Yes?"

"That law book was not in that drawer when our men searched it, and the bottom drawer of that filing cabinet was full when they investigated the accident."

"They're sure? Couldn't have just been a muddle in the investigation?"

Birdsong scowled. "They're sure."

"What about the picture of Marielle?"

"The sergeant admits they could have missed that behind the cabinet there. They were investigating an accident at the time, not a murder. They missed the deuced passageway, that's for certain."

"Hardly something one would expect to find," Drew conceded. "So what is your theory now, Inspector? Obviously we're well past the lovers' quarrel idea."

"Looks that way."

"But if it is someone after whatever he can steal from Farlinford, why the bit about Marielle, if that's her name? And whyever would he kill Constance?"

Birdsong returned the list of missing items to the folder, his thin lips twitching beneath his heavy mustache. "You may not have all the answers, Detective Farthering, but you do ask some very good questions."

It was a short drive southwest of Winchester to Chandlers Ford. The Merchants Bank and Trust was a small but reputable organization long established in a dour Georgian building on Winchester Road just down from the train station. Drew had never heard of them. And though it was not far from Farthering St. John, he had not often visited Chandlers Ford.

Birdsong showed the woman at the front desk his identification, and he and Drew were immediately shown into the manager's office. There they were greeted by a middle-aged man whose portly physique and florid face spoke to his keen enjoyment of good food and fine wine.

"Good afternoon, gentlemen, I am Joseph Grambs, the manager. You must be Chief Inspector Birdsong." Birdsong shook his hand, and then Grambs extended his hand to Drew. "And you are . . . ?"

"I'm Drew Farthering. I am one of the directors of Farlinford Processing. My stepfather is Mason Parker, the managing partner."

"I see. Well, I hope you can appreciate our position in this matter, Mr. Farthering. The papers were in order, if you'd care to review them. And as you say, Mr. Parker is the managing partner of your company."

"Yes, he is, Mr. Grambs," Drew said with a smile. "Might we sit?"

"Oh, yes, certainly."

Drew and Birdsong sat in the pair of leather chairs that faced Mr. Grambs's imposing mahogany desk.

"Now, Mr. Grambs," Birdsong began, "if you don't mind, I'd like to hear exactly what happened."

After taking his seat behind the desk, Grambs began, "Well, as I told your man on the telephone, it was the end of last month. Our Mr. Rodale received a call from someone claiming to be a Mr. Lincoln at Farlinford Processing. He said he wanted to sell some bearer bonds the company had held for some while now, and asked if we could accommodate him. As it was rather a large amount, Mr. Rodale came and spoke to me about it. I told him that so long as they had the proper authorization from the directors of the company, we would be happy to make the transaction. That afternoon a messenger arrived with the bonds and a declaration from the board of directors approving the sale."

"And you're contacting us now because . . . ?"

"Well, after I heard about the goings-on at Farlinford, I thought I'd better make certain I didn't have possession of stolen goods."

Birdsong narrowed his eyes. "May I see the declaration?"

"Certainly."

Grambs took an official-looking document from a file and pushed it across the desk. "You'll see it's on Farlinford's stationery and signed by two directors as required. Very aboveboard."

Birdsong inspected the paper and then handed it over to Drew. It was indeed on company stationery, signed by Edwin M. Rushford and David Lincoln.

"Do you know if those signatures are genuine?" the chief inspector asked Drew.

"I really couldn't say. Did you happen to see the messenger, Mr. Grambs?"

"No. Mr. Rodale dealt with him."

"And Mr. Rodale was the only one to speak to the man on the telephone?"

"He was."

"Is it possible to have your Mr. Rodale come in here for a moment?"

"Of course." Grambs stood and walked over to the door of his office. Poking his head through the doorway, he said to the woman at the front desk, "Miss Stapleton . . ."

"Yes, Mr. Grambs?"

"If you would, please ask Mr. Rodale to come to my office."

"Right away, sir."

A few moments later, Mr. Rodale stepped into Grambs's office, shielded behind the sheaf of files and loose papers he carried in both arms. "You wished to see me, sir?"

Grambs introduced Drew and the chief inspector. "They'd like to ask you about the Farlinford matter."

"Certainly, sir." He juggled his papers to allow himself the opportunity to push his wire-rimmed glasses up on his nose. "How may I help?"

"Tell us what you remember," Birdsong said, and Rodale dutifully repeated the story Grambs had already related.

"The Mr. Lincoln on the telephone," Drew said, "what sort of voice did he have?"

Rodale thought for a moment. "Nothing unusual, I suppose. Rather an ordinary voice."

"Young or old?"

"Sort of middling, I'd have to say. Or perhaps a bit more on the young side, but not much."

Birdsong made a note in his book.

"And the messenger?" Drew asked.

"Young chap. Looked barely out of school."

"What sort of voice did he have?"

"Oh, I shouldn't think he was the same one on the phone. Working class, going by the way he spoke. And he didn't say much, anyway. Just a hasty 'Package for you, sir' and 'Sign here, please,' and he was off."

"You didn't pay for the bonds in cash, did you?" Birdsong asked.

"I should say not. We gave the boy a check made out to Farlinford Processing."

"Has that check been deposited?"

"It has," Mr. Rodale said. "It was cashed at the bank in Otterbourne that same day."

"Another bank with which Farlinford has never had dealings," Drew said, and Birdsong nodded.

"The messenger, was he from a service?" Drew asked Rodale.

"Not that I could tell. He didn't have a uniform or anything of the sort. I thought he'd been sent over from your firm."

Drew sighed.

The chief inspector removed some photographs from his pocket and spread them out on the manager's desk for Rodale to see—pictures of Lincoln, Mason, Rushford, Peterson the gardener, and even Nick, along with three or four others Drew did not know. "Do you recognize any of these men, Mr. Rodale?" Birdsong asked.

Rodale studied them for a minute or two, then slid one of the photographs back toward the chief inspector. "I've seen that man. I know I have."

Drew leaned forward in his chair. "Really? Where?"

"Give me a moment, Mr. Farthering. I'll think of it."

Drew glanced at Birdsong, but instead of the excitement he expected to see on the chief inspector's face, there was only mild disgust.

"That's Detective Inspector Cook from our fraud division. We put his picture in there so as not to unduly influence any of our witnesses."

Drew sighed once more.

"Cook, Cook," Rodale mused, tapping his chin, and then he beamed at them. "Ah, yes! He won the cycling race they held at the fair in Highbridge last summer. Bested their local chappie by a good fifteen seconds. Grand day, that was."

Chief Inspector Birdsong stood and thanked the two men for their time, and then Drew followed him back onto Winchester Road.

"A slippery fellow, this Lincoln," Drew said after he and the inspector had driven toward Winchester for some minutes in near silence.

"We'll have him," Birdsong grumbled, grinding the gears as he shifted into third. "Don't you worry, Mr. Farthering."

"Where do you think he's got to just now?"

Birdsong frowned, considering. "If he was smart, he'd be long gone by now. Grambs said they bought those bonds at the end of last month."

"But we know he was in Winchester no longer ago than Friday, when he broke into the office."

"True enough."

"Why do you suppose he hasn't made good his escape to South America or China or some such?"

"Obviously he was after something at Farlinford. Question is, did he find what he was looking for?"

Drew nodded. "And if he didn't, where is he now, and will he be coming back for it?"

— Sixteen —

n his own car now and heading back to Farthering Place, Drew considered the question of where Lincoln might be secreting himself since his supposed death. Searches at Farthering Place had turned up nothing. Where else might he be? Somewhere close enough for him to prowl about the place at night, skulking in the wood or climbing trellises into upstairs windows. Drew hadn't actually checked the trellises around the house, but he supposed there would be broken tendrils and scuffed or damaged bits of wood or brick if someone had climbed one.

On a whim he drove past the drive up to Farthering and headed into the village instead. Of course, the lad he'd seen climbing down from the window at the inn couldn't have been Lincoln, even if the man was a wizard at disguising himself. Still, if a boy could climb a trellis, so could a man. It couldn't hurt to make inquiries. Any clue would be welcome, and perhaps all wasn't as advertised at the Royal Elizabeth Inn.

Mrs. Burrell started when she saw him at the back door of her inn.

"Mr. Drew! What are you doing here? Wasn't anyone at the front to see to you?"

Drew removed his hat and stepped into her kitchen, into the simmering, tantalizing smells coming from a variety of bubbling pots on the enormous iron stove.

"I didn't go up front, actually. I came to see you, if you'll forgive the intrusion."

She smiled a little uncertainly and pushed a limp strand of graying hair behind one ear. "I'll be happy to help however I can, of course, but—"

"I was just having a look in your garden, to be perfectly honest, and I was wondering if you could tell me if anyone's been climbing down that trellis from that window there?"

"I should say not," she huffed. "That little rapscallion who helps round the inn climbed up it a few days ago, and didn't I half tan him when I caught him at it."

"What was he doing?"

"Said there was a pound note caught up there and he went to bring it down. I won't have him up there spoiling the ivy and tramping his mud back through the inn."

"And was there a pound note?"

"Funny enough, there was. I checked to make sure there wasn't nobody missing of it, then I couldn't do nothing but let the little rascal keep it. Heaven knows what he'll be wasting it on."

"When was this?"

"Oh, Friday, I suppose it was. He'd been warned not to get into mischief, not if he wanted to keep his job. Mind you, I can find another little imp to do the fetching and such round here if he doesn't behave, and I told him as much."

"Quite right," Drew agreed. "Is, um . . . is he about at the moment?"

"I sent him to gather up the breakfast things from any of the rooms as ordered up. Shouldn't take a minute, but he takes his precious time, he does. Those should have been down long ago."

"Mind if I pop up just for a bit and talk to him?"

The woman smiled, splitting her face into two crinkled halves. "'Course I don't mind. He'll listen to you, I don't doubt. Remind him of where his heathen ways will end him up. Tell him a layabout never comes to any good."

"Yes, well, I'll have a talk with him. Don't you worry, Mrs. Burrell. What's the boy's name?"

"May as well be Mischief Maker, if you ask me, but it's Eddie. Eddie Jenkins."

"One of the Jenkinses from over by the mill pond?"

"The very same, sir."

"Right. Thank you."

"You send him down with those dishes too when you're done, sir. He'll be all day about it otherwise."

"Right away."

Drew hurried up the stairs and found the boy tottering down the hallway with a trayful of dirty breakfast ware and three pairs of boots to be blacked. It was a heavy load for a ten-year-old.

"Well, you must be Eddie," Drew said, smiling, and the boy stopped and nodded, big dark eyes uncertain under a mass of lank black hair.

"I'm Drew Farthering and—"

"I know who you are. You come from up at Farthering Place."

"That's right."

"I ain't done nothing."

"Of course not," Drew said as he took the tray from him. "I just thought you might be able to help me with something."

"You oughtn't do that. It's my job."

"That's all right, Eddie. I don't mind helping you a bit, too."

"Did that man and lady really get killed at your house?"

"I'm afraid they did."

The boy dropped his eyes and fussed with the lace on one of the boots he still had slung over his shoulder. "My mum's dead, too."

"It's a tough go, isn't it?" Drew set the tray on the floor and gestured toward the two Morris chairs that graced the little alcove in the hallway. "How about we sit right here and talk a bit?"

The boy shook his head. "I ain't allowed. I might get the chairs dirty."

"Come on now," Drew urged. "If you do, I'll make it all right with Mrs. Burrell. Fair enough?"

Still looking as if he were about to be scolded, the boy sat down. Drew joined him.

"Now, this is better, isn't it?"

The boy nodded, obviously certain that it wasn't.

"Now, Eddie, I understand you got in a bit of a jam with Mrs. Burrell awhile back. What was that about?"

"Didn't mean nothing by it. There was a pound note up in the ivy in back of the inn, and I went to fetch it down."

"A pound? How do you suppose it got up there?"

"Dunno. I thought maybe the wind got it. One of the guests, the gentleman with the white mustache, he was looking up at it, figuring what it was, and said I might as well have it if I wanted to go up. That was all. I didn't steal it, and I didn't break nothing."

"I believe you. Do you know the name of the gentleman with the white mustache?"

The boy shook his head. "But he's in number twenty-two, 'long with the other gentleman that don't come out."

"Never?"

"Well, in the late mornings, I think. But only for a bit. And he's all wrapped up, like he's ill."

"Yes, I heard that he wasn't feeling well. Have you been in there yet today?"

"Not yet. I couldn't carry anything more, so I thought I'd take this lot down and then do the evens."

"Is he out now?"

"Him and the gentleman with the mustache, yeah."

"I see." Drew smiled again. "What do you say we go take a quick look round number twenty-two, and then I'll help you clear up the evens? How would that be?"

The boy narrowed his eyes. "If you take something, I'll be the one getting the blame."

Drew put one hand upon his heart. "Upon my word, Eddie, I won't touch a thing. I'm just curious about how the gentleman knew there was a pound note up there, and I should think it quite worth another pound if you'll let me have a look round. What do you say?"

"I dunno . . ."

"Just one little look. Help a fellow out."

With a sigh the boy led him down the hall to the door labeled 22, and with a turn of the passkey they were inside.

The room was unremarkable as hotel rooms go. Situated in the oldest part of the inn, it was a corner room with two windows, one above the back garden, the other overlooking the roof of the new addition, and farther on, the churchyard and Holy Trinity itself. Under each window was a single bed and night table. Both beds were in need of making up. As explanation for the acrid odor in the air, the ashtray on one of the night tables was overflowing, and the other, though empty, was still grimed with recent ash.

On the table in the middle of the room was an assortment of dirty plates and cups, and a crumpled napkin lay on the floor under one of the chairs. Drew picked it up. There was a large water spot on one corner, and in the center of it, a tiny pinkish smudge.

"Tell me, Eddie, was there another napkin when you brought up breakfast today?"

"I dunno. There should have been, but I don't bring up the breakfast unless Maggie's sick. I just clear up."

He started picking up the dishes, but Drew stopped him. "Just let me have a quick look first."

One of the occupants of the room had been decidedly hungrier than the other, but of course anyone who was ill was likely to suffer a loss of appetite. Half a cup of cold coffee sat next to the nearly full plate, and Drew took a moment to examine it. Something had been wiped off the inner and outer rim of one side of the cup, something that had left a sticky, slightly greasy residue. There was nothing like it on the empty cup or plate.

Drew went to the window and looked down on the trellis he'd seen Eddie on a few days before. He'd certainly made a mess of the vine and the paint with his climbing. He'd scuffed up the sill, too.

"How far did you climb up here, Eddie? All the way to the window?"

"Oh, no, sir. Just enough to reach the money. I was standing just about where that drainpipe bends. Then somebody yelled at me from the street, and I nipped back down. That was when Mrs. Burrell caught me."

Drew swallowed down a chuckle. "Bad luck, that."

Eddie started to empty the ashtray that was full, but Drew stopped him and examined the remains.

"Hmmm. I say, Eddie . . ."

"Yes, sir?"

"Does this room have a bath, or do they use the one in the hall?"

"No, sir. Mrs. Burrell said they was very particular to have a room with a bath. Can I take away the breakfast things now?"

"Yes, that'll be fine." Drew pointed to a door across from the one that led to the hallway. "Through here?"

Eddie nodded as he began stacking dishes, and Drew pushed open the door. The bathroom was perfectly empty, including the little medicine cabinet, except for the towels and the sliver of soap provided by the hotel. Even the wastebasket, apart from a small paper bag, was unoccupied.

Drew opened up the crumpled paper and looked inside. It too was empty, but the inside was coated with what looked and smelled like cigarette ash. Drew smiled to himself. So that was it.

He walked back into the main room.

"I say, Eddie . . ."

The boy was in no position to answer any more questions. As it was, Mrs. Burrell had him by one ear, her face the picture of affronted authority.

"Mr. Drew!"

Drew smiled, the appealing, apologetic-but-mischievous smile that always softened the hardest of female hearts, especially the middle-aged ones. "Sorry, Mrs. Burrell. I know this doesn't look exactly on the up-and-up and all, but well, you know, everyone's been a bit curious about this Flesch chappie, and I didn't think it would do any harm just to—"

"I don't see as it matters, Mr. Drew, what you think, begging your pardon, sir, if our guests think they can't leave their rooms and have us keep them private for them. Be still, you." Her face red and shining from the effort, she shook Eddie by the ear, pinching a little harder to keep him from squirming away. "Now, Mr. Drew, sir, I think you'd best be going before Mr. Whiteside and Mr. Flesch come back and find there's been goings-on in their room while they were out. And here I thought you were going to set a fine example for the boy."

"I didn't do nothing," Eddie whined, and Mrs. Burrell shook him again.

"The blame is entirely mine, I assure you," Drew said. "I was going to help him gather up the breakfast things so he could get them down to you quickly, as you asked." He tried the smile again. "I'm a hopelessly curious creature. Anyone will tell you so. No need to take it out on him."

Lips pursed, she pushed Eddie toward the little table. "You clear off those dishes and get them all down to the kitchen, and don't you let me hear you say boo."

He scrambled to do as she said and was out of the room in a flash.

"It really was all my doing," Drew said once the boy was gone.

"Well, I can hardly be surprised to see that young scalawag up to mischief. I was taking a chance trusting him in here in the first place. I only did it long of his mother passing on and all. But you, Mr. Drew, and a gentleman born, as well! I hardly know what to say."

"But I—"

"No, sir, I think there's no need of saying anything more. If you'll just leave me to my work as I try to put things right before the reputation of my hotel is put in further danger, I will thank you."

Chastened, Drew made one last apology and then hurried out into the hallway and down the front stairs. He slipped a five-pound note into little Eddie's hand as he passed him, and then he spied Maggie, the girl who did most of the scrub work at the inn, cleaning up at the bar.

"Hullo," Drew said with a tip of his hat. "Has it been a busy morning?"

The girl gave him a shy smile. "Not really, Mr. Drew. Hasn't been much of anybody round the place today. But then we haven't started serving the drinks yet, either."

She wiped down the bar and started cleaning the ashtrays. Only the one closest to the end had anything in it.

"Do you tidy up here every day, Maggie?"

"Yes, sir. Mrs. Burrell won't have it no other way."

"That's a lot of ash for a slow day, isn't it?" Drew asked, taking a quick look at the cigarette butts before she dumped them into her trash bin.

"Suppose it is. Some folk smoke one after another, you know."

"Was there a lady in here today?"

Maggie frowned for a moment, thinking. "Not as I seen, Mr. Drew. 'Course, I was helping in the kitchen and taking up trays most of the morning, so I suppose there could have been. Why?"

"Oh, that's all right. I'm just a nosey Parker with too much time on his hands." He gave her a wink and, setting his hat on his head at a jaunty angle, went whistling out into the street.

Drew pulled the Rolls into the garage at Farthering Place and switched off the engine. Before he could get out, Nick strolled up to him.

"There you are. Did you and old Birdsong turn up anything?"

"Not much," Drew replied. "Just more Farlinford property being sold off. Bearer bonds this time."

"The ones they took from Rushford?"

"No. This was before that. Seems all this has been going on for some time now."

"Doesn't selling something like that take high-up approval?"

"They were signed by two directors properly enough."

"And the signatures are good?"

"The inspector and I drove up to Farlinford to verify just that. Lincoln's was genuine. Rushford's was not."

Nick frowned, not saying anything.

"What is it?" Drew asked.

Nick didn't answer for a long moment, and then he merely shook his head. "Nothing. Nothing yet."

"Tell me."

"Really, if it were anything worth mentioning, I would tell you."

"Father Knox," Drew cautioned him, snatching the well-worn list from Nick's coat pocket. "See? Right here. 'The stupid friend of the detective, the Watson,' that's you, 'must not conceal any thoughts which pass through his mind.' Now, my Watson, reveal all."

He smiled when he said it, but he gave Nick a look that allowed for no begging off.

Nick ducked his head a little. "I'm not all that stupid."

He said it with a laugh, but when he looked up again, Drew could see a flicker of pain in his eyes.

"I say, old man," Drew said, flustered, "it was only meant to be a bit of a joke. I'd never really—"

Nick quickly shook his head. "Don't be a cretin. I know all that. I just . . ." He blinked hard. "Mr. Parker's been good to me and my dad. About as good as your father was. I don't want to—"

"You don't want to get him into trouble," Drew finished for him. "Lincoln's blatantly involved, Rushford's been grossly made to look so, but where's Mason in all this? Someone in authority has to be behind it."

Nick sagged against the car's fender. "More and more, I can't help wondering. It's an awful thing."

"I know." Drew started to pace again. "I've noticed things,

just little things, things I wish I hadn't seen. For Madeline's sake. For mine."

Nick looked up. "I didn't think about her. She's pretty stuck on him, isn't she?"

"He's like a father to her. I don't know if she'd take it kindly if I were to prove he was a murderer."

"But if he is, Drew . . ."

"I've thought about it a lot. At first, when we thought it was just Lincoln who had been killed, I tried to convince myself that it was all right, that the scoundrel got no more than he deserved. But the more I tried to think it, the more I couldn't. Once a man has justified cold, willful murder, he can justify anything. And it's not just one murder now. It's Clarke and Constance and McCutcheon and maybe even that Chinese girl in Edmonton. If Mason's the killer, or in league with him, he has to face the law for what he's done. Madeline will just have to understand that." Drew let out a slow breath and then slapped Nick on the back. "Come on, old man. Let's go into the house and hash things out over some of Mrs. D's cake. Whoever is in this with Lincoln, he's bound to give himself away. We just have to catch him at it."

"He can't bally well get round us forever," Nick said. "Especially not with Miss Parker helping out."

Scowling, Drew pushed him out of the garage and along the walk toward the house. "You just carry on being clever, then, and I'll keep my conclusions to myself."

"I don't know why she should upset you. She's a good egg and not subject to the vapors and other annoying feminine maladies."

"You remember how Diana Wheaton used to make you feel? If she was along, you'd five-putt every hole on the course."

A look of wistful fondness came across Nick's face. "Ah,

Diana. I wonder how she and her aged captain of industry are faring these days."

"She made her bed and no doubt must lie in it. You got off easy, if you ask me."

"It never would have done to have her on an investigation like this one, I'll give you that much. She'd have fainted dead away at the mere mention of murder. Never in a million would she have offered to help solve one."

"True enough." Drew smiled a little wistfully himself. "Madeline is a plucky one, isn't she? You know, I really don't mind having her along, even if it does muddle my thinking a bit."

"Perhaps she'd like some cake along with us. It couldn't hurt to have another brain churning away at the problem, could it?"

They went into the house and were immediately greeted by Dennison.

"Ask Mrs. Devon to serve us tea in the library, would you, please, Denny?" Drew said. "And invite Miss Parker to join us, if she will."

"Very good, sir."

"All right, Nick," Drew continued as they headed toward the library, "let's suppose Lincoln and his yet-unknown accomplice have decided to bankrupt Farlinford. Why would Lincoln's *ghost* appear here at Farthering Place? It couldn't have benefitted him to scare Anna out of her wits that night. What could he have been after?"

"Well, it couldn't have been a ghost. Father Knox rules them out as a matter of course. Perhaps Lincoln didn't find what he was looking for when he broke into Rushford's office." Nick opened the library door and stepped inside. "Perhaps he thinks Rushford brought it with him here, or perhaps . . ." He slowed to a stop, his voice trailing off.

Drew looked at him, puzzled. "What—?"

Nick cut him off with a quick gesture toward the draperies. There on the left side, just visible under the heavy gold fringe, were the toes of a pair of men's shoes.

Drew motioned to him to keep talking.

"Of course, we don't know that yet," Nick said, quickening his stride once more.

"No, not enough evidence. Not to be certain." Drew gestured with both hands, indicating that they should approach the intruder from opposite sides. "But there is always something that gives the game away, an inscription on a ring or a left-handed golf club, or perhaps a poorly concealed pair of shoes—"

They pounced at the same instant, and the lavish curtains and attendant lace sheers tumbled with them out the open window and into the damp flower bed. Drew thrashed in the near-blackness and caught hold of someone—a sturdy, flailing someone who seemed equally set on pinning Drew to the ground. Drew struggled under the heavy brocade, determined to keep his crushing hold on the lurker, but the other man struggled just as fiercely.

"Hold him! Hold him!"

Drew could hear Nick's muffled voice somewhere beyond the sea of antique gold that blinded him and tightened his grasp in response.

"Ugh!" Nick huffed. "He's got a grip like iron!"

With a sudden burst of realization, Drew threw his opponent onto his back and then shoved the suffocating draperies to one side. Blinking up at him was a startled-looking Nick.

"I thought as much," Drew grumbled. "I knew he couldn't be crushing the life out of us both at the same time."

Nick sat up. "But where did he go?"

"I suppose he took himself off once he suspected we'd spotted him. Or perhaps . . ." Drew went back to the library window and looked down at the floor. The shoes were still there. Empty. "Perhaps he was never there."

"That must have been quite a sight," Nick said, rubbing his head as he leaned into the window beside Drew. "All that was missing was the amusing coconut-like sound when our empty skulls collided."

"And I suppose we've rather neatly obliterated any footmarks that may have been left in the garden, as well," Drew said. "I'm glad our Miss Parker wasn't witness to our antics."

"Who says?"

Drew looked up to see Madeline standing in the doorway, laughing silently. He drew himself up, a picture of wounded dignity.

"Madam, you are no gentleman . . . and for that I am profoundly grateful."

With a smile of his own, Drew stepped back over the windowsill. Nick hopped into the library after him.

"Did you see anyone?" Drew asked.

"I'm afraid not," she admitted, coming over to the window beside them. "I got here only in time to see the two of you beat the curtains into submission."

"No, look here," Nick insisted. "Someone was back there. Listening."

"*Maybe* someone was back there," Drew corrected.

Madeline examined the shoes, not touching them. "Do you recognize them?"

"Could belong to anyone," Nick said, "but it wouldn't be hard to compare them to anybody's here."

"True enough." Drew glanced out into the garden once more. "If he's staying here. Suppose it was Lincoln again, looking for whatever he was after in the first place. Where's he been keeping himself all this time since he was 'murdered'? We've searched the house, and he doesn't seem to be here."

"Perhaps he's staying out in the wood somewhere," Nick offered. "Or in one of our cottages."

"Like Peterson's, you mean."

Nick shook his head. "No. I can't see that in old Peterson. He's not the kind to kill for money."

"Maybe not for money," Drew said, "but there's no telling what a father might do because of his child. Of course, the only one he'd kill because of Opal would be Lincoln. It's hardly likely he'd be hiding him, is it?"

"Well, he's not registered at the Queen Bess, that's for certain." Nick sprawled out on a chair. "That would have helped enormously."

Madeline's face suddenly lit. "What if he is?"

Nick sat up straight. "What?"

"Why doesn't anyone ever see this Mr. Flesch? And why would Mr. Whiteside, a man with connections to Farlinford Processing, *just happen* to come to Farthering St. John right now? And why . . ." She broke off when Drew grinned. "I'm not kidding."

Drew squeezed one arm around her. "Of course you're not, darling. I was thinking along those same lines myself earlier today. I even went to the Queen Bess to see what I could see."

"What made you go there?"

"I don't know." Drew shrugged. "Just a hunch, I suppose." He winked at Madeline. "Perhaps it was divine guidance."

Nick scowled. "That's hardly cricket. Father Knox says the detective must never have an unaccountable intuition which—"

"Oh, bother Father Knox. Do you know what I found?"

Madeline narrowed her eyes at him. "What?"

"Our Mr. Whiteside has a lady friend."

Nick burst out laughing. "No. Are you certain?"

"I managed to get a look round his room. Traces of lipstick on the dishes, despite efforts to wipe them off, lipstick-marked cigarette butts bagged up and dumped into the ashtray in the bar, that sort of thing. And evidently our mystery woman has gone out the window and down the trellis at least once."

"How do you know that?"

"Seems old Whiteside put a pound note up there and then pointed it out to the boy that works at the inn. Told him he could have it if he cared to climb up for it. Best way to account for any marks his inamorata may have left, don't you think?"

Nick frowned. "Why go to all that trouble? Couldn't he just have said she was his wife? Who's to know the difference here?"

"Perhaps she's got a husband," Drew said.

"From around here?" Nick shook his head. "Who else would know her?"

"It's probably that girl from the tea shop," Madeline said. "That Kitty."

"Now, now, darling. Mustn't be snide. I'm sure old Leicester would have noticed if his wife had disappeared for that long, don't you think?" Drew considered for a moment. "I suppose all we can do is keep our eyes open."

"Besides," Nick added, "the police would have surely investigated if they thought Lincoln was hiding out at the Queen Bess. They've been combing the area for him for days now. It is combing that they do, isn't it?"

"I believe combing *is* the preferred term," Drew replied. "No doubt they'll want to know about our little tête-à-tête with the intruder in the curtains and have a look at the shoes. I suppose I ought to telephone our chief inspector at once. Excuse me a minute, darling."

Madeline smiled. "All right, but don't be gone long. I don't like being left alone with a murderer around."

Nick drew himself up melodramatically. "Well, I like that."

"You can stay here and protect me from the killer," Madeline said, laughing. "Or at least throw yourself into his path until I have a chance to run away."

"Yes, do that, old man," Drew said. "And we'll make sure our grandchildren know the sacrifice you made to ensure their eventual existence."

Nick straightened his shoulders and resolutely adjusted his tie. "You have at least to name your firstborn after me in that event."

"Unless it's a girl," Madeline said.

"Especially if it's a girl," Nick insisted. "Nick's a fine name for a girl. Quite sporty, if you ask me."

"You two hash out the details," Drew said. "I'm off to telephone the inspector, and then we'll see what we ought to do next."

He went down the hallway, intending to telephone from his stepfather's study but found Mason in there on a business call, something about drill bits and viscosity and other things with which Drew was unfamiliar.

"I'll go upstairs," he half whispered when Mason noticed him there in the doorway, and he pointed to the floor above them. Mason nodded and returned to his call.

Drew headed for Constance's sitting room and her private line.

"I'll call you the minute I get something."

Drew stopped outside Constance's door. The voice he heard was soft, distinctly American, a young man's voice. Besides Whiteside, Drew didn't know of any Americans in the area, much less here at Farthering Place.

After a brief pause, the voice said, "Right. They'll have to be able to prove it."

Drew waited a moment more. Then, hearing nothing, he flung open the door.

The room was empty.

He hurried to the door to the bedroom and pushed that open. It was empty, too.

He went through the door that led to the hallway from Constance's bedroom, surprised to find it unlocked, and then opened the door to the guest room next to it.

"I can be of service to Mr. Farthering, please?"

Min stood there, coatless, with a flatiron in his hand. A pair of gentleman's trousers, Rushford's no doubt, were spread on the bed to be pressed. No one else was in the room.

"Did anyone come through here, Min?"

"No. I see no one." Min set the iron down on the hearth and hurried into his coat. "Please forgive state of disarray."

"No, no," Drew said. "That's all right. Carry on." He turned to the door and then back again. "Min, did you hear anyone on the telephone just now?"

"Telephone? No, no telephone that I have heard."

"Very well then."

Drew went back into the sitting room and opened the connecting door on the other side. No one in that room. Whoever he was, if the American had gone out that way, he would be well away by now.

With a flash of inspiration, he snatched up the phone. "Hello, operator? Did you just put through a trunk call from this number?"

"Yes, sir. Shall I reconnect you?"

"Why, uh, yes. Yes. Please."

A moment later there was a click at the other end of the line. "Hello?"

"Ah, yes. May I ask to whom I am speaking?"

"Who's this?"

The voice was male, clearly not English, and rather surly upon such short acquaintance.

"I was just wondering . . ." Drew winced as the other phone slammed down, and then he jiggled the switch hook. "Operator! Operator!"

"Operator."

"Ring that number again, please, and hurry."

He waited, pacing a semicircular path in front of the little mirrored telephone table. It was taking too long this time.

"Are you there, sir?"

Finally. "Yes?"

"I'm sorry, sir, but that number doesn't answer."

"I just spoke to someone there."

"I'm sorry, sir. Shall I keep trying?"

"Yes. Definitely. Ring me back if you get anyone."

"I certainly will, sir."

He paced awhile longer, still waiting, and then he returned to the library.

Seeing him, Nick stood up. "Did you reach the inspector?"

"Not yet, no."

"No?"

"Someone was using the line."

Nick sighed. "I suppose it was too much trouble to telephone from the kitchen or upstairs."

"I did go upstairs, actually," Drew said. "Mason was using the phone in the study, so I went up and found Constance's telephone engaged, as well."

"Who . . . ?"

"That's what I would like to know. I overheard only a couple of sentences, a man's voice, but not one I recognized." Drew glanced at Madeline. "And it was definitely American."

She caught her breath. "But there aren't any—"

"Precisely. No American men staying here at the house. So where could he have come from? And where could he have gone to?"

"And you're sure he's not still in the house?"

"Don't worry, darling. Stalwart Nick is going to get a couple of the men and have a look around."

Nick blinked. "I am?"

"Yes. That's after you call the inspector and tell him what's gone on here and present him with our mystery footwear. Still untouched, of course."

"That's all very well," Nick said, "but what will you be doing?"

Drew smiled at Madeline. "I thought a certain charming young lady and I might wander down into Farthering St. John and catch up on the gossip, perhaps stop by the good Queen Bess and see if our Mr. Whiteside is still visiting."

Madeline took his hand and stood up. "Are you sure we shouldn't stay and see what happens here? I mean, if some-body's in the house—"

"If somebody's in the house, Nick and the others will see to him. You'd better get your walking shoes."

She looked down at the stylish little silver sandals she was wearing. "You don't mean for us to walk all the way there again, do you?"

"Why not? It's not far. Just a pleasant stroll." He turned her toward the door. "Now hurry on up and put on your sturdiest, most unfashionable shoes, and we'll see what lovely scandals we can hear about over sweet old Mrs. Beecham's garden gate."

She hurried up to her room and returned a moment later wearing a pair of the most hideous, sensible shoes he'd seen on anyone younger than sixty, and a daisy-strewn, black straw hat to make up for the shoes. Soon they were walking down the tree-shaded lane that led to the village.

"Oh, she's not there," Madeline said, scanning Mrs. Beecham's garden. "And I'm sure she could have told us about anyone staying in the village."

"Not to worry, darling," Drew told her. "There she is at Mrs. Eversleigh's next door, nattering away."

They hurried over to the rose arbor, where the two women sat talking.

"Good afternoon, ladies," Drew said, smiling as he removed his hat. "And how are you this fine day?"

"Good afternoon, Mr. Farthering," Mrs. Beecham said. "Oh, do come in, the two of you. How are you, Miss Parker?"

Drew opened the little iron gate for Madeline and then followed her into Mrs. Eversleigh's garden. The owner of the garden was a wizened, frail little woman, a sharp contrast to the plump, hearty Mrs. Beecham, but she seemed just as eager to gossip.

"Yes, come in," she said, her black eyes snapping. "Sit down."

"We can't stay but a minute, Mrs. Eversleigh." Drew pulled up a wicker chair for Madeline and then took one for himself.

"This is the American girl I was telling you about, Madge," Mrs. Beecham told her neighbor. "Miss Parker, we were just talking about the terrible goings-on at your uncle's company."

"Hello," Madeline said to her hostess, and then she nodded at Mrs. Beecham. "Yes, it was pretty terrible."

"And that poor man who was attacked, how is he today? He is staying at Farthering Place now, isn't he?"

Drew fought off a smile. There was nothing the ladies of the village missed. "He is. At least for a day or two. The whole thing was rather unnerving for him, as you might understand."

"It's a wonder we're not all murdered in our beds," Mrs. Beecham said, one hand over her heart.

"If we were, it wouldn't be any less than I've expected every night since the war," Mrs. Eversleigh put in, sounding mournfully delighted at the prospect. "The world's never been the same since."

"No. No, it hasn't," Mrs. Beecham sighed, and then her expression brightened. "And where are you two young people off to this afternoon?"

"We heard there was another American visiting," Drew said, "and Miss Parker thought she'd see if it was someone she knows."

Mrs. Beecham frowned. "Another American?"

"Oh, no," Mrs. Eversleigh said. "At least no one I've heard about."

"Nor I," Mrs. Beecham confirmed. "Why, even the ones we had have since gone."

"Have they?" Drew asked, glancing at Madeline. "When was this?"

"Oh, this morning, so they say," Mrs. Beecham said.

"And we never did get to meet that Mr. Flesch," her neighbor added. "He must have been very fond of his wife to be still so grieved."

"No one got to meet him?" Madeline asked.

"No, dear," Mrs. Beecham said. "He had all his meals brought up to him the whole time he was here."

"Well, Mr. Whiteside did say he took cold after he'd got here," Mrs. Eversleigh said, "although he did take the air some mornings later on. Still, such a shame to come all this way and never see anything. At least he didn't end up like Mr. Martindale. Once he took cold, he was here one moment and gone the next."

Mrs. Beecham made a sympathetic clucking noise. "Poor Mr. Martindale. And he was such fun at cards. He'd pretend he was holding one sort of hand and drop little hints about it. Made one feel so clever to have figured it out, and so foolish later to find he had won with something else entirely."

"And where did they go this morning?" Drew asked, turning over in his mind what she had just said. "Mr. Whiteside and Mr. Flesch?"

"Mr. Piggot at the station said they got tickets to Southampton. Sounds as though they'll be going straight back to America."

Drew stood, pulling Madeline up with him.

"I hope you'll excuse us, ladies. I've just remembered something I must see to." Drew replaced his hat with a brief bow. "It's been lovely seeing you both."

"Yes, good to meet you, Mrs. Eversleigh," Madeline called as Drew hurried her out the gate and toward the center of town.

"Young people are always in a hurry," Mrs. Beecham sighed, and her neighbor nodded.

"I tell you, it hasn't been the same since the war."

"Where are we going?" Madeline asked, struggling to keep up.

"If Whiteside and the supposed Mr. Flesch are still in Southampton, they may be worth talking to." Drew crossed the street, making a beeline toward the police station. "What the ladies said just now about their friend Martindale dropping little hints to set them wrong . . ."

She caught her breath. "You don't think—"

Drew pushed open the door to the police station and saw Police Constable Applegate at the desk. "You've got to ring up the police in Southampton, Jimmy, before Lincoln gets away."

— Seventeen —

In another minute, Applegate was on the telephone to the station in Southampton and then to Chief Inspector Birdsong at Farthering Place. Soon the constable and the chief inspector were on their way to the coast, with Drew and Madeline reluctantly in tow.

"It makes perfect sense," Drew insisted. "If Lincoln was supposed to be dead, he'd have to hide somewhere, but it would have to be somewhere near enough for him to carry on with his mischief. It would be easy enough for him to check into the Queen Bess as Mr. Flesch before he was supposedly killed in the greenhouse. Then all he need do is slip out via the trellis, show up at the house as Lincoln, kill Clarke to take his place, and slip back to the inn. And there's poor little Eddie to unwittingly cover his footmarks."

"Then Whiteside is in on it, too," Birdsong said.

"Obviously. But why?"

"The money, of course." The inspector wagged his thick finger in Drew's face. "We're not talking a few hundred in blackmail anymore."

"I realize that, but why? Whiteside's a rich man. He needn't do another day's work in his life if he doesn't like to, even if he lives a hundred years more and doesn't make another farthing."

"Some men's greed knows no bounds," Madeline said.

"Still, murdering for it?" Drew shook his head. "He doesn't at all seem the type."

"You're always saying you can't tell about people," she reminded him.

"Perhaps it's a game to him," Birdsong said. "See how much he can get away with and never be suspected."

"Then he oughtn't have been so clumsy with his tales about poor Mr. Flesch." Drew crossed his arms over his chest, struggling to keep a calm demeanor. They were close now.

"And what about the things in the room?" Birdsong asked. "The lipstick marks on the cigarettes and the napkin."

"Red herrings," Drew said. "What better way to turn suspicions the wrong way round?"

It wasn't long before they were in Southampton and, soon after, at the dock of the ship next leaving for New York City. An official request for a look at the passenger list showed a Mr. Whiteside and a Mr. Flesch booked for a first-class cabin. They had not yet checked in.

"The ship leaves in less than an hour. They'll have to show up soon."

"No need to worry, Mr. Farthering. I have men set up at both ends of the pier and on the ship itself. They won't be slipping away from us at this point."

As if they had been summoned, Whiteside and his companion showed up a few minutes later. Whiteside was his usual jocund self. His companion, shrouded in an overcoat and broad-brimmed hat, was still an enigma.

"All right," Birdsong said, and with a nod to the two waiting constables he stepped forward and took Whiteside's arm. "I'll have to ask you to come with me, gentlemen."

"Here now. What are you doing?"

"You are Mr. Jonas Whiteside of New York City?"

"Yes. And who the devil are you?"

Birdsong showed him his identification. "I am Chief Inspector Birdsong of the Hampshire Police. Now, if you and your *companion* would come along quietly—"

"I won't! I'm an American citizen and I'll be hanged if I'll come quietly. You there! Farthering! Tell these idiots who I am."

"It's not a question of who you are, sir," Drew said. "We do have some concerns about the elusive Mr. Flesch here."

The two constables already had custody of the man in the overcoat and hat. They hadn't yet attempted to remove the dark glasses and muffler that concealed his face.

"We're both Americans! We've broken none of your laws, and you have no right to hold us!"

Already a little gathering of the curious was taking place around them.

"You'd best come along, sir," Drew counseled. "And do stop shouting. No need to lay this all out in the street as it were."

"What are the charges, Inspector?" Whiteside demanded. "What laws have we broken? You can't just arrest us for nothing!"

"Perhaps our Mr. Flesch can clear everything up for us," Drew offered. "If you'll just remove your hat and those glasses, sir . . ."

"You can't do that," Whiteside protested. "Mr. Flesch has been very sick. It's a wet day, and it won't do him any good to catch a chill on the trip home."

Birdsong was obviously unimpressed. "Then we'll take him down to the police station and see he gets out of the damp."

"It will have to be one way or the other, sir," Drew said.

"What sort of country is this?" Whiteside roared. "It's barbaric!"

Birdsong merely went up to the suspect in the overcoat and pulled off his hat and glasses. "All right, Mr. Lin—"

There was a general gasp.

"That's Lucy Lucette, that is!" a man cried, followed by a rising babble of agreement.

The woman displayed her perfect smile to the crowd and shook loose her wealth of golden hair. Then she bit her full lower lip and tucked in her chin so she could give the inspector a coy look through her long, curling lashes. "I suppose you think I've been a naughty, naughty girl, Inspector."

"I think you'd best come along now, miss," Birdsong said. "And you, Mr. Whiteside."

"Publicity stunt," Drew said, fuming.

Madeline squeezed his hand. "Now, you know your Agatha Christie did just the same thing not five or six years ago."

"They don't know that for certain. She said she had a nervous breakdown and didn't know what she was doing. This . . . this so-called actress hasn't any such excuse."

"Well, they haven't actually broken any laws, have they?"

"I don't know that it isn't an offense to sign a hotel register under a false name," Drew said, adding a sanctimonious sniff for good measure.

Madeline snuggled against him in the back of the police car. "You have to admit, it worked pretty well. She's been all the talk since she disappeared. I'm sure *Arabella's Gilded Cage* will be a smash hit."

"But Whiteside! A man his age ought to know better. Especially with her climbing down trellises just to go gamboling about in the fields at night because her artistic temperament demands it, and him thinking he has her safely tucked out of sight."

Madeline smiled. "A man his age rarely knows better when it comes to a girl her age."

"And what in the world could she see in him?"

"I'm sure there are millions of reasons she would find him irresistible. All of them in his bank in New York City."

"And if this motion picture is a success, and he's backing it, then there will surely be a few million more," Drew observed. "The two of them should be beaten to death with the penulti-mate issue of *Silver Screen*."

"Why not the latest?"

"I might want to read that one."

"You're just mad because you didn't have everything figured out like you thought you did."

"Well, she may scheme all she likes. She'll never be another Constance Collier. Why, in ten years no one will remember the name Lucy Lucette. Perhaps five."

Madeline sighed. "It would have explained everything so neatly. Now we have to start all over again."

"Not all over. We just have to figure out where Lincoln has been hiding himself all this while, and where he plans to strike next." Drew turned to the chief inspector. "Did your men ever check out that cottage Mrs. Chapman sometimes lets out?"

Birdsong looked weary. "They did, I'm afraid. They spoke to the lady and to her tenant, a fellow from Ipswich. Definitely not Lincoln."

"Not Lincoln in a false nose and glasses?"

Birdsong pursed his lips. "No."

Before long, they were overlooking the village of Farthering St. John. Drew leaned toward the front seat and tapped Constable

Applegate's shoulder. "I say, Jimmy, would you mind popping us up to Farthering Place before you go back to your duties?"

"It's not really official police business, is it, sir?"

"It's all right, Applegate," Birdsong said. "Drop me at the station here first and then take them on up. It's not far."

Drew gave him a rueful smile. "Thank you, Chief Inspector. I feel rather embarrassed running you out to Southampton for nothing."

"Let that be a lesson, young man. I'm not saying it wasn't an interesting theory on your part, but you'd better let the police see to this investigation from now on. Every time we have to go chasing wild geese, that's time the real murderer has to think of how to get away."

Chastened again, Drew spent the rest of the drive back to Farthering St. John in silent contemplation of the quandary that remained to be solved.

P. C. Benson was waiting in front of the police station when they pulled up. Seeing his urgent expression, Birdsong put down the car window.

"You've got to go up to Farthering Place, sir. Right away. Mr. Parker is dead."

Drew felt Madeline's hand tighten on his arm, and he put his free hand over hers.

"What happened?" Birdsong asked.

"I don't have details at the moment, sir. All I was told is that he and Mr. Rushford had a quarrel and, defending himself, Rushford killed him."

"No," Madeline whispered.

Drew pulled her into his arms. "Hold on to me, darling."

She didn't cry. She didn't ask any questions. She merely clung to him, unmoving, hardly breathing.

"All right, Mr. Applegate," Birdsong ordered. "Farthering Place and quick as you can."

— Eighteen —

Several constables from the chief inspector's office in Winchester were already at Farthering Place by the time Drew and Madeline arrived. Dennison hurried down the front steps as soon as Birdsong's car slowed to a stop.

"It's Mr. Parker, sir."

Drew felt the pain in the very center of his heart grow even sharper. "Yes, I know."

"Where is he?" Madeline sped up the steps before anyone could stop her. "Where is he?"

"Madeline, darling . . ." Drew sprinted after her. "Wait!"

They rushed through the entryway, past the open door of the parlor, where Rushford was slumped in an overstuffed chair, being attended to by Min, past the maids and footmen clustered, frightened, in the hallway that led to Mason's study.

He was still sitting at his desk, still upright, with his arms hanging limp beside him. His head lolled to one side, but his eyes were open, startled, and his throat was a well of blood. The ivory-handled letter opener was still protruding from his neck. And scattered all around him were papers from the office: notes and formulas and columns of figures.

"Don't—" The words half strangling him, Drew held Madeline closer, pressing her face to his shoulder so she wouldn't keep looking at the horrible scene before them.

"Don't anyone touch anything," Birdsong ordered as he came in behind them. "And clear those people out of the hallway."

"When we heard the row," Dennison said once he had dismissed the staff, "we came in and found him just that way, Chief Inspector. No one's been allowed to tamper with anything, except we did put Mr. Rushford in the parlor and send for Dr. Wallace to see to him. As you might imagine, he was most distressed." He turned to Drew and Madeline. "I'm very sorry, sir. Miss."

"Shhh," Drew soothed, stroking Madeline's hair, but she was sobbing and trying to struggle away from him.

"Uncle Mason . . ."

"You can't go over there, darling," he murmured. "We mustn't touch anything."

"We have to help him."

Her eyes were wide and desperate, and he tightened his hold on her. "It's too late."

"No, he's—"

"He's gone, Madeline." He cupped her face in his hands, forcing her to look at him. "He's gone."

At first she merely stood there, her grip on his wrists tightening in painful increments, and then her expression wilted and she huddled against him, sobbing once more. He pressed his cheek against her hair, wishing, wishing for the blessed relief of tears.

"You'd better take the young lady away, sir," Birdsong advised. "Perhaps she ought to go up and lie down."

"I want to know what happened," Madeline insisted, pushing herself out of Drew's arms.

"You're very upset, miss—"

"Yes, Inspector, I am." Madeline blotted her face with her fingertips. "I'm extremely upset, and I want to know what happened."

Drew glanced again at the body in the chair. "Good heavens, can't we discuss this in another room?"

Once he had locked the room and pocketed the key, the chief inspector left a constable on duty at the study door and went with Drew and Madeline and Dennison into the sunny morning room across the hall.

Birdsong took out his notebook. "Now, Mr. Dennison, I'd like to know what's happened here."

"The study door was shut, sir, so no one saw anything. But we could hear some of it quite clearly, even as far away as the library."

"Some of it?"

"Yes, sir. Most of it wasn't intelligible at all, as though they were both talking at once."

"Tell me, as nearly as possible, their exact words. The part you could understand."

"Mr. Parker said 'No. I can't let you,' and Mr. Rushford cried out something along the lines of 'You're mad. Let me out of here. Someone, help.' There was a loud struggle, and I came to see what was happening, but the door was locked. By the time I had opened it, Mr. Parker was . . ." Dennison glanced at Madeline. "Well, just as you saw him there."

"If the door was locked, how did you get in?" Birdsong asked.

"I have keys to all the locks at Farthering Place, Inspector."

"I see. And what did Mr. Rushford say when you came in?"

"He was so terrified, he could hardly speak at all. We gave him some brandy and called his man down to look after him. After a while he was able to tell us what happened. He said he'd found something."

The chief inspector scowled. "Found something?"

"Yes, sir. Begging your pardon, Mr. Drew, Miss Parker, but he said he'd found evidence that showed Mr. Parker was behind all the goings-on at Farlinford and here at the house."

Madeline shook her head but said nothing.

"Did he say what it was?" Birdsong asked.

"No, sir. He said only that he wanted to confront Mr. Parker with it in the hope that he would make a clean breast of it to the police and give himself up. He said that, instead, Mr. Parker tried to kill him."

"Was that how it sounded to you, Denny?" Drew asked.

"I fear it was, sir. I can hardly believe it of Mr. Parker. If you'll pardon me, sir, I wouldn't believe it of him if I hadn't heard it myself."

That was that, then. Drew shut his eyes. "I wouldn't believe it either if you hadn't been the one to tell me."

Still Madeline said nothing.

"Is there anything else we should know about the incident?" Birdsong asked Dennison.

"I regret I cannot be of more assistance, Chief Inspector."

"That'll be all. I suppose I'd best go speak to Mr. Rushford now."

Rushford brought the teacup to his mouth, trying to sip from it and eventually sloshing tea down his white shirtfront before Min took the cup from him.

"Just try to relax, sir," Birdsong told him. "I know this hasn't been pleasant for you, but we have to clear some things up and then we'll let you go up for a rest. I understand the doctor's been here already."

"Doctor?" Rushford muttered, staring at the faces surrounding him.

"A Dr. Wallace, I believe, sir," Min said as he tried to blot his master's shirtfront. "He left to get something from car."

Drew pulled up a chair next to Rushford's. "Do you feel up to talking a bit?"

Rushford's rheumy eyes filled with tears, and he clutched Drew's arm. "It was terrible. Too, too terrible."

"Yes, it's awful. Can you tell us what happened?"

"I found some evidence, some things in the files at the office. More assets sold, more mortgages taken out, things that couldn't be done by someone who wasn't a director of the company. It had to be him or me, and I knew it wasn't me. I just wanted to talk to him. Just talk. I wanted him to do the right thing and go to the police with what he'd done. I didn't want there to be more scandal than need be. I didn't like to do it. I was afraid that if I confronted him, he would . . ." Rushford glanced at Madeline, sitting ashen-faced on the sofa across from him. "I was afraid he would make away with himself."

"But you did confront him?"

"Yes. I told him I must have a word with him in private, and he locked the study door. So we wouldn't be disturbed, he said, but I think he must have already known I had found him out. I told him what I had seen and that he would have to go to the police, or I would do so. He said he wasn't going to let me do that, and he grabbed that letter opener. He . . . he . . ." Rushford tried again to drink his tea, and this time he managed to get a little of it down. He wiped his mouth. "We struggled and fought, and then somehow I overpowered him and got hold of it, the letter opener, and stabbed him with it. I'll never know how."

The chief inspector made a note in his book. "What happened next, sir?"

"I must have fainted. I really can't say. Next thing I knew, I was in here and the doctor and Min were standing over me. I can hardly believe it even happened. Oh, Parker. Parker . . ."

Madeline was weeping now, and Drew went to sit next to her. "Hold on to me," he whispered, kissing her temple, and she did.

"Anything else you ought to tell us, sir?" Birdsong asked.

"I don't know," Rushford moaned. "Don't ask me anything more. I can't tell you anything."

Drew looked at Birdsong, who gave him a reluctant nod.

"Go ahead and help him up to his room, Min," Drew said. "Did the doctor give him anything to help him sleep?"

"He want to give him something, sir, but Mr. Rushford not want to take it."

"Why not, sir?" Drew asked, and a look of terror came into the old man's eyes.

"I don't need anything, just another drink. Something stronger than tea, eh?" He laughed, a weak, mirthless laugh that ended in another sob.

"It's all right, sir," Drew soothed. "You go on and lie down. We'll see to everything now."

Min helped Rushford to his feet, and leaning on his servant's arm, the old man tottered out of the room.

As soon as he was gone, Drew turned to Madeline. "I'd like you to go as well, darling."

"But—"

"No, really, you must now." Drew stood, bringing her with him. "You've heard what happened. The rest is just routine investigation and writing the report for the police."

"But—"

"He's right, miss," Birdsong said.

"Please, darling." Drew kissed her temple once more. "I promise I'll come tell you if there's anything else to know. Either way, I promise I'll come up for a bit after the police have done. Shall

I have Mrs. Devon come to look after you? Would you rather have Dr. Wallace?"

Madeline shook her head. "I'm all right."

"Promise me you'll go up?" Drew said, wishing more than anything he could stay here, holding her in his arms until this first shock had worn off somewhat. "Promise?"

Madeline sighed. "I promise."

He escorted her past the locked door of the study and to the foot of the stairs. "I'll be up to see you soon."

She merely nodded and went slowly up the stairs without a glance back.

Chief Inspector Birdsong and Dr. Wallace were already in the study when Drew got there. Both of them were staring at the body in the chair.

"No question about the cause of death, I suppose," Birdsong said.

"No." The doctor adjusted his spectacles and leaned forward to get a closer look at the gash in Mason's throat. "Not in the least."

Drew steeled himself and came closer, too. Now was not the time for personal feelings. Nor for grief. Nor for rage against a liar and a hypocrite. Mason was dead, and this whole ordeal was nearly at an end.

He drew a hard breath and forced himself to look at the wound and at the letter opener that made it—that sharp, wicked little blade that he himself had brought back from Italy as a gift for his stepfather. He looked up from the wound and into Mason's face. His eyes were open, and in the corner of one of them . . . Drew bit his lip and turned his back on the grisly scene.

"Are you all right, sir?" Birdsong asked.

"Yes. Yes, I'm sorry."

Once more Drew steeled himself, and then he turned again to face the chair. There was no mistaking it, the single tear that glistened in Mason's sightless eye.

Liar. Thief. Murderer.

Drew's heart rebelled at the thought, but his mind could find no way around it. There was work yet to be done here. It would be a simple exercise in logic now, nothing more, and that mostly solved at this point. Lincoln would have to be accounted for, but he'd be run to ground in time.

"What have you heard about the incident so far, Doctor?" Birdsong asked.

"Only that the old gentleman and Mr. Parker quarreled over their business and, well, this was the result. Tragic."

"Mr. Rushford didn't tell you what happened?" Drew asked.

"No, poor man. He was almost hysterical when I arrived and could hardly speak."

"Then what would you say, judging from the physical evidence, happened here?"

"Judging from the way things are scattered about, and the bruises on Mr. Rushford's arms, I'd say the two of them struggled, one or the other of them picked up the letter opener, and of course it was Parker here who got the worst of it. Little wonder Rushford was so shaken up."

"Yes," Drew said. "He could hardly hold his teacup when he was telling us about it. He managed to spill tea all down the front of his . . ." Drew knit his brow and looked once again at the wound in Mason's throat.

Birdsong did the same. "What is it?"

"If they were struggling here at the side of the desk where all the papers are knocked about, so he could have fallen back into the chair like that, wouldn't the blood have spattered outward?" Drew asked.

"It would," the doctor said. "As you can see by these papers and such, it did."

"But not on the man with the weapon?"

"Of course on the man with the weapon. Him more than anything else. He could hardly—"

"But there was no blood on Rushford," the chief inspector said. "Not on his hands. Not on his shirtfront."

"Exactly." Drew pointed to the letter opener. "I was wondering why this struck me as odd, and now I think I know. Suppose Rushford and Mason were standing here arguing, and then Mason picks up the letter opener and the two of them grapple for it. Now suppose Rushford gets the upper hand and stabs Mason. He is a good six inches shorter than my stepfather. I would think any wound to a taller man's throat would come from below, but look at this."

The inspector and the doctor both squinted and leaned closer.

"It's straight on or even downward a bit," the inspector said, "as if he was already sitting down when it happened."

The doctor nodded. "Which would explain the, um . . ." The doctor glanced at something over Drew's shoulder. "Ah, the way it, um . . ."

Drew turned and saw Madeline peering into the window.

"Pardon me, Dr. Wallace." Drew went to the window and opened it. "What are you doing? You promised me you would go up to your room."

"I didn't promise I wouldn't come down again."

Her face was tear-stained, but her eyes were clear, and her mouth was set in a firm line that would brook no denial.

"Madeline, darling—"

"Somebody's been out here." She looked down at the freshly turned dirt of the flower bed that followed the exterior wall.

There was one distinct footprint and part of another leading away from the window.

Birdsong was immediately at the window. "You're right about that, miss."

"Don't disturb anything," Drew said.

Madeline's eyes flashed. "I'm not that dumb."

"Darling, please . . ."

"Stay right there, miss, if you will," Birdsong said, and then he called one of his men from the hallway. "Go round and bring the young lady in, and then send some of the lads out to search the woods. Mind the footmarks out there."

"Right away, sir." The constable touched the brim of his hat and disappeared.

"I'd let you in this way," Drew told Madeline, "but you can't get over here except through the flower bed."

"Someone was in there when Uncle Mason was killed. Someone besides Mr. Rushford."

"If you'll come with me, please, miss," the constable said, and with another touch of his fingers to the brim of his hat he took Madeline's arm.

"Bring her in here, Davies," Birdsong ordered, and with a reproachful look at Drew, Madeline accompanied the constable back into the house.

"She's right, you know," Birdsong said. "Someone else was in here. But if that's true, why didn't Rushford say so?"

Drew nodded. "It does seem as if the blow came when he was already sitting down. From above and maybe a bit from the side, as if the blow came from behind him."

"Which is why the blood spattered on the papers and not on Rushford." Birdsong turned to Constable Davies, who had just returned from outside. "Post a man outside Mr. Rushford's door, Davies. And one below his window."

"Right away, sir."

Drew eyed the chief inspector. "You don't think Mr. Rushford . . ."

"No, no." Birdsong thought for a second. "Good heavens, no. The man's scared out of his wits. If Lincoln is still alive and someone is in it with him, it would have to be a cooler customer than our Mr. Rushford. He'd have fallen apart the first time Applegate questioned him."

"But the evidence . . ." Drew shook his head.

Birdsong remained unruffled. "We'll just have to go up and have a bit of a chat with the gentleman."

"I told you what happened. I told you!" Mr. Rushford pulled his bedcovers up to his sagging chin.

"It won't do, sir," Drew said. "We know it didn't happen as you said. You may as well come clean."

"I tell you, I killed him. I wish I could say it happened some other way, but there it is. I killed him. I killed him! Oh, can't you give me a moment's peace?"

Birdsong eyed him coolly. "Certainly, sir. As soon as you tell us what really happened in there."

"Who else was in the room, sir?" Drew pressed.

"No one. There was no one. Why would I make up such a ghastly story? Why would I tell you I'd been forced to . . . to . . ." Rushford groaned and covered his face with his hands. "I don't know anything about investigations. I can only tell you what happened when I was there. If someone was in there before I came, how could I know that?"

Birdsong tapped the cover of his notebook with the little stub of a pencil he carried. "You say you struggled for the letter opener—the knife—and you eventually stabbed him to defend yourself. Is that right, sir?"

"Yes, yes. How many times must I say it?"

"There was a considerable amount of blood, sir. On the body and on the papers on the desk and the floor. Why was there none on you?"

Rushford looked panic-stricken. "I . . . I don't know. I tell you I just can't remember what happened after I killed him. Not until I was already in the parlor. I don't know."

"Excuse, please." Min bowed to the chief inspector. "I wash Mr. Rushford's hands after they call for me. They have very much blood on them."

"I see." Birdsong was clearly unconvinced. "Was that the palms of his hands or the backs of them? Or both?"

Min thought for a moment. "Palms of hands, sir. Very much blood."

"But not the backs of his hands?"

"No, sir."

Drew looked around the room. "Do you still have the shirt and coat he was wearing, Min?"

Min bowed. "I will bring them."

When Min returned with the garments in question, Drew spread them over the bed, across Rushford's knees.

"Have you cleaned these, Min?"

"No, sir. I have not yet had opportunity."

Drew brushed his fingers over the brown stains on the front of the shirt. "Here is where you spilled your tea a bit ago, isn't it, sir?"

Rushford gnawed his lower lip but said nothing.

Drew continued examining the garments. "Are you right-handed, sir, or left?"

"Right," Rushford breathed. "I'm right-handed."

"Hmmm." Drew looked over the right sleeve of the shirt and then the right sleeve of the coat, and then he leaned down, searching Rushford's face. "How is it that there is no blood on your sleeve, sir?"

Rushford burst into tears. "He'll kill me. God help me, he'll kill me if I say a word."

"Who, sir?"

"No, no, no." The old man shook his head and pressed both hands hard over his lips.

Drew took hold of his wrists. "Was it Lincoln?"

Rushford shook his head, making muffled wailing noises down deep in his throat, and Drew shook him a bit harder than he meant to.

"Tell me, was it Lincoln?"

The chief inspector put his hand on Drew's shoulder, pulling him back. "Let me see to this."

Drew immediately released his grip and paced to the other side of the room. "Sorry."

"Now, Mr. Rushford . . ." Birdsong gently moved the old man's hands away from his mouth. "You'll have to tell us, sir, whatever it is. You needn't be afraid. We'll have officers looking after you round the clock if need be."

Rushford's lip quivered, but he nodded and seemed a bit calmer.

"That's better," Birdsong said. "Now, tell us what happened this afternoon in Mr. Parker's study."

Rushford pulled up a corner of his sheet and used it to wipe his face. Min handed him a clean handkerchief.

"I . . . I went to talk to Parker, just as I said I had. I knew he was in this whole plot from the beginning, and I told him so. At first, he acted as if he didn't know what I was talking about. I told him what proof I had and that I was going to the police.

He said he wouldn't let me do that." Rushford looked up at Birdsong and then at Drew, his red-rimmed eyes filling again with tears. "It was Lincoln. He had been behind the drapes there in the corner of the study all along. Before I knew what was happening, he came up behind Parker in his chair there and stabbed him with that knife. Stabbed him right in the throat!"

"Steady on, sir," Birdsong soothed.

Rushford managed to compose himself again. "I suppose he'd grabbed the knife off the desk before Parker came into the study in the first place, in case someone found him hiding there."

Drew frowned. "But why would he—?"

"Let him tell it, Mr. Fathering," Birdsong said.

Drew sagged down into the overstuffed chair in the corner of the room, suddenly remembering how he had sat there the night Constance was murdered, wishing he could bury his face in his arms and cry. He'd have to tell Denny to remove this chair when this was all over.

"What happened after Lincoln stabbed Parker?" Birdsong asked.

"He told me I had better do just as he said or he'd give me the same as he gave Parker. He said he didn't want Parker around anymore. He didn't want to have to share what they'd taken. He said he'd been wanting to kill him anyway, and my showing up gave him the perfect way out. He said I was to tell the police I'd killed Parker in self-defense."

"I see."

"He said you'd believe me, Inspector, because I'd have nothing to gain by lying about it. He'd already made me tell you I was mistaken about hearing his voice that night at the office. He said if I convinced you it was Parker who'd done everything, then you'd stop looking for him. And if I didn't, he said he'd find me, wherever I was, and kill me, but not as quickly as he had Parker. Then he made me . . ." Rushford's face turned a sickly shade of green, and Birdsong took his arm.

"Made you what, Mr. Rushford?"

"He . . . he made me put my hands in the blood."

Birdsong gave him another moment to compose himself. "Then what did he do, sir?"

"We heard Dennison at the study door, so Lincoln went out the window and across the lawn. Into the woods, I suppose. I think I may have fainted then in earnest." Rushford wiped his face again. "I was so terrified, I was sure my heart would give out on me right there."

"Perhaps you should bring Mr. Rushford some brandy, Min," Drew suggested.

Min bowed and left the room.

Rushford let out a breath and then dredged up the tiniest of smiles. "You've been too kind, Chief Inspector. Really too kind. I know I should have come to you from the very first, when that mountebank said he wanted to be paid off to keep quiet about my taking that money from the company back in '22. It would have stopped all this from happening if I'd just stood up to him then."

"It's hard to say," Birdsong said. "It's been my experience that some men are just dead set on doing wrong. Thwart them one way and they'll try another."

Rushford's brittle smile faded. "He will get me in time, won't he?"

"Don't you worry yourself, sir. My men are searching the grounds and the woods for him. He can't hide himself forever."

"Did he say where he'd been all this while?" Drew asked.

"No." Rushford's lip quivered. "There wasn't time. It all happened so quickly. He'd killed Parker, Dennison was at the door . . ." He squeezed his eyes shut. "Maybe Parker had been hiding him, but I don't know how."

"We've searched Farthering Place more than once," Drew said. "Though I suppose an accomplice might be able to pull it off with a bit of sleight of hand."

"Never you mind that," Birdsong said. "We'll have the dogs on him now that we know he's out there. You just rest easy, Mr. Rushford. My men will find him."

Min returned with a snifter of brandy, and Rushford downed it with a little gasp. "It does sting a bit," he admitted with an apologetic smile. "Thank you, Inspector. I shall try as best I can to put all this from my mind. Oh dear, I shall never sleep again."

"Try to relax," Drew said, yet it seemed the brandy was helping already. Mr. Rushford was already looking groggy as his head sagged back onto the pillows.

Min went to the open door and bowed. "If gentlemen will please excuse . . ."

"Quite right." Drew stepped into the hallway. "Inspector, I believe we have some dogs to see to."

"Nothing, sir."

The young police constable stood stiffly before the chief inspector, his face blank.

"What do you mean, 'nothing'?" Birdsong demanded.

"I'm sorry, sir, but the dogs aren't picking up anything."

A pair of chocolate-and-white springer spaniels sniffed around at his feet.

"What did you give them?"

"Lincoln's trousers, sir."

"Which ones?" Drew asked.

The constable held up a pair of white flannel trousers. "These, sir."

"Those are the ones he wore the morning before the party, aren't they?" Birdsong asked.

"As best I remember, yes." Drew looked them over. "Are these the only white flannels in his kit?"

"Yes, sir."

"I expect they're the ones, then. What about the mysterious shoes we found in the library?"

"We tried those, as well. The dogs get nothing from them. They're either new or they've been carefully cleaned."

"What sort of dogs are these, Inspector?" Drew asked, scowling at the animals.

"What do you mean?"

"They look a bit seedy, if you ask me."

Birdsong drew himself up. "Maisie and Ranger have been on the force three years now. If they can't find Lincoln, he's just not there."

"No offense meant, Inspector," Drew hurried to explain, and then he bent down and touched the brim of his hat. "No offense, Maisie. Ranger."

Ranger merely looked at him with large, sad eyes. Maisie scratched herself under the chin, not even acknowledging his apology.

Drew looked at the inspector. "So, shouldn't they be out there? Finding?"

Birdsong muttered something to himself, then turned back to his constable. "Why aren't they in the wood by now?"

"I'm sorry, sir. We had them there, but they didn't pick up the scent. We brought them up here to see if they could get it from the footprints in the flower bed, but they still haven't picked up anything."

Birdsong took the trousers from him and held them down to the dogs, who eagerly sniffed them. "All right, Ranger, Maisie girl, find him. Go on. Find him."

Both dogs snuffled around on the ground for a while, in the flower bed and across the lawn in the direction of the forest, but soon they came back and sat at the constable's feet.

"You don't think he's tried to mask his scent, do you?" Drew asked. "I mean, with pepper or some such?"

"It doesn't seem so, sir," the constable replied. "Doesn't seem like anything's been disturbed apart from the prints in the flower bed there. I understand your gardener had turned it recently?"

"That's right."

"And you can see where our suspect carried a bit of the fresh dirt out to the grass here, but that's where we lose him."

Drew nodded. "Could he have gone back into the house?"

"That would be rather daft of him, wouldn't it, sir?"

"Yes, but if he's been hiding there all along, perhaps it wouldn't be so daft. After all, where would be the last place you'd look for him?"

"Come on," Birdsong told his constable. "Bring the dogs."

But a search of the house, from larder to lumber room, turned up nothing. They even searched poor Mr. Rushford's room. He was lying on the bed still, but had pushed all the bedclothes off himself, shoving them all to the side of the bed against the wall, cowering against them when the police came into the room, fretting and muttering to himself until, their search done even as far as the underside of the bed, they left.

By the time it was all over, the police photographers had finished with the study, and Dr. Wallace had taken Mason's body away. Tessa, who did most of the heavy work around Farthering Place, was on her hands and knees, trying to scrub the dark stains out of the carpet in the study. It would have to be replaced.

Drew didn't know if he'd ever be comfortable in this room again. Someday, perhaps, he would be able to look across that desk and not see Mason sprawled in the chair with that evil blade driven into his throat. Someday.

Madeline had at last gone to her room to lie down. He'd wanted to comfort her, to be comforted by her, but he couldn't afford that luxury just yet. Not with a murderer still on the loose. Besides, if he stayed with Birdsong and helped with the investigation, he wouldn't have to think about Mason too much. Liar, thief, and murderer.

"What now, Inspector?"

Birdsong stroked his heavy mustache, his brows drawn together in supreme displeasure. "I'll have him. By George and England, I'll have him."

He stalked off, and Drew watched him go.

"No, Inspector," he said to himself. "I'll have him first."

— Nineteen —

The sun had set before Madeline came downstairs. She sat next to Drew in the library, saying nothing.

"You should see the kittens, darling," he said finally. "They're getting bigger, and I expect their eyes will be open soon."

Her lips trembled into a bit of a smile. "Really?"

"Would you like to come see them? The little white fellow seems about ready to venture out on his own."

She wiped one eye with the back of her hand, still forcing a smile. "You like him especially, don't you?"

"He reminds me for all the world of my old Latin professor, Mr. Chambers. It's hard to say which of them is more like a stoat."

That made her laugh, but the laughter quickly turned to tears.

For her sake, for his own, he hadn't wanted things to turn out as they had. He'd wanted desperately to believe there was some other explanation for everything that had happened, but there wasn't one. There just wasn't.

"I'm sorry," he murmured, holding her close. He kissed her hair and then her cheek. "So, so sorry."

"It's not right," she sobbed. "It's not right. He couldn't have done it. He just couldn't."

"I'm sorry—"

"Stop saying you're sorry!" She shoved herself away from him, her periwinkle eyes flashing behind the tears. "Isn't this what you wanted? Isn't this what you were trying to prove all along?"

"Prove?" He shook his head. "I wasn't trying to prove anything except the truth."

"All of this . . ." She made a sweeping gesture, encompassing everything that had happened that day. "This isn't the truth. Not if you think it means Uncle Mason was behind everything."

He took a deep breath. "Then what does it mean? Who is behind it all?"

"I don't know," she admitted. "But it wasn't Uncle Mason."

"What else explains everything? Who else was in a position to carry this off as it was? Who else would have a reason to kill Constance and rob Farlinford?"

"I don't know. And I don't know why you would want him to be guilty."

"I never—"

"You're all in such a hurry to close this case, to fit it into your neat little explanation, you don't even look at all the possibilities. I thought you wanted to find the truth."

"I do, I just . . ." He could see that nothing he could possibly say at this point would soothe her pain, so he let a few seconds pass in silence. "What would you like me to do?"

"Find out the truth."

Sudden tears filled her eyes, and she ran out of the library. Bewildered, he let her go.

Drew watched Madeline as she stood at the head of the grave, pale and still, her slender shoulders slumped, her eyes shadowed and empty. He wished her friends, Miss Holland and even that

Brower girl, were here with her. She could probably do with a touch of the familiar just now, a touch of home. But she had refused to send a message telling them what had happened to her uncle. And when they sent her a telegram saying they had heard the news, she had fired back a reply telling them not to come, that she'd rather they finished their tour. So now she was alone.

It had been a tense three days since Mason's death. The police continued their search for Lincoln without the slightest progress, and their investigation of Mason's private papers was equally fruitless except for some personal memos, a jumbled stack of formulae and notes to do with petroleum processing that had unquestionably once filled the empty drawer in McCutcheon's filing cabinet. It wasn't enough to close the case, of course, but it made up the vicar's mind irrevocably. Mason was not to be buried next to Constance in the churchyard.

The Reverend Mr. Bartlett was very kind and understanding regarding Madeline's pleas, but he was firm. He could not, in the face of the strong objections of his parishioners and of his own conscience, allow a murderer to be buried in consecrated ground at the side of the woman he had murdered. The vicar was good enough to agree to a quiet service at a burial at Farthering Place, and it was all he could do under the circumstances. Considering that most people thought Mason should have been buried in the prison graveyard after being hanged, it was quite a kindness. Perhaps one day Madeline would appreciate it.

Drew ached to stand there beside her, to hold her gloved hand, to slip his arm around her and draw her close, but no doubt she would rebuff him. He had failed her beloved uncle. It wasn't rational, but there it was. If only there was some way yet to prove Mason's innocence. Drew wanted to believe. He did. Just as he wanted to believe the vicar's words, the words he'd last heard too short a time ago.

"In sure and certain hope of the resurrection unto eternal life . . ."

He saw Madeline's eyes close, and a single tear slipped down the sweet curve of her cheek, only to be lost in the blackness of her dress. But when she opened her eyes, there was again that expression of peace he'd seen at Constance's funeral, as if her hope truly was sure and certain.

Their eyes met, and she immediately looked down. Drew sighed. She was still angry. If nothing else was, that at least was sure and certain.

Soon fragrant lilies and clods of earth were laid over the casket and the funeral was over. Besides Madeline and Drew, only a handful of mourners had come to the little grove of willows that was Mason's final resting place: Nick, Denny, Mrs. Devon, Mason's man Plumfield, old Peterson and his missus, and a few others of the staff.

Peterson stopped briefly, hat in hand. "I don't believe it of him, Mr. Drew, sir. I just don't."

"I know, Mr. Peterson. This has come as quite a shock to all of us."

"There's something else you ought to know, sir. Someone's taken my wheelbarrow and my millstone. Out of the shed, mind you, and took pains to cover his tracks."

Drew sighed. "Anything else missing?"

"Not as I seen, sir, though I can't think what a murderer would want with them."

"Perhaps it's nothing to do with Lincoln and all the rest."

"That may be, sir." Peterson did not look convinced. "Just thought you'd better know."

"Yes, certainly. Thank you, Mr. Peterson."

"Respects to the family, sir." Peterson replaced his hat, gave the brim a tug, and then was gone.

A wheelbarrow and a millstone. The wheelbarrow to carry the millstone, like as not, but the millstone itself? Drew rubbed his eyes. He didn't know why anyone would steal those things. He didn't want to think of it anymore.

As the rest of the mourners filed past on their way back to the house, Drew acknowledged the condolences as graciously as he could manage, but he did not want their comfort. He wanted the comfort of soothing the heart he had so unwillingly broken.

"Talk to her," Nick hissed beside him.

"I can't," Drew replied through clenched teeth. "She won't— Thank you, Mrs. Devon. Yes, quite a shock to us all. Tea would be much appreciated, thank you." He glared at Nick over the woman's shoulder.

"Why not?" Nick asked once she was gone.

Drew glanced once more toward the graveside. Madeline was still there, alone now, with her head bowed and her hands clasped together and her black veil quivering in the breeze.

"She wants to be alone," he said, looking away. "And if she did want someone, it wouldn't be me."

"Fine," Nick said. "Then I'll talk to her."

"Nick—"

But Nick had already loped over to the grave. In another moment he was back. "She'd like to see you, if you don't mind."

Drew looked toward her once more. She had drawn her veil over her face now, so it was hard to read her expression, especially from where he stood.

Nick gave him a little shove. "Go on."

Finally, Drew set off through the wet grass. She didn't look up when he approached her.

He cleared his throat, but still she did not acknowledge him. "Madeline?"

"I'm sorry."

Her voice was only a whisper, and he leaned down a bit, wanting to catch her words and see her face. "What did you say?"

"I know it wasn't your fault." She lifted her eyes to his in remorseful appeal. "I didn't stop to think that you might be grieving, too. And I do want to know the truth. Whatever it is."

He took her hand. "I thought you would."

She nodded, and her hand tightened on his. "But I still don't think Uncle Mason was a thief. Or a murderer."

He resisted the temptation to go over all the evidence once again. "I know you don't."

She managed a subdued smile. "What are you going to do now?"

"Don't know," he admitted. "See if old Rushford and I can get Farlinford back on her feet, I expect."

"I mean about the investigation."

"Birdsong says he's closing it, except to still try to track down Lincoln. They're satisfied with the conclusions they've drawn."

She slid her hand out of his. "I'm not satisfied."

"I realize that. I didn't expect you would be."

"You knew him."

He knit his brow, puzzled. "Yes?"

"How can you leave things this way?"

"The evidence—"

"There are too many things that don't fit. Who was the American on the phone? Why would Uncle Mason send Mr. Rushford to the office to be robbed if the papers he wanted were already here in his desk? Why . . ." She pressed her handkerchief to her eyes and took a quavering breath. "I'm sorry. I do know it's not your fault. He wasn't your uncle. Or your father."

He took her arm to lead her away from the grave, away from Mack and Bobby in their earth-stained work clothes standing at the edge of the trees, shovels ready.

"It's all right," he soothed. "We can talk about it at home, if you like. You'll feel better with a nice cup of tea and some of Mrs. Devon's biscuits."

But when he took her home, they didn't talk about it. She sat mutely over her tea, taking no more than a sip or two before returning to her room.

She didn't come down to dinner, so Drew's only company was Nick. The good fellow made a valiant attempt to keep a cheerful conversation going, but getting little more than a word or two from Drew in response, he lapsed into uncomfortable silence by the end of the second course. As soon as the meal was over, Drew excused himself and headed upstairs. It was getting late, anyway. A hot bath and a sound night's sleep would help clear his thinking, he was certain.

"You knew him."

He thought of Madeline's words and the bewildered pain in her eyes as she said them.

"You knew him."

He sent Denny away and ran his own bath, laid out his own pajamas, but the activity did not chase away the picture of her. He *had* known Mason. He'd liked him, too. But was it rational to believe his innocence in spite of all the evidence to the contrary?

Stubborn, that's what she was.

"You knew him," he heard again, and closing his eyes he immersed himself in the bath water.

Still he saw her face, her pleading eyes. And he saw Mason. Kind, gentle Mason. Embezzling, scheming, murdering Mason.

"You knew him."

"Fine," he spat once he was forced to come up for air. "God, what does she want from me?"

He stopped himself. Before, he might have used that name thoughtlessly, as little more than an expression of frustration. But now, alone with nothing but the sound of the water that dripped from his hair, he knew it was something more. He drew his knees up to his chest and rested his forehead on them. "God," he whispered, "what do *you* want from me?"

"*. . . thou hast a name that thou livest, and art dead.*"

It wasn't someone else. It was Drew himself. Deep inside him, inside the hollow meaninglessness, he knew it. No wonder the words wouldn't leave him alone.

"*. . . thou hast a name that thou livest, and art dead.*"

He ought to be on his knees. Wasn't that how the humble supplicant was best received?

He stood and let the water run off him and back into the tub, and then he sloshed to the edge of the bath and stepped out onto the chilly floor. As naked and wet as when he had come into the world, he knelt there on the black-and-white tiles and bowed his head.

"God, help me. Show me something. Anything. I want to believe he was innocent. I want to believe you're there. I want to believe there's something right in the world. But how do I believe something I don't believe?" He laughed, a silent, convulsive little laugh from somewhere painful inside himself. "I suppose I must believe you're there, mustn't I? I'm praying to you."

He pressed the heels of his hands against his eyes and twined his fingers into his still-dripping hair.

"I don't exactly know what to say or what you want. I don't suppose I *could* say anything you don't already know. I only . . ." He ducked his head, feeling the hot sting of tears, fighting them, and then he looked up again.

"*. . . thou hast a name that thou livest, and art dead.*"

"Don't leave me this way," he whispered. Then he turned his face up. "I have it on very good authority that you accept all comers, no matter how slowly they come. Provided, of course, they do come. I hope it doesn't matter if they come to you because there's just nowhere else to turn."

Hadn't even the disciples in the presence of the Lord himself said there was nowhere else to go for the words of life? Drew took a hard breath and lowered his head again.

"Dominus illuminatio mea," he said, and a tear slipped down his cheek, only to be swallowed up by the widening puddle that surrounded him. "Oh, God, be my light. Show me something, anything to cling to. Lord Jesus—"

He lifted his head, abruptly breaking the prayer. There was a tapping at his door. He scrambled to his feet and grabbed one of the thick towels that had been warming at the radiator. He scrubbed the water from his face, and then, wrapping the towel around his hips, he hurried to the door.

"Yes? Who is it?"

"It's me." She hesitated for a moment. "It's Madeline."

"Madeline!" He reached for the doorknob and then stopped himself. "Is everything all right?"

"I need to talk to you." Her voice was soft and urgent.

"Uh, I'll just be a moment."

He snatched the towel from around his hips and used it to blot the water from his hair. He then toweled off his arms and legs and chest. Once he had thrown on his robe and thrust his feet into his slippers, he opened the door.

"Oh, I didn't . . ." Madeline felt the heat rise in her face. "I was hoping you hadn't gone to bed already."

"Bath, actually," he said with a pale imitation of his usual smile, and she wished he could have somehow been in his typical breezy mood. It would make everything else so much easier.

"I suppose I should wait until tomorrow."

"If you'd like," he said. "It would be a bit more conventional. Or if you'd rather, you can wait just a bit in my study while I put on something a little more suited for a lady's company."

She nodded, and he opened the door wide enough to admit her. In another moment he had her settled on the tufted settee under his window.

"I'd ring for some coffee or something, but no use scandalizing Denny this time of the night."

"I don't want any coffee." She shouldn't have come. It would be too easy now to lose her resolve, to say and do things she didn't mean or at least that she shouldn't mean. "I'll just wait for you."

He smiled again. "Won't be a tick."

In less than five minutes he returned to her, wearing dark trousers and a white shirt, socks but no shoes. He hadn't taken the time to put in cuff links or button his shirt at the neck. He hadn't taken much time to dry himself either, judging by the way his thin shirt clung to his back and how it had turned transparent enough in places to reveal the undershirt beneath.

He patted his slicked-back hair and sat beside her. "Bit of an improvement, what?"

"I sort of liked it the way it was," she admitted.

"Anything to please," he said, and with both hands he ruffled his hair into a spiky mess. "Better?"

She laughed, but she couldn't help the tears that sprang to her eyes.

He took her hand, cradling it in both of his. "What is it?"

"I'm going home."

"But I don't want you to go."

He said it as if that should be enough, and for a moment it was. No, she'd have to be strong now. She'd have to be strong.

"I don't want you to go," he said again, and he brought her hand to his lips.

How could she resist those lips and those eyes? She tried to pull away, but he clung to her hand. Then he pulled her into his arms.

"I need you," he breathed, and his breath was warm against her neck. "I need you as surely as I need food and drink and sleep to sustain my life. Truly. Madeline, don't go."

She hesitated, afraid. What men would say in the cold loneliness of night was often very different from what they claim to have said come morning. She reminded herself that deceit could come as easily from handsome lips as plain ones and tried once more to pull away from him.

Abruptly he knelt before her and took her hand once more. "Marry me, Madeline. I love you terribly."

She shook her head. "You can't mean that. We barely know each other. We—"

"I mean it. I know it's insane, but I also know what I feel." He pressed her hand with a passionate kiss. "I need you. I love you."

Her heart pounded, but she knew what she had to do. She managed an indulgent, half-cynical smile, and brought his hand to her heart. "And I love you." Her voice was husky and heavily accented, another imitation of Garbo. "Our souls are but two halves of one whole."

He took his hand from her and got to his feet. "It's cruel to tease."

His voice was soft and wounded. Ashamed, she stood and touched his cheek. "I only said that because . . ." She closed her eyes to keep them from spilling over tears. They were melting the last bit of her resolve. "I should never have said it, but I meant it truly. Every bit of it." She opened her eyes to see an eager, answering light in his own.

"You did?"

With a shy little nod, she ducked her head against his shoulder, breathing in the clean scent of him, of sun-dried linen and fresh soap.

He kissed her lips, tender and sweet, and then held her wrapped in his arms.

"I love you," she whispered, leaning up to kiss the corner of his jaw. "But I have to go."

He stepped back from her, and his eyes lost the pleading softness that had made them so hard to resist. "You're still angry with me."

She shook her head. "Not angry. Not anymore. Not really. I'm just sad and disappointed. I thought if no one else would champion Uncle Mason, you would. Instead you leave him forever branded a murderer and a thief. It's not right. I know—"

"You think you know, but people aren't always what they seem. I was very sure about my father, too." For a moment he didn't say anything. "I'm sorry about Mason. Truly I am." He looked down. "I guess I loved the old boy, too."

"But he would never have—"

"Look here, Madeline, I love your stubborn loyalty, your belief even in the face of hard evidence, but there has to be a time when you let it go. No matter how lovely the fantasy, we eventually have to grow up and see the truth."

She released his arm and faced him, her mouth set in a firm line. "And sometimes it's not the belief that is wrong, just the interpretation of the evidence."

She turned on her heel and started toward the door, but he grabbed her hand and turned her back to him.

"What do you want me to do?" he asked. "I tried. I wanted to believe he was innocent. I wanted to believe everything you believe. Do you know I even . . ." His mouth turned up in a little smirk. "I even prayed. I even . . ." He swiped the back of his hand over his eyes. "I got down on my knees like a schoolboy and begged God to show me, somehow, if there was some other explanation for all this. If Mason really was the man we all thought for so long that he was. If He was even there listening. And I thought you were my answer." He grimaced. "I must have looked quite the fool."

"Drew, no," she murmured, her eyes brimming with tears, and she squeezed his hand. "You can't—"

"I can."

He slipped his hand out of hers and went to the door, opening it to show her out, but she took his hand again.

He stood looking at her, that wounded disappointment in his gray eyes, in every vulnerable line of his face.

The tears spilled down her cheeks, and she reached up to caress his face. "I . . ." She smiled a little. "I think we should make a bargain."

He laughed half under his breath. "A bargain?"

"You asked God to show you if there was another explanation for all this, if Uncle Mason was innocent."

"Yes?"

"I've asked Him to show me if I was being foolish to believe Uncle Mason wasn't guilty in the face of all the evidence."

"And?"

"Well, one of us has to be right. We'll just have to both pray that He'll show us which one it is." Again she stroked his cheek. "But we can't give up."

He laughed softly and wrapped her again in his arms. "You will drive me mad, you know that. But it will be the loveliest, most wonderful madness ever to overwhelm a man."

She couldn't help herself. She started sobbing against his shoulder. "How can you be so wonderful and so horrible all at the same time?"

"Sorry," he said. "But you won't go?"

Again she couldn't help herself. She started giggling, giggling and crying and clinging to him. "I won't say I'll marry you, but I won't go. Not yet."

"Darling," he breathed, and he kissed her once again, sweet at first, but then with more and more intensity, dizzying her with kisses until he finally pulled away from her.

"Perhaps you'd better go, after all," he said, and her heart dropped.

"You want me to?"

"Just back to your room, darling." He took an unsteady breath. "You're far too tempting."

"And you're not?" She laughed and touched her fingers to his lips. "I can't believe we've known each other only a few days."

"Eleven."

"You're sweet to keep count." She touched his lips once more, aching for another taste of them, and then she looked away. "And sweet to not try to take advantage."

There was a hint of wry wistfulness in his smile. "We're both a bit too cut up just now to reason clearly, don't you think? I guess we could both use some comforting, but I don't want there to be any regrets between us. Not ever."

Tears again filled her eyes. He was only making her want him more. "I love you for that."

"I want you to keep on loving me." He wrapped her again in his arms, warm and tight, and then kissed her hair. "Come, darling. Time you got some sleep."

After he took Madeline to her room, stealing just one more kiss at her door, Drew walked back down the long hallway, his steps slow and deliberate.

"Which is it?" he whispered. "If you're there, if you're listening, give me a clue here."

"... *thou hast a name that thou livest, and art dead.*"

That one Scripture gnawed at him still. Why wouldn't it leave him alone?

"She says Mason's innocent. But the evidence says he's not. Well, which is it? Which of us is right? If it wasn't Mason, then who—?"

Something moved at the edge of his vision and then disappeared. Lincoln?

Drew sprinted after the apparition, a figure in black moving soundlessly into the darkness of the hallway that led to the other wing of the house, and with a final burst of speed, Drew caught it by the shoulders and spun it to face him.

"Rushford!"

The old man sagged against the wall with a whimpering cry, and Drew was forced to hold him up.

"Steady on, sir. I *am* sorry. I thought perhaps I'd nabbed Lincoln at last."

Rushford was white to the lips, but he managed a faint laugh. "And I thought for certain he had me." He pressed his hand to his heart, over the brocade bathrobe that was not actually black, merely a deep plum. "Oh, my word, young man, you should make your presence known."

"Sorry about that. Why in the world didn't you put on the lights?"

"It's rather late, you know. I hated to disturb anyone. I thought I'd have a bath to relax and found I was out of soap, so I just nipped downstairs for some."

"You look as if you'd already bathed," Drew said, seeing the man's hair, what he had of it, was wet.

"Yes, well." Rushford smoothed one hand over his head. "I had already gotten into the bath when I realized about the soap."

"You should have rung for someone. Shall I call your man?"

"I sent him back home earlier this evening actually. To see to some things for me." They had reached Rushford's room by then, and the old man put one hand on the doorknob. "You might like to know I'll be leaving tomorrow. Time we all got back to something like a normal life."

"I suppose you're right, sir. Though you're more than welcome to stay here as long as you like."

"You're very kind, but I'm leaving England."

"Leaving?"

"The chief inspector said I needn't stay until Lincoln's caught. They'll call me back over when he's brought to trial."

"Where will you go?"

"Back to Canada. I put my house up with an estate agent today and booked passage on a ship sailing tomorrow."

"That's a bit sudden, isn't it, sir?"

"Perhaps so, but I want to be somewhere out of Lincoln's reach. It's far enough, isn't it? And the police will keep us safe tonight, won't they?" He looked at Drew with tired, pleading eyes and grasped his sleeve. "I know I'm a coward. But I just can't live this way any longer. I have to have some peace, don't you see?"

"Perfectly understandable." Drew patted his hand, gently removing it, but Rushford clung to him, his other hand still on the doorknob.

"You wouldn't . . . you wouldn't come in and have a look round, would you? I know there's a constable posted and all that, but Lincoln's been so elusive."

Drew took his arm. Rushford's fears were making him feel a little unsettled himself. "If he's in there, we'll soon have him out."

Stiffening his spine and his resolve, Drew eased open the door. There was only stillness. "Seems quite empty, sir."

"Would you mind checking the wardrobe?"

With more indulgent confidence than he felt, Drew flung open the wardrobe. Relieved, he poked about in the meager contents. "Nothing here."

Rushford's eyes flickered toward the heaped tangle of sheets and coverlet on the bed. "You don't suppose . . ."

Drew pulled the coverlet onto the floor, prodded the sheets and, for good measure, looked under the bed. "I'd say you're safely alone, sir."

The color returning to his face, Rushford sank into an easy chair. "I daresay I'm an old fool, but with what happened to Parker and all . . ." He put one hand over his face. "I've got to get away from all this. My nerves are completely gone."

Drew poured an inch or so of the brandy from the decanter on the dresser and pressed Rushford's free hand around it. "Buck up, sir. You'll be away from here tomorrow. We'll see to everything here."

The old man downed the brandy, then grabbed Drew hard by the wrist. "Listen here, if I don't make it to the morning—"

"Sir, I—"

"Hear me out." Rushford's eyes were fever-bright, his face intent. "Lincoln's eluded everyone so far. He got to Parker even after we knew he might be about the house somewhere. If he gets to me, you'll be the last. You'll own Farlinford outright. It's fairly ruined at this point, but you can build it up again. You've enough of your father in you to make a go of it. You do it for him and for his father and grandfather before him. For all the Fartherings." His expression softened. "And for an old fool who hasn't anyone else."

It was deuced awkward, but Drew couldn't help feeling for the old boy, alone as he was.

"I'll give it a go. Don't you worry." He took a quick look behind the curtains, made sure the window was securely latched, and then went back to Rushford. "You'd best get to bed, sir. Sounds as though you've got a busy day tomorrow."

"Yes, I suppose I have."

Rushford drained the last drop clinging to the inside of his glass and then stood. He opened his mouth as if he were about to speak, closed it, and then opened it again. "I'm sorry about Parker. I knew Lincoln was a bit of a blackguard, but I never would have thought it of Parker. Never."

Drew nodded, weary with the thought of revisiting it all again. "Neither would I. I was hoping we'd find out he wasn't part of it at all, but it seems there's no getting round it now."

"No," Rushford said. "But you're young yet, Drew. You still have Farlinford. A great many young men have started with less." He laughed wistfully. "I know I did."

"Thank you, sir," Drew replied. "I might do just that. Good night."

A cleansing midmorning sun flooded the front lawn at Farthering Place, somehow making even old Rushford, with his little kit bag in hand, look steady and robust.

He took a deep breath and let it out. "I shall miss England, young man. Home and all that. But I just can't stay any longer, you understand."

"Of course, sir," Drew said. "Best to put it all behind you for good and all."

"Oh, and I have something for you. Just the final loose end."

He tucked his bag under his arm and reached into his coat pocket for a single sheet of paper, folded lengthwise. He handed it to Drew.

"What's this?" Drew's smile faded as he scanned the contents. "Sir, you can't possibly—"

"It seems rather that I can," Rushford said. "It's witnessed by your butler and your housekeeper. Perfectly legal and in order. I confirmed it with my solicitor by telephone this morning."

"But you're giving me your interest in Farlinford."

"Yes, I believe I am. Not that there's much left in it now, of course, but she's all yours."

"But, sir, there's no need for that. I'll try to get her running again, you needn't bother about that, but you'll still have your share. It's only right."

Rushford shook his head. "You know the agreement. No director can sell his interest in the company except to the other directors. That would be only you now, my boy. And the value of my half would hardly buy me tea and toast anymore." He chuckled. "Look at me. Since I signed that little paper, I'm a new man. I'm off to a new life and leaving all my worries behind me. You wouldn't begrudge me that, now, would you?"

"Certainly not, sir. I can't say I was expecting this, but if it's what you want . . ."

"You'll be doing me a great favor." Rushford took Drew's hand and shook it heartily. "Now, I must be off before my ship leaves without me. Goodbye, young Farthering. Make us proud."

With a nod of farewell, Rushford shuffled down the steps, carrying his kit bag in both arms now, like a boy off to camp.

Min was holding the door to the black sedan, his face as inscrutable as ever. "May I take your bag, sir?"

Rushford waved him away, scowling slightly, and climbed into the back seat.

Drew followed him to the car. "Don't you worry about Lincoln. The police will run him to ground in time. I still can't imagine where he could be, but they've checked everywhere, even that little cottage of Mrs. Chapman's. The police say she has a tenant, but it's some fellow called Barker come after trout.

Deuced shame, too. It would have been a nice, convenient place for Lincoln to keep himself."

"I didn't know there was a place as close as that. I wish you hadn't mentioned him again. That boat cannot leave too soon for me." Rushford mopped his forehead with his handkerchief and then managed a smile. "Here, now. Mustn't give way, eh? That blackguard is likely miles away and daren't show his face by day."

"That's the ticket, sir."

"Well, best of luck to you, young man. Drive on, Min."

Min ducked his head and closed the rear door. Then, with one hard look at Drew, he got into the front seat. In another moment, the sedan was out of sight.

Madeline came out of the house in time to wave after it, and then she walked down the steps. "What now?"

"You'll never believe it," Drew said. "He's signed all of Farlinford over to me." He showed her the paper Rushford had given him. "It will take some doing, but I think I'll try to make a go of it. Maybe I can make something of myself, after all."

"Uncle Mason would have liked that," Madeline said. "He always wanted you to come into business with him. He was very fond of you, you know."

She knew just how to sting his conscience. Just a little wistfulness in the eyes, a sigh in the voice.

"All right." Drew let the breath seep out of his lungs like the air from a punctured tire, and then he led her back into the parlor. Nick came trailing in after them.

"We'll start at the beginning once again." Drew forced himself to sound resolute and hopeful. "What evidence do we have that doesn't point to Mason and Lincoln being behind it all?"

"What about Mr. Peterson?" Madeline asked. "From the very first, he had access to the fireworks and the gun. Suppose his whole story about his daughter is a lie and he and she both are in it with Lincoln? He could be hiding Lincoln in his house right now."

Drew shook his head. "It won't work. I couldn't help wondering that myself and had someone from my solicitor's look into it for me. She was where Peterson said she was, in an even more wretched condition than he knew. We've got her in a sanatorium now, and when she's ready, she's to come back home."

"So," Nick said, "we could suspect her or her father of killing Lincoln, but it's not bally likely they'd be helping him. No."

Drew spent a moment drumming his fingers on the arm of the overstuffed chair. "The fingerprints," he said finally. "Or lack thereof." He narrowed his eyes, thinking. "Remember what Jimmy said? It couldn't have been more thorough if they had done it themselves."

"But why would they do it themselves? I mean, Lincoln, certainly, if he wanted to disappear. But why would Clarke? What would he have been thinking?"

The ringing of the telephone halted the conversation, and in a moment Dennison appeared at the parlor door. "You're wanted on the telephone, sir."

"Who is it, Denny?"

"He didn't give his name, sir. An American gentleman, if I'm not mistaken."

Drew leapt to his feet and hurried into the study, with Nick and Madeline on his heels.

"Hello?"

"Check out the cottage. Mrs. Chapman's. He's there. They're getting away."

"Who's there? Who is this?"

The line went dead.

"Who was that?" Madeline asked. "What did he say?"

"Hello? Hello?" Drew clicked the switch hook. "Hello, operator? Ring Mrs. Chapman at Lilac Cottage. No, I don't know the number. Hurry, please."

"Who was it?" Madeline pressed.

"That American. The same one I overheard before. He said— Hello, Mrs. Chapman?"

"This is Mrs. Chapman." The woman's voice was quavery with age, but pleasantly chipper. "Who's calling, please?"

"Drew Farthering here. From up at Farthering Place. I was wondering if I could ask you about the chap you have staying at your cottage."

"Mr. Barker? The police have already asked about him, you know. Perfectly nice young man from Ipswich."

"Yes, I've heard that. He doesn't happen to be a tall blond fellow with a mustache, does he?"

"You mean like that Mr. Lincoln they're looking for. Oh, no, that couldn't be Mr. Barker. He's dark, you know, and clean-shaven."

Drew sighed. "I see."

"The police showed me a photograph of the man they want. My young man here is nothing like him, especially in the chin. Dimpled on one side and all."

Drew clutched the receiver so hard, he feared it would break. "He doesn't happen to have a little scar over his upper lip, does he?"

"Why, yes. How did you—?"

"Don't . . ." Drew paused and took a deep breath. "Could you please go down to the cottage and see if he's in?"

"I'm sorry, dear, but he left last night. I went this morning to see how he was getting on with the trout, and he'd taken all his things and gone. Didn't even bother to lock up."

"Thank you, Mrs. Chapman. You've been a great help." Drew

rung off and stared at Madeline and Nick. "It's not Lincoln. It's Clarke. By heaven, it's Clarke. He must have shaved his mustache and dyed his hair."

"So it was Lincoln in the greenhouse all along," Nick said.

"*. . . thou hast a name that thou livest, and art dead.*" That was it.

Drew nodded. "And Rushford could never have seen him at the office."

"Or seen him murder Uncle Mason." Madeline put both hands over her mouth, her eyes wide.

Drew took her arm. "Are you all right?"

"Of course I'm all right," she said, shaking him off. "And you're letting a murderer get away."

"Good heavens!" Nick cried, and the three of them rushed into the front hall.

"Get the car, Nick," Drew ordered. "Madeline, darling, ring up Jimmy at the police station, if you would. Tell him to get hold of someone at the docks before Rushford gets there."

"Oh no, you don't," Madeline said. "Denny can call the police. I'm going with you."

"It could be dangerous," Drew warned.

"I don't care. I have a thing or two to say to Mr. Rushford."

Her full lips were set in a determined line he didn't want to resist, but he tried all the same. "He's already murdered at least four people. He's not going to stick at two or three more now."

"No, I don't suppose he will," she agreed. "That's why you're going to take that pistol Uncle Mason kept in his study."

"Well, I wasn't going to be so daft as to go empty-handed, you know." He couldn't help smiling at her. "All right, you can come, but be quick about it, and if anything happens, you're to drive the car straightaway back here. Promise?"

"Now, Drew—"

"Promise?"

She sighed. "I promise."

By then, Nick was in the drive and leaning on the horn. After a few parting instructions for the imperturbable Dennison, Drew and Madeline scurried down the front steps and leapt into the car. Nick hit the gas before Drew could even close the door behind himself.

"No use smashing us up before we even get to the road," Drew said, pushing his hat off his forehead and back onto the proper place on his head. "I daresay Rushford thinks he's got us all duped and there's no need to rush."

"I suppose," Nick agreed, "though it'd be a bit easier if he had a puncture somewhere between here and the village."

Madeline shook her head. "I just can't believe it. Mr. Rushford seemed like such a nice old man."

"I told you no one is ever as he seems," Drew reminded her.

"You also told me Uncle Mason was a murderer."

"I suppose I did," he admitted, and then he seized her hand. "I say, Madeline, can you ever—?"

"Good heavens." Nick wrenched the car to the side of the road, nearly throwing Madeline into Drew's lap. "I don't believe it."

There, just before the road turned toward Farthering St. John, was Rushford's black sedan. Rushford himself was standing beside it, looking anxious as Min bent over the motor, evidently making some sort of repair.

"Leave this to me," Drew said, and slipping his hand around the pistol in his pocket, he got out of the car. Madeline and Nick were right behind him.

— Twenty —

"Miss Parker! Drew, my boy!" Rushford called. "What luck to see you here! It seems we've broken down and my fool of a driver hasn't a clue what the matter is." Min did not look up from his work.

"Pity," Drew said coolly. "Perhaps you'd better come back up to the house with us."

"Oh, no, no," Rushford told him. "I couldn't possibly. My ship will sail without me if I don't get along."

Drew nodded. "Then perhaps you'd rather go to the police station. It's on your way."

"The police station?" Rushford laughed. "I don't know what sort of prank you young people are up to now, but I haven't time for it. I've got to move along or I'll miss my ship. Look, I'll show you my tickets."

He reached for the coat that was laid across the back seat and patted it down, rummaging for something. Drew tightened his grip on the gun he held, certain it wasn't sailing tickets Rushford was after.

"Are you looking for this, Mr. Rushford?"

Drew and Rushford both turned at the voice, the distinctly American voice Drew had heard on the telephone.

Rushford's face went ghost white. "Min . . ."

The chauffeur held the obvious object of Rushford's search: a little Remington derringer. And he held it pointed at Rushford.

"Min, you . . ." The old man wiped the sudden perspiration from his forehead. "You sound—"

"American?" Min asked with a wry smile. "I was born in Peking, but raised in Edmonton and then in Los Angeles. I went to college there. I didn't think it would occur to you that I might sound like anything but a China boy fresh off the boat. After my father was convicted, my mother sent me to live with her sister's family in Los Angeles. She wanted me to study, to be an American and know the language and not end up like my father." He looked at Rushford. "At the mercy of those who could speak well."

"I spoke for him," the old man protested. "Look at the court records. He would have hanged otherwise."

"And you would have let him if it had fit in with your plan. As it was, you needed to look concerned and, more than that, above suspicion." Min made an exaggerated bow. "Kind benefactor no hang poor Chinee."

"But you . . ." Rushford gulped, his frightened eyes darting from Min to the gun and then back again. "You wouldn't really—"

Min clicked back the hammer.

"Steady on," Drew said.

"You may have forgotten my father," Min said, not looking away from his target, and suddenly his voice, his whole demeanor, changed. "Poor, worthless father that honorable Mr. Rushford save from gallows? And sad little Lan Jing, with her seventeen bones broken and her windpipe crushed?" His eyes obsidian hard, he dropped the persona as quickly as he had put it on. "Let's just say this is for them."

"Min," Drew warned.

"Oh, don't worry. I won't kill him. I just want to make sure he gets what's coming to him. Sounds like it's going to be a lot more than even I expected."

Rushford sagged back against the car. "I don't . . . I don't know what all this is about. Certainly I keep that little gun for protection, but I was only going to show you my tickets. My word—"

"Where's Clarke?" Drew snapped.

"Clarke? Clarke's dead."

"I talked to Mrs. Chapman. He wasn't as of last night."

"What do you mean? Clarke's alive?"

"Looks like."

Rushford's mouth gradually closed. "Then it was Lincoln in the greenhouse, after all. And Parker and Clarke were behind everything from the beginning. Oh, my word."

"I think you'd best come along," Drew said, watching every nuance of the old man's face. He looked so bewildered, so mild and guileless, that this was all hard to imagine yet.

"Whatever for?" Rushford asked. "I can't help the police. I don't know where Clarke is."

"Perhaps not now, but you did."

"Drew, my boy, you can't possibly mean to think I'm somehow involved."

"If it was Lincoln in the greenhouse, how did you manage to be the only one to see him afterward?"

"Where's Clarke?" Nick demanded.

Rushford gaped again, his eyes watery, his lips trembling, and then his face changed. Looking as if he were fighting a laugh, he snatched the kit bag from the back seat of the car and tossed it into Nick's arms.

Nick snorted. "Well, he's not in there."

"There have been stranger things."

Rushford was almost chuckling now, and Drew didn't much care for that. He kept his eyes on the old man.

"Open it, Nick," Drew said.

Nick clicked open the latch and then held the bag at arm's length, his face screwed up in disgust. "Ugh."

"Open it," Drew repeated.

Nick set the bag on the boot of the car and rummaged inside. "Something in oilcloth looks like. Something nasty." He pulled back one layer of the covering and then another. Then he shoved it back onto the back seat, his face bloodless.

"What?" Madeline asked, trying to see over his shoulder.

Drew still didn't look away from the old man. "What is it, Nick?"

"Clarke." Nick swallowed audibly. "It's Clarke."

With a little smirk, Rushford winked at him. "You'll find the rest of him in the pond behind your wood. Do apologize for me to your Mr. Peterson about his millstone. I didn't want Clarke popping up before I was well on my way. Even with his hair dyed and his mustache gone, he would have been too easily recognized and my little charade would have been up. If things had gone as planned, I'd have had that bag into the sea the moment we reached deep water and my secret would have been safe." Hearing the jingling bell of a police car, he glanced up the road toward Winchester. "Ah, that will be Chief Inspector Birdsong."

⚬

"Well, Detective Farthering, your Mr. Dennison tells me you've found our murderer at last." Birdsong peered at Rushford, still being covered by the gun in Min's hand, and then at Min himself. "I'll take that. We'll see to him from here."

Min handed him the gun. "Whatever you say."

The chief inspector looked briefly startled by Min's American accent. Turning to Drew, he asked, "You're sure of your facts this time?"

Drew nodded toward the back seat of the car. "I think you'll find all the evidence you need in that bag there. It's Rushford's."

Madeline turned her face away, and Nick walked a few paces down the road, but Rushford merely looked on, smiling slightly, his eyes mild, as Birdsong and his sergeant looked into the bag. Afterward, the sergeant, white-faced, took the bag into custody and put it in the police car.

Birdsong peered at Mr. Rushford. "I take it this is your doing."

"Oh, I don't deny it, Inspector. I don't deny it. May I smoke?"

Birdsong's expression turned guarded. "Search the gentleman, Sergeant."

"I assure you, I have nothing." Rushford held his arms out from his sides as the sergeant patted down his pockets. "Min took my little popgun there. I haven't anything else."

"Nothing here, sir," the sergeant said, stepping back from the man.

Rushford took out his cigarette case. "May I?"

Birdsong nodded. "Go ahead."

"I suppose you'll want details," Rushford said as he lit up. "It was quite simple really. Lincoln and Clarke were both greedy and small-minded. It didn't take much to get them to join me, separately of course. Just a promise of easy money and no chance of being caught." He laughed. "I told them both the same plan. We were to make it look as if Lincoln had been killed and then make it known he'd embezzled everything from Farlinford. If he were dead, he couldn't rightly be prosecuted, and he'd never be pursued. And with him being so obviously guilty, no one else would be pursued, either. Naturally, he had to be the one to recommend Clarke for Parker's new secretary once I had given old Vickers enough for an early and very quiet retirement."

"You're saying Vickers had a part in this, too?" Drew said.

"Oh, no. I merely told him Parker needed a younger man for the job, but was too kindhearted to force him into retirement. Vickers agreed to take the money and pretend it was all his own idea. That was for the rest of the plan."

"And you persuaded Lincoln to be accomplice to his own murder," Birdsong said. "Clever."

"That was rather good, wasn't it?" Rushford said. "But the best part was when I told him I would arrange for Clarke to go out to the greenhouse to be killed so there'd be a body we could claim as Lincoln's. I said the gun would be waiting out there for him. And it's funny, because it really was. Poor fellow, he hardly had a chance. He didn't know I'd sent Clarke out there a quarter of an hour earlier to kill *him*."

"How did he get the gun?" Birdsong asked.

"Oh, that was no problem. Lincoln took the key from Parker's key ring the day before. Weaseled it in and out of his pocket, neat as you please, and Parker none the wiser. Lincoln always was a seamy little toad, hardly a step removed from any county-fair charlatan. I knew a bit of light-fingered work would come naturally to him. It was nothing for him to creep down to get the gun from the shed in the middle of the night after everyone at the house was in bed or too drunk to know what was happening. He hid it in the greenhouse just as I told him. Rather neat, I'd say."

"And the ring?" Drew said.

"I told Clarke to take it from him before he was killed and then replace it afterwards to make it look as if Lincoln had staged his own death. Nice little touch, I thought, though it took the lot of you long enough to catch on to it." He looked at the faces surrounding him as if he expected to be congratulated.

"Why did you kill Constance?" Drew asked, his eyes hard.

"Stupid Clarke. She wasn't part of the plan at all, but she went running after Lincoln that night. I don't know why. Perhaps it was to pay him the last of his blackmail and tell him there'd be no more. Anyway, she'd seen Lincoln going outside and meant to find him when she saw Clarke creeping in the back way. She didn't know Lincoln was already dead. I suppose you and the lovely Miss Parker were still in the greenhouse then. Clarke said she'd mistaken him for Lincoln and, seeing he wasn't, went back upstairs. Clarke knew she'd remember seeing him, and knew she'd remember it was after the fireworks. If she told the police later on, it would spoil the rest of the plan, you see? He said he went through the window into her room, meaning to strangle her or something, the fool didn't know what, and he found her fast asleep. With all that Veronol in her, it was easy to just put a pillow over her face until she was gone. Barely a struggle, he said, and not a mark on her. That silly girl listening to the wireless in the other room never heard a thing."

Drew felt Madeline's hand slip into his, and it took him a moment to realize he hadn't exhaled the whole time Rushford was speaking. He finally let the tightness in his lungs relax, and the air seeped soundlessly out of him. "And you killed Mason because he'd figured you out."

Rushford sighed and took a drag on his cigarette. "I didn't plan on that one, young man. I expected the police to blame him for anything they couldn't properly put on Lincoln, of course, but he was always such a nice chap, I hated to see him killed."

Tears filled Madeline's eyes, and Drew pulled her closer to him.

"So you were the one who killed him, after all."

"No, Drew, my boy. It was Clarke. He was searching the study when Mason asked me to come talk to him."

"Searching? For what?"

Rushford smiled. "Parker had figured it out, as you say, and doubtless he would have had to be killed after that. A quiet suicide would have been most convincing. I could have arranged that. I didn't like the stabbing. It was far too messy. Clarke was a fool." Rushford chuckled to himself. "Of course, if he hadn't been, I couldn't so easily have gotten him to fall in with my plans, could I?"

Birdsong crossed his arms over his chest. "So it was always you. How many is it now? Five?"

"Six, actually, if you count the Chinese girl."

Min muttered something under his breath. Not in English.

"Min's cousin," Drew said. "Yes, that must have been you, as well."

"She was a pretty little thing. She'd come up to bring Min's father his dinner from time to time, and I'd see her sometimes in the hallway. And all the while she taunted me with that delicate little body and those bewitching eyes modestly lowered, acting as if she didn't know what she was doing. It's been a long time, but I still remember." He held out his hands, studying them. "She broke like fine porcelain. I suppose I half expected it."

Min turned and stalked away, obviously needing to put some distance between himself and Rushford.

"I think I'm going to be sick," Madeline whispered, and Drew tightened his arm around her.

Birdsong cleared his throat. There wasn't the slightest trace of emotion on his face. "Edwin Morris Rushford, I arrest you on the charges of embezzlement and theft, and for the murders of Arthur McCutcheon, David Lincoln, Constance Parker, Mason Parker, and Merton Clarke."

Min quickly returned and gave the chief inspector a hard look. Birdsong shook his head. "I can't do anything about your cousin, I'm afraid, Mr. Min. That will have to be dealt with by the police in Edmonton. It's little consolation, I'm sure, and I'm sorry but they can't hang a man more than once."

It was the work of only a moment for the police to place Rushford in handcuffs and bundle him into the squad car next to the grisly evidence in the bag. The accused was pleasant and cooperative, but he had nothing more to say.

"You might want to take the young lady home, Mr. Farthering," Birdsong said as he got in beside his prisoner, "then come up to the station in Winchester to get this all sorted out."

Drew glanced back at Madeline. She had been determined to speak her mind to Rushford just a little while ago, but now, face-to-face with him, she had only stood in burning silence, keeping a tight, sometimes painful hold on Drew's hand.

"He's right, darling. Let me—"

She pulled away from him, leaning down to fix her eyes on Rushford through the open car window. "You killed Uncle Mason. You killed all of them." A tear slid down her flushed cheek. "Why did you have to kill them? You were already rich. None of them ever harmed you. Not to kill them for. Not Uncle Mason."

"My dear," Rushford said, and Drew thought for a moment that he was going to reach out, manacles and all, and give her hand a comforting pat, "it wasn't all about the money. It was a grand plan, though, and I'm quite proud to know I almost made it work. Can you even imagine what it's like to be forever thought of as nothing more than a harmless old man?" He faced the front again, his expression one of benevolent superiority. "You may drive on, Sergeant."

"Before you go, tell me what Clarke was searching for," Drew said, "at the office and in Mason's study."

Rushford merely winked and sat back in the seat.

The chief inspector shook his head. "We'll get it all out of him before long, don't you trouble yourself about that, Mr. Farthering. Go on, Davies."

"I guess you finally figured it out," Min said as they drove away. "I didn't know how much longer I could keep him here. If he'd gotten to the ship, there would have been no catching him. His ticket was for South America, not Canada."

Drew narrowed his eyes. "You were the one who called about the cottage. How did you know?"

"I almost didn't. I was cleaning up at Rushford's, ready to send him off to Canada, when I saw a bit of paper stuck under one side of the grate. It was just a little handwritten receipt from a Mrs. Chapman, partially burned, for rent on a cottage, and I swept it out with everything else."

Drew glanced at Nick, who started to laugh.

"Then I heard you talking about the cottage to Rushford," Min said, "and was sure Lincoln must be there, no matter what the police said. Once we'd gone a few miles, I told Rushford the car had broken down and I'd have to call a garage. Then I walked to a nearby house and telephoned you. I had no idea it was Clarke and not Lincoln."

"Why didn't you just go to the police with it?"

"I saw how much the cops listened to my father." He brought his palms together and made a mocking bow. "Honorable officers of law never believe poor Chinee against English gentleman."

"That's as may be," Drew said, a little edge to his tone, "but you could have told me. I'd have listened."

Min studied him for a moment, and then his expression softened. "Yeah, I think you would have."

"The police mightn't have listened anyway," Nick put in. "They were after Lincoln and never thought to look for Clarke."

"That was you on the telephone earlier as well, wasn't it?"

Drew said. "You don't have a trace of an accent. Well, besides American. Who did you call?"

"A policeman in Canada. My father's case was his very first assignment, and he's kept track of me and Mom over the years. After my father was killed in the prison, my mother just stopped. Stopped eating. Stopped drinking. Stopped talking. She didn't last long after that, no matter what we tried to do to help her. She had been so strong through everything, and I guess she just couldn't do it anymore."

"And was that when you decided to look into matters yourself?" Drew asked.

Min nodded. "That policeman was the only one who'd take the time to hear me out about my father. After Mom died, I went to see him. He let me look into the files on the case. Even he was surprised at how little evidence there was for a conviction. He couldn't get his department to reopen the case then, but he told me to let him know if I found enough real proof to make them look at it again."

"So that's why you came after Rushford."

"No." A smile touched Min's lips. "That's why I came after Mr. Parker."

Madeline caught her breath. "What?"

"I knew it had to be someone with access to the plant at the time. Someone who would never be questioned if he was there at odd hours. That was the main thing they used to convict my father, but it applied to other men, too. Powerful men. Not Bill Morrow, that's for sure."

"Who?" Drew asked.

"He was the man Lan Jing loved. The one who killed himself after she was murdered. He never kept her as his mistress. My mother told me he came to my father and respectfully asked to marry Lan Jing. My father said she was too young yet, that

320

they would have to wait, and he agreed. But he was just an engineer. He wouldn't have been able to get in and out of the plant without someone asking him what he was doing there that night."

"Then who—?"

"As far as I could see, there were only two men who could have done it. Directors of the company. Parker and Rushford. And Rushford had stood up for my father, kept him from hanging. I had no reason to suspect him. That left Parker, though the police in Edmonton said they had nothing to hold him on and he was a respectable gentleman."

"So you thought you could check up on him by working for Rushford here in England?"

"Sort of. First I tried to get a job at Farthering Place, gardening or something, but your Mr. Peterson doesn't exactly trust foreigners."

"No, I don't think he does."

"Then I tried at Farlinford, but they didn't have any use for me either, even though my degree is in chemical engineering."

"Well, perhaps they were full up."

"They'd just lost a chemical engineer, if you remember."

"Oh. Right. Sorry."

Min shrugged. "It's not your fault. Anyway, I decided Rushford was the next best thing since he's not far from the office and I was sure to be driving him places where he'd be in contact with Mr. Parker."

"How did he happen to need someone just then?"

"Rushford isn't the only one who can make it worth someone's while to quit his job."

"You have that much money?"

"No, but the Canadian policeman was able to find out a few things about Rushford's former valet that he didn't want publicized." Min smiled. "Information is sometimes as good as cash, don't you think?"

Drew returned the smile. One couldn't help admiring the man. "So, he was out, and you just happened to show up on Rushford's doorstep, willing to work at reduced wages."

"Exactly. Then Lincoln was murdered, and Mrs. Parker, and I thought I had my killer for sure, but it didn't add up. Then there was that little scrap of paper."

"Just that, eh? Rushford almost got away with it, too. Thank you, Min," Drew said, offering his hand, and the other man shook it.

"My friends call me Mickey."

Drew nodded, smiling. "Mickey, then. I suppose your Canadian policeman will be interested to know what's happened here."

"Yeah. Maybe. But like the inspector said, you can't hang a man twice." Min shrugged. "I guess once will have to do."

"I suppose it will."

It didn't matter now. Rushford was caught, Clarke and Lincoln were dead. It was all over. Thank God, it was all over.

Drew gestured toward the Rolls. "You don't actually need a lift somewhere, do you? To a garage or something?"

Grinning, Min got back into Rushford's sedan and turned the key. "Thanks anyway," he said over the purring engine, "but I'll meet you at Birdsong's office. I'm sure the police will have a few questions for me, too." Then he pulled out onto the road and sped northward.

"I want to go with you," Madeline declared before Drew could say anything. "If you take me back to the house, I'll just find some other way there."

Drew liked to think he knew when to make a wise retreat and merely opened the car door for her. "I wouldn't dream of leaving you behind, darling. Come on, Nick, old man. I still have more questions than answers."

They followed Min up to Winchester and ended up waiting with him in the same drab little interview room Drew had been in earlier in the week.

Before long, Birdsong came in. "I think we have most of it cleared up now, Mr. Farthering, thanks to you and our, uh, American friend here."

"Don't worry, Inspector, I am Chinese. But I'm an American citizen, too."

"Right. Well, you've been a great help, Mr. Min." Birdsong raised one eyebrow. "Though you might have let us in on what you were up to early on. You might want to know too that Rushford's confessed to more than your cousin's murder in 1917. Seems he made away with an Emily Evelyn Murdoch in London in 1921, and a Sheila Ann Dormer in 1928 right here in Winchester. Both of them young girls, they made the mistake of thinking him harmless."

"And you might have checked into the man staying at Mrs. Chapman's a little more closely, Inspector," Drew observed. "Might have ended this all much more quickly. And more cleanly."

Birdsong looked disgusted. "In fact, we did check into him. When we talked to the false Mr. Barker, he told us where he worked and where he lived in Ipswich. We telephoned his supposed employer and his supposed landlady. Both confirmed that their Mr. Barker was well-known to them and had gone on a fishing holiday. Of course, Clarke was acquainted with the man, knew he was going to be on holiday, and used his identity without Barker's knowing it. Funny thing is, the real Barker's been just over in Otterbourne all this while."

"I suppose Clarke, at least most of him, is at the bottom of the pond," Nick said.

"Oh yes. Rushford's being quite aboveboard about everything now. He'd arranged to meet Clarke out there late last night to plan how and where to divvy up. Once there, he bashed Clarke's skull in, dragged him out into the water, and hacked off his head. He then wrapped the head in oilcloth and put it in his bag. That done, he stripped off his own bloodied clothes and weighted them and the body with the stolen millstone and sunk the lot to the bottom of the pond. He returned to the house in his bathrobe. He told me he had just time enough to shove the bag under a table there in the hall before you caught him coming in."

Drew shook his head. "And he had me apologizing for giving him a fright. Good heavens, what an actor he'd have made."

"I'll say," the chief inspector agreed. "And when you lads searched the house, bless me if it wasn't Rushford hiding Clarke in his room. Even had him bundled into the bedclothes once, and you searching right there by him."

"What about the dogs?" Nick asked. "Why didn't they lead us to Clarke?"

"The trousers were Lincoln's," Birdsong explained, "so they wouldn't have Clarke's scent on them. And the shoes were new. Clarke had never worn them. Rushford had planted them in the library to keep everyone occupied while he and Clarke searched for the papers they'd been after all along—the formula McCutcheon had come up with."

Drew wrinkled his brow. "So McCutcheon wasn't in on the blackmail?"

"He never knew about it," Birdsong said. "The whole thing with the law book and the photographs was just to throw us off the real reason for McCutcheon's murder."

"And the pictures of Marielle? She's not my—"

Birdsong shook his head. "Rushford bought them at a second-hand shop, I'm afraid. She's nothing to do with you at all." Birdsong smiled ruefully. "I'm sorry."

Drew let out his breath, and Madeline squeezed his hand.

"Then Uncle Mason must have known about the formula, too," she said. "That's why he took those papers from Mr. Mc-Cutcheon's office and was trying to figure out what was in them that was so valuable." Her voice quavered. "And that's why they killed him. But what sort of formula was it?"

"Here's what he was after." Birdsong took some papers out of a file and handed them to Drew. "And he's taking particular satisfaction in not saying what it is."

Drew took a moment to look them over. "I can't make heads or tails of this."

Min lifted one eyebrow. "May I?"

"By all means." Drew handed the papers to him and gave the chief inspector a reassuring nod. "He's a chemical engineer, you know."

Birdsong didn't look quite convinced, but he held his peace until Min began to shake his head, his expression an odd mixture of astonishment and regret.

"It's a formula for catalytic cracking."

Birdsong narrowed his eyes. "What's that?"

"In the simplest terms, it's a process used to break down crude oil into usable components like gasoline. This formula would practically double the output from every barrel."

Drew's eyes widened. "The patent on that would be worth millions."

"Yeah, I'm sure it is." Min handed the formula back to him. "To the American company that's just patented it."

"What?"

"A French guy called Houdry just came out with this same thing with an oil company back east. They're supposed to open a new plant that uses this formula sometime in the next year or so. I've been reading up on it."

Madeline sank into one of the unrelenting wooden chairs that populated the room. "So Rushford killed them all for nothing."

She pressed her trembling lips together and looked up at Drew with tear-filled eyes. He knew she was hurting still, but she would be all right in time. He'd seen that in the sweet assurance in her face at Constance's funeral and at Mason's, too. She would be all right.

Rushford had nothing to look back on now but the lives he had destroyed, nothing to look forward to but the hangman's noose and the judgment that lay beyond. All to prove his own clever superiority, and for riches that had vanished before he could lay his hands on them.

"Vanity of vanities . . . All is vanity."

Drew considered the state of his own soul.

". . . thou hast a name that thou livest, and art dead."

Was it still just a name?

Finally, Drew brought Madeline to her feet and extended his right hand to the chief inspector. "I suppose that's it, then. Do you need anything more from us?"

"Not that I know of. You'll all be required in court, of course, but you'll be notified when the time comes." Birdsong gave his hand a firm shake before releasing it. "I'm not saying your methods would be sanctioned by Scotland Yard, Detective Farthering, but you've all been a great help. I'm sorry we couldn't have stopped Rushford before we did, miss."

Madeline nodded.

Drew also shook hands with Min. "What will you do now?"

"I'll go home."

"To China?"

Min laughed. "To America. I love and honor my homeland,

but I love and honor my home, too. America is where I belong now that I can finally lay my father and Lan Jing to rest. Inspector, you know how to reach me when you need me." He made a brief bow and was gone.

"We'll be going as well, Inspector," Drew said. "I suppose I've a lot of things to see to now."

Birdsong shook his hand once again, and then Drew and Madeline and Nick went out to the car.

"So much for all those commandments, eh?" Drew said, dredging up a thin smile. "I told you we'd break them all or very nearly. It was pure coincidence that Min heard me mention Mrs. Chapman's cottage, and you know what Father Knox would have said about that."

"Maybe not coincidence," Madeline said.

True enough. He had prayed, truly prayed. Why should he be surprised at an answer?

"Want me to drive, old man?" Nick asked. "You look all in."

"That bad, eh?" Drew took a quick look in the rearview mirror. "I see what you mean. Very well then, take us home."

He got into the back seat with Madeline, and they rode in near silence back to Farthering Place.

What was he going to do now? He was sole owner of Farlinford Processing, or whatever was left of it. Surely Rushford had stockpiled the proceeds from his thefts somewhere, and Drew supposed most of that would eventually make its way back to the company. He'd be on his own at Farthering Place, as well. It all felt a bit overwhelming to him at the moment. All alone.

Madeline linked her fingers with his and nestled her head on his shoulder.

Maybe he wouldn't be quite all alone, at least as long as she decided to stay, but there was still that hollowness inside him.

"*. . . thou hast a name that thou livest, and art dead.*"

When they got near Farthering Place, Drew told Nick to drive on into the village and pull up in front of the church. Then, saying only that he wouldn't be long, he got out of the car. He made his way up the walk alone and, removing his hat, went through the heavy wooden door and down the narrow center aisle to the altar.

"I don't . . ." He turned his hat in his hands. "I don't know where we go from here."

He stood there for a long while, bathed in the warm colored light that poured from the stained glass, from the Christ who waited, who had always waited, open-armed, to receive him. Then he dropped to one knee and bowed his head. He didn't know how long he stayed there, but at last he looked up again, feeling lighter somehow, smiling at the simplicity of it all.

"I don't suppose I actually have to know that part yet. I'll just carry on with the glorifying and enjoying then, shall I?"

He stood up, knowing Madeline was waiting for him outside. There were a great many things he wanted to discuss with her. Most of all, he wanted to tell her that the kittens had begun opening their eyes.

AUTHOR'S NOTE

Ronald Arbuthnott Knox (1888–1957), English priest and theologian, was the author of *The Three Taps, The Footsteps at the Lock*, and several other mysteries. But he's best known for his 1929 Decalogue, a ten commandments for mystery writers.

When I decided to delve into mystery writing myself, after years of feasting on the classic mysteries of the 1920s and '30s, I thought it would be great fun to write a book that intentionally broke all these rules, or at least bent them a bit. *Rules of Murder* is the result.

ACKNOWLEDGMENTS

To Agatha Christie, Margery Allingham, and Dorothy L. Sayers, the Queens of Classic Mystery, for being such a delightful inspiration.

To my wonderful dad, who loves my books even before they're written.

To my amazing agent, Wendy Lawton, for believing in Drew and in me.

To everyone who helped me throughout the writing of this book, even those I've lost touch with.

To all of you. I appreciate you more than I can say.

Julianna Deering is the pen name of multi-published author DeAnna Julie Dodson. DeAnna has always been an avid reader and a lover of storytelling, whether on the page, the screen, or the stage. This, together with her keen interest in history and her Christian faith, shows in her tales of love, forgiveness, and triumph over adversity. A fifth-generation Texan, she makes her home north of Dallas, along with three spoiled cats. When not writing, DeAnna spends her free time quilting, cross-stitching, and watching NHL hockey. To learn more, visit JuliannaDeering.com.